THE
BOOK·OF·BEASTS

A NOVEL

BERNICE FRIESEN

COTEAU
BOOKS

Edited by Edna Alford.
Book and cover design by Duncan Campbell.
Cover images: "Dragon (ceramic), The De Morgan Centre, London" (detail), photo by William De Morgan, The Bridgeman Art Library/Getty Images, and "Old Paper Isolated On White" by Gansovsky Vladislav/iStockphoto. Additional interior/back cover glyphs by Bernice Friesen.

Printed and bound in Canada at Friesens.

Library and Archives Canada Cataloguing in Publication

Friesen, Bernice, 1966-
The book of beasts : a novel / Bernice Friesen.

ISBN 978-1-55050-387-6

I. Title.
PS8561.R4952B66 2007   C813'.54   C2007-904327-5

10 9 8 7 6 5 4 3 2 1

COTEAU
BOOKS

2517 Victoria Ave.
Regina, Saskatchewan
Canada S4P 0T2

AVAILABLE IN CANADA & THE US FROM
Fitzhenry & Whiteside
195 Allstate Parkway
Markham, ON, Canada, L3R 4T8

The publisher gratefully acknowledges the financial assistance of the Saskatchewan Arts Board, the Canada Council for the Arts, the Government of Canada through the Book Publishing Industry Development Program (BPIDP), Association for the Export of Canadian Books, and the City of Regina Arts Commission, for its publishing program.

Canadä

for Colin and Alex and Jo
and for my father

"THESE ARE STORIES
OF THE MUTUAL CHARITIES
BETWEEN SAINTS & BEASTS..."

"THE BEASTS HAVE STILL
THEIR WAY WITH US..."

– H.W.

G⊙D was a little black-haired bastard named Timmy with wet sheet skin, bleeding gums, and fists full of iron oxide pebbles which he flung in James's face, each sting becoming a freckle. His mother told him it was God who'd given him the freckles, and it was true because he couldn't remember having freckles before Timmy started throwing stones. If freckles were so bad, at least they weren't his fault. He convinced himself they were caused by wounds, like the blood he saw on Jesus's side, flowing down the plaster of his mother's crucifix like bubbled spit. It was easier to look at Jesus's blood than at his own, and after he realized freckles were ugly – except on his beautiful mother – it wasn't easy to look at himself at all.

Skinny, big ears, red hair messed like the knots of hay sticking out of a cow's mouth. These were the things he heard about himself after he got into the habit of listening, when being seen and not heard became too boring. He told himself he didn't care, began scratching his face. Get rid of the spots. Even if his mother said she liked them, that they were delicious, especially when she was a dog, and licked them off his nose – see the freckles on her tongue? They tasted salty, she said, were delicate and crunchy like little potato crisps. Sometimes he was a dog, too, and so he scratched anyway. And then his father told him to stop that scratching, sit still, and he would, almost, until every adult eye was averted, and then his hand would strike like the tongue of a frog, and he would stuff another Jaffa cake in his mouth.

Everything was alive to him. Not just the neighbour's cat and his grandfather's King Charles spaniel, not just the ladybirds and dragonflies and earthworms, but the turnips wincing as they were pulled from the ground in his mother's garden. He made little playful screams whenever his mother tore lettuce apart for a salad, said *ouch, ouch*, when she chopped onions, misinterpreting her tears as sympathy for the poor vegetables. He refused to eat the tiniest grape from the vine, even though his father told him it would perish anyway. He kept it in a little baby-food jar in the fridge, and took it out to hold it in the palm of his hand and pet it like a kitten.

His first word, as a baby, had been *meow*, and he was a cat-sneak behind doors and beneath the tablecloth. His grandfather called his father a senseless dreamer – that *acting*, way back then, for God's sake – who should never have married a child who was such a harpy, whatever that meant. It seemed to mean an Irish woman who wore her red hair too loose, her blouses too tight, and who didn't care what she said in polite company – and Oxford was nothing if not polite in the late 1950s.

"What will people *think*?"

These words were spoken in tight-lipped British whispers after his staid and solid grandparents – unlanded, almost-aristocracy – gave a party. His mother leaped during the waltzes, took off her shoes, spun her circle skirt into orbit around her thighs, whirled through the arms of every man present, complained that there were no decent fiddlers in England, and that she'd much rather be dancing a reel on her father's barn floor. During a waltz, she sputtered her own jig tune, hands at sides, feet stepping and rapping, kicking and twisting, ankles bending, red hair whipping up and down against her turquoise back; her favourite colour was blue, any blue between sky and midnight. She was drunk, of course, and all his father did was smile – he was always drunker than she was – and whisper, "There's more life in your mother's little feet than in the whole of our class, James. Remember that. No matter what Grandpa says. Hm. It's good for him to be shaken up a bit."

And his mother liked shaking up his grandparents. At the next party, she crossed herself conspicuously, Catholically, when they said the blessing. She talked about plucking and eviscerating chickens over the shrimp cocktail:

"...have to scald the chooks in a pot of boiling water or you'd never get the damned pinfeathers out. And the *stink*."

She talked of her brothers and sisters scavenging for shellfish to get the family fed when times were bad, spoke her fury at the famine and the damn British colonials when she had deliberately drunken too much Madeira out of the Waterford crystal glasses, spoke proudly of poverty in front of the other (damned British) guests, the young squire with his shrunken country seat between Oxford and Woodstock (and on her mother-in-law's hard dining room chair), the don and his wife who was an *Honourable*, and the architect who could trace his ancestry back to Magnus Maximus, Roman governor of Britain. The cat-sneak heard every uncomfortable silence, every clearing of his grandmother's throat even when he was supposed to be *not* seen *and* not heard, sleeping in one of the upstairs bedrooms. He learned to cringe in sympathy with his grandmother's embarrassment: "Oh the scenes that girl makes!" even as he admired his mother's dancing, her devil-may-care laugh, her sharp hawk-eyes winking at him when she saw him hiding, listening, at the top of the stairs. Once, from behind the wing chair in the lounge, he heard the don refer to her as a nice bit of crumpet with a look of jailbait about her. Something every man should have, the architect replied.

But James was other animals, too.

When his mother sat in the kitchen, he slipped within her hair, became a mouse in red fuzzy grass, warm in a field under sunset.

One day, before Sunday lunch, he laid his ear on a grand-mother-given Royal Staffordshire Tea Rose and covered his head with another.

I am a clam, he thought, between two plates. And his mother and father would come into the room and laugh.

"Damn you," he heard his mother say. "I'm not good enough, am I? Bog Irish am I? I'll never learn what fork to put where for your stupid – I'm going home. I'm leaving now!"

"Bernadette, I didn't mean it like that, I only thought you'd like it. You never had a chance to finish school. Give you something to do now that James is getting older –"

"I don't remember why I – and you! Always with a glass in your hand. And now, nothing but me trying to be some English wife, and only good enough to be a servant – according to *some* people. I'm so lonely for home, for my sisters, for a friendly face."

He tilted the top plate, saw his mother through the doorway, crying, stabbing, stabbing, stabbing his father in the chest with her finger, trying to punch a hole in his heart that she could crawl out of. She cried as if she knew she was trapped there in his heart, her body tangled in his.

"I'd leave you! I'd leave you! Can't you see? Haven't you noticed? You've got me! You've got me. First with *him*, and there's going to be another, now! Where am I going to go but crazy with loneliness? All your stiff-upper-lip friends! And the bleeding queen for a mother-in-law – you think I can polish the silver enough for *her majesty*? For –"

"Another – a baby? Bernadette –"

"She wants to civilize me, does she? *Englishize* me? She thinks she can do it with silver and china and linen and other horse shit! That's what it all is! Trying to cover me with fancy shit so her friends mightn't notice me any more! Wants me to shut my flaming mouth if I've got nothing to say she thinks proper to hear! Nothing to say that's pronounced right! If I'd known all this before! If I'd have known what it'd be like to...to – well I'll shut my trap, then, and see how she likes me just staring at her. I'll shut my bleeding trap!"

She barged into the room, his father after her, and they stopped when they saw him.

"I am a clam," James whispered. His top shell slid off his head onto the floor in a white and pink shatter of tea roses.

Much later, he was a sandpiper, carrot-beak clenched in his front teeth, and he pecked his little sister in the head when she was only a baby, and she screamed and cried and his mother smacked him, hot on his backside.

Do what you're told, his mother said. Eat your vegetables, drink your milk, sit up straight. Do what you're told; don't do what you're not told. But there was so much of that – what she didn't say until he'd done it already: don't play with your food, don't tap your foot, don't drink from the pudding bowl, don't peck your sister in the head with a carrot, don't shriek like a seagull at your grandmother's dinner table so that she puts her hands over her head because she thinks there must be a bird careening through the open window.

How could he learn everything? Enough to be grown up? To avoid the smacks? To be seen *and* heard at his grandmother's dinner table?

He learned to comb his hair so it would be decent for the first hour of the day, tried, sort of, to eat the things his father said would stick to his ribs, and every night before he went to sleep, he lay on his back, elbows pointing out, hands pressing his ears to his head, hoping he'd wake with his ears laying flat instead of sticking out.

At St. Aloysius Primary, he learned Timmy was not God.

The spring of his eleventh birthday, he was standing on a storm-crossed playing field between Oxford and Headington when he saw his father, small in the distance, walking out of the ragged dancing monster trees toward him. James dropped the ball and took a running step to meet him, but then remembered he was with the other boys, and he was to be captain this time, finally what he deserved. His father wasn't supposed to come around and bother with him when he was with his mates, and this was the first real week of sky. The sun had been crazy hot in the afternoon, and the rising breath of the earth was thick, swirling the sky with creamy clouds that sagged blue with water and electricity and booming. None of the boys believed in death by lightning.

"Go on, then. You wanted to be the captain, so pick your team before we all have to go home for supper."

"Or before it rains again."

James stretched his leg and took possession of the ball, rolling it beneath his foot on the thick grass. Sam and Ian were his best friends, and both wanted the prestige of being chosen first, proclaimed the best player. Well, wasn't James himself the best? He was captain after all. And it was his ball, and he could run faster than any of them and he was smarter, too.

"Ian," he called. Ian turkey-strutted up beside James and turned to face the others.

Sam stubbed his fingers repeatedly on his corduroy thighs. He thought he was as good a player as Ian, any day, and he didn't talk with a stupid Irishness either, like Ian, the singsongy old lady voices he heard in the oratory – like James's mother. And James was supposed to be his best friend anyway, so what was he doing choosing Ian first?

"Harry," the other captain called. Sam reddened, thought about stomping away.

James watched his father coming closer. Why was he wandering around in the field when it was Thursday and he should have been looking after the book shop?

"Sam," he said. Maybe if the teams were chosen fast enough, and they got started, his father wouldn't take him off to the shop to sweep up. "Hurry," he told Robin, the other captain.

"Mick,"

"Tim."

"Kevin."

"James."

"Steven."

"James," his father repeated. James didn't move. His father was swaying, his face a pale shadow. "Come home."

"Why?" he asked, but his father turned and started back through the grass, scuffing over his own footprints. James ran to him under the new gloom of rain and the trees, where his father slid against an oak and told him his sister was dead, thrown through the windscreen against the car of an afternoon drunk.

His mother had lost an eye.

So much rain, you'd think you'd drown.

They had been two men trying to forget, eating canned mushroom soup, cream crackers, digestive biscuits, greasy chops and boiled potatoes, the only things his father knew how to cook: white and tan meals. When his father broke the last of the crystal tumblers and began drinking straight from the bottle, it was James who peeled the potatoes, put the soup on to boil.

It had been pouring the day his father brought his mother home from the hospital without Dymphna, raincoat over her shoulders, rain on the floor, a pillow instead of an eye, undercurrent of blue stagnant blood, a cast on her leg, a plastic polka-dot kerchief tied viciously around her chin. From that day on, his mother tied his knots so tight, James needed help undoing them.

It was shocking to see her without his sister – this was the whole family now. Shocking to see her in the unmatched clothes her husband had brought her, red hair torque-twisted and bunned, impaled with too many bobby pins. She immediately did their mound of men's dishes, crutches against the counter, her flat stomach against the sink, cold white-bellied arms cut and now wet-bandaged, clung with soap. She banged the dishes as if her arms had taken all the dancing from her broken leg – hard dancing like feet trying to hurt the earth. Dymphna should have been swinging around her legs, sucking fat four-year-old fingers, or licking sponge cake batter from a spoon.

Bernadette put plate after plate in the rack, suds sliding down the china, and then there was the clink of the silver her mother-in-law had given her.

"Mother?" James said, not knowing that his English accent, that the word itself, was a judgment upon her. Irish children would not say "Mother," but "Mam." He wanted the cocoa she always made him in the evening, wanted to know things would go on as they always had.

"Mother?"

She knew she was alone. Even her little boy was becoming like them, like her husband, like the Protestants.

She finished the dishes, hung up the towel, turned, and James believed then that she was completely blind in her seeing eye also. The eye filled with tears, wallowed in stillness, sent a shiver up his back.

His father was standing by the kitchen table, shoulders and heart forward, arms ready to embrace her, a glass still in his hand.

"I have to go home," were the only words she spoke.

"Of course we'll go. Of course," his father said, his words gusting with whiskey.

But she only stared at him with her single eye, an eye which froze instead of flashed, then took herself upstairs, no hug for James, no kiss for either. Man and boy heard a door close, and shortly after, the crash of glass. They rushed upstairs to find the bedroom door locked – the mother-and-father room of cries in the night, of some strange sort of pain James could not imagine. In the bathroom, the mirror of the medicine cabinet was shattered, the shards crashed into the sink, toothbrushes and the remains of a clay mug in the middle of scattered reflections. In the wastebasket was the square pillow of cotton gauze and tape, crusted with blood.

His father threw himself at the bedroom door, crying "No! No! Think of James if you can't think of me! It wasn't you! God doesn't bring his judgment down like that! Bernadette!"

James, his cheek against a corner of wall, couldn't move. His mother opened the door and let the knife of mirror fall from her hand. There was a thin cut across her other wrist, dark pearls of blood, but it was the stabbing hand that bled the most; she squeezed red from the fist clenched against her heart.

She was remembering his birth among strangers – one of whom was his father – his birth to a banished woman, a girl of sixteen, his birth to a woman who didn't know, then, if she wanted him. Her own father was now only a roar in her ears; she had been his favourite, and had betrayed his love to come here to Victor, to England...to this mess.

Poor James. Poor little boy. To have come out of nothing, the great dark nothing – and then to meet the void within his own mother.

He was part of her when he was living inside her body, and after, the little arms, the little hands she couldn't stop caressing, were still hers. He was the only thing that was truly hers; her son who was becoming like the English, her son who could turn Protestant. She saw him dying, saw him flinging his way to hell.

And she, damned as a suicide.

She looked at him, and this time he knew she could see.

Her eye ate him – and the other one was just a hole, a scabbing mess as if it had been clawed out by some huge bird.

"I'm here for you, James. I've come back from the dead for you."

She reached out her bleeding hand to him and he couldn't shut his eyes, couldn't take them off the hole in her face. He heard the sound of blood dropping on the hardwood like a tapping finger.

"FOR IF THE DARK PLACES OF THE EARTH
HAVE ALWAYS BEEN FULL
OF THE HABITATIONS OF CRUELTY,
THERE HAS ALWAYS BEEN
A SPRING OF MERCY IN MANKIND."

– H.W.

THE air of Ireland was the whitest rain: mist, almost cloud, falling. Cattle and sheep walked in the small, irregular fields, over the green rolling shoulders, hips, bellies and breasts of land. The walls dividing the fields were backbones, the best of them topped with upright slices of slate, mortar between the vertebrae, the worst of them upright shuffles of slate flake, splashed with grey and white lichen or overgrown with jumbles of fern, blackberry, white trumpeted bindweed and waves of fuchsia.

The country of long memory and the living wills of dead men.

James saw everything through the finger-drawn animals on the steamed window of the bus: green flashing horses and deer and dogs and seagulls with a blur of white water-droplets between them, animals made of the flashing grassy distance. His mother beside him was silent, her face closed like her eye. He licked a freckle off her arm and chewed, swallowed. She bent and bit one from the tip of his nose.

"Are you bored?"

He nodded and she pulled a small notepad and pencil from her purse.

"Monster?" she said.

"You go first."

She made a fat body, a blister body, a body like a huge teardrop with a neck that ended in a point.

"Onion man," she said. "Is that what he –"

"Onion bum." James drew a bum crack as she laughed, then a tiny pin-head on the tip of the neck, with hair spiking up from it, and a toothy smile floating above. "His head is too tiny for his face."

"You're good at the drawing."

"You mean *I draw very well*, mother."

"I *mean* you're the very devil at it."

She ruffled his hair like she usually did when he corrected her English, but there was something else in her face – what he could see of her face within her kerchief: something blue and cloudy, the way she would look outside if it was the fourth or fifth day of rain, and sigh.

She drew frog flipper hands, and he drew big toenails on elephant feet. She drew big batty eyelashed eyes and he drew a belly button – a monster outsie big as a marble, bum and belly both on the front of the monster body.

They got off the bus in Killaghmore, the bus driver lifting down the suitcases into the square, an open area of potholed asphalt surrounded by brightly painted shops and pubs. It was the place his mother grew up, the place she and his father met, but it wasn't much. One car passed, then mostly horse or donkey carts, traffic patterns marked out with manure, lumpy, runny, and run over. Men and women paced between the shops, their eyes on the newcomers and the weather, wondering. His foot was asleep so he stamped the tingles out and caught his mother around the waist.

"Stop, now," she said, grabbing through the contents of her purse. "I thought I brought my –"

"I'm hungry."

"Yes, I know."

The journey had worn them out – all day yesterday on the train, from Oxford to London to Liverpool, all night on the ferry, sleeping in fits and starts, and most of that day on trains and motorcoach. The canvas shopping bag of apples, sausage rolls, sandwiches and biscuits that James was in charge of became lighter and lighter until his mother emptied it of crumbs, shook out the waxed paper, folded it and put it in her purse. He thought it was strange to get on the bus in Cork without a crumb, then to be locked up, speeding along. Who knew when they would get off?

"Dad should have come."

"You know he has to mind the shop."

"But I sweep up for him. I –"

"Hush up, now."

"Where's the Anglican church?"

"Church of Ireland it's called here. The steeple over there. See? It was the Catholic, you know. Before it was stolen from us by the English."

"Tell me the story of you and Dad."

Her hand strayed up to her face, to her scars which had taken on an unnatural redness against her flushed face.

"You're not to speak of that. Not here. Not ever. Understand?"

He didn't understand. He nodded.

It was two weeks since the doctor had sawn away her outer white leg, a hard cocoon James had covered with pencil-crayon drawings of cars, horses, and dragons. Her inner leg appeared like a new one: wrinkled, healthy if pale, churning life after mummification. It had been days since she removed the bandage, the half-mask, at his father's request. On one side she was still herself, her striking angular face smooth as her soft arms. The other side was something that wasn't her, a nest of fresh red scars turning slowly to old white scars around the glass eye, skin lumpy, shining, the lids no longer forming an almond, but a skew-lashed diamond on its side. She had seen her son's horror, raked her hair over her face and wailed.

She smoothed her lips red with the lipstick she'd found, shook out a fresh head scarf – the colour of a calm sea – and tied it too far forward around her head, letting the excess form a tunnel for her face. She led her son into the spirit grocer's, leaving the baggage beside the door.

The shop was tiny, its uneven floor of green linoleum blackening with wear. On one side was a bar made of planks, running on to form a counter and hold a cash register. Built-in cubicle shelves filled the walls to the ceiling, where the wood was cut out in sturdy gingerbread fretwork.

Gingerbread, James thought.

Everything was covered in layers of thick brown paint, so many layers, corners were dulled, edges made obscure and sticky-looking.

Molasses.

He wandered, examined objects, read labels: pitchforks, sheep dip, (*sheep* dip?), hen tonic, knitting wool, frying pans, tea and sugar, bread and butter, soap and starch, among other things, and whiskey and stout behind the counter. A decaying man sat on the stool behind the cash register, frayed woolen elbows on the only wood rubbed clean of paint. The tweed cap on his head covered his dirty faded hair and the dandruff that was not already on his coat collar. His hands were thick, his nails broken and grubby, and he held his foam-topped glass of Guinness preciously, his black but golden apple.

"Somethin' I can do for ye?" His smile showed a black mouth with a few stumps of slick, glistening, brown teeth.

"Soda bread." His mother turned her head here and there, examining, avoiding. "This one."

"Righ-et."

"And some biscuits."

"Just got the Jacob's in a fresh tin from the man," he said, his voice mild and musical, as if he was talking to himself. "And would ye be wanting any cream crackers?"

"No, just biscuits. A half pound. Those," she said, pointing into the big tin he had opened, "and –"

"Ginger ones," James said. "To keep our hair red."

She flashed a smile at him through the blue kerchief tunnel and whispered, "To take to your Grandpa Cahalane – his favourite." She put a shaking finger to her lips.

"Lucky boy," the man said, winking at James as he weighed the biscuits. His mother folded them in a crumpled sheet of waxed paper that had held sandwiches the day before.

"Ye wouldn't be from around these parts, now?" he said, peering at her, craning his neck to the side, then down, trying to see inside the kerchief. She ducked her head to shuffle through her purse again. "Something familiar about ye. The voice, maybe."

"England," she mumbled, put money on the counter and took the shopping bag out of her purse.

But you *are* from here, James wanted to say, outraged because his mother was wrong and the truth of the matter was within him, dancing to get out, to show that he, himself, was right, and oh, how he loved to be right. He opened his mouth, but she silenced him with a glare, made him hold the bag open while she put the food inside. The angry face of a middle-aged man poked through a curtained doorway and vanished so quickly, James wasn't sure he'd seen it – but he must have. The curtain was still swaying, remembering.

"Ah, righ-et," the old man said. "Righ-et. There ye go. God bless."

Outside, Bernadette picked up the suitcase and paced across the square. James followed her down the corner street with a grey-tasting empty-stomach burp, and with his carpet bag and all that was inside it – his new book on the animals of America that his father's cousin sent from Canada, his pencil crayons, his plastic wolf teeth. Where was the Protestant deanery where his great-uncle had lived? He was not to talk of it. He opened his mouth and closed it, confused by two kinds of hunger.

"Mother, I want to eat *now*."

"Now, now, now. Not yet." She walked with her head down, avoiding the gaze of everyone they passed. Out of town, they took a side road that passed over a brown, swollen stream. She led him onto a path beside the water into a cave of trees.

"It's still here," she said, and sat on a rotting bench, motioning him to sit beside her. She looked toward the road, then broke off a moon-sliver piece of the round flat soda bread, the paper bag crunching. Crumbs fell with the shakings of flour that was thick on the bottom of the loaf. James ate the top raisins first – swollen hard and burnt – then the top brown crust, exposing the white flesh and soft raisins of the inside. Then he ate the rest, his tongue and lower lip on the bottom ashy crust, dry with flour, the inner bread soft and sweet. It was almost as good as his mother's.

"That man in the shop has been there ever since I can remember, though sure his son must be running it now. My father used to have a pint with him while my mother shopped. I wonder about his wife. You'd always see her there. She might have died."

"You know him?" He held the last bite of bread in his mouth, amazed. His mother had always been a friendly person. She would start up a conversation with anybody, even in shops, talking about the poor vegetables, or the damn government, a lack of reserve and decorum his gentle little English grandmother disapproved of.

Bernadette pretended not to hear, tore at her chunk of bread, her lips curled back over sharp teeth, trying to save her lipstick.

"Drink from the stream."

He drank brown water. A year ago he had been shopping with her and she had seen someone from Ireland, from home, from Killaghmore itself.

"God bless us! Nuala! Nuala McGovern! I can't believe my eyes!" She grabbed James's arm in a claw grip and ran with him across the street. He was used to her boisterous voice, the enthusiasm that made his father smile and his grandparents raise their eyebrows, but this was double the usual amount. His mother rushed to embrace the woman, who endured it, then took a step back.

"Bernadette!" A smile crossed the woman's round face and left it. "Never thought I'd see ye again." The woman was visibly pregnant but had become much heavier than she should have. She shifted her weight from one foot to the other.

"What are you doing here? When did you leave home?"

"Oh, guess ye wouldn't know. Me and Jimmy Gillespie, we got married. Two little ones so far. He came over to work as a builder a year or so back, and me and kids, now, settling in. Just in Oxford for the day, ye know, bit of a sightsee. Mam's visiting us in London looking after things."

"How is everybody? Anything changed? What's the news? Has Colm –"

"Oh, I don't know." The woman glanced at James, then looked past them down the street. "Things pretty much go on as always. I'm meeting Jimmy a fair ways up. Should be going."

"You'll come in for a cup of tea tonight then, tell me everything," his mother said, scribbling her address on a corner of an envelope she found in her purse.

The woman nodded and walked away, but she and Jimmy Gillespie didn't show up for tea. His mother was as furious as she'd been overjoyed to see her.

"Barely knew the young *cat*. This is what they do now with hospitality! Didn't tell me a thing! You'd think she'd be happy to see someone from home! Eat these!" she ordered James, pointing to a pile of fancy white bread sandwiches, the crusts cut off, the filling creamy, chickeny – exactly like the ones his grandmother served. "They'll be terrible tomorrow." He and his father had eaten them all, thinking it would make her feel better, leaving the fruitcake and shortbread, the things that would keep.

Wind blew water down on them: rain trapped in the leaves. She handed him another chunk of soda bread, this time from the thicker middle of the loaf, mostly the soft inside. He squashed some of it with his fingers before putting it in his mouth, molded it like clay.

"Don't play with your food."

"Dad says I'm experimenting. Like a scientist. Like cousin Lawrence in Canada in the wilderness, all the wolves out to eat him." James champed on the bread – open-mouthed, like a wolf. "Why aren't you happy to be back?"

She shook her head, let a gust of breath out her red, red lips. She was wearing her best dress, best shoes and Sunday coat, but she still didn't want anybody to know her – as if her hair was in curlers and she was running out to buy eggs. Was she afraid the man in the store would see her bad eye?

"Did we pass the deanery? Was the –"

"You're not to talk of that. That was your father's story, anyhow," she snapped. "Tell it to yourself if you need to hear it."

He was suddenly aware of the wide space between them on the bench. When he looked up, he caught her dead eye in its red bed and looked away. The kerchief had blown back from the right side of her face and she couldn't see that her blind eye was exposed. Glancing at her was frightening, dangerous. Sometimes, in the first second, he didn't recognize her.

His father, Victor Edward George, named after the latest varieties of European monarchs, often lost his reserve after supper and too many brandies. His hair, usually water-combed straight back, sagged in blond strings over his temples – the kind of limp hair that seemed to sag over the foreheads of the most dissolute of aristocrats – or aspiring aristocrats. He put his arm around his young son like a new-found drinking friend, told the most important story of his life as if James had never heard it.

"Naughty lad I was at King's College. Fell in with the acting crowd – though I couldn't get on the stage for fright. But I could assume a character, become someone else. I wasn't shy when I was Julius Caesar. Romeo was never shy, or the Duke of Urbino, or Casanova, or Faust. I folded me up and put me in my pocket. Hm." Every now and then, Victor would punctuate his stories with a "hm," a little burst of wonder mingled with humour. "In the pub, I was Mercutio. Wore black, spent money on whiskey, failed my examinations, and fell in – hm – well, your grandparents shipped me off to Dublin, to Trinity College, to forget her – to try again. Wouldn't even let me come home for the summer. Had to go to Uncle Rodney's, where he was dean. Hm. What a place. Hovels everywhere. The middle of nowhere."

"And I thought I was getting Mercutio, or however the hell you say it," his mother would accuse. Around this point, usually in the middle of darning a sock, in the middle of the story, she would get up and leave the lounge, her red hair flying behind her like hot, angry wind.

"Freckle-faced girl!" he would shout after her, then lower his voice. "Strong slender arms. She smelled of milk. Hm. That haze of red hair around her shoulders like an outrageous sunset, going down, almost, to her waist, and a way with a willow switch on the back of her donkey. The slow crunch of her feet on the gravel, and then the sway of her..."

This was James's favourite part of the story, when his father seemed to be reading romance out of the air, making his beautiful mother even more beautiful. Sometimes Victor would open his hands like a book, fingers spread, and elaborate further on Bernadette's sea blue eyes, on the way the town was – the donkey carts upsetting down the church hill, the chickens in the street.

But the last time Victor told the story, he got lost, even his imagined drinking friend vanishing, his pipe going out, his hands creeping up to cover his head, a man trying to hide from himself, talking to himself. Why had James wanted to think about this story? Why couldn't he stop?

"She wasn't like an angel. Something sharper. An eagle. Not Venus, but Hera, a goddess, keen, knowing. Killing. *Hm.*" The noise was no longer humourous, but sad, bitter. "A face like a sword. You wouldn't know it until it cut you open, disemboweled you. Painful...brilliant. How could a face like that be *young*? Be any age? The tick of all those clocks as we climbed the stairs to my room. I didn't know she was so young. I was such a bumbling idiot and she was too young to know. If I had...I...I almost left her behind when she was in the Ladies at the Cork railway station. Terrified. What my parents would do when...I didn't know she was so young. Hm. But not too young to have a baby, oh no. Those clocks. Dark wooden boxes, little coffins, ticking, measuring our footsteps up the stairs. Casanova, Mercutio, they all abandoned me, even Mephistopheles – that's out of character for the devil. I couldn't remember how *Victor* would behave. Where was Victor? Hm? Where had I put him? Where is he now? Poor frightened girl expected the man I'd pretended to be and I couldn't even find the frightened boy. I fell in love with her like no Casanova would have."

The continuation of the story was their marriage – a "Gretna Green" marriage on the run; Victor took her first to Scotland because a sixteen-year-old could marry there without her parents' consent, took her to Gretna Green, a town near the English border famous for its elopements, famous for its "anvil" priests who, as in the way of blacksmiths, forged lovers together like iron. James's grandparents gave up on Victor's education, and bought him a book shop. This was the father James knew, the book-merchant who knew more about literature than a man behind a counter should, a man with the right props – the antique books, the ledgers, the nib pens, the old maps and prints, the bidding skill at auctions. Victor soon forgot they were props. He escaped into them, his own little dramatic production, because he found they suited him. He was able to take his shy self out of his pocket and unfold.

"She was fifteen. *Fifteen*. I didn't know. Those clocks. And now she hates me."

No, James thought, felt the orange blindness of shutting his eyes too tight, shutting out the fading blue grey of the clouds, his mother tearing bread with her teeth and red-rimmed mouth at the far end of the bench.

But she kisses you, James said to the father he saw in his head. She kisses you *hard*. He had seen it more than once when they thought he was playing in the garden – that disturbing crush of face into face that made James turn away. She couldn't hate him.

"You don't," he said.

"What are you talking about, James? You're daydreaming." Bernadette tried to dust the flour off her brusque hands, but they were wet from the beginning drizzle and she made white paste in her palms – white paste that smeared up her wrist to the fierce red cut-mark. "No bleeding use." She wiped her hands in the grass. "It's a long way, so we'd better start walking. It'll be dark, soon."

The road was a slope, and with the rain, a stream. The ditches rushed with water beneath the nervous grasses, God trying to flood them away, their two of a kind.

Her roaring father was in her ears. He was already an old man when she left, his face creased from a life of hard weather. She half expected, half hoped, he would be dead. She didn't want him to see her like this. Her earliest memory was of being a child of three, riding across the kitchen on his huge shoe with her arms wrapped around his leg: thump-sweep, thump-sweep. She was his baby, the only child he could sit back and enjoy once his sons were old enough to help with the farm work. Until she started school, she rode on his shoulders, was part of him, even when he stopped in the street to argue:

"Me little Bernie here could do a better job of the damn government! What d'ye say, pup? Would ye like to be the prime minister? The *Taoiseach*?"

"No! I want to be a princess!"

All those men, young and old, laughing with her, loving her, her father's red-haired – red-winged – faery.

Growing up separated them, her beauty becoming less and less childlike. She worked in the kitchen at her mother's insistence, learning what a girl had to learn, until that horrible day when her father found out there was a baby inside her. "Go, then," he said, shaking, pointing, his fury as much about blaming himself for spoiling her, as much about getting her safely away so he would not be able to hit her. "You've turned your back on me, and I won't keep you if you want to leave so badly. Go then!" She wouldn't have gone if he hadn't pushed her, shut the door behind her.

She would never have left him.

No. This was just the way she wanted to remember it, wanted to erase all his yelling, erase how he seemed to stop loving her as she grew away from faeryhood to womanhood, as she grew beyond his control.

She hoped he was dead, shook herself. Bad luck to wish that.

"I'm the raven who deserted Noah," she said, warning her son. "They might not be happy to see us."

She told James about the houses they passed. They were stone, some whitewashed an eggshell colour, some very poor, with only one room, the kind in which all cooking was done over a naked turf fire. A few of the farms looked better, with many small outbuildings, and he saw one rare tractor to replace the work of horses and donkeys.

"This is good land. Folks get poorer as you get away from the shore and the towns. Some in the hills never come down but for the big fair in July."

They stopped once for his mother to heave the suitcase onto a dryish patch of road beneath a sycamore. She scuffed through its contents for his raincoat. It was quiet, not like the city. He felt the sluggish heave of cattle beyond hedge and wall, the thump of their steps through the earth, up through the soles of his shoes, saw them through an iron gate sludged with black paint, the thick, wattle-necked beasts chewing the grass, concentrating on one of many stomachs.

Stomachs.

The bread was a small dry lump in his stomach – not enough – and only made him hungrier.

He put on the coat and they walked. When the rain stopped, the clouds tore open, and a cool wind came through the shredding sky. The sun burned on the clouds, was slipping beyond the horizon.

They turned up a narrow, grassy, seldom-used road, a boreen that was like a flat-bottomed valley, stone walls holding back the earth of the fields on either side, fuchsia overgrowing everywhere.

"Lord have mercy. They have the electricity now. Do you see that house at the top of the rise?" His mother pointed through a thinning of the fuchsia, then reached down to her stockings, soaked below the knee where the hem of her coat flapped. "That's where I was born. You'll meet your – your grandparents soon – and what a sight I'll make. Lord. I don't know if I can do it, now."

What James saw was a fall of roofs and angles, tiny houses and sheds that seemed to have clumped together like magnets. They were black against the dim sky, yellow light glowing through the windows. It didn't seem right that he should have another set of grandparents, and he felt a surge of loyalty to the ones he had always known: his grandfather's gruff humour and refusal to wear socks because of some mysterious happening of the Great War, his grandmother's soft wrinkled hands, her gentle, off-key operatic voice, and the Jaffa cakes she bought for him. He loved even the look of near-to-fainting shock on her face when his mother swore: "Dymphna! Where the hell are you hiding?"

"I won't like them," James said.

"You will if you try."

"I don't want to."

"You have enough to go around, James. If you love the one, you won't be depriving the other. You can love two grandfathers and be all right."

"And be all right," he muttered.

"What?"

"What?"

"Don't do this to me," she said, shaking her head, water flying from it.

"This to me."

"Don't start up. Not now."

"Not now."

She raised her slap-shaped hand, but changed her mind, switched the suitcase to the slap hand, her purse to the opposite shoulder, and walked faster, then slower, then faster again until they were at the edge of the yard.

"My arms must be three inches longer," she said, making him laugh in imagining it, laughing because it was something she would have said before the accident.

"Sorry," he said, "about starting up."

She strode across the cement and grass of the farmyard and left the suitcase in the dry under the eaves. He looked down at the water beads on his polished shoes. His mother's shoes now squished with the water that had run down her legs. Her knock on the door was barely audible. Why didn't she fling open the door and announce their coming the way she burst into his grandparents' house in Oxford? "Here comes your *Celtic horde*, like it or not," using what she called "Victor's fancy-book words."

"It's been twelve years," she whispered to the air. "They aren't expecting us."

She hit the door again with her knuckles, harder, then opened it.

"Make a wish," she whispered to James, what she told him to do whenever he stepped over the threshold of a house he'd never been in before.

They walked through the porch, into the kitchen, James wishing, exhausted, that this wasn't *here*, but *home*, wishing also for steak and kidney pie.

His eyes opened and his heart fell. His other grandparents had an entrance hall with a stairway, golden wood floors, India carpets, a crystal chandelier in the dining room, and also had Mrs. Tupper, a housekeeper who cooked everything from curry to lobster.

This kitchen had a low ceiling, thick walls and recessed windows, all painted stark white, with cold grey checker-squares of slate for a floor. There was a deep, square, porcelain sink in one of the window alcoves, cupboards, a counter along a wall, a few old chairs, and a long wooden settle behind a table covered with oilcloth. The air smelled of milk, raw meat, and smoke from cigarettes and the large peat-burning range, and it vibrated with tin-sharp radio music, an over-fast jig that only his mother might have attempted to dance to.

Through a low doorway came the oldest woman James had ever seen, a white enamel jug of milk in her hands. She was a gnarled tree with a thin, white thunderstorm of hair. The curl of her dowager's hump was so pronounced, her head seemed to be attached to the front of her throat. She raised her eyes from the cotton dress that shrouded her with blossoms and James could see an absent-minded outrage there.

"Oh," she said, her face changing abruptly when she saw them. "Oh," she said again, more softly, her eyes round, her mouth round, "Oh," more a gasp than a word, as if the sight of them had caused some terrible physical pain.

His mother felt for his shoulder and pulled him against her wet coat.

"If you don't want me, if things haven't changed, I'll go. Mam? Do you want me to go?"

The old woman's hands moved on the milk jug. "It was your father who wanted that. Not me, no. I never wanted ye to go. I never did...even though ye've treated me as if I were dead. *He's* been dead these five years, God rest his soul."

"He's dead," his mother said, shut her eyes because it was bad luck to have wished it and have it so.

"Ten years without a letter?" the old woman yelled, slopping milk on the slates.

"Mam!" His mother rushed to the old woman whose face withered with scowls and confusion. Bernadette caught the jug and they held it between them. "I'll never go against ye again, Mam, I swear it. I swear."

The old woman shook her head, not in refusal, but in disbelief at the whole of what she saw, her lost daughter standing before her mutilated, her last baby, born when she was forty-six. Bernadette let go of the jug and ran to the sink to get a rag to mop the floor. Watching her daughter wipe the floor, the old woman gathered herself. She wasn't the oldest woman on the hill, but she looked it, after ten children, two dying in infancy, and more than half a lifetime of giving her share of milk over to her young ones, her back curling over from the want of it. Her name was Grania. Even her daughters called her Granny sometimes, after teaching their children to do so. She lifted her eyes to stare at James.

"And who is this?"

"Your grandson, Jame – Seamus."

His mother stopped wiping, lifted her nylon-covered knees from the cold stone. There were only looks, then, each of them glancing from one person to the other, looks that drew a triangle, attempted to connect all three people after so many years – grandmother, mother, grandson – old woman, maimed daughter, reluctant boy.

"Well, well," the grandmother gusted, her eyes unable to settle. "Ye'll have a cup o' tea, then," she ordered, swallowing, and swished her hand toward an empty chair at the table.

"Go J...Seamus. Warm yourself. The best spot there."

James sat where his mother pointed, on a bench by the big Aga cooking range. Beside him was a box of hand-cut peat bricks, brown and speckled like dog turd. The heat they gave off in the range was cozy, woolly, prickly.

"Have ye eaten? Has the boy?" were Granny's next orders, disguised as questions.

"Only a bit of bread after the bus, Mam."

Granny shook her head. "Damned eejits." She went to work cutting bread and making tea.

"Mam, I couldn't eat – now – for God's sake, don't put on a fry for us."

"Well what have ye eaten then, today – roast pheasant – to say *no* to a bit of egg and sausage?"

"Nothing, Mam. Nothing, really."

"Well, ye know where the eggs are, and Paddy's comin' in for his tea. Go on. Five – six, then."

Bernadette opened the little cupboard and took out a small, yellowed ceramic bowl, a paler chip on the edge.

"You haven't managed to break this then, all these years?"

James watched his mother smiling, smiling, but crying at the same time, her mouth twisting in ways he'd never seen before, and he sucked in air, and more air, until he stopped breathing, and he was frozen, couldn't breathe out, his chest trembling, his arms rigid. He couldn't go to her to comfort her because it hardly seemed like her.

"Go on. Go on! Haven't got all bleeding day!" Granny said, her voice harsh, wiping a tear away from under one eye with her knuckles. She slapped jam on a piece of brown soda bread and put it on a plate, then put the plate on James's lap. He stared at it a moment before she seized his head with both hands and forced him to look into her bleary eyes. They were blue, dull like another kind of skin, with soggy yellow drifts of something in the corners. She exhaled whiskey and reeking fish. He wrenched away.

"Well, don't get the jam on yourself," she said, offended, and scratched another chair across the floor to the table.

A man came through the door with a burst of rainy, night-smelling air. He was tall, thick-shouldered, and softened throughout with a small layer of fat. The hair sticking out from under his tweed cap was beginning to grey, as was the stubble on his face – almost a week's worth – and high on his cheeks were two tufts of curly whiskers. Before he could shut the door, a dirty, dripping, black and white mongrel puppy skittered across the floor.

"Get it out, Paddy! Get the filthy thing out!" Granny yelled.

"Sorry, Mam, the weather, 'tis desperate, and the pup, he's a young one. Had his tail stepped on by a cow and 'twas bleeding bad. Scared he'll get infected."

"Well he don't look in a bad way now. Shut him in the porch then, shut him in the porch until I can give him a wash. So long as he doesn't eat the shoes."

He caught the dog and was carrying it under one arm, back to the door.

"Paddy," Bernadette said, coming in from the pantry with her bowl full of eggs. "Paddy."

He turned, confused.

"Lord." He shook his head and squinted at her scarred eye. "Lord, it's Bernie! Aw – *Jasus*, girl. *Jasus*. What's happened to ye?" He caught her in his free arm, pressed the dog's snout against her ribs. "Ye never sent a word – aw, nothing – and I was mad at ye for years. I thought I was never going to see ye again."

"I'm sorry. I'm sorry. I thought –"

"Nah, nah. He's dead. Long time. The bad's finished with now. Is over." He shook trouble away with his head. "Lord, Bernie! Lord!" His eyes were almost closed, his smile wrung with grief when he examined her damaged face.

"Paddy, get yourself to the table so ye can sit and eat, then," Granny said, coming close, churning her arms in front of her to separate them.

"But Mam! How can I –"

"Ye'll eat because the bacon's already fryin' for ye! Don't I always throw it in the pan the moment ye come in? No matter what bleeding –"

"A'right, Mam." He shut the dog in the porch, then pulled a great wad of white handkerchief from his pants pocket and blew his nose wildly. After washing his hands in the kitchen sink, he sat in the chair at the head of the table. Granny finished the fry, Bernadette helping her heap the hot plates, then setting the most loaded one in front of him: toast, fried potatoes, sausage and black pudding, rashers of bacon and huge fried eggs, their yolks more yellow than the sun, their edges crispy brown lace.

"So tell me everything," he said, through a mealy mouthful of potato. He ate from the front of the plate to the back, as if the food was as uniform as oatmeal. A drip of yolk rolled down his chin when he didn't flip a rubbery slice of egg into his mouth fast enough. He rasped it off his stubble with his knife, then licked the knife clean. He listened, filling the fork with egg and putting it in his mouth, then stabbing a disk of black pudding with his knife and putting that in his mouth, eyes mild beneath the hat he'd forgotten to take off.

"Paddy, this is my son, Seamus." His mother motioned for James to get up and come closer. He didn't. She only called him Seamus when she was angry. "Seamus! Do as you're told."

"Sure, but I think the boy's afraid of me," Paddy said, wiping the corner of his mouth with the heel of his hand. "Will ye not come to sit beside me so's we can have some good *craic*?" His voice was sleepy, and his wink was like a tic of his face.

Bernadette nodded to James, set his plate down, and he went to sit beside his uncle. His plate held only an egg, a strip of bacon, and some fried potatoes. He gazed into Paddy's plate as if it was the future.

"So, young man..." Paddy said. He held out a crusty shining sausage on the end of his knife. "Am I to understand this is your first visit to Ireland?"

"Yes, sir." James pulled the sausage off the knife.

"And do ye like it well enough, then?"

"It's nice," he said, glancing at his mother, wondering whether she could tell he was lying. Ireland was rainy and tiring, and uncomfortable on an empty stomach, and his granny scared him a little. He bit through the sausage, cracking its skin, chewing the sweet, greasy meat.

"I see. So do ye like the hurling, young Seamus?"

"He doesn't know what that is, Paddy. They don't have it in England." His mother was wiping the cleared table with a knitted rag. "Cricket and football is what he knows."

"Ah, well." Paddy chewed his bacon.

"Why do you have hair way up there on your cheeks?" James asked, his uncle's interest making him brave. "Why don't you shave it off?" He had never seen whiskers up so high on a man's face and had an urge to touch them. Did they grow that way only in Ireland?

Paddy cocked his head in surprise and moved his eyes comically in an effort to look at his own face. "Sure, but I never thought about it. Didn't seem like a place a man should have to shave,

beneath the eyes. Wouldn't think of shaving me forehead either –
if there was a hair growing on it. Oh, pardon." Paddy removed his
hat and put his palm over his receding hairline. "Getting old,
Bernie. Never thought I'd be one o' them old bachelors."

"Mother says hair on a man's face is disgusting."

"Seamus!"

"Oh, she does? Bernadette! How come ye never told me the
ladies think that? If I'd known, I'd have been married by the time
I was twenty-five."

"It never was your hair, Paddy, dear Paddy."

"Now, your mother," Paddy said, putting his arm across the
back of James's chair, "she's a fine one, and lucky ye are to have
her. Ye ever seen her dancing? She's a mighty dancer. The boys,
they were all after her when she was a young one."

"For God's sake, Paddy!" Granny said.

"Only ones that can dance like that have some faery in them.
Did your mother warn ye there were faeries in the family?"
Paddy winked again.

Granny turned away in disgust. She wasn't eating with them,
but washing a few dishes in the sink, wiping tea cups, saucers,
and plates in whirlwinds of white dishcloth and clattering them
in stacks on the counter.

"Ye have the faeries in England?" Paddy asked James. "Now,
don't tell me ye haven't heard of the little people."

"Babies?"

First Paddy, then the women, burst out laughing.

"He doesn't know about blarney either, Paddy, so easy," his
mother said.

"Faeries, Seamus. Little wee people, about so high." Paddy
swished the air at James's waist with his bitten-nailed hand.
"Make nothing but trouble. Don't ye listen to them pot-of-gold
stories. They'll sour your milk, and spoil your meat and make
the moths eat holes in the bottom of your britches!"

"Yeah, sure."

"The lad doesn't believe ye," Granny sputtered. "You're
raising him to be a skeptic, then, are ye, Bernie?"

"My – my mother-in-law thought me superstitious, didn't like me telling those stories. And maybe he's too old for that, now."

"Take ye around tomorrow, Seamus, to meet the lads," Paddy said. "No use in ye spending your time in the house with the women. They'll wear your ears out. Ye can come and help me and Dermot wi' the cows."

He didn't really *want* to help with the cows, never having been on the same side of the fence as one, but he guessed it might be better than staying with his mother, who was acting so strange, and with his granny, with her hard-voiced orders and angry face.

They put him in a tiny upstairs room where the window sat in its dormer at floor level, hunched under a slant of ceiling. He sat in it with knees poking up, toes bent against the thick plaster and stone of the opposite side. Outside was the yard and the barn, and beyond, the lights of the farms down the hill, like campfires, and then the dim Viking burning of Killaghmore. He didn't know that in the morning he would be able to see the ocean. Even though his body was vibrating with too much travel, too much newness, and too little sleep, he refused to cry. The sound of rain encouraged the brown water and tea to strain at his bladder. He went into the dark hallway, but behind all the doors there were only beds, so he went to the stairs, light shining up dimly from the kitchen, and stopped. They were all still down there, talking. He sat on the top step, then slid down to the next, and the next, so he could hear and not be seen.

His mother was telling them about his father, the book shop, his grandparents in their big house – oh, the fancy china and cut glass, and a housekeeper, no less – and the motor holidays each summer, and then she started on about him, what a big healthy baby, how mild he was – tears, of course, but rarely a tantrum even when a toy was broken – how he had to know everything, would cry in frustration whenever he made a mistake or she had to finish a sentence for him because his mind was so full of ideas trying to get out that his mouth couldn't catch up, and how smart he was, what an imagination, how good he was at school, and it was *such* a school, too. He could tell she was avoiding the other part of their story, the part about his sister, the part about the accident. When she finally began to tell it, he squeezed his eyes shut so hard, he thought there would be no room for the tears to seep in, but they did somehow, and he let them come, let them fall, the only way he could cry without sobbing, without making a sound. It was hard to listen and cry at the same time, but he managed. He could tell his mother cried, too, though her voice was as tight as his eyes.

"...not your fault, Bernie..." he heard his uncle saying.

"Well, whose, then? Whose? It's just what I've done. My life...I wasn't a worthy mother...so God is punishing –"

"Bernie –"

"I didn't want her at first – not either of them, and now – God forgive me."

He couldn't hear anything else, couldn't understand anything else he heard, because he understood this.

"Are ye all right?" Paddy was peering up at him from the bottom of the stairs.

"I'm looking for the lavatory." He wiped his face quickly with the palms of his hands.

"Ah. Right. Ye don't want to use the potty under your bed?"

"No."

Potties were for children.

Paddy went through the kitchen, slipped his bare feet into the large shit-crusted Wellingtons in the porch.

"The bog's out beside the barn. Ye have boots?"

James shook his head and followed Paddy into the rain, feet cold and tender on the cement.

"Ye can make water anywhere ye like, but this is where ye do the other business."

"This is it?' James said, aghast. The tiny moonlit shack seemed to lean into the wind. Inside was a seat with a large hole in it. How could he sit there in the reek that was already making him gasp?

"I'll be off to the house, now. Sure but ye can find your own way."

James relieved himself and walked back past the barn. A strange yipping noise came from the open door, and he peered in to see the nearest stall with its wall to ceiling barrier of chicken wire. He could just make out the form of a young fox in one corner, so still, staring back, waiting for him to go away. Cold fingers of rain tapped his head and shoulders on his way to the house.

He stopped inside the porch. The light in the kitchen was out. The others seemed to have gone upstairs to bed. The puppy jumped at his legs, and he sat and gathered it in his arms, the wet from its fur seeping through his pajamas, first cold, then warm. He held the little dog tightly, and it licked and licked and licked his chin in a way that would have had him laughing an hour ago.

He had been working hard to teach himself not to cry. His grandfather said he was too sensitive, was forever telling a story about what he was like when he was three, too far back for him to remember. It had been Christmas. He had peeled a mandarin orange out of its green wrapping paper, then out of its skin: so many blankets for it to curl up in. Someone had said something about the poor orange being eaten – the poor little baby pieces he found between the usual-sized segments, only about the size of his thumbnail. He refused to eat the baby pieces, folded them between his hands and told everyone he was hugging them and that they were sleeping in his arms. He had not been able to stop crying when his mother told him the mould would eat his precious darlings if he didn't, and he wanted to eat them, but wanted to save them at the same time. Neither his parents nor his grandparents had any patience for the knots of remorse he tied himself up in.

He listened to the sound of muted voices coming from somewhere above him. They must have forgotten he was still outside, even his mother.

But then, she hadn't wanted him.

James woke shivering in bed, under blankets that seemed to suck damp from the air. He blew out of his mouth to see if he could see his breath.

One side of his mouth.

Other side.

Invisible.

Foot stomping, Granny's terse commands, and Paddy's mumbles came from somewhere beneath him.

"Si'down," Granny said, when she caught sight of him standing on the stairs, hands behind his back, teetering between going in among near strangers and going back to find his mother. "D'ye hear me?"

He sat across the table from Paddy who was folding his toast and marmalade and eating it like a sandwich, dripping butter and orange sweetness into the crumbs on his plate. His hair tufted up in places and stuck to his head in others. He looked younger without his old cap in spite of his greying hair.

"They's your work clothes?" he asked James.

"Yes." He'd put on his comfortable clothes because his mother wasn't up to tell him what to do.

"All set then." Paddy gave him a "how are ye" wink as Granny set the steaming bowls of porridge in front of them. She slapped her hands on her apron harder than was necessary before she picked up her cup of tea, the only thing she was having for breakfast, the first of many throughout the day.

James sadly contemplated the lumpy grey sea of oatmeal before pouring on a little milk and putting the first spoonful in his mouth.

"Walking over to Castle Field today – ye'll want to see the ruin – to see how some calves are doing. Vet give 'em injections yesterday. Going to see your uncle Colm. Ye'll meet some of your cousins." Paddy spat a drop of milk as he spoke.

"Stop!"

James dropped his spoon. His mother was standing in the doorway in her blue, almost black, Sunday dress.

"Don't swallow! Spit it out!"

He breathed in a lump of porridge, then coughed it from his throat into his plate. There were red painful whorls inside his squeezed-shut eyes.

"Jesus, Mary and Joseph –" Granny said.

"That was your first bite, wasn't it? You didn't swallow any of it, did you?"

His eyes were watering and he shook his head.

"Good. So you can take communion at Mass with me."

"But it's Saturday."

"Ye'll not backtalk me. Not here in front of me own mother."

He sat back, away from his food, hunger filling him. *Me own mother.* His mother was beginning to sound like them, these Irish relatives who hadn't known he existed. Her eye was tired and raw-looking next to its immutable glass companion.

"Upstairs and change your clothes. Be quick about it!"

He did what he was told.

St. Fachtna's Church looked like the biggest stone in the grave-yard. It was plain and mossy, surrounded by trees and wall, was halfway between the farm and the sea. Beyond it was a ruined tower, some outpost of a long crumbled manor house. He felt faint from lack of food, a characteristic of morning Mass; God wanted you to fast for three hours before you ate His body. Ate Him. Ate God. Maybe He didn't like getting all mixed up together with bits of pork and bread and slimy egg and sloshed into milk and por-ridge oats. James could understand that; maybe God would have to take yet *another* bath. James chanted the prayers trying to keep from laughing, because God had egg-sodden belly-button lint and cereal in his ears, and a chunk of bacon jammed up his nose. How could he get himself all back together after being chewed up by however many people? That would really be a miracle.

The altar boys clanged the bells as if they were calling the cows home, keeping everyone awake. His eyes wandered, settling on things; the windows were made up of dirty little diamonds and cobwebs and the shadows of leaves, except for the new stained glass one beside him. Jesus held a lantern, knocked on a door. At the bottom was a scroll with a dedication he could not read. The floor was brick-coloured tile in the centre and sides, but wood beneath the pews, grey with dirt and old washings. The priest wiped the chalice with the white folded cloth more thoroughly than Granny wiped the dishes. His voice was deep, adenoidal, on the verge of a yawn. James yawned. He rubbed his nose, dislodged something that made his breath whistle with each exhale.

He missed the stone semicircles of saints, angels, bishops and kings that lined the curved wall behind the altar of St. Aloysius, back home in Oxford. Whenever he was bored, he made a game of imagining who they all were, made up stories about them, once staged a fight in which the kings and bishops hit each other on the head with their orbs and maces of state, giggled until his mother put her hand over his mouth, but that made him giggle harder. St. Aloysius was pocked all over with whimsy and horror, from the huge marble goblet at the back filled with holy water, a skin of slippery green algae on the bottom, to the spikes pounded through the soft marble palm of Christ's hands, to the windows bright as sun-backed sheets of paper, crossed with lead, to the black-clothed Jesuits, their scarred old faces.

Whistle. How long could he keep a nose whistle? He had never tried before.

He yawned again. His mother's eyes were closed. He thought she should be looking at the priest. Was she going to sleep? No. Her lips were moving. Her real eye was shiny and wet when she opened it. At least her kerchief was tied tight, covering the bad eye. The thought of strangers looking at her and turning away was unbearable. He'd seen them do it on the bus; he'd done it himself. Hot shameful blood filled his heart, made it feel swollen and purple. He supposed she had to go to Mass. She couldn't just stay in the house for the rest of her life. Her lips moved more and he could hear she was saying something different from what the rest of the people were saying. She had the wanting, *wanting*, look of the crazy woman who came to Mass at St. Aloysius and walked the aisles the whole time, kneeling at each chapel, babbling something else when she should have been synchronized with the rest in the Lord's Prayer.

People *were* looking at his mother, now. The blood rose from his heart, flooded his face.

Whistle.

They stepped outside with the others, mostly women and old men with wrinkled necks, clouds scudding above them through the blue. Grania was walking down the road toward them, a thick grey woolen cloak over her shoulders, the wind blowing her dress against her knobbed legs, her head hunched down and stuck forward.

"Going to bathe me corns in the sea. The only thing that does them any good."

"Isn't that cloak too heavy for a day like today, Mam? Sure, but you'll get it full of sand."

"It's cold near the sea!" Granny snapped, and clutched the edge of the cloak as if Bernadette had threatened to take it from her; the cloak had belonged to her grandmother, and became hers on the day she was born.

Bernadette bowed her head. "Shall I go with you?"

Granny waved her away, bumped through a jam of old women outside the gate of the churchyard, nodded to some, shoved when one got in her way. James watched her shamble down a path beside the graveyard wall, toward hills split with a triangle of fishy green ocean. From behind, she looked headless.

"We're going the other way," his mother told him, when she saw him watching, straining to explore. "Your uncle Colm is down the other way. Weren't you going to help Paddy with the cows today?"

"What kind of help do people *need* with cows?"

She laughed, grabbed his arm, rubbed his back and chest. He rubbed her stomach.

"Oh, to paint on the spots. To tie on their tails. To put in the *moo*."

"Silly Mo-*ther*."

He found himself walking up yet more hill roads. She took the last hunk of soda bread out of her purse, gave it to him, and he stuffed bit by dry bit of it into his mouth.

"Susan will have the kettle on. Not to worry. We'll go this way," she said, going through an opening in a wall. They crossed a field, then passed through a gate made from an old iron headboard of a bed, its black paint bubbled up with rust. Soon, they came to a copse of dead, ivy-strangled trees scratching the sky. She led him to a place where it looked as if people had been dumping garbage. Shreds of faded cloth hung from bare branches and there was a pile of stones covered by bits of plastic and glinting metal. He was very close before he saw a few coins and a trickle of water flowing from a pipe into a mossy barrel. Around the barrel was a dirt path worn through the grass and a wooden platform spanning the puddle of water where the spring became a stream.

"This is St. Fachtna's well," his mother said. "Here." She handed him a small blue plastic rosary, the one he had seen around her Queen of Heaven statue. "Follow me."

They circled the well on their knees, three times in three rosaries. He drank from the dribble of the spout and watched his mother take a small ruffled blouse from her purse – Dymphna's – and snag it up on a branch as high as she could reach. Strange to see her jump like that, her stockings muddy around lithe ankles.

"She's in heaven, James, and – and we're still here." Her eyes closed – even the blind one.

He said a prayer for his sister, hoping she was happy, then thinking no one would be allowed to be unhappy up there. He had forgotten how lonely and bored he had been before she was born, when it was just him in the house, and his mother and father's sporadic fights, when everyone seemed to pay too much attention to him, whether he cried too much, was too sensitive, was too this, too that. Of course he and his sister had fought sometimes, when she copied him, when she followed him around like a puppy and he couldn't take it any more, but they had been together, somehow, against the adults, against the grandfather that poked them in the back with his finger to make them sit straighter, against the lot of them obsessed with forcing vegetables into their mouths.

At his uncle Colm's, his mother sat in the kitchen drinking tea and listening to Colm's wife Susan tell her about their five children. The baby Susan held on her hip wiped his drippy nose on her breast. A girl slightly younger than James stirred an evil-looking black liquid in a pot on the range and stared at him. Susan deposited the baby in Bernadette's lap and worked around the kitchen with a swift calmness, her eyes mostly on her visitors, as if she knew the room so well she could make lunch with her eyes shut. Once when she passed James, she gathered up his hands in her own and folded a cellophane-wrapped butterscotch sweet within them. Colm was late coming back from Killaghmore – buying cattle purge, she said. James found Paddy in the barn when the sweet was almost gone, when it was a tangy little knife on his tongue.

"Ready to go then, after your bit o' prayer?" Paddy asked.

James looked to see if he was laughing, but he wasn't. Three boys were clustered around Paddy and a large cow that was secured behind a wooden fence next to the barn wall. A horse was pulling wisps of hay from a box in the corner, reins brushing the floor.

Whistle. He rubbed the sound from his nose.

"Lads, this is your cousin Seamus from England. This big fella here is Dermot. That's John – both Colm's boys, and this here's Liam, that's your Auntie Maureen's. The young two are your own age exactly."

The boys said a sullen hello. Dermot was a big awkward boy of about sixteen with thick shoulders, a roll of fat around his middle, and small pubescent girl's breasts which he stuck out with an uncertain aggressiveness. He looked nothing like John, who had a gentler face, a body made of twigs, and a thin, asthmatic wheeze. Liam was dark-haired like his cousins, his small face twisted by a sour, lopsided mouth and suspicious eyes. All three wore threadbare, conspicuously mended clothes, very different from James's muddy-kneed church corduroys.

"What are ye staring at, mucky-pants?" Dermot demanded.

"Nothing."

Paddy made a grab for a teat on the large quarter of the cow's lopsided udder and she whipped him in the mouth with her greenish, shit-filled tail. James had never seen such an ugly colour in all his life.

"Pah! Dermot, hold that thing away, will ye?" Paddy wiped his face with the back of his coat sleeve. The big boy grinned and grabbed the tail.

"Shite for your dinner," Dermot said, and John and Liam laughed.

"None o' that talk, now, and I don't care if it *is* a barn you're in." Paddy's voice was too soft to put fear into them, but they stopped grinning.

"Sorry, Uncle Paddy," Dermot said immediately, small eyes contrite. Paddy never gave any of them a cuff, and they loved him for it.

"Now, Seamus. This here cow's got a blocked quarter. Y'see?" Paddy pointed to the udder, caked with cracked earth and dung, and squeezed the teat, spraying a fouled yellow milk jet at the dirt. The cow jerked against the wall, then against the creaking boards of the fence and tried to kick Paddy. She hit wood. "Get over, ye eejit!" he said, putting his hand through the fence and pushing against her ribs. "Ye ever milked a cow, lad? Over there in England? Something tells me ye haven't. Here. See if ye can get a squirt out of her." Paddy got up and made his way to a trough of water to wash his face.

James looked at the cow, thinking she would be disgusting to touch, especially the part he was supposed to touch, the teat on her great, hanging, excrement-smeared bag, the most sex-part of a cow he could imagine.

"He's scared o' cows," Liam said, squinting his eyes and laughing.

James bent, gripped the balloon end of the teat in his hand, and squeezed. It felt awful, a finger with no bones. The cow jerked and Dermot let the tail go, the shitty end whipping James in the forehead.

"Sorry 'bout that. Sorry. Sorry," Dermot said, crooked-toothed and gleeful, a gust of wind finding its way through the open doors of the barn to press his shirt against his wobbling chest. John laughed with a wet sniff of his nose.

James glared at them as he wiped the shit with the sleeve of his tweed jacket.

Dermot grabbed the tail and raised his eyebrows. "Your Irish baptism." He snickered and hit his little brother in the chest with the back of his hand. John, still looking sag-eyed and obedient, hit him back in the groin.

"Ow! Ye little shite!"

"Shite," he muttered, laughing, glancing again at a hole in the knee of Dermot's pants. The word was shit, not shite.

"Something the matter with the way I talk?"

"No."

"You sound like the English prime minister on the radio. You a Prod?"

"A what?"

"Protestant. A fookin' Protestant."

"No."

"He sounds like the fookin' Queen."

"What are ye going on about now?" Paddy said, back from his wash, his face dripping. "Ah, never mind. Sure, but I'd be worse off for knowing."

Paddy finished emptying the cow's quarter and the boys slapped its rump and *yahed* it from the barn.

"Nothing more to do boys. Ye've got the day off. So go someplace where ye won't get into trouble, or at least where I won't be the one to catch ye. Go on. Before I find something else for ye to do. Why don't ye take young Seamus fishing in the bay?"

"Fishing!" John said. "I –"

"Nah. Da' wants that gate over to Cassidy's mended," Dermot said. He was staring at his uncle and the well-dressed, bluster-haired boy who seemed stuck to his side.

"Does the fookin' Queen go fishing?" Liam hooted, already running from the barn.

"Well, I guess we can take our tour then, lad," Paddy said, his big hand giving his shoulder a squeeze as Dermot turned his back and pulled his brother by the arm. "Not to worry. They'll warm to ye."

They walked up the hill together, surveying the little stone-boxed fields, Paddy talking cows and rain, milk and meat. James turned now and then to see the ocean, the changing view of the cliffs, the little skim of yellow beach on the other side of the town, the bay opening up beside it and disappearing inland toward the mouth of the river Tare, the three boys running with fishing rods down a boreen toward the sea.

They came after the evening meal – a Babel of women who, to James, seemed to be speaking a foreign language – one after another, in pairs, carrying babies, pulling children by the hand, his mother's sisters, aunts, cousins, nieces, neighbors.

They had heard she'd returned.

"God save all here," one of them might say as she ducked her head into the kitchen, not bothering to knock, then "Mother of God," when she saw his mother, the scars around her glass eye marring her beauty that was scarcely past teenage beauty, beauty that reminded them of how jealous they once had been, beauty that still shamed their thickened jowls and middles and backsides and ankles and hair hastily tied up in kerchiefs.

"Jesus, Mary, and Joseph. Your poor eye."

She stood up from the table, arms folded tightly in front of her, as they touched her gently, two fingers on her shoulder, a

palm on her cheek, a kiss beneath the corner of her lip, sometimes an entire, tentative embrace, tears falling freely.

They didn't ask. They had already heard it all – the car accident, the eye, the little girleen in the grave. They had suffered,
but she had suffered more, and suffering was what the Lord had
done, and suffering – didn't the priests say it made you wise?
Learned about life? Suffering was a blessing, indirect, of course,
from God, a blessing they prayed to be spared.

Bernadette helped her mother get bread and jam, biscuits
and tea, cups and saucers, whiskey and *poitín*. Its name meant
"little pot" in Gaelic, and like the other sort of spirit, it was difficult to capture or define. It contained sometimes only sugar,
yeast and water, but perhaps treacle, hops, barley, or even potatoes, and was always overproof, illegal, volatile enough in the
bloodstream, but explosive with the help of its glass bottle, a
cloth wick, and a match. Of course, local alcoholics would be
horrified at the idea of using it for such a purpose: not while
there was petrol to be had.

The women expected to talk, but Bernadette did not talk,
instead walked about with a rag to clean up spills, or with the
teapot to refill cups, or with the knife to cut and butter more
bread. The women expected talk, so they talked, laughing to
show brown tooth-stumps and gaps, gesturing with cigarettes
and stained fingers. The table became littered with dirty plates
and cups and saucers full of ash, a half-full bottle of whiskey
placed in the middle like a vase of flowers, smoke drifting above.

They talked of deaths, marriages, and lots and lots of children. There were accidents and wrongs to tell Bernadette and re-
tell each other, every angry word savoured like the first sip of tea
from a fresh cup. Road accidents, farm accidents – Eamon
Decoursey lost his leg in a binder. And wouldn't ye think the doctors with all their fancy medicine could've done somethin' – it's
1965 after all – and what's poor Fidelma goin' to do with him
hobblin' about the house all day? Sure, but the oldest boy can
take over the farm, but d'ye think Fidelma will ever let him bring
a woman into her house? Helen Muloney's sister-in-law's uncle's

son in Dublin, walkin' to his flat, and doesn't he get knocked on the head and killed? *Killed*, would ye believe? Frank Kelly had a miserable time with the shingles. They start up around the sides of ye, and when they meet in the middle, yer *dead*! Liam Rossa driven over by a tourist on the west mill hill. I don't know why they don't keep them foreigners out o' here. We's an island, isn't we? When Mary was at hospital in Cork, didn't she see a darkie on the street in his pajamas? I don't know what we're goin' to do! Kathleen goes to visit her sister in Clonakilty, and the sister goes off to work, tellin' her there's a chop in the icebox that she can cook if she wants. Have ye heard o' such treatment? No sister o' mine would get away with treatin' me like that and expect me not to complain. Imagine, a guest, left alone and told to cook for herself! Malachy Collins cracked Patrick O'Toole's head in a punch-up in a pub in Skibbereen. Somethin' to do with *the troubles*.

"But we won't go into that now," one of them said, looking at his mother, then him. Outsiders.

James found himself gnashing on a piece of bread and black-berry jam, the seeds crunching between his teeth, found himself sitting on the stairs with the rest of the children, sitting beside one of his aunt Susan's little girls. She snorted a string of snot back into her nose, arranged her doll's dress, and dabbed its mouth with a bit of her own bread and jam.

"What's your doll's name?"

The girl squirmed shyly, leaning her head low over the doll, biting her lips. Poor Dymphna had been shy, would hide behind him in the street sometimes, her small hands clutching his elbows. Without even thinking, he began to talk to the little girl like he used to talk to his sister.

"I had a doll named Spot."

"Wha? Sure tha's a dog's name. Ye don't call a doll a dog's name."

"Sorry. I guess it wasn't a doll. It was a little stuffed dog. Had stripes so I named him Spot..." James frowned and looked puzzled as if there was something wrong with what he had said and he couldn't figure out what it was.

The girl began to giggle.

"Her name's Bridie."

"She like ginger biscuits?"

"Sure."

"She's a good dolly? Cry a lot?"

"She cries WAAA!"

"Oh, she's loud. How do you stand it?"

"Rock her."

"What, like this?"

He took the doll and held it upside down by its legs and moved it back and forth gently.

"Nah! Not like that!" As she reached for the doll another hand shot out from above and knocked it down the stairs. The girl whirled and hit the arm of a boy of about eight. "You stupid arse," she yelled, and ran down the stairs to get her doll, bumping a toddler, who tumbled two steps to the floor and started screaming. The mothers rose up, but as soon as they'd gotten everyone calmed down, someone else started to cry. James hadn't noticed one of the young women was carrying a bundle in her arms. She got up and began to pace back and forth, jiggling, joggling, the bundle. James caught his breath. He could play with a girl his sister's age without feeling like he wanted to cry, but he hadn't encountered a small baby since his sister died.

Dymphna had been born when he was seven. His mother would walk to his school pushing the pram, his tiny sister screaming out her colic, nothing working to calm her, the look on his mother's face desperate: "She's got bellyache again." They would get home and he would hold out his arms, and his mother would put the heavy flannel bundle into them, and then take such a long time extracting her own arms from the tangle of her son and daughter, separating her own body from the bodies of her children, because the flannel was so clinging, and her wool coat was so rough. James had the strength to carry Dymphna for five minutes, up the street and back, up the street, out of the house, so his mother could have five minutes of quiet. Always, halfway up the street, he would begin to cry, too, because it wasn't fair that someone so small should have bellyaches that were bigger than she was, bellyaches that lasted all day and all night. She hated the pram, liked to be carried, and if he sang to her, she might be sleeping by the time he got back. He would sing "Happy Birthday," because wasn't she only just born?

Once, a wasp went for her, wanting soft baby flesh, and he had put her down on the soft grass and slapped it dead in the air between his hands, the sting only making him proud – as if its pathetic little sword could really stop him. Once, a big dog came up to them and began poking and prodding her, interested in the smelly thing that had recently happened inside her diaper. He was terrified. He thought the dog was trying to get at her to eat her, and he'd held her close and roared at it, kicked at it, looked madly around for a stick that he could stab it with, kill it in defense of his sister. Fortunately the owner came running with a leash. His scalp pin-prickling, his hair almost standing on end, James would have done anything to that dog, going into some sort of killing frenzy like Cúchulain, the hero of many of his mother's Irish stories.

The Irish woman's baby cried, and it was Dymphna. And who was it that said, after she died, that she would never suffer any more? He raged at the tears coming into his eyes, because why should it be good that she was dead, and why should she have to suffer to live? He fought, and fought, and fought the tears, putting bread in his mouth, taking a gulp of sweet, milky tea, pretending to scan the room so his right eye would crush itself, almost by mistake, against his shoulder, and then he could rub the other, as if an eyelash had fallen into it.

"So, what age of man are you, young fellow?"

He rid himself of the tears just in time to realize one of the women was asking him a question, and all eyes were on him.

"He's ten," his mother stated, emphatically.

"Oh, Mother. You know I'm eleven. My birthday was only in March." His voice sounded strange in the low-ceilinged room, almost snobbish, so different from the Irish accents. No one spoke again for a long time. The women were thinking back, calculating months, years.

So it was true. She *had* been pregnant when she'd run away.

There was just his mother's voice, then, shaking, talking too fast, twisting the rings on her finger, a bridal set, making the small diamonds in the curved gold settings point straight out from the back of her finger.

"James – Seamus. Wharram-Young." Her words buckshot through her mouth. "My *married* name. We call him James in England, you know." She turned her head so she could glare across the room, then laughed uneasily, crazily. "Aren't the English for the fancy last names? Double-barrelled! But – but my husband was – is an understanding man for all that. James was baptized in the *Church*. The Catholic Church. By a priest."

No one spoke.

"All right. All right. So you see. So there. You think even the anvil priests up in Scotland would marry us? A girl with no papers to prove she was sixteen? Well I wasn't, was I? I was a child. I was fifteen. And you can think what you're thinking, think it until the Judgment Day. Go ahead. Go on. It wasn't that we didn't try. Doesn't the trying count for anything then? They couldn't stop us from buying the rings in Gretna Green, though, and promising before God, vowing to stay with each other forever. There it is. I'm sick of all the lying we had to do just to get the priests over there to baptize...the lying to his kin..."

Wild and quick looks flew among the women, their rock-formed stillness and tight, blameful lips.

"What are you looking at? Get out. Get out all of you then!"

The first to rise were the ones who were preparing to go anyway, the ones who condemned her, the ones who wanted to keep their children, especially their daughters, from such scenes, such ideas. The next to rise were the ones who didn't know what to think, whose own consciences bewildered them, or who rose only because the others had risen first and decided for those of weaker mind. There were only two women who rose to go to

Bernadette: Susan, and an older one, one that James had noticed before because of her acne-scarred face, her beautiful smile contradicting all her pockmarked ugliness.

"Oh, Annie," his mother said, letting the woman embrace her.

"Don't worry, little darling. Those others have nothing to be so proud of."

Susan and Annie left later, only after Bernadette assured them again and again she would be all right.

Once they were gone, she shut herself in her room upstairs. James knocked but she wouldn't come out. She wouldn't say a word. He knocked and knocked because he had always believed his parents had been married, didn't know what to think of himself, now that he was illegitimate. Illegitimate, they said: it meant fatherless, but how could it mean that? He had a father. It meant something else, something that wasn't well-defined in the dictionaries, wasn't well explained to children of his age. It meant something that was only whispered about, meant something pitiful, shameful, meant, somehow, that he had never been a real person.

He knocked and called to her because the chill seeping into his backbone was swelling under his lungs, making it hard to breathe, making him feel colder than he had ever felt in his life.

"How many more days?" he whispered carefully to his mother the first time she left her room, midmorning, to go out to relieve herself, to take a bit of tea and toast, "When are we going *home*?"

"The end of the month," his mother told him, after a long silence, holding her head in her hands over her plate full of crumbs, before going back to shut herself into her room. "I don't know how many days."

He followed her upstairs and stared at the door.

That spring, only a couple of weeks before Dymphna died, they had been playing on the walk in front of the house, and he had seen a bird's nest in the old tree two houses down. The mother and father bird kept bringing tangles of twitching drag-onflies and writhing knots of worms in their mouths to the crying chicks, and the chicks kept crying, ravenous, their little beaks open to the clouds as if the whole world couldn't satisfy. It was easy to climb up to them – this had always been his favourite tree – so Dymphna helped him grub up worms from around the spent daffodils in front of their house, and, fingers clotted with clay, he climbed up again and again to help the parent birds, to dangle worms into the tiny ravenous beaks as his little sister looked up at him in near worship.

He stared at his mother's door and took a step back, retreated down the stairs.

The day after he'd fed the baby birds, he'd gotten up early and found one of them dead on the walk, the others dead in the nest. For those two weeks before Dymphna died, the death of those innocent bird-children had been the worst thing that had ever happened to him in his life, the worst thing he had ever done. He spoke of it to no one, succeeded in distracting Dymphna so she did not think to play the mother bird game again.

He would leave his mother alone, if that was what she needed. Best sometimes, to leave things alone.

But living things didn't always know what was best for them, did they?

Paddy had gone out to the barn, Granny to the garden. He counted the days to the end of the month on the Callaghan's Hardware calendar in the kitchen.

"Fifteen, fifteen, fifteen," he chanted as he walked through the ill-kept fields, kicking the poisonous orange heads of rag-wort. The day was endless, made longer by the chanting, but he couldn't stop because there was no one to talk to but himself, nowhere he wanted to be but by himself. The next day he chanted "fourteen, fourteen, fourteen," clambering over gates made of old bedsteads and knots of twine, watching his granny's farm from further up the hill, watching her dump a dish of potato peelings into the pigpen, watching his cousins carry buckets of milk into Susan's house. The day after that – his mother still in her room – he chanted "thirteen, thirteen, thirteen," walking past cows that lifted their saliva-strung faces from the streams. The fields, the small stone rooms, were filled with green pillowy grass, and in the distance, on the headland, the green turned to thick vivid paint. That day he went all the way down the hills past the church, through the cleft in the cliffs that led down to the little beach where Granny bathed her corns.

There were gargoyle cormorants above him on the rocky towers, gulls hovering over the lip of the cliff to catch the wind, and clouds smudging into being as the air moved over the land, land that stubbed his toes with stones, that scratched him with brambles, shivered him with empty winds. Sometimes he breathed the black-green stink of rotting, fly-ridden seaweed, and sometimes the pure drugging ozone of air blowing from the water. He watched the eerie, powerful silence of each eyeless cobra-headed wave as it rose and raced to throw itself to death on the land: wave shadows, wave beasts, faceless, mindless beings – or waves not things, maybe, but things that happen. He came to like the steep slope of sand, even though it seemed to be trying to slide him into the sea. He liked the places where the rocks were wet, black, sun-hardened licorice.

Licorice.

In the distance, he saw the slabs of land hunching out into the sea, carrying the farms, the fields, the walls, on their great backs, the rock breaking off at the edge of the water like dark chocolate.

Chocolate.

He found shells like fine bone china, mussel shells the colour of deepest water, clam and barnacle, scallop and limpet, oyster shells with mother-of-pearl linings that he slid salty over his tongue. He filled his pockets, dug, but could never get at the living things burrowing away from him in the sand. Mollusks: the proper scientific word his father taught him. His father liked proper words, scientific words, and the books that held them. James would sit on the arm of his father's chair, too big to sit in his lap, and his father would show him marvels of the world, read him true stories of the creatures God didn't mention as He went speeding through creation at the beginning of the Bible – only six days – to concentrate on humans instead of rock forms and limpets, wave-wash and kelp-bed. He had asked his mother to phone home so he could tell his father about it all, but she only said "Do you see a phone in this house?"

He sat and leaned his back against the barn sometimes, watching the chickens stampede whenever Granny threw a dish of scraps out the door, letting the chicks step into his open palms and nibble salt from between his fingers. If it was raining, he would go into the barn and throw bits of straw for the puppy or watch the young fox as it prowled its cage; Colm had shot and wounded its mother and Paddy had found it, the only survivor of the den after its crazed and dying mother tried to move her family to a safer place, biting the other two to death. Every day, Granny went to the barn to stare at it, to make sure Paddy hadn't let it go. She threatened to kill it herself, because if anyone was going to eat her chooks, it was going to be her. Once, when that stall had been the home of a pheasant that had knocked itself out on the kitchen window, Paddy had come home to find it cooked for his supper.

Sometimes James would happen across Paddy and follow him in whatever he was doing, often just checking on cows in this field and that. One day, Paddy took him to a little copse of trees on the side of the steepest part of the hill and got down to crawl beneath a bush. James followed, lying on his stomach beside his uncle to see a hole in the dark earth a few yards away. Paddy put a finger to his lips. After a few minutes, there was a snuffling sound from the little cave and a badger cub came out followed by three others. James watched them root around in the grass and tumble over each other as they waited for their mother to come home. He heard a strange noise and glanced at Paddy. His uncle, face buried in the crook of one arm, a twig tangled in his hair, had fallen asleep, and every few breaths, a snore came out of the folds of his dirty jacket. James watched the badgers for a few more minutes, until he grew restless. Should he wake his uncle? He crept out from under the bush and began his aimless rambles, alone again.

As he walked, he'd glance up now and then and search the sky for airplanes that might have taken off from Heathrow airport, or maybe even from somewhere in Europe; it seemed the modern world he'd left was skipping over Ireland. His granny's house had no telephone or toilet. He'd only seen a few cars, and he felt this as a deprivation in his boyish soul. There wasn't even a railway near the town – and he had so loved his Thomas the Tank Engine books when he was small – but there were many horse and donkey carts. Sometimes he imagined he was a time traveller, and that by coming to visit this country, he had actually leaped back to a time before he was born, before even his father was born, and if he tried to phone his grandparents, he'd end up talking to his grandfather as a young boy.

After the first few days he learned to be within calling distance at mealtimes. He had been confused at first, because Granny called lunchtime dinnertime, and she called dinnertime tea, though it was different than the many other times for drinking a cup of tea. The big meal, dinner, was at noon, then there might be a cup of tea and biscuits in the afternoon, and then tea was around six, and it might be sandwiches or a fry-up of eggs and sausages if Paddy had his way. His granny's shouts made him run and shrink at the same time: Seamus! Dinner! Where the hell are ye?

She would always be sitting at the kitchen window, cup of tea on the sill, a patch blanket piled on the floor beside her, a pin-glinting corner of it draping her knee. The food would be waiting on the table, or in the big oven if it was to be kept hot. She would look him up and down and find fault somewhere – a grass stain, a patch of mud on his pants, a bruise on his arm. He would open his mouth to protest.

"Don't say it. Isn't it always something like that with the boys?" She waved his attempted explanation away. The first day she slapped his chest with the back of her hand.

"Eejit. Didn't they teach ye enough to save your good shoes?" She backed him into the porch where the coats hung, the floor littered with workboots and women's overshoes. "Take them off! No wet dirty shoes on my floors!"

"Paddy's boots are too big for me!" he protested, struggling out of his shoes, the word "idiot" outraging him more than the slap. In the barn he had been using a pair of Paddy's enormous old Wellingtons, a hole in the toe of one. They were impossible to run in.

"What's wrong with going without? We did in my day, but ye think you're too rich, do ye? I had eight children that lived..."

"And you hated them, too?" He looked down to find something to revenge himself upon and kicked a boot past her legs, littering dried mud and dung on her newly washed kitchen floor.

"Disrespectful! Divil's seed!" She caught his arm and raised her hand, but Paddy came in. She pushed James away. "The boy has his – his mother's bad temper. And he's spoiled. Doesn't know how hard it is to come by things."

"Come on, boy, it's back to the barn with us."

"No, no, Owen. A letter came from Mary in America. Ye have to read it to me! And dinner almost on the table."

"Paddy, Mam."

"Eh?"

"Sure. Give it here."

Paddy read the letter to her as she pinched James's ear, handed him the broom, and supervised his sweeping.

His mother hardly ever came to eat, and the kitchen was silent with her undiscussed absence.

After untangling herself from the blanket, Granny would get up and take the plates of food out of the range. She clapped them down on the table, poured them cups of strong, lukewarm tea, then sighed with the attitude of one stuck in a hated job. "Eight children I had that lived. Lord bless the work! Shouldn't I be done with it by now – but I know me duty, b'Jesus."

"*Me duty, b'Jesus*," he whispered, mimicking her West Cork accent, angry that she was there instead of his mother, her sharp eyes pricking him from their sagging bags of flesh, angry that even his bruises couldn't wring sympathy from her – some grandmother.

"What are ye? A mockingbird?" Grania rummaged in the sink, then fell upon him with a soapy cloth.

"Ow! My mother –"

"Your mam's not well. She needs her rest. Ye'll not be bothering her now."

"But –"

"Whisht! Hush up. Clean your plate like a good boy."

The meal was bacon, or roast beef, pale boiled cabbage or mashed turnip, and always potatoes, all drowned in lumpy rubbery-skinned gravy. He ate to fill himself, lay the gravy skins on his side plate with the potato skins, left the cabbage in its swim of brown liquid.

Sometimes he hovered near the bottom of the stairs, undecided. Paddy would come and put a gentle hand on his shoulder, suggest going down to the strand or to the town for an ice cream. Once, when Paddy was gone, Granny intervened.

"Don't be bothering your mam about nothing."

"I have to –"

"She's a wounded animal, boy. And they can be dangerous. You go near her and I'll run ye through with me little sword." She brandished the big mending needle that was stuck in her flapping apron.

He turned and slammed out the door, leaving half his meal and the sound of her crackling laughter.

"You're too easy to tease, boy!" she called after him. "Come back and finish your dinner! I won't do it again! Don't pay me no mind!"

He ran out of the yard, kicked his feet down this road and that, almost trying to lose himself. It was lonely without his mother between the stone walls, and walls were always around him, keeping him out of the fields, keeping him from seeing the ocean sometimes, making him walk in the direction they wanted him to walk. He wanted to go down to the town, down to the water, but sometimes the road he was on wouldn't let him, veering him west around the hillside past tumbled stone houses. He finally climbed over a wall to head toward shore, but there seemed to be only more and more walls to climb after that, until he came to the edge of a cliff. He sat in the grass, wind and the cries of seabirds desolate in his ears. He hoped that birds had souls, too, tried not to let himself fall back into another cycle of remorse about the ones he had overfed: *too sensitive* his grandfather would say, gripping his pipe in his teeth, stiffening his back until he seemed remarkably tall.

The first thing he had ever killed was a toad he caught next to the lily pond in his grandmother's garden, one that only seemed big to him because he was four years old. He would open his hands to gaze at it, and it would leap away, back into the grass. He would catch it again in both hands, open a peephole with his thumb so he could press his eye to the opening and look at the little thing's snout and eyeballs and tiny blister-toes, but see little in the darkness. He would open his hands again and the toad would jump again. Finally, he caught it and held it too hard. At first he thought it had shat in his hand – silly thing to be frightened of *him* – and then realized the mess wasn't coming from its bottom, but from its side. He shrieked, dropping it, then wiping his hands in the grass. It wasn't moving. He had taken its life – its *life* – had stopped its huge happy jumping and the delicate movements of its toes on the palm of his hand. His grief grew more and more frantic because what he wanted was to turn time backward, go to the moment before his last grab and snatch his hands behind his back instead. Why couldn't he do it? He could do so many things, but he couldn't undo any of them. Why couldn't he *undo*? He *had* to undo. It wasn't fair if he couldn't undo. He was trapped for the first time, a child trapped by time and its single relentless direction. He threw himself to the earth, screaming out his desperation, trying to escape, trying to beat reality into submitting to his will, flailing his arms and legs, though there were no ropes that bound them.

A gull hovered above him, motionless in the updraft of wind coming off the cliff. It cried, and its fellows cried, and he cried back, again and again, trying to get the sound exactly; not everybody could be fooled as easily as his English grandmother. Birds had to have souls. They were the most soul-like things he could think of. If God was all good, as they said, if he righted all wrongs, then birds did have souls. The bird babies would grow their feathers and fly, at last, in heaven. What would heaven be without birds to sing and soar above with the angels?

But then, toads would have to have souls, too, and he imagined the angel version of them, with cool warty wings.

He laughed, listening to the gulls.

After a long afternoon of wandering, he was exhausted by the time he got back to the house. Paddy was sitting by the kitchen table, his big dirty wool feet stretched in front of him, smelling of cows and tobacco. He wiped egg yolk off his plate with a chunk of brown soda bread, his evening tea often another huge fry-up.

Granny set a plate of soda bread and biscuits in front of James and poured him a cup of tea, and as soon as he was done, told him to go to bed.

"Do what you're told."

He looked at Paddy to see if he objected. Boys of his age were never sent to bed right after tea, but Paddy didn't seem to object to anything.

"G'night, lad," was all Paddy said.

"*Don't be botherin' yer mam about nothin',*" he muttered to himself as he tramped up the stairs. There was no one telling him to wash his face and brush his teeth. One night he overheard Paddy talking: "...it's her nerves – got a bad case of the nerves – one of them breakdowns," and he began to eavesdrop, trying to find out whatever he could. Another night, he got into his pajamas and was cold, was about to climb into the small sagging bed when he heard a sound from his mother's room. Sometimes, in England, his mother would cry, and after she ran away and shut a door behind her, he would ask his father what was wrong.

"That's just the wind," his father would say.

Night after night, the wind blew stronger. He could hear his mother through the thin plaster and lath, praying or muttering at first, then crying and howling through his fitful sleep. In the morning, he and Paddy and Granny would look at each other with weary, haunted eyes, disparate creatures sheltering together from a storm, unequal to the forces of nature. Paddy and Granny could no longer ignore Bernadette's state, had to talk about the sudden and terrible cloud that had appeared above them; talking is also a kind of shelter, a kind of shelter that James needed also. They told him how it all began, and James re-examined every word of every story at night, when he couldn't sleep.

As a child, no one could keep her in a room. She'd be off, even at the age of two, learning early to work the latches, standing on tiptoe or dragging up the nearest chair. Neighbours would pass and see the baby girl standing on a chair in the doorway, the door swinging wide, and they would always veer toward her, arms involuntarily stretching out – the chair was so high, and suddenly the door coming away from her like that – it looked like she was standing at the edge of a cliff, for she was such a tiny cherub, red curls fluffing around her head, pale tattered skirts fluttering. She'd be immediately snatched from behind by her sisters Maureen, Annie, Mary, or Orla, but she'd be off again soon. At first her sisters loved chasing her purely because of the sound of her laughter: baby laughter, angel laughter, the sound of pure and utter happiness. But then, they began to lose her. Once, they found her running barefoot through the ruts on the other side of town, only a slope away from the ocean. "Who's going to sit on her today?" Grania would demand in the morning, and pick one of her older daughters to be responsible, the girl knowing her life was forfeit if she lost the baby of the family, the petted and adored little Bernie, still with the sweetest little feet that could fit in the palm of your hand, the baby who screamed and struggled away from every adoring embrace, too many embraces; she would much rather crush her own doll to her thin little belly than be trapped in anyone's arms. She was mad to get away – all those sister-hands hanging on to her from well before she could remember, keeping her from running off, her sisters' bodies on each side of her in the bed, so she could not climb out in the middle of the night.

When she got older they couldn't keep her at all. She would be off through the fields and hedges, coming back only when hunger and thirst tangled in her belly, the pain making her cry with rage, coming back with her red hair a tangle of twigs and spent grasses and leaves, coming back soaked to the waist in sea water, her bare feet blue with cold, crusted with the blood from walking the low-tide broken barnacles, smeared with the chicken dirt from the yard. Someone, maybe two, would have to hold her while her mother washed her with water that was a bit too hot, lye that stung too much, and then the worst thing, the salt that was rubbed into the cut. She would kick and hit and struggle and scratch, her fingernails almost useless, short and sandblasted from digging for clams, softened by the sea. Her pain and rage only flung her farther, and when she cut herself again, she would shriek in anger at the anticipation of the cure, rage at the wound done to her body, and keep it a secret as long as she could until she was finally caught and the scolding she got tore open her heart. With all her running about, her wounds barely healed. Grania screamed at her, afraid for her last baby, told her she would die of blood poisoning if she wasn't more careful, using volume and fury for emphasis, trying to be heard through the girl's own wrathful crying. *Take care or you'll die, you'll die,* but the girl just wouldn't listen, wouldn't stay at home to attend to her chores, was forever tearing up her legs on the brambles, was down every day on the strand in the summer, standing thigh deep in the water, letting the waves pick her up and push her toward shore even though she, even though none of them, could swim. Once she tore her leg open as she tried to crawl through a barbed-wire fence, her skirts gathered around her waist, but her sash forgotten. It caught and pulled her back, raked her thigh over the barbs, scraping open three deep rusty tears. She couldn't hide the wounds for all the blood on her dress, was afraid she'd bleed out, her life drain away, so finally showed herself to her mother, who dressed her wounds in silence. Her father locked her in the pantry, said she could come out only if she promised to keep to the paths for a month and not go down to the sea. She stayed there for thirty-five hours, her will only broken by the smell of her own shit in the bucket.

"I can't breathe," James heard her shout on the worst night of all, the wind battering itself, breaking its wings against the walls. He heard her window bang open as if the wind was finally escaping from the room it had locked itself in, letting the rain rush in. After that, there was silence for a while, then a kind of keening, the sound of a wild thing still trapped in a cage.

James sat up in bed; the indecision of going or not going to her tormenting him. How many more nights of this could he bear?

"It's hard to bear the judgment of all them women," Paddy had said the night before, pushing away his empty plate with his knuckles, glancing at Bernie's heaped, untouched plate; Granny was piling Bernadette's plate higher and higher the more meals she missed, as if purposely torturing herself with the idea of wasted food, giving herself greater reason to be enraged, to grouse about her daughter.

"That girl never had any sense. Wouldna' eat her potatoes or hardly anything a'tall. Skin and bones. Neighbours thought we couldn't feed our own children. Would eat nothing but white raisin bread, and that with lashings of jam!"

Paddy glanced at James. He had been given permission to leave the table and was sitting at the window with a book he'd brought from home, doing his best to appear oblivious while his mother was under attack. Paddy and Granny had both been looking at him more carefully lately, as if he were a refugee, as if he were a boy walking away from the same car accident that killed his sister and might collapse at any moment. Paddy lowered his voice.

"I told ye, ye never should have been forcing her. That made her worse, only."

"Eh? What ye still doin' out of bed, then?" James looked up. Granny pointed at the stairs with a crooked finger and he put down his book, but went up the stairs only to sit at the top. The words from below mingled with the sound of his mother's sobbing behind that door, now a room full of rain.

"And what did you know about it then, eh?" Granny's distant voice a pointing finger at Paddy. "...all of seventeen when she was born."

"– almost grown up...my little girl, too...just saying, remember after Da' locked her up, the way...slapping herself...she started biting her hands?"

"Oh, if she wanted attention –"

James slid quietly down the stairs, not caring if he was caught, cupping his hands around his ears to hear everything.

"Mam, wasn't it just the way ye taught her? All that yellin' and slappin' when she was sick to her stomach at the sight of food, when she'd hurt herself on something...I saw her keep on doing it to herself. Sure ye taught her this: that when she was suffering, feeling as bad as she could feel...ye taught her to hurt herself more."

"*Ach.*"

"Well, what else could it be, then, what she did years ago? Goin' for an impossible man. Goin' for what would hurt her and everyone else, the most? And goin' for it the way it would hurt the most, too."

Going for his father, having a baby, him: what would hurt everyone the most.

That worst night of all, her voice came in waves, inaudible prayers, punctuated with cries of pain: "I can't breathe! I can't bear this stillness!"

James got out of bed and sat near the window, where the rain was shattering itself against the glass, her shouting and the echo of it in his head: "Why didn't you kill me, too? Why didn't you bury me with her?"

People said that it was quiet in the grave, but these were words to cry poor Dymphna awake, jagged and sharp enough to slit a throat.

"Oh, I know, *now* what I am," he heard, her voice the loudest it had yet been, drowning out the downpour. "I've been shown. I've –"

The agony of her twisting scream was terrible, and he put his hands over his ears, for it was as if she was wringing her own neck. "Whore!" she shrieked, again and again and again, but the sudden silence after she stopped was worse; he half believed she had vanished with her voice, that God had heard her prayers and struck her dead.

His door opened slowly and revealed her pale face rising out of the shadows, her haze of hair colourless in the dim hall light, drained of life.

"I'm sorry."

She stumbled toward him, sank down on the cold hard floor, her bare foot icy where it slid against his own, her sacklike nightgown bone-white, her body shifting uncomfortably until she wound up on her knees in front of him in the alcove, the black window dank with condensation beside them.

"I know it's God I'm supposed to confess to, through the priest, God we hurt when we sin, but I've hurt you the most. I've been committing whoredom every day of your life and calling it holy marriage."

He swallowed, his throat dry, felt his own cheeks heat with blood as she folded her hands and bowed her head.

"Dear Lord, I'm sorry. I never truly believed. I never thought of how short life was. I never knew about pain, or my own frailty, James – mankind's frailty. I used to despise piety, what I thought of as old lady piety. Maybe I was just too young. I've been raising you all wrong. I've been leading you toward Hell. But that's over with. If you can forgive me, I'll know that God can."

He nodded, wide-eyed and she took him in her arms that were so strangely cold beneath the cloth. She smelled of ashes and honey, of a beeswax candle just blown out. He felt her long relieved sigh, the gentle wind of it.

"What time is it? What day is it?" she said, and then released him far enough to be able to look at him, her own face haggard, her eye bright, full of joy. "We're going to start right now, James. I've neglected to teach you to say the rosary every day. Come."

She took the beads from around her neck and led him to kneel by the bed.

"Holy Mary, Mother of God..."

She helped him count the beads, the words not completely in his memory. His fingers slipped over the smooth brown wood that looked like some kind of sweet. She had been crying, but now she was better. She *had* to be better, so his heart would stop breaking. He leaned his head against her shoulder and felt how she was shaking, shivering.

"Oh. I know now. I finally know *why*, now. God took her while she was too young and innocent to be tainted. He took her to heaven. He did it to save her from me. He did it to call me to repentance, so that I could save you, so you could go to heaven, too."

James shrank back, horrified; God killed Dymphna so he could go to heaven? He shut his eyes; he couldn't bear to think of this, even though the words were coming out of his own mother's mouth. Was she blaming him? No, she was blaming herself, but...but he had always been told that God was good.

Her breaths were coming faster. She laughed, confused, talked about how suddenly this was all coming over her: joy in the belief of God's forgiveness, the passion that was the love of Jesus's passion, his holy wounds, his saving blood, the wind blowing her back into God's green arms. She felt the storm of faith and piety, and hated what she had loved before, hated her foolish youth and its illusion of love that was really lust, she saw now, only lust.

James watched her fall in love with hating herself.

She wrapped her arms around her ribs, then around him, held him hard, as if sheltering him.

The next day his mother came out of her room – but it wasn't her. There was something in her face he didn't recognize, some new light behind her smile that was as hard as her glass eye in its bed of scar tissue, a way of holding her head that was a fraction of an inch higher than before. Instead of having breakfast with him she went to Mass every morning. Their time together began to be filled with rules; prayers instead of talking before bed, Bible lessons instead of stories. She seemed to require a new kind of obedience: quicker, more thoughtless, preferably with a smile of some kind, false or not. His nerves rubbed raw, he would have done anything she wanted to help her keep from crying, to make sure she was happy.

Some of the women began to come back to the house in the evening – *her* presence wasn't going to stop them. What right had she to order them about? Wasn't it the old woman's house? Hadn't they been going there forever to drink their tea and have their fights, and hadn't this *other* one, this prodigal daughter, just returned?

James began to get to know them and their strange intermittence, all noise one moment, all stares the next: stares at him and his mother. Of course he knew kind Susan and her flock of children, the way she was consistently overwhelmed with their demands, that, if she got a moment of peace, she just sat back and listened, never contributing to any argument. He began to sort a few others out of the group; his cousin Liam's mother, a fat, scowling, red-faced woman, was always turning down the volume on the white plastic radio. Her hair was tied back so tightly it stretched the skin of her forehead and raised her eyebrows in surprise, which created a problem for her in maintaining her foul demeanour. James thought she looked a bit sick, or like she was straining, trying to do something, silently, motionlessly within her body. He thought maybe she was constipated. His favorite was Annie; everyone's favorite was Annie. She was the one who looked shot-blasted in the face with pockmarks, looked frightening until she happened to smile, and then her face would burst out with such happiness, she was radiantly, eye-squintingly beautiful, and James knew she loved everyone, loved everything in the world, even him. The best part of her was her laugh. She was blessed with an overactive funny bone, people thinking she was either a bit daft to laugh at things that weren't funny, or that maybe, in fact, in this one respect, she was smarter than all of them. She would laugh, and the rest of them would smile, and think, *now what on earth is so funny?* and then she would really get going and her laugh would "go chicken," they called it, rise from a little cackle to a piercing, strangulating intake of breath, so close to the sound of a proud laying hen, that no one could keep from laughing at her, even if they didn't get the joke in the first place. Annie was the life of every party, but she would only be able to come if her husband drove her over from Skibbereen, if he had business, or fancied a pint in town.

Bernadette remained stiff-backed and silent as she ate her bread and tea. The women all seemed to talk at the same time. Granny smoked, drank tea or white lemonade adulterated with *poitín*, contributed to the conversation with greatest fervour when speaking of violence and disease. "Whisht!" Granny insisted sometimes, waving a hand. The radio announcer was talking about the North, and silence was immediate, eyes focused on their hands in their laps. Little had happened for years, the old men getting too old, the revolution frustrated by disorganization, the rest of the world moving on into the sixties, but the people of Ireland still waiting, listening for the boys, the Volunteers. All were related to or knew men who'd been involved, who'd been in jail, and some knew men who were killed by the Black and Tans in the twenties, killed just for the hell of it by these ex-soldiers and ex-convicts who'd been sent over by England to suppress the revolutionaries.

"Lazy young sods!" Granny exclaimed one night. "Doesn't anyone believe in Ireland for the Irish any more?"

"Whisht!" Susan said, her eyes darting in James's direction.

"If *I* was *Taoiseach*..." Bernadette said, with an angry toss of her head that James recognized as his mother's old self rearing to the surface, "I'd never let –"

"*You?*" said Maureen, scowling. "You'll never be anything but what you *are*."

Bernadette got up immediately, and for a second, James thought she was going to slap her sister's face, so set was her jaw, so righteous her eyes, but all she did was reach for the teapot. She filled teacups, whiskey glasses, cleaned the saucers of ashes – moved around the table, her face trembling in resolve, trying to harden herself into blankness. Most of the women didn't seem to know how to look at her, their arms folded, their eyes cast elsewhere. She washed dishes, her movements doubly brisk, cleaned obsessively until the newest cigarette stub was the only thing out of place in the entire kitchen – and yet James knew the look of the room would still shock his other grandmother; paint peeling, plaster lumpy, lines of dirt embedded in the cracks in the stone floor, teacups thick and chipped. Under the sink his mother found bleach and poured it into two teacups to clean the tea stains, making the room smell like the hospital she'd been in, making James cover his nose with the palm of his hand and breathe in the smell of the day that had rubbed off onto his skin: salt water, dirt, grass. He watched her behave like his grandmother's housekeeper, a woman of low class, a woman who didn't eat at the same table with them. What had happened to her? Where had the mother he loved gone? He couldn't help but think of the way his sister and everything about her had vanished.

One night, after he had gone to bed, their little Oxford house thumped, rumbled – a stomach digesting. The next morning, he looked into Dymphna's room. It was empty, except for the bed and the dresser. No sheets, no clothes, no toys. Dymphna's dolls and teddy bear were gone, and so was her small unbreakable juice glass, plastic with bright cherries and oranges prancing on thin legs around the rim. She had been erased.

Annie offered his mother a cigarette, and he could hardly believe it when she took it and started to smoke, rolling the glowing end expertly on a cracked plate to get the ash off.

One evening only Annie came, and after she drank her cup of tea, she stood up and got her coat.

"We'll be late for the bingo then, Bernie. Come on."

"I won't go," his mother said. "If they don't want to hear me, I won't speak. See how they like it. Two-faced bitches! Coming here and treating me like that and then going to Mass saying *forgive* me, Lord, for I have forgiven. Bitches!"

"The Lord knows their hearts, Bernie."

"Can you go to Hell for such a little thing, I wonder?"

Granny was putting on her cloak, hanging a little black purse in the crook of her arm.

"Come on, Bernie," Annie urged. "It's only the bingo. There'll not be time for talking. You won't have to look at the rest of them much."

"No, no. James, you go."

He widened his eyes at her, shook his head.

"Ah, sure." Annie turned to him, her cheeks crinkling. "My, but you're getting brown and healthy-looking! Mam, this boy has been outside all the time he's been here, but has he been out for a bit o' fun?"

Granny frowned. Her face crumpled like the velvet hat on the back of her vulture's head.

"Well, I've got a bit extra," Annie said. "Do ye want to come to the bingo, Seamus? Look! Ye come with me and ye'll get your very own bingo card. Maybe ye'll win the jackpot."

"Sure, but he's not dressed for it. And the bingo's no place for him." Granny wasn't ordering this time, was uncertain.

"Go. Just go," Bernadette, said. She was looking pale tonight, her red hair bunned tightly at the back of her head. She stood, held herself together with slender arms folded across her stomach, and went up the stairs, leaving James more alone than if he had been by himself in the kitchen.

"Ye go and put on your shoes and jacket and ye'll be fine. Go on!" Annie said.

He obeyed partly out of spite, because his granny didn't want him to go, partly to run away from the edge of the widening sea between himself and his mother. It was something different, too, than forever wandering in the fields and on the strand, thinking about his sister, and trying not to think about her, missing his grandparents and his father, and trying not to miss them so much. There were so many people around him, but he felt so lonely. He didn't know them. They didn't seem to want to know him. But he liked his aunt Annie, her sunlit smile, the way she embraced his mother without thinking, and yet, somehow, with great thought, turning to stare certain other women in the face. His wet shoes squeaked as they went down the hill.

"*Sure, but he's not dressed fer it,*" he whispered so no one would hear, mockery of his grandmother wicked and stinging in his cheeks. "*Dressed fer it.*"

The MoonStar Dance Hall had a sign surrounded by light bulbs with a painting of a comet zooming into the sky. It was new, cheaply built out of cindercrete blocks, and its sometime use as a dance hall was frowned upon by many of the priests and elderly women. They thought it was too far out of town, the fields around it too dark, places where boys and girls could meet at night and get into trouble, but this didn't keep either the priests or the old women from going to the bingo nights.

Annie squashed James into the queue between herself and the padded hips of a big middle-aged woman. She gave him a handful of coins, mostly pence, and he paid for his own card. They hurried through the passage to the auditorium.

The floor was linoleum-covered cement, dusted with the silt of dried mud, lined with rows and rows of metal and curved plywood chairs, the kind that hooked together to form straight rows. At one end of the room was a stage with heavy blue velvet curtains, round theatrical lights like black popped eyes, the bingo machine, and more rows of chairs and people. Most were women of all ages in skirts and cardigans, their hair "done" days ago, already frizzed and flattened in places, or twisted back in buns, or pressed under gauze scarves. The men were older and tieless, some in jumper sweaters, some in pale green shirts and rumpled green suit jackets dusted with dandruff, arms folded over soft round bellies, hair combed in damp strings over shining scalps. There were a few restless children yanked into sitting position on the floor by young mothers grasping younger arms. The serious players had two or three cards clipped to thin pieces of plywood. Cigarette smoke curled and flowered in the air currents.

There were few seats left. Granny spotted two and they pushed past others to take possession of them. Annie waved him on.

"Hurry then, and look for a place to sit before they're all gone. We'll meet ye at the doors at the end."

He walked down the side aisle scanning for empty chairs. On the stage, he found the last empty seat in the middle of a row and squirmed past many thick, stiff knees to get to it. He sat between a frowning young woman and an upright man with a hooked nose and the longest eyebrow hairs he had ever seen. In front of him was the carnival-painted bingo machine and the crowd gazing up from the auditorium. He could see Annie at the back of the hall, but his granny was too short and stooped to be visible. The balls were scrambling in the glass box, making a popping sound. The bingo caller came out from behind the curtain carrying his own chair and arranged himself behind the machine, one foot on a rubber mat, one on his chair. His ears stood out from his shorn head like wrinkled flesh bowls.

Ear bowls.

James could see these ears on the dinner table, bigger, filled with boiled cabbage or potatoes, crinkling with hot pain or swallowing the whole meal.

Gulp.

The bingo man pressed a button and picked up the first ball.

"Eight and one, eighty-one," he shouted over the gamblers, who hushed into concentration. James marked his card with a stripe of his pen.

"Four and two, forty-two."

The woman beside him crossed her legs, sucked on her cigarette, and blew the smoke at him through the side of her mouth. He leaned back.

"On its own, number seven."

The numbers, the idea of winning, hypnotized him for the next ten minutes. He shook himself out of this trance, stretched the crick in his back, and looked out at all the bent concentrating people, involved in a kind of meditation almost as frequent as prayer. Two seats ahead of him there was an old man with creased, quilted skin on the back of his neck, his white hair sparse, poking out like pins. The bingo man called more numbers and the woman beside James tapped her card. She had to get one more number to win the line and so did he. Thirty-four, he thought, thirty-four, in the same incantation as his "How many days until home" chant. He had never won anything in his life, and he wanted to be the winner, wanted thirty-four so badly.

"One and three, thirteen."

"Check!" shouted a woman in the middle of the hall. A lanky teenage boy with a bony jaw and bright pink pimples pushed himself away from the wall and leaped off the stage to get to her. The boy leaned over the excited woman and shouted out her numbers to verify them. A winner. The woman beside him clenched and opened her fist. She had needed number fourteen.

After an hour of number calling, there was a break. The women in front of him passed biscuits and cigarettes to each other, and when one turned her fading blonde head, he recognized her: Susan, Dermot and John's mother. He looked at the others. One had dull red hair, and the other was enormous – Maureen, his mother's meanest sister.

"...desperate weather," Susan was saying. "Me and Maureen...to the door...it was lashing! Positively lashing!"

"– some of them lovely ginger ones, and a sack of brown sugar."

"– *her*, those airs...*English* voice –"

"Isn't it always the way?" Maureen cut in, half turning, her chair creaking under her. "...Bernadette to be ashamed...how can she show herself out the house..."

He stilled his breathing.

"– damaged goods –"

"– sure but it was his –"

"That man of hers...and Protestant...ne'er-do-well...now it's being pious she's wild with...likes of her shouldn't be owned a'tall –"

"Aye," said the scrawny red-haired woman, hands working absently at the knitting taken from a bag beside her. "...Catholic...forgive...that little one of hers...the creature in agony was."

"– horrors is that eye...used to be such a beauty."

"– wrapped up in their own faces...that's lost, it's the whole of themselves..."

"– I *am* sorry –"

"– she's home for good now to take care of Mam and Paddy. Never going back, she says...have them in your house ye'll have to –"

Home *for good?*

"– don't think much of –"

"– raise the boy a proper...when his father...the boy's soul –"

Maureen threw her cigarette butt on the floor and stomped on it with her tan plastic thick-heeled sandal. It spilled its hot ash blood under her swollen ankle beside a dead grey worm of a mop string, a pencil stub and a crushed biscuit.

James let his head fall back and he saw a huge, long-legged insect battering itself against the white wall. He was never going home. He couldn't deny it. His mother had told another lie. Had told *him* a lie. And she had told him that God killed Dymphna so he could go to heaven. The clay-damp of his shoes seeped up his legs, chilled his bones. Stay here forever? Alone like this forever? What about his father?

"On its own, number two."

Silence in the hall again except for the bubbling of the balls and number after number.

"Three and three, thirty-three."

"One and nine, nineteen."

"Four and five, forty-five."

He shut his eyes on his panic. The balls tumbling in the box sounded like rain. He heard the thick Irish voice of God chanting random, meaningless numbers.

"...GO BAREFOOT THROUGH THE FROST,
PEERING UNDER HEDGES
FOR SUCH SMALL ANIMALS
AS MIGHT BE HELPLESS
WITH THE COLD."

– H. W.

BERNADETTE'S eye was now always ardent

and rain-brimming when she looked at her son. The warmth of her narrow, bony nun's hands held his face, barely touching, and he would forget to move, only saying *please, please, why can't we go home?*

Every evening after the rosary, she sipped a thin kiss from his cheek and told him his father wouldn't come. His father had given him back to Jesus and the Holy Church. It would be a sin to hope to be anywhere but here, in Ireland, God's green cradle.

"Elsewhere is Hell," she would say, then shut her soft lips like an eye.

Everlasting burning for him then, his body torn limb from limb, fingers flaming like candles; hope doomed him, his nightly prayers of escape doomed him. His soul shrank from her new, strange, fanatical words, even as he held on to her arm, sometimes tried to shake the mother he remembered out of this praying, tall-standing, aloof woman, tried to pry open her folded arms, tried to get her to chase him.

His missing father was a hole shot through him, heart-sized. He could no longer go to the book shop to sweep, to shelve new books, things he did well that made him feel clever. He could no longer sit with his father in the evening with old maps, things so precious they had to be handled with gloves, looked at with a jeweller's eyepiece. All parts of his life were gone. No school and friends and gentle British neighbours. No sister. No grandparents. He was lost in the empty Irish country, all the foreign air between green sea and greener hill, women with cawing voices, and Paddy, who only talked about cows and hurling. In spite of what his mother said, he expected his father to come for both of them, any day, even if he was a Protestant, even if he was as wicked as his aunts said he was.

One night, when she came into his room for the rosary and to tuck him into bed, he said, "I'll write a letter like I write to Grandma and Grandpa when we go to the seaside. He'll come and take us home."

"You will not. He doesn't want you," she said, fed up with his yearning, with her own guilt at keeping his father from him. "You'd just be bothering him. He wants to forget you. And it's for the best. Think of her. The Little One. You don't want to go to hell like all the unbelievers. You don't want to end up in Limbo either. You want to be able to go to heaven someday, to see her. Come on. Get into bed."

"I don't want to go to heaven!" he screamed, and waited for her slap, the slap that never came, because she had changed, only touched him as if he were a baby, her hand clinging to his cheek, steering his arm, keeping him, caressing his body as if it belonged to her and not him, forcing him down to eat at the table or up the stairs to his bed: hands that didn't recognize him, his status as an eleven-year-old.

"Seamus, you don't mean that, you don't." Her hands were rain-cool on his shoulders. "Everyone knows. The postmistress knows. She's a God-fearing woman. She'll not send your letters. Not to a —"

A Protestant. A ne'er-do-well. A goat.

Victor's words: she hates me.

Like last summer when they drove from their usual place on the Northumberland coast, up to that island that was only an island at low tide, the water so far away across the seaweeded rocks, it vanished in distance.

The sea unseen.

Lindisfarne Island, a sandstone ruin of a church, its reddish walls wind-blasted and swirl-carved, and a castle on a crag, Dymphna begging for ice cream, ice cream, *I scream.*

"The English always peering at their own bones, their old broken body – some empire – staring at broken this, broken that," his mother grumbled, sitting in the car out of the rain while James and Victor and Dymphna prepared to walk from the parking lot to the castle.

"But Bernadette, I brought you here because it's Irish – it started off that way. This place had the second monastery the Irish monks built on the islands of Britain. They wrote the Lindisfarne Gospels, one of the most beautiful books in the world. You Irish converted us. I thought you knew."

"A fat lot of good it did us."

And later in the car, James ate some cherries and Bernadette told him to wait for supper, but then his father said he wanted some cherries too, and began to eat. James kept eating cherries and his mother didn't speak to any of them for the remaining three days of the holiday.

Do what you're told.

Or else.

She *did* hate them.

His father the Prod.

Her son the disobedient.

"Into bed. I don't have time for this."

He twisted from her cool, hard grip, but her hands were reaching for him, backing him into the side of his room where the roof pitched down toward the floor. His head struck the ceiling and he flailed his arms, whipped at her hands until she cried out and stepped back to sit on his bed, rubbing the pain from where he had struck her – something he couldn't believe he had done. He buried his face in her lap and held on to her, what remained of her.

"I'm sorry, I'm sorry," he whispered into the sway of skirt, the warm place where her legs met, terrified she would change more, stop speaking to him, vanish as completely into her own head as his father and sister had vanished.

He stole a few pence from his mother's purse in the morning. He wrote a letter, bought a stamp, challenging the postmistress, staring deep into her eyes, and mailing the letter through the slot. She could pick it up and throw it away whenever she wanted. He held her eyes as long as he was able.

"Please," he whispered.

❖ ❖ ❖

The bonfire night of Midsummer's Eve came, and the strangeness of this old country, his new country, burned into his skin with the heat of the fires. He stayed close to his mother as she shuddered between excitement and uncertain disapproval; the day after was the feast day of Saint John the Baptist, but it was always celebrated in the ancient way, the night before, wasn't really about John's birthday at all, was just cloaked paganism his mother said, a celebration of the sun's long-lit summer fire in the darkness of the night, a celebration of Áine, Irish goddess of love. Granny raged back from the barn one July day because the fox was gone; Paddy had released it.

"Well, you cooked my pheasant. I wasn't going to let you kill my little foxy lass as well," he said, his face calm to all Granny's shouting and justifications: that she had cooked the pheasant the day after it arrived, before he could get so attached to it.

"Well, I didn't cook your bleeding duck, did I? Years ago. And what's the difference between the pheasant and one of them hens, eh? Ye see *them* every day, don't you?"

When the fox still hung around the yard, when Granny

complained, he said nothing. When the fox killed one of the hens, he said nothing, walked out of the house as if he had known this would happen all along, enticed it near with some meat, and caught it in an old horse blanket. Back in the kitchen, he wouldn't let his mother help clean the wound on his hand where the fox had managed to bite him, and shut himself in his room, not coming down for tea, ignoring Granny when she climbed the stairs to accuse him of sulking. He did the same thing the day a rich man from Cork City, who kept a menagerie, took the fox away. James was sad, but knew how sad Paddy must have been; he'd gone into the barn one cold day in spring and found Paddy curled up on his side in the stall, taking one of his little naps, snoring softly, the half-grown fox lying against his warm thick back, ears pricked, eyes wide, almost protective, knowing James was coming by the sound of his footsteps in the gravel.

The haymaking began and then it was over. Sometimes in the kitchen, he could forget where he was. His mother would make soda bread like she used to in their small bread-pan shaped Oxford kitchen, making the table thump and squeak with the kneading, nip off a bit of dough with her fingers, and pop it into his mouth. Sometimes, she sat with him, buttering a slice of the loaf hot out of the oven.

"Ye'll go to school and make lots of friends, you know. Sometimes people feel alone, but it's only for a little while."

He drew in the flour, finger-shaped lines that went nowhere, that were filled with the scarred wood of the table.

"I'll hate it. Nothing but stupid cousins. They smell like cow shit."

"Seamus!"

The first morning he left for school, Paddy chased him down in the yard and handed him a letter.

"Since you're going to town anyway, I don't suppose ye'd post this for me?"

James looked down at the letter. It was addressed to a woman named Eileen in Clonakilty. Paddy drew his hand across his nose, looked around, scratched.

"Ye see, Seamus, it's an important letter. But no one's to know. No one in the house, even. When ye live with a bunch of women, it's hard to get your privacy. Now, ye'll post that? Ye'll keep me secret?"

"Sure," James said, curious, but hushed by his new knowledge of how important a letter could be. He watched Paddy jog away, red-faced, to get his mare, Lizzy, out of the barn and start the day.

"*Keep me secret*," James said.

Streams of children trickled down from the hills, converged in the streets of Killaghmore, flowed down to pool dejectedly in the rooms of the convent on the other side of town. The first thing that had outraged him was the fact he was going to be taught by nuns, which seemed a step down from Jesuits, however much he disliked the stern brothers at St. Aloysius. Then, as he walked, there were girls everywhere, and they didn't filter away, but processed in small groups in the same direction as the boys. He stared at them and he thought they were staring back until he saw that everyone was staring at him – the girls with red-splotched cheeks who flung pebbles at the pub signs and over the bridge into the mouth of the river Tare, the boys who pushed each other into puddles. The girls and boys entered the same building, the same lemon-waxed hallways, the same rooms of paint-fumed air the nuns and lay teachers herded them into. A fat nun with a clipboard attacked James with questions, then grabbed him by the collar and escorted him to a classroom. He found a seat in the middle of the room so he wouldn't be on the edge, left out.

"Why are the girls here?" he asked the boy sitting across from him, ignoring the droning nun.

"This is a girls' school, ye eejit," was the hostile whisper that came over his shoulder. His cousin Liam was in the seat behind him. John, to the left, had just stuck his finger in his nose and was wiping it on his corduroy thigh. "Was only a year ago they let boys keep going after primary. S'why Dermot still goes."

James turned away. The only people he knew at school wanted nothing to do with him, and he had to go to school with girls. It was *outrageous*. That's what his grandfather would have said. Nothing was as good as England. The way people talked was a joke. The school was a joke. Even the Catholicism was a joke, its anemic altar boys bell-clanging, cow-calling, the substance of God into the host, the priests scruffy and yawning. He remembered something he'd overheard his grandmother say; it was natural for low people to dislike you, when you'd been born a gentleman. *A terrible snob she was*, his mother always told him, and he had never wanted to be like her, to be anything that his mother disliked, but now he was here, and he was unacceptable, even to his own cousins, and snobbishness did something for him: made him feel included somewhere else, gave him an excuse for hating them back, these cousins who wouldn't take him fishing, who had seen him every day on the hill and run in the opposite direction.

"*S'why*," he whispered.

Sister Ignatius directed the class to open their readers to a story called "Fionn Mac Cumhail."

"Why don't we ask the new boy to read first?" she said, speaking as if there were several people stuffed into her huge, stiff habit and she had the honour of speaking for all of them. She ran her finger down a page in her ledger. "Seamus Wharra...-Wharram-Young. Mr. Young, please read the first page."

He read, conscious of his pronunciation. He'd show them. He was good at something better than cows and slops; he was good at books, like his father.

"Ye have a good reading voice," Sister Ignatius said. "You're English?"

"Yes."

He ate the lunch his mother had packed for him, two hard-boiled eggs, some buttered bread, a jar of milk. The boys gathered on the playing field for a game of hurling, and James watched from the trees beside the school with a sinking heart, trying to catch on to the rules, how to use the big flat stick to hit the little ball, when to grab the ball with a hand and for how long to hold it.

After school, he tried to lose himself in the streams of children going through the town, but his cousins ran up behind him in the square.

"English he says he is. It's the arse end that's English. Me da' says it's how ye tell a Prod a mile away."

He turned without willing it. Liam was grinning. Dermot was puffing his chest out from the rest of his fat-muscled body, and behind him was John, pale and wheezing. They started speaking Gaelic at him, sputters of words that came cursing, insinuating, out of their mouths. He turned away, but found himself surrounded by boys he didn't know. Their eyes were sticks that they prodded him with. His clothes were so much better than theirs. He had some of John's twig-frame, but his face was mostly his father's, foreign and British with a high forehead and cheekbones, a face nobody knew between a scrawny neck and weedy hair, fly-away red.

"Thinks he's so smart," were words he caught in English. "Half Irish, and he can't even understand what we're saying."

They laughed, John's laugh weak, asking for approval.

"His name is Warren, like the rabbit warren by the strand – cause his mam breeds like rabbits."

"Seen yer mammy's cunt lately? Every man in town has."

"Yah, I was there t'other day," Dermot said. "His mam's a good fuck. And cheap. Didn't charge me a copper."

James screamed at them, hardly knowing what he was saying in his rage, a gibberish of things his mother read him out of the Bible and some things he'd read himself. "Vipers! I'll curse you and God will strike you down! Whoever pisseth against the wall will have his thing cut off –"

His words were frightening, blasphemous, had the sound of a real curse.

"Take it back," Dermot ordered.

James shook his head, aware of all the children backing away superstitiously, aware of adult faces looking through the spirit grocer's windows.

"Take it back, or I'll show them how much ye like your own shite," Dermot said. His hand was already leaping through air.

Dermot forced him face-first into a puddle until he was almost gulping the mud. Writhing, choking, his lungs, his brain exploding, he thought he'd die. Finally, Dermot jerked his head back by his hair to show his face, his tears.

"There. Why don't you go now and get Paddy to show ye around. Show ye *your* fields, now?"

Dermot walked away and the others followed. James waited on the edge of town, wiping the mud from his face on his sleeves, waited until he couldn't see anyone walking up the hills, and started to run.

He ran like an animal escaping from open ravening jaws, dropping his bag of books as soon as he realized he was carrying it. He took the road the bus had come on, remembering a sequence of places – first Cork City, then Dublin, then the port in England at Liverpool, and everyone knew where Oxford was. He could get on a bus in Cork and go, and go home, and never have to see any of his filthy cousins again. He ran hard, crazy, lungs burning, the back of his throat tasting of blood, too afraid to hitch rides from the postal truck, the bread truck, the milk truck. He refused to greet the men who passed him with their donkey carts, concentrated on the strides that took him away from the hated people, the place he could never belong, never want to belong. The road curved around the bay, the Tare's tidal estuary that was tracked at low tide with transparent rivers of fresh water over mud, combed pates of green sea-hair between the channels, then the road rose into a cleft between two hills. By the time he'd reached the top, he was gasping, unable to pull enough air in. He saw only hills and more hills, cliffs and sea. He couldn't see Cork City.

He remembered he had no money.

He beat his head with his hands when he couldn't stop crying, squeezed his eyes shut so hard, his eyes flared with false lights and he thought he might never see again. He threw his feet out in giant steps, letting gravity pull him down the other side of the hill. Somehow, he would get there. He had already stolen from his own mother. If he could get enough to eat to get him to the ferry, maybe they would let him work his way across. He would do anything, anything. And if his father sent him money, maybe... There was some sort of pub further down the road amongst a cluster of other buildings. He ran on, opened its door carefully and peered in, noticing the phone on the edge of the bar. The barkeep was talking to someone at the far end, and the few farmers barely looked up when he came in. He dialed home. Oxford.

He heard a few ticks, some uneven tocks as if he had put a broken clock to his ear. He had never heard of country codes, had never made a reverse charge call, had never imagined such an old phone.

"That phone is for the use of hotel guests only."

James put down the receiver. The woman peering through the door behind the counter had a receding chin and thin brown hair parted down the middle.

"I was trying to phone England, and it didn't work."

"And sticking me with the price of it! Look at yourself! Covered in mud. Did your mates make ye do it?"

"I have to phone my father. He'll pay."

"I don't know the numbers for England. And if I did...say – you're Bernadette Cahalane's boy. Why don't ye get back home and help your poor mammy? She'll not be pleased with ye for being out so late – and in such a mess."

The postmistress, and now this woman, and his mother and granny, and everyone against him. How could he run? He couldn't even call his father. Ireland was a dank green jail with a castle-moat of pitching sea.

He walked out. He had never felt despair before, even when his sister had died. Now his sister was dead, and so was his father, his grandmother, his grandfather, every friend he'd ever had. Everything he had ever known was dead – dead to him. This must be what it would be like to be dead himself, he thought. Dead, but still awake. The clouds were getting darker, bluer. He wanted to stay out in the wet blue forever, catch one of those colds his mother talked about, catch another and another, a hundred colds that would knock him down, lay him out in the grass so he would never have to go back to his granny's house again.

He guessed he should turn back, but he couldn't make himself, figured something had to happen if he could just keep walking in the right direction, even if that something was walking all the way home to England, stealing carrots out of people's gardens, cleaning out barns – he could do that; he'd helped Paddy once – for a meal and a place to stay. And he'd think about the ferry when the time came.

He kept on walking. Every time he came to the top of a hill, he was hopeful, drew in his breath at the sight of the endless ocean between the headlands under the overcast sky – so many kinds of darkness – his heart falling when the town up ahead did not seem big enough to be Cork City.

Clonakilty, the signs said, measuring out distance in miles and quarter miles. If he walked all night, at least he would be warm, and then maybe he could sleep some during the day – find some good hay and slip under the ropes and sheet that kept the wind from blowing it away, sleep cozy with the farm cats under the sun-warmed canvas – if only he could count on the sun. He was so tired. His legs ached from the effort of heaving himself up the hills, and from braking on the way down to keep himself from pitching forward. His chest hurt from breathing, from suffering. He would not turn back. No.

Now and then another walker coming from the town passed him and said, "Howrya." He heard the beat of hooves.

Paddy rode up beside him. James glanced up, shook his head and kept walking. So did the mare. He watched his feet and the hooves of the horse beside him for a long time – he didn't know how long. He noticed his bookbag was hanging from the saddle horn. He remembered there was an apple in it. He stopped walking.

Even with his sore muscles, it was easy for him to catch the toe of his shoe on top of Paddy's big boot in the stirrup, and swing up behind him; he'd done it so many times that summer, going with Paddy to check the fields, to mend the fences, to watch the badgers. He held on, his hands not quite meeting around Paddy's wide waist, and pressed his face against Paddy's back, his tears wetting the wool of his uncle's coat. Disoriented, numb, he found himself not turned around and heading back, but somewhere in the town of Clonakilty, in a big hot kitchen, an old man and woman sitting at a table, a smiling middle-aged woman putting a hasty meal of ham and leftover cabbage and potatoes in front of him. He ate, then ate the blackberry tart and cream, and drank cup after cup of milky tea. He put his coat back on when Paddy said it was time to go. The mare plodded home, tired from her hasty earlier journey, and from the weight of two.

They began to ride through mist as twilight deepened, and then the mist turned to fine rain, barely there, sharp and sparkling on his face, the tingle after the numbness of a limb that has gone to sleep. It was what snow should feel like. He was grateful for it. It cooled his face, hot with shame, kept each breath from sticking in his throat; he'd failed miserably, causing only trouble and worry. After about an hour, Paddy moved the reins and clicked his tongue and the mare stumbled down through the ditch, then through some bushes, onto a trail that would take them over the last hill, home, without having to parade past the convent and through the town. James forced his hands to meet around Paddy's big coat, held his uncle tighter, because the terrain was rougher, but more because Paddy hadn't said anything, not in accusation, reprimand, or punishment. James pledged his eternal love, eternal gratitude, as he listened to the horse's muted footfalls on the peaty earth, because he knew Paddy was never going to say anything, wasn't that kind of man.

It was after midnight when they came home. They stood in the porch, shedding overcoats and shoes, a voice inside the house coming closer until the door swung open and there was Granny, James amazed by the look of delighted relief on her face that vanished abruptly. She put her fists on her scrawny hips beneath her thin dress and cardigan.

"Jesus, Mary and Joseph! Where have ye been? Your mother's *beside* herself. Have ye been rolling in the mud?"

"I fell."

"I'll tell ye, I'll never get used to having a boy in the house again! I'm not having ye track that into the porch! Outside! Outside! Take off your pants!"

James scrambled as his granny churned her arms, snatching his pants, snatching at his shirt, rubbing at his wet, muddy hair with a kitchen rag.

"...and I don't care who's passing by to see your underpants! Filthy! Filthy! Now..."

Granny dragged him into the warm kitchen and he stood, shivering by the hot range. She wiped his arms and face and hair with a washcloth, dipping it into a basin now and then, clouding the water browner and browner. He looked up; Paddy was gone.

"Now fly upstairs and put on your pajamas before I get the whip out of the barn! And your mam up crying in her room."

He ran almost naked upstairs, desperate tingle at the back of his neck, feeling Granny behind him, as if she was young enough to give chase. There was exhilaration in the fear, in the freedom he felt in hating her. "Whip out o'th' barn," he muttered to himself, because he could take it, could take Granny's naked anger a lot easier than whatever he knew was stewing, waiting for him, within his mother's heart.

He dressed and stood a moment outside his mother's door, hearing nothing, knocking finally, opening the door.

She was lying on the floor in front of her bed, curled up like a baby. She saw him and got up, and took him, held him.

"I couldn't go down, you see. I was praying you were alright, and I couldn't go down to see if...if..."

They stood, listening to each other breathe, his mother's rosary beads in her hand, hard against his ribs like a handful of rocks, her cheek against his wet, gritty hair.

"Did you run away?"

"I was just going home."

She cried then, hard sobs that shook them both, and she began to mumble things as she shook her head: *no*, and things he couldn't hear properly, bits about being thankful, being grateful, being unable to stand, what? Losing him, losing him as well as his sister.

His heart bucked suddenly. Why should it matter to lose something she barely noticed any more? Wasn't she always praying, lost in her housework, chasing the priest down to question him on something more important than he was? Wasn't she sometimes still holed up in her room, coming to the door and opening it like a wild creature at the edge of its burrow, looking suspicious, ready to attack something, anything, barely even recognizing him?

On the chest of drawers was a collection of icons, some of which he had seen before. There was a glutton Christ child in chipped plaster and golden robes, a wooden crucifix, a framed picture of the sacred heart, a blue mantled Virgin wearing a crown – the Queen of Heaven – and a tiny brown monk in a plastic bubble, like the crisp, ancient corsage on his grandmother's dresser in Oxford. He was suddenly afraid his mother would leave him to become a nun.

"Oh, child," she said, and pushed him away, holding his shoulders tight in her fists, "You're mine. You're all that I've got. You're everything to me. I can't live without you."

He reached out then for the rest of her, the rest of her that she kept at a stiff arm's-length. This was what he had been longing to hear after their first night in this house, that night she said she hadn't wanted him at first. *Now* she wanted him, and finally he felt safe.

He got to her, wrapped his arms around her. She couldn't hold him tight enough – and yet and yet, the next day, when something of a miracle happened, when Paddy walked to school with him, walked him into the Mother Superior's office, had her dial his father's number, and they both left him alone with his father's voice, all he could do was cry, cry for his father to come and take him home. His father's promises to do just that, his father's sobs blurred into his own shaking relief.

After that came the waiting, days and days of it, until a week had gone past, and then two. Then he remembered the way it had been, sometimes, with his father, with promises, with entire conversations, entire evenings. One night, months ago, he had asked his father for what he wanted most in the world: a golden retriever puppy; hadn't they said they would get him a dog once Dymphna was out of diapers, once she had learned to be gentle with animals, once she didn't need naps any more so the barking wouldn't be waking her up? Of course, his father said. Yes, of course. I'll talk to your mother about it.

No, his father said the next day, no – not that a dog was impossible – but no, James, they had never had any such conversation.

A few days later, after school, he saw Dermot with a girl in a little copse of trees by the convent wall. Dermot had pulled the tails of her blouse out of her woolen skirt and pushed his hands beneath the cotton, inched his fingers up her white ribs.

James walked up the hill, almost not seeing, not hearing, as he made his plan, thinking back to some of the books he'd seen in his father's shop, the magazine one of his Oxford friends had stolen from his big brother, paralyzed by his own single-minded will to do something, anything, to punish Dermot, to revenge himself.

That evening at tea, Granny was brooding, her teacup half empty, the glowing coal of the cigarette nearing her fingers. Paddy was reading a letter aloud from a cousin of Granny's in America. Bernadette was up from her chair every few minutes, cutting more bread, pouring more tea. James swirled his leftover dreg of tea and leaves, watching the muddy trail it left on the sides of the cup, watching gravity take the liquid back to the bottom. He began to talk, first about his schoolwork, then the book he'd borrowed from the library, then the strange things he'd seen his cousin doing with a girl. The adults stopped breathing. The peat burned silently in the range, in the hard hollow room. James described what he'd seen in detail, and also described what he hadn't, pretending to be as ignorant of sex as they assumed he was. The throats of his audience turned to stone.

"...I thought he was going to pee, but –"

"Enough! Stop it! His granny put her hands over her ears, then over her face.

"But he –"

"What are they thinking of, putting girls and boys in the same schools?" his mother protested, her brusque hands stopping, for once, in mid-air, the teapot a scalding weight above him. "That's what comes of education when it's *free*! Free! Government run, is what it is! Immoral! Godless! Sodom and –"

"Why can't –"

"No, dear, enough," his mother said, fighting tears of outrage that her little son's innocence should be destroyed so soon, managing to set the teapot down and sink back into her chair. "It's Dermot who's done something wrong. You were right to tell us."

"But what –" James turned his eyes to Paddy who looked back wide-eyed and helpless before swallowing, mustering himself.

"Nothing ye need concern yourself with."

James did his best to assume a look of outraged curiosity.

"Who was the girl?" Granny demanded, her eyes nailing him to his chair. "Who was the little tart?"

"Leave him alone, Mam," Paddy mumbled.

"I could only see the back of her – and it was through the trees." He tried to keep his voice calm, but he hated his granny, always finding fault, always there, at him, in rage and ugliness.

"Don't ye see how the thing has upset him, Mam?" his mother said. "To see a sight like that at his age. No doubt he ran away as soon as he saw. Didn't you, James?"

"Yes."

"Ye must have seen her. Come on!" Granny reached out with her sagging skinned hand and he leaned away.

He hadn't thought about this. He hadn't been prepared to bring down two with a lie only meant for one. Should he say her name? They might not believe him if he didn't. "I don't know all the girls names yet – I –"

"Well ye can tell us what she looked like, then. Come on! Come on!"

"I think...I think..." he said, surges of blood in his temples. "It was the girl from the spirit grocer's."

There was silence, Granny and Paddy finding each other's horrified eyes, Bernadette, puzzled.

"Oh, God," Paddy whispered, looking away, "Oh, Jesus."

Granny muttered and sloshed whiskey in her rinsed-out teacup.

"Now, ye understand ye aren't to speak of this again to anyone?" his mother said.

He nodded. He listened to their frantic whispering from the top of the stairs when they thought he was going to bed, becoming more and more frightened. What had he done? What had he started? Some avalanche of people colliding furiously into one another that he, that no one, could stop? The only words above a whisper were Paddy's exhausted "I'll go, I'll go," the outside door slamming with wind.

James got up in the middle of the night, almost knocked on his mother's door to confess, to ask her for forgiveness, to ask her to get him into the heaven he knew he had thrown away with a lie. As he stood on the landing, his granny's door swayed open so slowly he thought he wasn't seeing it. It was the only door in the house that didn't squeak.

"So. You're a little spy," came a crackling whisper through the dark. He could see her pale vulture's silhouette as she leaned against the doorframe. "I didn't see it before, with all that fancy talk of yours, fancy clothes. Ye little *spy*."

He leaped into his room, heart thumping, knowing God would never save a liar, especially a liar who refuses to confess his sin. But his granny didn't come into his room like the witch she was, to scratch his ears with incantations. The most frightening thing was that while she had accused him of being a spy, and possibly a liar, she hadn't sounded angry. She'd sounded amused: an enjoyer of wickedness.

Granny didn't fall asleep soon either, needing less sleep at her age. It was one of the reasons she kept the hinges of her door well oiled, so she could go to the kitchen, make herself a cup of tea without waking anyone, go for a walk if the weather was fine. She had told James that she liked walking at night when no one could see her. If no one could see her, no one could talk, and she might see a few things herself.

The next day, James didn't see Dermot. He overheard John talking about the terrible beating his brother got. Dermot never came back to school. Colm had decided it was about time Dermot started helping on the farm full time – rooting up the ragwort from the furthest fields – to hell with the so-called education he was getting at the convent. A convent was no place for a boy, at least a boy like Dermot. Dermot had protested the parts of the accusation that were false, but did not deny the identity of the girl.

Her name was Deirdre McAnenely and she was thirteen. She had a thin dark face, a beautiful, straight, aggressive nose, and a thick fringe of black hair that hung nearly down to her waist. It was the blackest black James had ever seen, black with blue glints, a shine that reflected the sky like the deepest water. The only child of the spirit grocer, she was like her mother, Fiona, who was rumoured to have descended from a shipwrecked sailor of the Spanish Armada.

James kept his eyes open, skirted Colm's farm on the way to school, ducked into the hedges whenever he saw Dermot, which was more often than he'd like. James wanted him to vanish into the fields, but saw him once or twice a week. Often, James would come back from school and search for Paddy, only to catch sight of Dermot beside their shared uncle, checking on a heifer's hoof, or carrying a bucket of oats meant for Lizzy. He avoided the barns at milking time.

He also stopped going into the spirit grocer's to buy peppermint sticks because Deirdre might be working there with her father. He watched her from a distance, despised her for letting a boy like Dermot touch her. The sight of her terrified him with guilt and a horrifying kind of pleasure.

On his way home from school one day, James had to hide from Dermot for nearly an hour in a hedge, finally entering the kitchen with a monstrous hunger. Granny was sitting in her old blanket-padded chair by the kitchen window. Her head didn't turn when he slammed the door, and it was his intention to get through the kitchen as quickly as he could before she might chase him back outside or to the kitchen sink for a wash, blowing her old woman's smell around him.

Paddy came in from milking and began scrubbing his hands in the sink, cleaning his nails with an old toothbrush. There was a bramble leaf in his hair; it must have been a good day for napping under a bush.

"You're not watching for the Guards again, Mam?" Paddy asked without a backward look, the soap hard and round and slippery in his big hands.

"They're still out there watching *me*, so why shouldn't I be watching them?"

"The Guards aren't in that sort of business."

"The Black and Tans are."

"Mam, I keep telling ye – it's the Guardai now. The police. They're to keep us safe. The time of the Black and Tans is over."

"I've still got something up m' sleeve! They'll not catch me with me head a-hanging out in the rain, Owen. I may be an old woman, but I can always be of service. There were women alive before my time who'd preserved the heads of English soldiers in vats of sheep's grease!"

"Agh," James said.

"Paddy, Mam."

"Eh?"

"Ye called me Owen."

"Oh, yes. Right, right. Paddy."

She watched him sit at the table to read his luxury of a pre-tea time newspaper, the *Cork Examiner,* second-hand, from the town doctor.

"And ye'll read me anything about the troubles in the paper, won't ye Paddy?"

"Yes, Mam."

James loaded the top of his school books with ginger biscuits and treaded over the cold kitchen floor to the stairs. The first step creaked.

"Eh? What are ye doing with all them biscuits? Tea time is coming when tea time is coming. Don't ye know about the poor children in China without a crust of bread for themselves? Don't ye know about our very own poor. I tell ye, along this road, up into the hills, there are houses with dirt floors, six people in one cold room!"

James sighed – this sounded like one of his mother's old tirades about what the English did to the Irish – and he made his way back to the cupboard, his tongue and stomach kicking against him. He unloaded all but two biscuits into the tin.

"Come here," Granny ordered, hand beckoning, neck stooped, eyes on something beyond the window.

He looked at Paddy.

"She's a good one to have on your side. Go then."

He set his books and biscuits on the table and came carefully. Her hand found his arm and pulled him beside her to the window.

"Ye see that?"

"What?"

The window framed the most beautiful view from the house: farms and fields and tumbling walls of stone and bramble and fuchsia stretching down the hill to the plateau and then the plunge of cliffs at the sea edge. There was the castle of Castle Field, an ivy-covered, dark-windowed cube of wall without roof or floor. To the left was Colm's house, and far below was Killaghmore, the river Tare, the bay and all the small boreens that scoured their way through the hills. A round crumble-topped tower marked the copse of trees where the old church lay in its walls and tombs, and to the right was the hollow where his mother's holy well lived in faded offerings of tattered clothing. It was raining, the sky blue and heavy, darkening the hills, every slate roof shining silver black with wet depth and distance.

"What do you want me to see?"

"The foreigners, boy! Do ye not see them in their fancy car at the Murphy's?"

He searched, feeling her stir with impatience until he saw the tip of a green car poking out from behind a barn further down the hill.

"Are they in the –"

"They both went into the house. Two of them, man and woman. Couldn't see if 'twas Mary's son come from America with his new wife, but I'm laying bets – hasn't she been going on and on about them coming? Couldn't get the glasses out soon enough."

James looked into her lap. She was clutching a set of World War One field glasses like the pair his father used to take on their summer holidays. One of the large lenses was cracked clean across the middle and the leather strap was in a knot where it had broken.

"Here, boy. Take a look. Come on." She steered his body to the window and between her knees, in spite of his reluctance, and held up the glasses. "Well, take them! Can't do all the sainted work meself."

He took the glasses, afraid of her sharp voice in his ear, and looked through. He could see nothing but green blur.

"How is it? Here." She moved and forced him to share her chair, then made adjustments to the glasses. "Look through just the left one with your right eye." He felt her vulture head move to the other eyepiece; they were ear to ear. "What can ye see?"

"The ocean. Gulls."

"Good. Now ye keep holding them up, but let me move them." She swung their eyes along the coast to the west. "There's the land," she breathed. "Ye cannot destroy the land though the English have tried to take it from its people. This is where the first people came to Ireland with King Partholan and Queen Dealgnaid."

"Queen Dalny?"

"That's about how ye say it. When they came they had to fight with the demons – right there, ye see the tower, where its shadow falls on the slope? Where the man is walking – oh, that's young Tommy O'Brien. His father was a bastard – that's where Rury, the son of the king and queen, killed a demon in the shape of an eagle and a snake. There was snakes in Ireland before the coming of Saint Patrick, don't ye know. But getting the demons out of the country didn't help them in the end, because they all died of the plague and 'twas nobody to bury them but one man, Tuan, brother of the king, and he was too worried about getting eaten by the wolves to wait about."

She moved the glasses along the cliff and let both their eyes rest on the castle.

"Ye want to know how we got all this land? During the famine, everyone was leaving, starving, and we were the ones that stayed, took the land they left. Ate grass, even."

"Ye *canna* eat grass, Mam," Paddy interjected.

"They ate grass when it got very bad," she shouted, hurting James's ear, "because they knew the old magic that let them get food from even the stones, could bait fish hooks with twigs and catch salmon."

"More stories, Mam." Paddy was relaxed in the way he bickered with his mother, as if they were husband and wife. "There are some that say we could stay only because we were in so tight with the Protestant landlord – the overseers – did a bit of the dirty work for him."

"Lies! Jealousy! So read the stories in your newspaper, then, and leave the important ones to us, why don't ye?" Granny shook her head and continued. "Then, after the rising, the Protestants was all afeared to get out of the place, and the one that had most of this land was a fool and out of brass, and me father bought his land for a song, took the roof off the great house and let the rain in. That's what the castle is, all tangled with vines. Wakefield House. There used to be a ballroom with crystal chandeliers and mirrored walls, hunting trophies and grand staircases, and underground passageways for the servants. I saw it all."

"Why did he take the roof off?"

"Some say the neighbours was jealous and told him lies, that he wouldn't be able to pay the taxes on the great house, but I think it was from religious feeling, to keep himself away from the Protestant wealth and filth – hunting trophies! all them rotting animal bits – to ruin the last of what remained of them. I don't regret it. Ivy is far better dressing than silk for a good Irish wall. Sure, but what could I have done with so much floor except be scrubbing it all the time?"

She swung the glasses to the east, skimming the houses of the town, the convent school, and the hills behind. "Ah, right. I was telling ye. So Tuan went over all the land, for there was no one else but him, and he lived so lonely until he was old and grey and decrepit, and one morning he woke up and found his head was heavy, spiny with horns." She thrust her knobby, contorting hands up beside her head to demonstrate. "He had changed into a stag, was young and strong again."

James made a sound, a derisive snort.

"Do ye want to hear the story or not? Hush up, then. He became the king of all the deer in Ireland."

"Sure. Deer don't have kings."

"Disrespectful! They did a long time ago – and ye weren't around a long time ago, were ye? Well your granny was, and the damned deer had kings, so there. And cut the smiling."

He bit his lips together so they disappeared into his mouth, but couldn't stop smiling, the corners of his mouth crinkling up, gusting with spit.

She swung the glasses along a far road to an intersection, where there was a little clot of houses with a pub and a shop.

"Well, would ye lookit who's coming out of MacMahon's over to Bally Cross! Ye see the old man? That's Spuddy. They called him that 'cause he was a digging the taties all his life. Hasn't been seen outside his house since his wife died months back, and now look at him out at MacMahon's having a pint! Good on ye, Spuddy! You're not dead yet! See, if this were a Sunday, they'd be playing a score of bowls between MacMahon's and Cooney's across the valley."

"What's that?"

"Road bowling. Two men go throwing an iron ball to see who gets furthest down the road with the fewest throws."

"What about Tuan? What did he do when he was king of the deer?"

"Well, he watched people come on the island, watched them be born and die, and finally they all died again, and then he turned into a wild boar. And then he was young again. And he changed next to an eagle when he got old, and – look there's a hawk! Ye see him above the head? He's looking for fish for his children – and when Tuan got old again, he turned next to a salmon, and all the while, the people of Ireland came and fought, and lived and died, and soon Tuan was caught and a princess ate him for dinner. Then, a most wonderful thing happened. Inside the princess," she clutched James in the belly, "he turned into a baby, and was born a man once again, became a king, and was a great friend of the Christian monks. He's one of your grandfathers."

"Can I move the glasses now? Is it my turn?"

She sighed. "Go ahead, boy. Don't know how much of these things sink into your brain."

He swung himself over the sea, into the clouds, then down into the square of Killaghmore. There, in the market the month before, he'd seen the prettiest Connemara pony, rich red brown and almost as big as Paddy's mare. He swept back and forth, closer and closer. Halfway up the hill, there was Dermot, trudging down the boreen to his father's house, as much a part of the landscape as the stone walls and bony-hipped cows. Suddenly aware of his granny's hand on the back of his neck, he startled and shook her off. She lit a cigarette and he smelled the sulfurous match – rotten egg. He raced his eyes through the sky and didn't see his mother walk into the yard carrying a bag of groceries, her head hunched further under her kerchief from all the hiding she did in town. She refused to let him go on some of her shopping trips, and he was all too ready to stay ignorant of the looks people gave her, though he had the urge to follow her, to protect her in some way he couldn't imagine.

"Here comes Bernadette in for her tea, and Paddy waiting, and I haven't even got the scones made up! Get on up to your homework! Give me the glasses."

"Can't I keep them to look out the window? I won't drop them."

"No, ye canna!" she shouted. "Up the stairs with ye." He let go of the glasses and retreated to the doorway as she flailed her finger at him. "You're not to touch these ever, d'ye hear me? Not unless I'm there, and I've told ye. I'll kill ye, otherwise."

He held on to the door frame and looked into her bagged, angry eyes, his neck still warm from her hand.

"No you wouldn't. You're just full of talk."

She nodded, mouth grim, but softening. "Here, then, back-talker. Ye can have them to look through when I'm in the room and no one else but Paddy or Bernadette around – if ye keep it a secret. I tell ye, I'll *give* 'em to ye someday if ye try hard at school...if ye bring your books home and read your granny a good story now and then."

He thought about it while sitting in her chair, field glasses in his hand, as he watched her mash the potatoes for the scones and put the kettle on to boil. He would do that. He found himself wanting to read her stories.

The next day after school, he found a rack of sun-bleached weather-worn antlers on the floor of his room.

He put them to his head, snorted.

Everyone came to drink tea.

Nice cup of tea, *lovely* cup of tea, *beautiful* cup of tea.

Every cup of tea they had was praised as lavishly as the last – all the same every day cups of tea. It made James laugh.

The life of the household moved around him and his mother unchanged. Many evenings, the kitchen filled with female relatives, always Susan and her young children, Maureen, his sour, overweight aunt, and Agnes, who looked like a younger version of Granny, who was always knitting with wiry hands and ordering around a stunning variety of silent, rebellious-eyed, teenage girls. Annie, the scar-faced woman with the ravishing smile, was there if she could get her husband to drop her off on his way to McGovern's pub in town. Sometimes their neighbour, old Mrs. Murphy, came over with a huge soft brick of cake called "sponge." Now and then, two venerable rickety cousins of Granny's helped each other up the hill to drink glasses of her generously poured whiskey. Men dropped by often because they knew the food would be there and the kettle was always on the range. Every few weeks, the thick-spectacled yawning-voiced priest from the hill parish visited, making a hasty retreat in the early evening when the kitchen filled with too many women. Paddy often stayed in the kitchen and put up with his sisters' teasing, or retreated to the lounge to read second-hand newspapers if he decided he could afford the luxury of two fires in the house. He went to the pub once a week, on a Friday or Saturday, so when the house got too noisy on Thursday, he'd sit in the dark cow-smelling barn to smoke, or walk down the hill to talk to Colm. James would wolf his tea and bread and go to a corner of the kitchen and whatever books he'd taken out of the library.

His mother whirled the dishcloth, checking for dust above the door frames, became her toiling body, became a servant, piety pinched tight into the centre of her sharp face by her silence. Her narrow fingers sometimes found the bridge of her nose and squeezed it even tighter. She began doing things that made their new life seem too permanent. She had gotten permission from the priest to tell Bible stories to the young children immediately after Sunday morning Mass. He attended Mass with her on Saturday morning, evening, and Sunday morning. She volunteered him for altar boy duty, which he performed sullenly, fainting from hunger one Sunday morning.

One afternoon, after the roast beef, mashed turnips and potatoes were eaten, all the gravy mopped up with pieces of bread, and the sweet, custard-drowned cake and blackberry preserve savoured with cup after cup of strong tea, his mother called James back into the kitchen.

"Time ye started helping," she told him. "You bring the dishes to the sink. I'll wash, and you dry."

There was a knock at the door, and James let in the yawning, adenoidal priest, Father O'Griofa.

Granny grunted, flashed a resentful look at him from her chair by the window where she brooded over her last cup of tea. Brooding was taking up more of her time as Bernadette rushed, when her nerves weren't bad, to take on more of the chores.

"Ah, Father. Ye should time your visits more cleverly," Bernadette said, with one of her old smirks of irony. "Didn't we just put away a lovely roast beef. Ye'll have a bit of pudding and a cup of tea, now, won't ye?" She didn't take the time to dry her hands and rushed around the kitchen dripping, assembling another dish of sponge cake, custard, and blackberry preserve. "Won't ye be sitting down, Father?"

Father O'Griofa sat at the table uneasily. He always gave the impression that his spirit might be too large for his body just as his body was too large for his clothes. He moved carefully to prevent the seams from ripping.

"Ah, don't trouble yourself, Bernadette. I'm just after me dinner. I didn't come on a social visit. It's an ill wind I'm blowing in on, I'm afraid."

That yawning voice. James yawned.

Bernadette set Father O'Griofa's bowl of custard and cake in front of him, poured his tea, and sank her hands into the hot wash water again.

"Someone, one of the mothers of the children in your little class, has demanded I talk to ye or she would do it herself. It seems her little girl was upset by something ye said this morning. Something about devils, and she's been crying, frightened out of her wits."

"I don't tell them anything but the truth!"

"That may be, but there are some truths the little ones aren't ready –"

"My – my little girl – ye can die any time after you're born."

"I'm not saying they shouldn't be taught, gradual-like. How to behave and such. The Ten Commandments. But it's their baptism that justifies them before the age of decision, Bernadette."

Bernadette washed a plate, kept shaking her head, swung around and pointed a dripping finger at the priest.

"We are called to preach the Gospel to all, and it's *good* for her to be frightened. That's what will keep her to the path when she's *past* the age of decision. Father, I was never afraid when I was a girl. I should have been afraid! Look at what I – look at what happened –"

"Bernadette. This lady is not the first to have spoken to me. I'm not talking about your good intentions. I'm talking about *ways* of doing things. And ye talk about what happened to ye! Some of the ladies don't want ye teaching the children at all because of it. If I'd known of all this fuss..."

Bernadette plunged her hands into the wash water again, teeth clenched.

"It might, I think, be the best thing, if ye take a little rest from teaching. Ye've just come out of a shocking time. I know ye want to do good. We'll talk about what ye can do later, after ye've rested a bit. Making yourself healthy so ye *can* do God's work, is also God's work, ye know. Best be going."

"I'm not *healthy?*"

She faced him, her mouth contorting, forming and unforming words. The priest rose and left, his pudding uneaten, his tea untouched. Bernadette shook her head over the dish-water, her tears dropping into the white soapsuds. She cried so often now. James leaned his head on her shoulder, but she kept working, her arm knocking against his ribs – her body always working. Was there nothing he could do to make her feel better? Helpless, he left her to her work, stuffed the priest's portion of cake into his mouth, forced his already overfull stomach to take it, so she could wash the bowl.

James missed his father most in the small Killaghmore library when he opened a book that smelled of mildew. It was a com-plicated kind of missing – a deep, hopeless yearning made more painful by the anger and the feeling of abandonment he attempted to bury.

The library was in one room of what used to be the town courthouse. The walls had been damaged by perpetual damp and the pale yellow paint was coming off in huge, curved shav-ings wherever the plaster was still intact. The floor was harle-quined with red and black diamond tiles, too solid a foundation for the sparse shelves of books and the atmosphere of mould. Three tall arched windows looked out onto the square and pooled light in the centre of the room. The library had a few interesting books. His favourites were the art books, similar to the kind he used to look at with his father, books that were beau-tiful, books that made him feel calm, somehow beloved. James managed to convince himself he wasn't hiding when he hurried to the library after school and sat in a window alcove watching the other children splash past in the silver downpours of autumn.

He watched the civilization he was trapped in. There were donkey carts filled with empty milk cans, a few cars, town women trotting from one shop to another, holding their arms against their bodies for some protection from the wet. Most didn't own raincoats because women weren't expected to leave the house much. He watched men entering McGovern's pub, sometimes with their sons, slowly carving a place for the boys in the adult world.

He would close his eyes on his jealousy, or turn them toward another book.

The second day of a cold Atlantic gale, he ducked into the library and left his raincoat in a sodden mass inside the door. He didn't feel like looking at any of the books he'd looked at before. Reading itself seemed too much of an effort on days like this. He sat in the window and watched the rain bullet down, angled by the wind. The sturdy, pucker-lipped librarian, Mrs. McGinty, was cutting pieces of thick green tape and applying them to the spines of decaying books. He listened to the snip of the scissors and the open-mouthed roar of water on the cavern roof. His eyes were almost closed when he noticed a new object in the room. It was a small glass-topped display case like a low pulpit, the legs thin, delicately touching the floor like the hooves of a small deer. He walked over. There was a book inside, pages spread open.

"I can take it out for ye to look at," Mrs. McGinty said, "seeing that there isn't anyone else around and as long as ye don't tell. I can't do these things for everybody, but you're one of me best customers."

She had to pry up the hinged glass door with her letter opener.

"It's just come from central library. It's touring to all the libraries in Cork, ye see. It's a copy of a very famous Irish book called the *Book of Kells*. See the photographs of the pages? All in colour. The real one is supposed to be very old. Maybe from the time of St. Patrick."

He wanted her to stop talking and give him the book. She let him take it from her, but followed him back to his seat.

"They say the monks wrote it. Ye can't read it – I tried – but it's supposed to be part of the Bible, ye see. The monks painted it, too. Even the copy is very expensive, so ye'll have to be careful with it. Next month it'll be over to Skibbereen."

Some of the pages were mostly words, but there were pages entirely of pictures and twisted designs, and even the word pages had their drawings. There were little cartoon dogs and eagle monsters grappling with nets and knots that were snakes, spindle-nosed and claw-footed. There were curve-backed, pop-eyed men with see-through kilts and long toes, Celtic-knotted into the bodies of letters, and small brown-eared, blonde-haired faeries. There was the black, stretch-boned, limp-winged devil, alone against a flock of apostles embroidered almost beyond recognition with blue and gold lace, wedged against the throne of Christ, who was protected by glum-faced, goggle-eyed angels with squiggle hair, all welded to God's red chain-link halo. He liked the snoozing sideways men at the ends of paragraphs, arms folded with palms on shoulders, bodies spooling in knots, scaling into the tails of mythic fish – maybe Tuan before he was eaten by the princess? – and Alpha and Omega flying away, gripped in the sharp feet of a hawk. Even the insides of the *A* and *O* were coloured in, doodle-bright, as if his sister had gotten hold of the book and attacked it with crayons.

"Lovely book isn't it? Lovely pictures." Mrs. McGinty was standing over him, but he was in the world of the book and didn't hear.

He found loll-tongued monsters, eyes all blue iris with curved noses like exotic feather pens, fox-fish heads, a fish snipping through the thin scrawled belly of a cat, a huge old man sitting bowlegged in an armchair, book in lap, starbursts exploding around him, his fists extending to the edges of the page, round pink-ankled feet at the bottom, the whole innards of the book a wonder-language, the holy mystery of heaven. Was this the life beyond? James's heart was laughing, aching.

"...and there are the other religious books we have in the library, the translations of the Bible. Lots more good books we have all the time. Ye ask the priest, too. I'm sure he'd let ye look at some of his own."

He looked up at Mrs. McGinty and wondered how long she had been standing beside him, talking. If there were more books, he hoped they would have pictures like these.

"The thing about the Irish, ye see, is they've always been good at writing the books."

It was the next Saturday that he noticed his mother's strange smile – a pleased, clinging kind of smile – as she rested her eye on him. He took another mouthful of potatoes and gravy, then stirred his fork through the thin dry skins on his side plate. She should have been staring at Paddy. He was dressed up in a white shirt and navy tie, his thick soft neck pink and clean, his face shaven except for the two tufts high on his cheeks, and the little grey drifts of whiskers the razor had missed. His hair was water-combed straight back, his eyes on his meal, his cheeks blushing pink. Granny was ice-lipped, crashing plates down on the table, pots into the sink, then propping herself against the counter to gaze aridly at Paddy, sucking tea, sucking tobacco, blowing smoke.

"Aren't ye going to eat, Mam?" his mother asked, her brogue now purely Irish, no softening from the years spent in England. "Sit yourself –"

Granny slapped the air with the back of her hand, silenced her daughter. Paddy put a forkful of cabbage in his mouth miserably, as if his mother had cooked him a plate of straw. He cleaned his plate quickly, and Granny banged a bowl of apple pie smothered in warm custard in front of him. He pushed himself away from the table, got his coat in the porch, and stepped back into the kitchen to put it around his big shoulders.

"Are ye sure ye don't want anything from Clon'?" he said, fingering the money for his bus ticket.

Granny shifted her hanging vulture head to look at the wall. "Ye didn't eat your pie."

"Ye'll give Orla our love," Bernadette said. "That's another aunt of yours, James. Ye've got more cousins in Clonakilty."

"Joy," James said.

"Disrespectful!" his mother snapped, the exclamation re-learned from her mother.

"Back late," Paddy mumbled, and ducked his head into the rain.

James read in his room in the afternoon. He was wearing two jumpers and had folded a blanket under him on the floor so he could open his book in the square of misty window light and still be warm.

Granny was gone when he came down for tea. His mother didn't think there was anything to worry about, that she had probably gone to visit her cousins.

"Besides, it'll be nice to have tea together, just the two of us. I'm glad."

He put his chin on his hands on the table and watched her get the tea, stoking up the range; she seemed almost her old self. He loved the time he spent with her in the kitchen, usually with bites of chewy bread dough or bowl lickings, or gingerbread he could cut into men, raisin buttons pressed into their bellies. Cold rain pelted the windows, fogged with mist. He tapped the hard slate floor with his feet.

"Oh, didn't I forget your cod-liver oil this morning? You should have reminded me."

He smirked, shook his head.

"Come on, now. Here you go."

"You first."

"All right. You know how I love it." She swallowed the oil, and licked the tablespoon clean. "Tonight, I'll dream of fish."

He swallowed his. "I'll dream of monkeys."

"*Monkeys?*" She laughed. With one finger she swirled the hair on the top of his head, following the red whorl.

She put the tea, toast, biscuits, and his once-a-day glass of milk on the table – good for his bones, she said. She had forgotten to stir the milk, so the cream curled buttery and thick on top, and the milk underneath looked thin, bluish. He ate his toast and blackberry jam first, then dunked the biscuits, cream swirling. Drinking it with something sweet was the only way he could stand milk, especially if the cows had eaten something strange, giving the milk a sour, grassy taste.

"T'other day I was talking to Mrs. McGinty, the woman over to the library."

He knew the way she would look on this visit, peering through a paisley tunnel of cloth to see where she was going, still afraid to show her whole face and its fading pink ripples of scar.

"She says ye spend a lot of time there after school."

"I figure Paddy, he doesn't need me to help with the cows with all –"

"Shh. It's all right. I'm not scolding ye. She says ye like reading the holy books. Said ye looked at one for over an hour, and it wasn't even in a language ye could understand."

He looked at his glass and stuffed another biscuit into his mouth. The last time he had gone to town with her, she had gripped his wrist the entire time, as if he might break into a run any second – or as if she might. He didn't want to run away any more, even when he thought he saw his father, thought he recognized the back of a stranger in town: broad shoulders and well-made tweed jacket, the height, the accent. Each time was catching his heart on a nail.

"This love of the holy books – it's a sign, Seamus. It's the call." She held him with her eyes – her eye. "I always knew ye were special, different from the other boys. I'm praying the Lord will give ye a vocation."

What was she talking about? He couldn't bear the intensity of her eye and looked at the glass one on purpose, to take the power away. It was as moist and glistening as the other, as a pearl onion, and his own eyes seemed to feel cold and hard in their sockets.

"Of course you're very young, but once God has called ye, ye must never forget, like Adam and Eve, who ran from their duty. Ye must go to Him, Seamus, and see. Think about the Judgment Day. Will ye be able to say that you tried to obey God in everything he asked ye to do?"

Was God asking him to do something? He couldn't say he was a very obedient boy, but God wasn't very good at explaining Himself. And He wasn't very good at granting prayers.

"They didn't die," he said, and he saw his mother startle, put her hand on the table for steadiness. The word *die*. He thought of Dymphna, the time he'd pecked her in the head with the carrot, the times she'd pinched him, hard. "God said if Adam and Eve ate the fruit they would die. And they didn't. They ended up knowing everything, just like the snake –"

"No, no. But they did die. Not right away. And they lived lives of pain for it too. It'll take ye a long time to understand. If ye become a priest like He wants, ye'll understand better than any of us."

She sat beside him and held his hands, her palms hot and dry from her teacup.

"God wants me to be a *priest?*"

"Why else would he put the love of the holy books into ye?"

Was that it? He didn't know anyone else who read as much as he did, and he did love that book with the pictures. The Jesuits, the nuns, spoke of the priesthood as the goal for the best of them, the greatest thing a man could aspire to.

"If ye became a priest, ye could do so much good – telling people when they're wrong and such, helping them be better. Ye could even become a missionary. Ye could go anywhere in the world to help people. Help the poor people in China, in India."

"I could...go? Away?"

Go *home.*

Her hand was in his hair making him look at her, into her eye.

"Give your life to God. I'd be so happy," she said.

She'd be happy. He could make her happy.

She gathered him into her arms and smiled harder and harder until she spilled a warm teardrop of water onto his ear, water that was sad water, but glad water at the same time, a wetness that dissolved him, made him shiver with knowing, with some kind of enlightenment.

That night, he lay in a coma of awareness, his sins swimming before his eyes, all the things he hadn't been able to tell in confession: hating Ireland, being angry at his mother when she was doing everything for him, writing to his father, telling tales about Dermot. What if he'd wrecked Dermot's life? What if Dermot had been meant to be a doctor or a lawyer and had ended up a cowhand?

Could a priest be a liar *and* a bastard?

He got out of bed to write his father again, wrote, and crossed out, wrote and crossed out, crumpled the paper and threw it against the wall. Why *would* his father want him? He tried to remember the exact sound of his father's voice. It was gone. Even in his memory, his father was vanishing.

His breath came in trembling waves, air moving him, shaking him, as if he were a small stone clattering back and forth in the surf. He thought of his father and hated him, his father who had thrown him into the waves and didn't care whether he was drowning.

But he knew for sure his mother wanted him, now. And God wanted him, and could never, ever stop wanting him.

James came into the kitchen on Saturday morning to find his mother bent, clasping her ribs with crossed arms. A column of steam was shooting unnoticed out of the kettle on the range, and Granny was smoking away, not thinking to make the tea, tending a pan of crackling bacon. Paddy's plate was already empty, wiped clean of all but one streak of egg and a few toast crumbs.

"He'll not go to Mass this morning, Bernie," Granny said. "Sure, but there are plenty of other things he could be doing just as holy as that! I'm not one for forcing it down a child's throat. Surest way to make him hate the whole bleeding – once a week is the commandment, and anything beyond should be your own choosing."

"But he's an altar boy, Mam! And if he's to be a priest! He's said so, ye know. It's not just me own wishful thinking!"

"Jesus, Mary and Joseph! A boy like that knowing what he –"

"Mam," Paddy warned when he saw James in the doorway. "It's himself."

"Lord, Seamus! Make a noise when ye come into a room. Ye scared the b'Jesus out of me!"

"Mam!" his mother exclaimed, lifting her head. "Blasphemy! I'll not have –"

"Disrespectful! Don't ye go turning into an old woman on me. Who let ye swear when you were a young thing?" Granny seized the kettle and swung it over the teapot, poured, then cracked a couple of eggs into the pan with the frying bacon. They fried hard: the sizzling sound of rain. "Sit," she ordered James. "We're going up Kilmoney Hill today, if it stays fine. So eat until you're full." She caught his eye with a grim wink and he frowned. Whichever of the women won, he couldn't do what he wanted. And he was sick of eggs.

He sat, tried to look into his mother's face to see if she was angry, but she turned away. He *should* protest against his granny. He should *want* to go to Mass.

But he didn't.

Bernadette pushed her chair back and left the house. James watched her through the window, crunching through the gravel on her going-to-Mass heels, the chickens running.

Paddy waited for his tea, scowled at James when Granny's back was turned, and made talking mouths with his hands.

"Gabby women," Paddy whispered. "Gab gab gab."

James grinned in spite of himself, cut into his bacon, put his fork down.

"I'm sick of eggs. We've been having them every day, for – for ever."

"Unthankful *and* disrespectful!" his granny blustered. "We eat them because the hens lay them, and we've got more than enough, thanks be to God. We're rich, boy, but ye can't just let things go to waste! Wouldn't ye be bored with nothing but potatoes every day, twice a day, or maybe not every day? There've been times! And how boring would it be to have nothing to eat a'tall? Like the Famine? And it's not every day! What about them nice sandwiches your mam made us last night? Lettuce and onion and ham and that nice salad cream? Ye don't get things like that every day!"

James ate his eggs, spilled salt on the table and drew in it.

It was a cool, damp morning, blue sky breaking through the clouds as they swept up into the hills. James kept the wind out of his ears with his hands and followed behind his granny as she laboured up the north pasture. They climbed the tumbled walls in familiar, worn places where the whitewash splatters of lichen on grey slate lay free of brambles and fuchsia. The puppy, now a half-grown collie-mongrel, lanky and laughing-toothed, bounded along with them, propelled itself off the walls and rocketed around the tiny fields. Granny had forbidden the others to bring it into the house, but once, home from school early, James had seen it lying beside Granny at her mending, gnashing a crust of bread into its mouth.

After Granny managed to get down from the second wall, she took the handle of the basket from the crook of her arm. "Make yourself useful," she said as she thrust it at him. "And whatever ye do, don't look under the cloth." A grim Irish wink.

He thrust his hand under the dishrag, found a bundle of food, a hot jar of something, then pulled out the field glasses.

"Not yet! Wait 'til we're above the last farm before ye take 'em out. Nobody's supposed to know, ye see."

He hid them, let the wind whistle into his ears and mouth, ran up the next wall and leaped down through the smell of wet grass. He didn't know why he was happy to be out with his granny, of all people. Missing Mass nagged at him a little, and he tried to think of God – God who made everything, the grass and the stones and the sky and the clouds, God blowing into his ears in the wind, God tasting like rain and sea on his tongue. He almost stepped in a fresh pile of cow shit; God made that, too.

"Ye see the fancy new tractor pulling all that hay?" Granny caught him by the collar, steered his head with her hand clamped on his scalp. "That's Martin O'Donovan, and don't ye think he'll have it known he's the richest farmer in the hills! The horses not good enough for 'im! He's forgetting about hay-making. Says he'll put the green grass in big barns and let it sour like some do cabbage – to hell with worrying about the rain. He'll have th' cows all giving sour milk!"

James twisted away from her, leapt the next low wall.

"Seamus. Watch it ye don't break your leg. Or the glasses."

He swung around. "My name is James."

"Oh, now. Aren't we the bold one. And why should I be calling ye James?"

"Because it's my name." He started to feel sullen and childish for making demands. His mother would not approve, and this made him angry. Was it too much for him to have his own name? Should he be mocked for wanting it?

"And it's the name of some of them English kings! What's wrong with your Irish name?"

"I don't want one."

"King James!" she taunted.

"The king of all the deer!"

He dropped the basket in the grass and left her, furious, climbing back over the wall. He could always go to the strand on a Saturday morning.

"Seamu – James! *James!*"

He stopped. His granny's voice was crackling, slow, embarrassed to be humble.

"Won't ye come up to Kilmoney Hill with me? It's the best place to look. I need ye to carry the basket. I'm gathering some leaves for me swollen ankles."

When he turned, she said, "I'll call ye whatever the hell ye want me to. Pick up that basket."

"Go to hell yourself, then. Carry your own fucking basket!"

Her mouth flew open. The word "disrespectful," formed on her lips, but instead, her chest began to heave. He was afraid something was wrong for a moment – her heart stopping – but she slapped her leg. She was laughing, wheezing.

"Exactly like your mother," she said. "Exactly like me. Exactly. *James.* The Lord's revenge – give ye a child exactly like yourself! Ye get the red hair and ye get the temper that comes with it! Ye can come with me if ye like."

He watched her walk away up the hill in her dead husband's huge boots and her own swooping monk-cowl cloak, her head stooped so far forward, it disappeared. He picked up the basket, rested his hand under the cloth on the glasses and followed. When she turned, it was one of the few times he'd ever seen her without a twist of sarcasm in her face. Her smile was pure.

They walked to the top of the hill, then along the high path to the next hill.

"Them down there," she said. "People in town. They think I'm a witch, but ye pay them no mind."

"Why? You look like a witch."

"Divil! Get out of it! It's these trips with me basket! And they say I'm a black rabbit – don't go to Mass enough for their taste. Some of them out to win me soul back – ha! They get the ideas in their heads! Care nothin' about me sittin' there for an hour when I've got the terrible backache!" She bent and cut a bunch of weeds with a knife he hadn't seen her carrying, and threw them in his basket. "They say I've been making witch's poisons and love potions and such. But ye pay them no mind, now. 'Tis jealousy. Grumbling. A woman's not supposed to inherit the biggest farm on the cliffs and marry a man from away, a man with no property of his own. Some went saying he was nothing but a bleeding tinker, but he wasn't! And Lord knows there's nothing wrong with some of them tinkers anyway! The good Lord made us all, me boy, and remember that! The only piece of advice ye'll ever get out of me!" She snipped a few more stalks and flung them in the basket, shaking her head more and more violently. "There was plenty of men around here who wanted me farm, b'Jesus!" She shook her knife at James. "And a poor snivelling lot they were – even Murphy! Jake-of-the-Pub Murphy, not Eli, our neighbour. Didn't deserve more than an acre betwixt 'em, but there's no making a man wise."

When they came to the next wall, she nipped off a few dying bramble leaves between her thumb and the blade.

"They're good for swelling and for burns. Now, boy. Take out the glasses."

He tightened his hand and pulled the glasses from the bottom of the basket. He put them up to his eyes, his feet already turning him like a lighthouse, and he swept the horizon faster and faster, land and sea close against his eyes, flying dizzy.

"Stop the foolishness and look at something worth it."

"What?"

"Look on the roads. Tell me who's going places."

"I don't know anybody."

"Ye will."

He saw Killaghmore, first half of it, then the other half.

"There's a priest getting on the bus."

"That'd be Father Thaddeus gone to the home in Clon' to visit his poor sainted mother. What else?"

"A bunch of men going into McGovern's."

"The regulars! We've our share of drunkards in this town. Make trouble, get thrown out of the one pub, go to another. Was a time me own man would be there on a Saturday morning, but thank the Lord, it didn't last. Enjoy yourself, James, but never show yourself a fool. That's the only bit of advice ye'll ever get out of me. What else do ye see?"

"But you drink a lot."

She threw her fist in the air.

"Sure! but there's a difference between a lot and *a lot*! You try to bear me old spine without a glass or two! Go on and look! What else do ye see?"

They examined the rest of the town, the farms, and the tumble of walled fields that sloped down to the small cove west of Killaghmore. They walked until they came to a ruin at the top of the last hill in the string. One gable-topped wall remained standing, as tall in the middle as a man on another man's shoulders. Tumbled stones and low walls were scattered around it, the ground muddy and marked by the feet of cattle between thick patches of grass. There were many hoof-shaped puddles.

"This was where the old monks was, back when they paid no mind to the Pope – they knew what it was about all by themselves. They made the holy books here 'til the whole place burnt down – 'twas the devil's work, to be sure. The Church was made of stone, and only the devil can burn a stone – and the books was all burnt up, too. See?"

She stooped and jabbed a ridge-nailed finger in the oval hollow of a stone. It was filled with green algaed water and the reflection of speeding clouds.

"Here's the well stone. God keeps it filled with water. A *miracle*." She crossed herself: forehead, heart, shoulders. After a moment, she pushed him in the chest with the back of her wet hand and pointed. "Here, go on, now. 'Tis a blessing."

He dunked his fingers and crossed himself.

"You could have gotten the leaves from right near the house," he said, scanning the length of coastline with wind-stung eyes.

"Sure, but the spying wouldn't be as good."

"Sure, but the *spyin'*," he mimicked. "Wanted me farm b'*Jasus*."

"Rascal. Would ye like a kick in the head, would ye?" She slapped him fondly on the arm.

They stayed at the top of the hill for the next hour, gossiping about the small men-ants they saw so far beneath them, sitting on the rocks, wrapped up together in the big cloak to eat cold scones and drink warm milky tea from the jar. They walked down the other side of the hill to the cove and made their way home by road and strand. Granny pushed the herbs to one side and filled the rest of the basket with carrageen moss, the seaweed she gathered from the shallow rocky pools whenever she was there at low tide. She offered him a piece to chew, but he stuck out his tongue and made a face as if he were dying. He filled his pockets with shells, marvelled at the warmth, the sun scattering the clouds for the first time in October, God in the wind, moving the waves.

He knocked on his granny's door the next evening and measured his steps into her room. It was sparse: a chair with her perched upon it, a big iron bedstead with her nightgown spread and ready, a chest of drawers, a rag rug, and an ancient iron-bound trunk which was open, filled with balls of wool and spiny nests of knitting. There was a black and white photo on the chest of drawers: a row of children in front of Granny's house, getting taller and taller until the oldest stood taller than the man who must have been their father. The children were alternately freckled and clear-faced, clothes neat, but poor, two other boys besides the tallest one. Granny got off the chair on stiffened joints, walked to the picture, and pointed to the smallest girl.

"Ye see your mam in that picture? She's the youngest. Weren't more than three or four, then. There's all my children that lived. Eight of 'em, except my poor Owen." She smoothed her wrinkled finger down the glass over the second tallest boy, who squinted wickedly, one corner of his mouth curled up. "Ran away to England to join the war, the fool. As if there wasn't enough fighting to be done right here. Buried in Germany somewhere, or France. And there's me Paddy, taller even than his dad. The other boy, that's your uncle Colm, but ye wouldn't know it, that Susan of his keeping him so fat. Them two love-birds. And there's Mary. Went to England during the war and married a soldier from America. Writes to me. Often! Says she'll send a ticket someday and take me to Florida. But they're not well off, ye see. There's Maureen. A weight problem she has.

Tries to be cheerful, but for that husband of hers, always going on about how much she eats. Bad for her nerves, he is – makes it worse, only – turns her into a right bitch, he does. And that's Agnes, such a good girl. Here's Annie, the rascal over to Skibbereen. And that's your aunt Orla, the one Paddy goes to visit in Clonakilty. She don't come back much, now. Think she's ashamed of her family. Always too big for her britches. Married a Guard, she did, and a swine of a man he is, too, wouldn't ye know it."

"*Wouldn't ye know it,*" James whispered.

"Comes from a twisted family. Twisted," she said, squinting her face, screwing her index finger into her temple. She opened the top drawer and shuffled out a few more photos, one of his grandfather holding a chain of fish, one of an even older man, his great-grandfather, kneeling by a fallen stag, its neck curved, its antlers held in his arms. "Well. Now you're here. Go on then and tell me what ye want." She went back to her chair and sat in it with a grunt of relief.

James lay on the bedspread, a collection of rags like the rug, and opened his book. He saw Granny's eager neck stretch as she peered at him, and he began reading her the story of Fionn Mac Cumhail and his magical powers of second sight, which he got by chewing his "thumb of knowledge." She sat in the hard wooden chair, her slippers off, caught in the middle of going to bed, folding her unbuttoned cardigan across her chest with her green-veined fists. He stopped in the middle of the story when he saw her nodding, smiling.

"You know this one already."

"'Tis no matter if it's a good story. I like old Fionn."

"But I wanted the ending to be a surprise." He rolled over on the bed, lay the backs of his hands on the two pillows, but that didn't feel right. He twisted again, hung his arms off the side of the bed, looked at the picture.

"You didn't say anything about him." He pointed to the man standing beside the younger, taller, straighter, fleshier version of his ever-scowling granny. "My grandfather? What was he like?"

Granny folded her arms, leaned back. Her voice was dreamy, cold. "He was a pretty man...clever man. Liked the women too much, and that turned me into an angry one for a time."

"Just for a time?"

"Disrespectful! He was a patriot! Hid the guns in the field with the bull. Can't have a better guard than a bull."

"*Guns?*"

"Sure! Take 'em off the ships from America in the dark of night and get them to the patriots! Not just guns, neither." She slid her feet back into her slippers. "Don't ye look at me with a face all dropped open like that. There was times when it was a furious working, and times ye had other things to think about than throwing out the English. That look on your face! Ye think you're English? Nah. No more than I am, boy. Look at your hair, for God's sake. You're as Irish as they come."

"I'm English!" he said, thinking of his hateful Irish cousins, thinking of their poor clothes, their peasant homes. "I am not Irish!" He hated her again – just a little – her turkey wattle neck, the knobs of arthritis in her knuckles, the way she grinned when she baited him. Strangely, he enjoyed this anger scudding red through his lungs, throbbing his heart, and the cold air he sucked through his teeth. He didn't feel he could allow himself to be angry at his mother, but anger seemed to be what his granny enjoyed the most. It made him feel equal to her, made him know that he could tell her anything, do anything, and she would still tug him over to the window to look through the field glasses. She would always lay her warm hand on the back of his neck.

"James, James. Ye've got the voice and the father and the name of the English, the snobbery of 'em, and the years spent away. But you're *here*, and you're *mine*. Mine. Me own grandson. Like it or not."

"I hate it," he said, though he was smiling.

"That's good for ye then. Ye want to know about your *Irish* great-grandfather, *my* father? Me mother bore only one baby and died of it. That was me. I got the house, the farm, and all the love of my father, the friendship he would have given a son, and when I married, I lost his name. This is Pearce land. *Pearce.* I am a Pearce, though my children have the name Cahalane. Mild as milk my father was. A saint he was. Never lifted a hand against anyone and he was murdered by the Tans. Declan moved into this house, my father's house, when we married, and the guns came too late to protect my poor father. Even that red hair of yours is Pearce hair. That's *my* red hair ye got."

"You don't have red hair."

"Oh, but I did," she said, one corded hand straying up into the halo of fine white wires that exposed her scalp as much as covered it. "And a glory it was to me. Bright like yours, thick like your mother's. Declan loved it. A good husband, for all of his weakness, but he had a temper on him. Only came at me once in anger, and I had to break his nose for it. I have a temper meself, don't ye know. Happened in the kitchen, and all I could grab was a lump of turf. Should have seen him laughing and crying and bleeding at the same time. Doomed him to a life of sin, I did. He had to lie until he died about how his nose got crooked like that. Said it had been the bull that done it."

His great-grandfather, the murdered saint.

His grandfather the liar, the gunrunner.

His granny with a lump of turf.

Thwack.

"*I have a temper meself, don't you know,*" he said, trying to get the sounds, the words, exactly right, rolling across the bed giggling, bruising his shoulder on his book. "How come you can't read?"

"Oh! Did I ever say I couldn't? I like people to read to me, is all. I can get by. Know when a letter is for me. Know what to buy at the grocer's."

"But you can't read papers or letters. Paddy always has to read them to you."

"But I know the best stories from hearing them. Reading was a luxury. It wasn't as important then, when I was of an age to learn things. Getting yourself fed and clothed was hard enough, and when a woman starts having the babies – well. Ye know what they told me, the priests, back then? That it was a sin to save my life by having fewer. Something in the Bible. 'He who seeks to save his life shall lose it. He who loses his life shall save it.' Women were supposed to kill themselves having twelve, fifteen children if they were able, and back then, I believed it. As if it isn't hard enough for a woman to lock her man out of the bedroom. Those icons in your mam's room, they were mine, but she's welcome to them. Isn't a woman here, except me now, who'll question a priest even today. Look at poor Susan. She'll have a brood, a litter, like me! Poor animal! Lord knows how many women in my mother's day left large families to fend for themselves, died thinking they'd get a better place in heaven for it. That's a kind of selfishness too, I think. But I'm going on about things ye wouldn't understand. What did ye ask me?"

"Reading."

"Oh, reading! There's always someone about to read things for me, and there's always some that knows things without having to read a'tall."

"But it's so easy. ABCDEFGHIJKL –"

"What's come over ye? Eh?"

"Repeat after me. Don't you know your ABCS?"

"I know them well enough."

"I'm going to teach you to read."

"Ye are, are ye?"

In her face was skepticism, but a softening, an innocence, a kind of hope.

He lay back on the bed, didn't notice the door swing open and his mother come in. Her arms were folded, tight.

"It's his bedtime, Mam. Come on, Seamus."

"Let him be. He's a comfort."

"He's got school in the morning. Seamus?"

James sat up, his mother's voice warning him.

"He'll stay a little longer," Grania said evenly, looking at the blank wall. "He wants a story before he goes to bed, better than all this prayer...and he wants his old name back. I think we can call him James. Sure, it won't hurt us any, give us the English germs, eh?"

His mother stood, suddenly displaced in her son's life by the old woman she had sworn never to disobey again.

"I – it was because of you, I started the *Seamus* business. What would you have said to an English name at first, eh? When we barged in here unannounced? *Seamus?*"

He didn't want to go, didn't quite understand why. His reluctance sprang from more than being a boy not wanting to go to bed. Without his father, his mother had complete power over him; there was no one he could appeal to when she wrapped her hand around his wrist and pulled. He didn't move, didn't speak, thought himself heavier and heavier, sinking into the blankets of his granny's bed. And then, he knew it was too late to move, to erase the stillness that was disloyalty. His face rose to meet hers, the torn away eye, the eye of her mind, seeing her son deny her for the first time.

She slammed out of the room.

Why could he never do what was right?

Granny leaned back in her chair. She told him the story of the woman she was named after, *Gráinne Mhaol Ni Mhaolmhaig* – Grania O'Malley – Queen of the Western Isles, Pirate of the High Seas, Terror of the English, a Celtic savage dressed in furs who faced down Queen Elizabeth the First in her castle, told her to leave Ireland alone, and Ireland would leave England alone.

Bernadette spent the next day in bed.

James felt her above him when he was in the kitchen, her angry heaviness pressing the top of his head flat, making it ache.

He brought her jar-bouquets of leaves, cups of tea that grew cold among the icons on her dresser. He read to her from his school books and was ignored. Accused.

She was up the next day whipping around the house,

bleaching the teacups, washing the curtains, the walls, burning his eggs black.

"Jesus, Mary and Joseph!" Granny complained into her cup of tea. "All I said was the place had missed its spring cleaning. Ye don't have to do the whole bleeding thing during breakfast! Gets an idea in her head and there's no talking to her!"

James took his school books and fled.

When he came home from school, he found Bernadette standing, ready, her overshoes on, her kerchief tied extra tight. In the darkness of the cloth he could see her smile; what kind of punishment would this be?

"Would ye like to go back to town with me, James? Feel like I want an ice cream."

Her voice was false, too cheerful. She said nothing on the way down the hill.

Every leafless tree she passed was a grasping old woman's claw, sharp, scratching, judgmental. She thought everyone must be watching her from their windows, judging her as she judged herself; there goes that woman, *that* kind of woman, the kind of woman who deserves no child, the kind of woman who should have her children taken from her. Usually she made this journey herself, insisting on it; somehow, she thought James would be safer without her, would blend in better without standing beside his sinful mother, the two of them so lonely, without a man beside them, not a family at all.

"We can go to the warren first – the strand. I know ye like watching the waves."

They sat on the sand above the silver grey breakers. No one else was out – it was too windy, the clouds too heavy and threatening. She had a small bag of roasted chestnuts and biscuits with her – the kind of little picnics she used to bring when they went for a walk by the river in Oxford, skirted the colleges and watched the punts and the odd game of rugby. She took out her notebook and James grabbed it and began to draw. She was doing everything he liked to make him remember the way life was before Ireland – to make him remember that she was the only one here who shared that life. She was the possessor of that life.

"Seamus...James," she said, watching him draw his dragon on paper rippling in the wind. "Don't you think it would be a good idea to start drawing nice things instead? Here."

She took the book and over the beginnings of his dragon body, started feathery wings. In every way possible, she wanted to start filling his mind with good things, with good stories – Bible stories – not the kind he'd hear from his granny. When she ran out of room on the first page, she started over on the next.

"Okay. You, now. Make a nice face. A kind face."

He drew mechanically. The dragon body had been the beginning of something really good – maybe his best yet.

"Now." She took the notebook from him. "How do I show that he's wearing a shining garment?" She drew a robe, drew lines from it representing sunrays. "Now you. Draw a harp."

"I don't want to."

"*Seamus.*"

"I want to make my own. That book in the library – it had monsters, too. Strange things. Even though it was part of the Bible."

He turned the page back to his dragon, now ruined. He tore the page out, crumpled it, and the wind blew it into the dune grass.

"You *said* we were going for ice cream," he said, as if he didn't believe her, didn't trust her even that much. They brushed the sand from their clothes and walked back to town.

"When we first came, you wanted to see the deanery."

As he shaped his ice cream cone into a spiral with his tongue, she led him to the Protestant dean's residence, the biggest, richest-looking house in town. She pointed at the window of Victor's one-time room, showed him the arched kitchen doorway, talked about all his great-uncle's clocks ticking.

The clocks. Measuring their steps up the stairs: his father's words. Why did these words stick in his mind? There seemed to be a great weight behind them, a wall about to tumble in.

"You're too young to remember when he died, aren't you?"

"Who?"

"The old dean. Your father's uncle Rodney."

James nodded, stuck his tongue into the top of his perfect spiral-licked cone, spoiling it so he could eat it. "Can we go in?"

"Oh, no, no. The new man, he doesn't know us. They're Protestants, the – I'm not that strong. I don't know I could take it, James. Sometimes – do you know those times I'm in bed, I can't even bear to think of making a cup of tea – it's too hard for me, then, everything's too hard, too much – as if it would kill me."

She stopped speaking, her thin arms around her stomach, and watched her son, who was getting that look in his eye that she dreaded, when he lost all timidity natural in a child, the look he gave her when he was about to talk back. Ever since he was small, he had to have an answer to every question, and he would force himself between her and whatever she was doing at the kitchen counter, his eyes aimed at her like arrows.

He saw movement behind a lace curtain. He walked to the kitchen door and banged on it, hard, wondering why he was doing it – trying to make his mother stronger? Or trying to break her?

"James, no! They're busy. The –"

"My uncle used to be dean here," James said to the short, dishwater-faced woman who opened the door. "Can we look at the house?"

Bernadette wouldn't go in, though he stood at the door and beckoned to her. She had wanted to show him the building, claim him with her possession of the past, but hadn't wanted this, her son venturing into her memories beyond her control. All she could do was rush up and take the cone out of his hands so he wouldn't get ice cream all over the house.

There were no clocks, not any more.

The dark wood floor creaked under his feet and he was aware of the tall ceilings, of the abundance of air and space around him – as if he were tiptoeing through his father's mind. There, the stairway. There, at the top, his father's room. There, the beginning of the story. Only now, after overhearing *this*, deducing *that*, did he understand that the story was about his illicit conception. There, he was made. His parents made him.

His mother waited for him outside, ice cream flowing over her fingers to drip into the gravel.

"Well," his mother said, on their way home. "That's over and done with. We'll have to take more of these walks. Have picnics. Go to the well, maybe."

He nodded because he knew she wanted him to, wanted him to think that everything would get back to normal now, that they would be friends again just like they had been in England.

He slipped his hand from hers, found a pebble to pick up, a stick to poke into the roadside stream, anything to lag behind.

"James! Jaaames!"

He leaped from his book at the sound of his granny's murderous screams. He ran down the stairs and found her pacing through air acrid with tobacco and peat. She was in her flannel nightgown and dusty felt slippers. Paddy wasn't back from his Saturday evening at the pub yet, and his mother was already praying in her room.

She jerked her hand up in front of his face. In it was a muddy envelope that had been torn open and the page of the letter from inside. The name at the bottom was Paddy's.

He gasped.

"Found it in the porch behind me bag of extra clothespins. So ye know something about this?"

He'd forgotten Paddy's letter – his letter that was to have been a secret. How? It must have fallen out of his clothes that night he ran away, that night when Granny had almost torn his dirty clothes off his back. Should he snatch it and run? Would it matter? What could be in it that could be so bad?

"Now, you're one for the tittle-tattle. Read *that*, me little spy!"

"It's not yours!"

"It's in me house, it's mine! Here!"

She grabbed him by the arm and forced him into a chair.

"Open it, boy! Read it!"

"It's not for you. I forgot to –"

"And a damn good thing ye did. Here! Read it! Read it or I'll kill ye!"

He grasped the thin sheet of lined paper, wrinkled but clean. Dear Eileen, it began, the writing careful with big rounds in the letters.

"Out loud, ye!"

"Dear Eileen. It's been so long since we've seen each other, with the haymaking and all the poor weather. Can you get away from the shop on Saturday? It's no good to meet at Nolan's any more because Timothy has started to go there with his mates from the Guardai, and you know what a laugh we'd give them. He'd tell Orla, and before you know it, Maureen would know, and then Mam..."

As he read, Granny's grip on him weakened and her chin sagged lower toward her hollow breastbone.

"...Love, Paddy," he said.

"Love!" Granny spat. "All this while he's been lying to me! I knew it! Visit Orla, my eye!" She cut into James's elbow with her nails, and as he struggled to get away, she started flailing him with words.

"Company-keeping! It's always a bad business if it's a secret. There's nothing worse than chasing around after women, boy, when ye should be past it! No good can come of it, ye can be sure."

She let him go, her voice destroyed by deep nicotine coughs of mucus into her handkerchief. He ran up the stairs. His mother's door was locked. He bolted his own door, sat in his window shaking, and watched for Paddy to come back from town.

Loud voices woke him.

"Eileen Rooney, Mam. Orla's husband's cousin. Ye know her family. Her father has –"

"I know them, a'right! And I know the kind of people they are! One of them at the mental hospital in Cork! And I don't know what's wrong with your head if ye think I'll allow that woman under my roof!"

James slid out of bed and tried to see them through the key-hole. Granny was in her nightgown, her feet bare and white on the floorboards. Paddy was beneath her, halfway up the stairs, his big face red from more than the cold.

"I'm going to marry her."

"She's old. She'll not give ye children."

"What's wrong with ye? Ye think that's all a man wants?"

"How *dare* ye talk to me like that – of things like that!"

"*What* things?"

"Well, ye won't be bringing her here to live!"

"That's right, I won't."

She reached for the banister, took a long breath. "Where'll ye go then? All ye got is this land," she said, beak-and-claw cruel, hooking his flesh. "And it's not yours, yet, is it? It's mine."

Paddy didn't move.

"I got another son, ye know," she whispered. "And he's got sons. Plenty enough men to farm this land."

He shook his head, tears curdling, wrinkling his face.

"We can – further up the hill – Colm's old house –"

"Not her. Not here. Not on *my* farm. I won't have it."

"Mam – ye don't even know her."

"Oh, I *know*. I know."

"This is why I kept it secret. It's just like when I was young and wanted Fiona, and ye did everything ye could to make us unhappy with each other."

"Not me! No. Is it my fault she wanted the town life? Seems to have a happy life with the spirit grocer."

"McAnenely's a dog! A devil of a man! And you bleeding well know it!" Paddy shouted. James was shocked, not thinking such anger possible for Paddy.

"Well, she didn't cry much when she left ye, did she?"

Paddy looked away. "I'm going to marry Eileen. I've already asked her. I'll go to Clon' tomorrow and we'll tell her parents."

"Ye got better things to do than –"

"Ye knew her name before I told ye. How was that?"

"I – the boy –"

James threw open his door, startling them both.

"Jesus," Granny cursed, "Mary and –"

"I didn't want to read it. She made me." He hated his granny for making him guilty, for making him an accomplice in this torture.

"Ye little rat. If it wasn't for your poor mother, I'd –"

"Nah. This is *you*, Mam," Paddy said. "Just you. Don't go blaming him. I was too young to go against ye with Fiona, but not now. Look at yourself before your mind gets as bent as your back."

He started climbing the stairs again, and she stepped forward, leaning on the banister, standing in his way.

"You're my first," she said, stumbling over words that were too full of passion for her to utter to a man who was only her son. "You were always so much like my father. Ye took all his good parts and left his bad, his..."

Paddy pushed past her, glancing at James. "We can talk about it later."

"There's nothing to say! Ye can't do it to me, Paddy! Not to your own mother! A woman coming into me house to take it over, to make me a laughingstock! And the children ye *might* have from an old –"

"We'll not live here. How could she stand it?"

"But ye can't leave me alone! How can ye?"

"Ye'll not be alone. Ye've got Bernie. Ye don't have to hang on to –"

"No! I don't have Bernie. Nobody's got Bernie, not even the boy. Bernie doesn't have herself any more! She's lost! Ye know what she used to be..."

Paddy pushed past her to get to his room.

"Go to bed, Mam."

"Ye'll get out of this house in the morning, Padraig Cahalane! And I'll look after th'cows meself! And Colm's boys! Ye'll have to hire yourself out to whoever'll have ye! Ye'll not be able to support that woman, and she'll go back to her mammy, she will!"

Paddy shut his door.

"Get back to bed." Grania swung her white storming head toward James and he leaped back into his room. He heard the creak of the floorboards, and peered out once she'd closed her door.

He made his way down through the dark to the kitchen, felt for Granny's knitting bag by the window, took the field glasses from their hiding place and threw them on the floor beside the range. He crashed an iron poker down on them again and again, a grain of glass sparking up against his cheek as he heard his granny's bare feet pounding down the stairs.

"CONSIDER, I PRAY YOU,
IN THIS EXAMPLE OF IT
THE POWER OF CHRIST,
WITH WHOM EVERY BRUTE BEAST IS WISE,
AND EVERY SAVAGE CREATURE GENTLE."

— SULPICIUS SEVERUS, *DIALOGUES*, H. W.

GRANÍA'S anger called up all the gales of winter. She spoke to no one but Bernadette and the dog. She renamed him Patrick, after the saint, partly to annoy the priest, but mostly to make Paddy angry, who was also named after the saint. St. Patrick spent more and more time in the kitchen, waiting for the touch of her hand, hoping for handouts. She gave up on cooking, fed the fire in the range only occasionally, but sometimes threw on so much turf, Bernadette was afraid the chimney would catch fire. They alternately froze and baked, but mostly they froze. Storms threw salt mist into the air and carried it far inland, making their skin sticky, clammy, wiping out the view of the ocean for days. Granny's daughters visited less and less. They stopped taking her to bingo because she yelled at them constantly, her consolation for forcing herself to remain silent with the two she was really angry at.

Paddy and James went into a sort of hiding. They left the house at the earliest opportunity, James to school and Paddy to the barn or the fields or Colm's place, depending on the rain. After school, James went to find him.

"So, ye've come to help with the cows?" Paddy asked him the first day, when James slipped into the dark, stony-aired barn.

"I guess so." James put his books on the slate ledge beneath the only window, the place where sparrows broke their necks in the summer. The chicken-wired stall now held a crow with a broken wing that eyed them beadily. Its feathers had been churned, crumpled: it looked like an unmade bed that had been set on fire and put out by a deluge as well as a good beating with a blanket. Paddy had found it under a rusty ten-gallon barrel after the worst storm of the winter, the hurricane-force winds blowing down a half-rotten chestnut near town, downing electrical lines throughout West Cork, and chasing whatever wasn't tied down into the stone walls. The crow perched on a smooth grey branch from a dead oak that Paddy had dragged into the stall and wired to the side. It peered at them first through one eye, then turned its head to see if they still looked the same through the other eye.

"Good thing you're here. I'll be needing more help. Colm's leash on ol' Dermot keeps getting tighter and tighter." James remembered the fight in Colm's yard, Dermot big but backing down, Colm screaming into his face that he was his boy, *his* boy, and Dermot would work with *his* stock.

Paddy was sitting on an old backless wooden chair with a cigarette and a cup of Bernadette's strong, steaming tea. Beside him a large puss-eyed calf was tied to a ring sunk into the stone wall.

"Here, then – not like I was counting on ye – but I need ye to help put these drops in the calf's eyes."

Paddy crushed his cigarette on the dirt floor, then positioned himself beside the calf. "There, ye are," he crooned to it as he smoothed its neck with his hands. "It'll be over in no time. A little raindrop in your eye. James, ye see the bottle on the pail over there? Go and get it slowly, then come over to me. The lid is an eyedropper, and when I have the calf's head, I want ye to put two drops in each eye."

Paddy smoothed his arms around the calf's neck, and when it tried to jerk away, he had it, neck in the hinge of his elbow, its body against the wall. It kicked and spat miniature cow outrage, a series of panicking groans rising to sharp squeals, but Paddy's huge shoulders held it fast. Paddy nodded and James came forward, stabbing tentatively with the eyedropper until the calf was blinking and its face was wet with medicine. Paddy untied it and gave it a slap on its bony rump to get it outside.

"Good job. I knew ye'd be good with the cows."

James laughed, knowing he'd gotten very little medicine where it was supposed to go, loving Paddy's gentle smiling irony.

"Granny's not really going to throw you out?"

"Nah. Doesn't look like it. She can say the words, but *doing* the throwing – that's another thing. A miserable business, eh? Maybe it'll be over like winter, but it's going to be cold yet a while."

Paddy kicked a waft of hay, and watched James run to the door; he'd glimpsed his mother. He could feel the weight of her going down the hill, could feel the gravity of her; this was one of those times he was not allowed to go. He listened to Paddy saying *hello* to the crow, trying to teach it to talk. He took a step, then another, and was after her, through the rain.

Bernadette was going to get the mail.

Maureen, too large to go unnoticed except by the overwrought or the entranced, saw Bernadette in the post office receiving a letter that she read, then tore up and threw away in the bin beside the counter. Bernadette turned and was confronted by the huge pink-flowered, wool-sweatered lump of disapproving sister who had no shame, could not imagine having shame, who leaned into the bin with effort and retrieved the scraps. Bernadette watched her piece three of them together and read, her round face stretched by the tightness of her bunned hair, stretching even more in surprise.

"How come it's a woman who's writing you, not your man?"

Bernadette rushed into the pelting rain, arms crossed in a death-posture over her chest, away from the queue of villagers in the post office. Maureen charged after her.

"Bernadette! What kind of game is this? Ye owe the family an explanation!"

"Oh, and you're the family, are ye? It's you I owe, is it? For not having been *under control*. For shaming you!"

Bernadette swerved away from a couple coming toward her, ran across the square, low overshoes splashing through shit-stained puddles, thick grey cloud hanging above her; for the last few days, there had been no day, only night and evening, only dim downpour.

Maureen followed her slowly, her face saddening, joined her under the spirit grocer's awning.

"Well, what I did," Bernadette hissed, "did it change *your* life? Did it hurt you in any way at all? Or did things go on as if I was never born? What the hell do I owe you? You're the one that told Dad. You're the one that made him throw me to the English – and I not even old enough to –"

"What's happened to your man? Something's happened to your man, or he'd be out here after you, after the boy. Something happened to him in that accident as well? What are ye telling –"

"He's –" Bernadette shook her head too hard, for too long. "I should have known. He was always – and so this is my proper punishment, isn't it? Public humiliation! Talking of these things in the middle of the square when ye don't even talk to me in our own mother's house! Forgiveness is never –"

Neither woman saw James, hiding around the corner of the store, having followed her all the way into town for the first time. He had already seen one sister walk past her without a word. She didn't realize that she had changed, that she was physically in hiding, that it was almost impossible for people to talk to a woman who always had her face hidden in deep blue cloth, who was always on the quivering verge of prayer.

"For the love of God," Maureen said, her voice exhausted, letting loose all her frustration. "Go home, Bernadette, go back

and straighten up whatever it is that's wrong. Keeping those letters from the boy –"

"There's no home! Not any more. If there ever was!"
Bernadette wrenched her head, scooped air into her sodden blue
kerchief with a gesture that used to fling her hair, show that she
was too young to have a son so tall. "Aren't ye supposed to obey
God over man? And didn't Jesus ask us to forsake our families
and follow him? Didn't St. Peter himself leave his wife and family
to become a disciple? Didn't Jesus forgive Mary Magdalene who
had been a prostitute? Blessed are they that mourn: for they shall
be comforted! You want my *public* humiliation?"

She walked into the middle of the square, her voice keen, rico-
cheting off the buildings. People stopped. There were roadside
preachers who passed through now and then, shouting about brim-
stone and hellfire, but this was the first time they heard a woman's
voice raised – and one of their own women. Even the men blushed
for the disgrace of it; the loud voice of a woman cried of madness,
and there she was, her shrieking head shrouded in paisley cotton.
Maureen fled. Bernadette went through the Beatitudes.

"Blessed are the meek: for they shall inherit the earth...
Blessed are the merciful: for they shall obtain mercy. Blessed are
the pure at heart: for they shall see God... Blessed are they which
are persecuted for righteousness sake: for theirs is the kingdom
of heaven. Blessed are *ye*, when men shall revile you, and shall
say all manner of evil against you falsely, for my sake. It's all
about *me* isn't it? But it's all about you, too!

"Blessed are the merciful!" she called again and again, taking
a kind of pleasure, feeling relieved, in control of her ultimate
humiliation – what she had been fearing for so long. Her clothes
were streaming-wet by the time James came out of hiding and
took her by the hand, led her home.

He pulled his hand from hers as soon as he was sure she
would keep on following.

"*Letters*," he said brutally, not looking back, conscious of his
back turned on her, his throat clenching closed. He heard her
silence, how full it was.

"I do send him a letter now and then. He doesn't answer them; he's drinking himself to death. That's what your gran says. He's dead to us now."

Good, James thought, and went to the window – not that his father, who wouldn't come for him, might die – but that his father was also suffering. He could see almost nothing outside, through the water, condensation on the inside of the glass, storm on the outside.

Autumn rained into winter, and Grania used her silence brutally. James heard her speak only once to someone other than his mother and the dog, when he caught her in the barn talking to the crow, saying "Hello...hello...*hello*, ye daft eejit!" The weather forced Paddy inside in the evenings but he spent more and more time at the pub. It was too cold for James to do his homework in his room, so he had to work at the kitchen table, close to the range, in the same room as his granny's poison-aired presence. His mother sat beside him often, watching what he was doing, smoothing his hair. He could hardly think with her hand upon his head, could hardly bear the weight of her attention, but could not muster the cruelty it would take to shake her off; he might make her cry, make her hide in her room. He felt only relief when she got up to make tea, to dust, to spoon the sizzling drippings over the roast, to sweep the floor.

Paddy wolfed his dinner one Saturday after a morning of riding Lizzy from field to field, restacking tumbled stone walls, stopping in for a cup of tea and gossip with his sister Maureen in her little hovel of a house, and then to see Susan before coming home. He was getting a lot of work done while avoiding Granny. The rain began blasting against the windows and Granny was sitting in her chair, tearing the seams out of one of her old dresses, shredded threads wafting onto Patrick's scruffy black and white back. Paddy got up from his gravy-smeared plate and made a show of stretching.

"It's a dirty day," he said.

"Best stay in, Paddy," Bernadette told him. "No reason to make yourself sick."

Paddy ran his hand over his stubbled face, gave a brief scratch to the small tuft of whiskers beneath his right eye, movements which made James think Paddy was looking for a newspaper, contemplating a good, relaxing read.

"James. You're twelve, aren't ye?"

"Almost. In five – four months."

"Nah. Today you're twelve. That's plenty old enough to have your first pint. Do ye want to go through this lashing to the pub?"

"Paddy, he's too young. And starting him on the drink like, like –"

"Nah. Murphy had a drink with his boys when they were eight or nine. 'Tis a matter of opinion, is all."

"Murphy is the worst drunk this town –"

"And that's a matter of opinion as well. I know it's not the usual thing, but it's just for the *craic*. Do more damage to force him to stay in a house like this," he said, glanced at his mother, who ripped seams with greater violence, the veins in her hands swelling. "Tying him with apron strings, you are, Bernie. I'll not –"

Bernadette threw down her dishrag and Paddy stepped close to her, whispered so James couldn't hear.

"He's not getting on with the other boys, Bernie. Told Colm to meet me there with his John. Don't know what else I can do."

"But the pub, Paddy."

"What, are ye? Going to take the pledge, Bernie? Make him take it too? Cut him off from everybody but yourself?"

She shut her trembling lips.

Paddy turned to James. "You're going?"

James got his raincoat.

"Don't catch your death," his mother yelled after them, into the wind.

McGovern's, one of the town's three public houses, was a welcome roar of sound and light when they got in. There was a huge fire in a blackened cave of a fireplace and gatherings of smiling windblown farmers, still with cow shit on their boots. James walked through pockets of air, smelling smoke, then sweat, then shit, then beer, then whiskey, and combinations of all. A huge man swung toward the door and displaced air that was filled with the smell of rotting teeth and shaving soap. Above the cigarette smoke was the aura of peat and the throb of its warmth. It was sensed as much as smelled, inhaled, absorbed. It prickled the skin, scratched the throat, welled against the crumbling plaster walls that were held together by thick layers of green paint.

"Colm!" Paddy called, and James saw his huge uncle overlapping a stool at the far end of the bar, one rubber boot on the floor, one wedged on the stool rung, hanging by its heel. Beside him was his son John, looking even thinner and more asthmatic sitting beside his mound of a father. James stopped walking and glanced around the room. Dermot was nowhere to be seen. Paddy slipped behind Colm, breathed deliberately on Colm's smooth bald head and polished it with his sleeve.

"Ha! There ye go again!" Colm grinned as he hit his brother's hand away.

"Thinks he's devilish funny," said Oliver McGovern, the equally hairless bartender. "But the hair is leaving him, too – just a bit slower-like."

Colm swung around at the friends laughing behind him, farmers and fishermen who were taking their turns patting his head.

"I'll take all of ye at once! Learned karate from the King of Siam when I travelled around the world! Hi-*yah*!" he screamed.

Paddy sat and James took possession of the stool beyond him, putting his two uncles between himself and his cousin. John stared at him with glum eyes. James returned the stare, slowly crossing his eyes.

"A pint of Guinness," Paddy told Oliver, "And a half for himself, here. Is that all right?" he asked James.

"Sure," James said. John took a drink from his glass, a full pint, and licked the foam from his lips, grinning because he had more than James was going to get. James watched the barman pour the beer, filling the glasses a little, then letting them rest, pouring, then resting, finally topping them up and letting the beer relax – what looked like a cascade of liquid falling through creamy air bubbles – before setting it on the bar.

"So, got your message and here I am, Paddy!" Colm spread his big arms. "What's so important that –"

"Patience, there." Paddy peered around the room. "So, no one's in with a paper?" Sometimes in a pub he was able to peer over the shoulders of men who could afford to buy the *Southern Star,* the *Cork Examiner,* or the *Irish Independent.* "You read the *Examiner* yet? What's the government up to?"

"Fuck all. Same as usual –"

"*Fook all,*" James repeated. "*Shite,*" he said to John, and grinned: it was only John, and Paddy was there; James felt safe. He reached up and pulled a bit of straw off Paddy's collar.

"...you listen to the radio." Colm signaled to Oliver. "Another pint. Sinn Féin would do better to give up on abstention. Let them vote like a government's supposed to. How long have we been waiting for Ireland to be one? The stalemate's doing neither country any good. Just because we're independent and want to get something done down here doesn't mean we're forgetting about those poor sods in the North who got stuck up there with the murdering Prods. Get the fucking English –"

"Careful what ye say in front of the boy, Colm. The old men'll go on waiting until they're dead and buried and refusing to play their harps in heaven until the Lord gives in and erases the border. No matter what the radicals –"

"I'm not radical!"

"The truth is – like it or not – the Republic is glad to be rid of the Protestants, and rid of the mad Catholics locked up there with them. That's the only way we can have peace down here, is if they all stay in their little box up in the North."

"I wouldn't let Mam hear ye talking. If she had a bomb, she'd light a fire under a few particular so-and-sos."

"Like all the other oldies. Too old to go out and fight themselves, angry at the young ones who've got more sense. It's the sixties, for God's sake. It's peace we want. A better life. I say it's war on poverty now, and wasn't poverty always the enemy? Not enough land and grub to go around. A poor man will as soon reach for a gun as a loaf of bread when he knows the gun will get him as many loaves of bread as he wants."

"And didn't we always have the poverty because of the land-lords? There's things that get results, and if ye've got a gun on your side, that gets results. Ireland is one island. Thirty-two counties. Should never have been divided." Colm looked around, lowered his voice. "Nothing's going to happen if the Volunteers keep wandering around in a haze. They've barely shot a gun in five years. It's nearly driving me crazy waiting for something to happen. I thought when the boys shot at the boat at Waterford last summer, we were off again, but there's nothing. What have we been doing? Teaching our sons not to love their country?"

"No!" John insisted.

James took his first sip; it was strong-tasting, of cream, and yet of cinders, just what a man should drink. He was determined to learn to like it. He smeared a puddle of spilled beer into a swimmy spider, remembering his mother at a dinner party in Oxford yelling about the damned British *to* the damned British, not giving a shit, a *shite*, what anybody thought – not like now.

"There are times for fighting, and then there are times for farming." Paddy took the first sip from his glass, wiped the foam from his lip with the back of his hand.

"So quote me something else from the Bible! It was always the time for farming with *you*, Paddy. *You* never tried. For God's sake, ye were born during the Civil War. And Dad a regular war hero and Granddad killed by the Tans."

"We don't know that for sure."

"But Mam knows. She's sure of it, so I am, too. Fucking convicts in uniform. Dead men in every ditch. And never in your –"

"What do ye want of me? You're the angry son. What are ye going to do about the lazy son-of-a-what Volunteers?"

"Me?" He glanced at his son. "Ye know what I've done. I've done plenty."

"Did you kill people?" James asked, incredulous, unable to imagine this of his roly-poly uncle.

Paddy threw him a warning glance. "And if it wasn't for Susan ye would have gotten yourself killed. Ye would have landed in jail your whole life. And a fat lot of good ye would have done there. Ye've shown more loyalty to your country by feeding your children than what ye got up to before that. If there's one bit of good that ever came out of that terrible business with McAnen –"

"Watch yourself, Paddy, before ye make me listen to that name again. I know I complain a lot, but that's all I can do any more. Five young ones. God knows, there might be another on the way." Colm reached over to tug his son's ear. "Besides, it was Owen was the real angry son."

Paddy sat back, nodded.

John and James watched, silent amid the sound of beer glasses clumping on the wooden bar, the easy talk of farmers and their laughter. His mother was right. Damned landlords. Damned British. James shook off thoughts of England. He was almost breathless at his entrance into the adult male world. The mention of guns thrilled him. He found John's ingrained patriotism funny, though he was jealous of how John could be possessive of his country. Did James have a country any more? Paddy never talked politics at home, however hard Granny flailed him with her voice and deepest desires for revolution. His mother often tried to stop his ears from hearing Granny's ranting over some news item on the radio about complacent politicians, about Orangemen parading in the North. Stop his ears so he would only hear what was *nice*. Stop his ears only now when it used to be her, back in England, doing the ranting.

"To Owen," Colm said, "A man forever young." He held up his new pint and took a drink.

"They don't teach ye a lot of the way the world works in school, do they?" Paddy said to James and John. "You're probably better off. Maybe when you're grown up and running the country ye can figure out something better. Shouldn't be talking about this now, anyway. First time out and all. Someday everybody's going to be like you, James, a mixture. No man can fight against himself."

"Sure, sure. Same argument we have every night, b'Jesus. James! So, young James," Colm said, turning to him with a delighted curl of his shoulders. "You and me, we haven't had much chance for conversation since ye arrived. And I'm sorry that it has to start out in such bad company in McGovern's!" Colm hitched his eyebrows as high as they would go, opened his mouth, and laughed madly. The bartender balled up his teatowel and lobbed it at Colm. James grinned. Paddy had told him stories about his uncle.

"And I'm sorry to have to tell ye, that while I was out in the field this morning, what should I see but the faeries making off with your underpants! 'Ho!' I says, 'Get out o' that!' but they turned their backs, dropped their pants and farted the tune to 'When Irish Eyes are Smiling' – that's seven faery arses I seen all at once! Me record! And I've seen a few! They yelled they never saw such holey things in all their lives! Holy! They knelt to say a prayer to them. Holy underpants! What d'ye think o'that?"

"As long as they took the dirty ones."

"Aha!" Colm laughed – bellow and explosion – and gave James such a congratulatory slap on the back it sent air belting out of his lungs. Even John laughed.

"Ye've got the wit! Ye've got it! No one can tell me you're not an Irishman! Not with that hair, neither!"

"Ah, Colm. Stop being such an Irish cliché."

"What the – where you get such fancy words from?"

"I'm associating with a more educated kind of person these days."

"Hey, boys," a man called to them, and broke away from the group of up-roaring young men in their twenties.

"Michael," Paddy said in greeting.

The man was in his forties and already had a mild whiskey-stagger. He grinned in spite of the bitter lines around his mouth, his nose as red as the tongue of St. Patrick the dog; Liam's father the dog-nosed, James thought.

"Teaching the young ones what the Saturdays are for?" Michael said.

"Got to learn sometime," Colm answered. "And where's your Liam, then?"

"I never take him Saturdays. Saturday is me own day."

"Like every fucking day," Colm muttered.

"And how's Maureen?" Paddy asked, being polite, having talked to her only that morning. "She's not been at the house lately."

"Same as always. That's why I'm here." Michael laughed and swung toward the group of young men he'd just left. He put one hand on the bar to steady himself before going back to gain their attention. He mumbled something to the nearest one, who bent his knees and threw his head back in mirth.

"He's not getting away with that – slandering me sister to me face!" Colm said, his face heating up as he got off the stool. Paddy grabbed his thick arm.

"Drink your beer."

"She's our sister, and I don't care – he can't say those things in public."

"Even when he's right?"

"It's not only her."

"I know. He uses her like a servant, sleeping, eating his meals, but he doesn't sit long enough to have a chat with her even. Don't know whether it's her that's made him, or him that's –"

"He's chewing up the whole family. *Jasus*, ye know how it gets around. I want to hit him. Just once in my life. We could get him outside in the dark. No one would know. If ye'd go with me."

"You hit him and what's going to happen?"

"He'll hurt for a week, that's what."

"No. He'll hit *you*, then ye'll hit *him*, then he'll hit *you*. Do ye see where I'm going? In circles. Like the rest of them in the North." Paddy sipped the dark stout from underneath the foam.

"I give up. Lord love ye, but *you're* what's wrong with the Republic."

"There's nothing wrong with Paddy!" James protested, not speaking the rest of the thought: *Big. Fat. Windbag.*

Colm sat on his stool, hunched his shoulders down around his beer. He lifted his glass to his lips, tipped back further and further until he put the glass down and the little sluice of foam slid to the bottom. "Another," he said to the barman.

"Slow down," Paddy said. "The boys ye know. They've got to get out of here early."

"Sometimes, Paddy," Colm began, elbows propping his thick shoulders on the bar, "I look at ye, and don't believe ye can move. When you're sitting there arguing, I can't even remember ye coming in or walking or anything. You're like a fucking Bible chained to a pulpit. Ye never change what ye do. Ye do what ye always done, and that's nothing. Ye never do nothing. Ye don't throw a punch when ye've wanted to. Ye never do nothing so ye never get nothing. Look at ye. Almost forty-five, aren't ye? and still –"

"I'm getting married," Paddy said.

"The fuck ye are." Colm laughed. He turned to John and James, whose mouths were open like their ears. "There he is! Do ye know how many mothers wanted him for their daughters? Paddy's mighty strength! When he was young, people said he'd lift the six foot of earth off his own coffin. That's something for a dead man. But when he's *alive*, that's when he doesn't move. Not even when it comes to the women. And doesn't Mam pull his reins like a –"

"Jake Murphy's lending me his fancy car and I'm bringing her home tomorrow to see everybody. Mam doesn't know. You're not to tell her. Ye just bring your family over after Mass. Bernie'll make ye a cup of tea, and me and Eileen will show up for dinner. Everybody's coming already. Stopped in to see Susan this afternoon. The sisters are all bringing something."

"*Pad*dy. You're joking me." Colm let one of his hands drop to the bar, into the smeared rings of spilled Guinness. "Paddy?"

"It's true, b'Jesus." Paddy's smile was big, quavering.

"Paddy." Colm started to laugh. "Paddy, ye old bastard! How did ye –" He grabbed the bar. "Is she –" He looked at his son, then at James, embarrassed. "Lord. Come on. Let's go into the snug. Can't talk about such things around here."

Colm took Paddy by the sleeve and pulled him to the front corner of the pub where there was a small walled booth open only to the bar. Colm and Paddy disappeared inside. Involuntarily, James and John's eyes met in the gulf of air above the two empty bar stools.

Dermot wasn't around. The bar, the uncles, the excitement of politics and laughter had erased their wariness.

"I can drink more than *you* can," John asserted above his glass, his thin neck rising from a too-wide collar, making him look like a scrawny young bird.

"So?" James had finished his black, smoky, almost bloody-tasting half-pint, and could already feel the alcohol in his brain, the slightly swimming inability to focus.

"So what we have is a contest here," Michael broke in. He moved from the group of young men and sat beside John, breathing into his hair. "Oliver, two pints and two Paddy's for the boys."

"Don't ye think ye'd better ask the fathers first?"

"What? I'm their relation," he said, hunching his eyebrows when he looked at James. "And only one has his da' with him. Isn't it your job to sell the stuff? None of your business who drinks it after."

Oliver stared at him.

"All right. Just give it for me mates over there in the corner. Pour."

Oliver poured the beer, and while it rested, he sloshed out two measures of Paddy's whiskey in small heavy glass beakers.

"There ye are, boys. The whiskey first. Now we'll see who's the man of ye. Down without a breath!"

"Ye don't have to do this, boys," Oliver said. "Enough, Michael. Take it to your mates. I'll throw ye out –"

James threw the whiskey back like he'd seen others do it. It burned down his throat, and his gasp came before it had all drained away, droplets entering his lungs and making him cough, helpless. John was already gulping the stout. James hacked the last raw droplet from his lungs and took the beer glass in both his hands. The beer got thicker, heavier, with each swallow. He put his glass down to rest, but John was still drinking. Gulp after gulp, his thin knobbed pigeon throat convulsing slower and slower, until he gasped. James had the urge to poke his bobbing Adam's apple to see what might happen. John put the pint glass down with only a quarter of the beer left in it.

"The winner!" Michael cheered, raised John's limp arm and wobbled it in the air. "Come on. You're not finished yet."

John drank, then looked up squinting, his face white and uncertain. James watched, fascinated, as John shifted on the stool, gripped the edge of the bar, dug his chin into his neck, turned, and vomited onto the slate floor. First, it was a big foaming rush and splash, then smaller convulsions pattering close to the stool legs. The farmers fell silent. Michael fled out the door. James caught the first whiff of stomach acid and his own throat opened sickeningly. He pinched his nose, staggered to the door of the snug, and knocked, everything he saw being a bit slanty, tipsy for the first time.

"Always had a weak stomach," Colm said after they left the pub, after spending his anger in threats yelled after Michael's retreating backside. "You with the hay fever, and everything, eh? Ye were a bit of a fool to do that, weren't ye, son?"

They trudged through the rain, making their way back into the hills, the sun already down at five, twilight leaving them. Colm, Paddy and James walked abreast and John trailed them miserably, contemplating a possible hiding place in one of the many sad, dripping haystacks.

"Don't tell anyone," John whispered to James as they stepped into Colm's kitchen to take their tea with Susan. James knew there was no point to secrecy. One or two members of every family for miles had seen John's disgrace.

"We'll stay and read the papers," Paddy said as he munched Susan's sugar cookies. The baby, now almost a toddler, squirmed in her arms, upset her tea on the table. Helen, the nine-year-old, leaped up to get a rag from the sink. Brenda, the four-year-old James liked to talk to, hung her nose over the lip of her teacup and blinked at him. He turned his head now and then, his head swimming through alcohol, expecting Dermot to walk through the door.

John feared the same thing. Dermot was bigger, older, stronger, bossed him around. Dermot thought his asthma made him weak as a girl, laughed at his boxes of junk. James was more his equal, no matter where he had come from, and James hadn't laughed at him, even though he used to laugh at James.

"I got some things upstairs to show ye," John said. "Things I been doing."

"Run along then," Susan said, as she lowered the baby into the high chair. "Put your plates in the sink."

James climbed the creaky stairs to the room John and Dermot shared. John sat on the floor and pulled a heavy wooden crate from under his bed. It was filled with stones. James gazed, thinking of his own seashell collection in an old jar by his window, seeing his antlers.

"They're better-looking when they're wet."

A hundred small stones were in the crate, all of them remarkable in some way. The biggest was a white and black pebbled piece of granite, smooth and perfectly egg-shaped, obviously the prize of the collection. John picked it up.

"Got this one last summer when we went to the regatta at Schull. I fooled people. Told them it was a petrified egg. It happens to trees ye know, turning to stone. And this one." He picked up a sea-smoothed finger of slate that looked like a carpenter's pencil. "This is one of me favourites."

James raked his fingers through the stones, deep green, grey-flecked, white, rosy, most of them beach-clattered, rounded, smooth as eyes.

"I looked this stone up in the library – see?" John picked up a milky angular stone. "This one's quartz. It can grow clear, like glass, like diamonds. Here."

John deposited the stone in James's hand, then, afraid James might be getting bored with stones, pulled another crate out from under the bed. Its contents made James start back. Inside, was the perfectly formed skeleton of a hook-beaked bird of prey, its joints bound with fine copper wire. James touched the skull with tenderness, respect.

Tuan was an eagle.

"Found it in Castle Field and Dad helped me connect all the bones that weren't still stuck where they were supposed to be. He thinks it's a kestrel. I got owl feet drying over the range, feathers and everything. I like the animals even better than stones. Dad says maybe I'll be a scientist or an animal doctor, but I want to be a farmer, like him. Sister Angeline says scientists have to live in the city."

They heard the creak of the stairs.

"Rocks in your head," Dermot said, and thumped his shoulder against the doorway. "Ye have fun at the pub?"

James caught his breath and said nothing; John's eyes slid around the room.

"Get out of my room, ye little English fuck," Dermot said, his voice pleasant, reasonable.

James stayed where he was, his hand in the crate, fist closed around the egg stone. It was heavy, nothing but stone shell all the way to its core. His arm seemed a lot longer than usual, hardly seemed to be a part of him, seemed to be drunk in its own separate way. Dermot made no move for fear of Colm in the room below.

"Dermot? Where are ye, boy?" called Colm from far below. "You come back down and explain a few things to me. Haven't ye been a real dog in the manger, now? Just because you're done with school..."

They listened to Dermot crash down the stairs. Colm berated him for trying to keep John from doing his homework, ignoring the lameness in a heifer, for being God-knows-where when he was supposed to be checking on the fields.

"Ye'll do the work I tell ye!" were Colm's last cries before the boys heard a door slam.

"He'll find out about you throwing up," James said. "Everyone saw it."

"I know," John said. "No matter what, he always finds out."

James thought about this all evening, the smell of John's nausea coming back to him. Not even John's stones, and new friendship, not even the sweetness of being almost twelve, of being almost a man in Paddy's eyes, could keep his mind from leaping to what might happen if Dermot always found out.

The women were in bed when James and Paddy got home, so Paddy filled the big kettle to the brim and piled turf into the range.

"So what do ye think of the Guinness?"

"It's all right."

"Just as well you're not crazy about it."

"How come Dermot didn't go to the pub?"

Paddy exhaled, a long *phoo*, that seemed to go on forever.

"Dermot doesn't like his dad enough to drink with him. Colm...he and Susan didn't know what to do with him – spoiled him early on, let him do as he pleased. And other things. Ah, it's hard for two men like that to live in the same house, both a bit fist-happy. Strange, them two being so much alike."

James wandered over to his granny's chair, looked at the basket of knitting that should have been hiding the field glasses. The window was pebbled with fine drops of condensation. He rubbed a dark moon on it with the side of his fist and looked out at the black colourless world as if he had lost something. Or was about to lose something.

"You're bringing her here tomorrow?"

"Looks like it," Paddy said, pulling the shirttails out of his pants. "I'm going to have a wash now, and I might stay up late. Might not even go to bed, so ye better get some rest."

"I want to stay up."

"All right then, but ye missed your bath. The women'll have ye up and be soaping your ears mighty early in the morning. Maybe making sure you're not a slave to the drink yet."

Paddy got the wide metal tub from the porch and set it on the floor. He hung a tiny round mirror from a nail sticking out of the middle of a cupboard door, gathered a bucket of clean cold water, basin, soap, scissors, an old safety razor, and a towel. He made himself and James a pot of tea and mixed the rest of the hot and cold water to a comfortable temperature. James watched him shave carefully, twice, even the tufts of whisker high under his eyes, then pinch and prod and smooth his neck with his fingers. He left no little drifts of greying whiskers this time. Peering into the mirror, lifting one lock of hair, then another, he snipped the ones he didn't like until, by his own strange aesthetic, he was satisfied. He clipped the little hairs growing in his nose, and tried his best with his ears, but eventually gave up. By crossing his arms and grasping his shirttails, he removed his shirt over his head, a large gesture that puffed sweaty air against James's face. Paddy's back was broad, strong, and hairy between the shoulder blades. James hadn't thought about Paddy having a body under all his dirty work clothes.

James got up.

"After you get married, for sure you won't be living with us any more?"

"For sure."

Before James got to the top of the stairs, he could hear the fall of clothing, Paddy stepping with naked feet into the washtub, the splash of water.

Susan was the first to arrive after Mass, with a great basin of potatoes, Helen carrying the baby, and Brenda complaining about a boot full of puddle water. Susan and Bernadette washed the potatoes as the range began to give off hot rich smells of roast beef. Agnes arrived with her husband Niall and her assortment of resentful, freckled girls. Raucous Annie came next from Skibbereen with her stern husband and Rosie, their only daughter, in a car with wing fins on the sides.

"And how's this boy of yours, Bernadette?" she called, too loudly, too friendly, trying to set an example for her sisters. "Jerry, why don't ye take the boy out to look at the car?"

Jerry mumbled something, fled into the lounge, and pounced on one of Paddy's old newspapers.

"Right, then," Annie said, wiping her rain-wet, scarred forehead with the back of her hand. "So give me a job."

"Has there been news of a flood, then? *Sacred Heart!* Is this house the ark?" Granny demanded, finally, from her window, unable to be silent when something was going on that she didn't know about.

"Lord, but she's in a mood," Annie said to Bernadette.

"Ye haven't been getting out like usual, Mam. You're not used to us any more. Here comes Maureen!" Susan said, as the door banged open in the wind. "So we decided this would be the day to come to *you.*"

"Eh," was all Granny replied, stretching her fingers in her lap, picking up her soft, spiny nest of knitting and throwing it down again.

The kitchen was filling with daughters and grandchildren, the girls whispering, squealing, the boys trailing in smells of stolen cigarettes. Some were wide-eyed and chattering, some sullen, some crashing into their cousins, chasing them, spitting, slapping and giggling. James stayed at the table near his mother, helping peel potatoes in the sometimes blinding noise, dreading the almost certain arrival of Dermot and Liam. They slammed through the kitchen door, John trailing behind, the latest of arrivals; they ignored him. John cast a nervous eye on James now and then, lifted the corners of his mouth when he thought no one was watching. Bernadette filled the kettle again and again for tea, opened the range door to spoon the roast's juice over it, cut slice after slice of white raisin soda bread. Every little while Granny flicked out her hand like the tongue of a frog and reeled a small child onto her lap, to be grilled on school work and told a story, then sent away with a tweak on the nose.

"Rosie! Give us your party piece," Granny called out. She pointed to the seven-year-old girl with huge blue eyes and red, windburned cheeks. "Ye promised me ye'd learn a song for Christmas. Has she been keeping it up, Annie? Come on. Let's hear it."

Rosie, aggressive, precocious, stepped on a chair and began screeching "The Rose of Tralee," above the rest of the screams and chatter. The boys began to boo.

"Shut up!" Dermot yelled. "What! Who told ye you could sing? Get off the stage!"

"You should be on the stage!" Liam said, pouncing on the hackneyed joke. "Or the bus, anyway. There's one leaving at half-two!"

Rosie began to cry, which increased the volume of her screeching. Granny got to her feet, a ball of wool tumbling from her lap, arms waving at the jeerers.

"Ye little bastards!" she screamed, though Dermot and Liam were taller than she was. "Look at what ye did! *Jesus, Mary and Joseph*! But I'll take the lot of ye out and *horsewhip –*"

And there, in the doorway, was Paddy and his woman.

Rosie's crying and the children's noise trailed away. There was a gaping silence.

"Mam, I'd like you to meet Eileen," Paddy said.

The woman's brown-gloved hand was tucked into the crook of his elbow. Paddy seemed taller than usual, his hair greased into place with something that made it look darker, made him look younger. He was tieless, his shirt buttoned tight. In his grey Sunday suit and old wax coat, he looked every bit the cleaned-up farmer. The woman was in her late thirties, tall, with broad clumsy hips and feet that didn't quite fit into her large, high-heeled pumps. With her free hand, she steadied a brown pillbox hat on top of her curly wind-damaged hairdo. She was dressed in dark ash-pink. Her face, though smooth and round, red and pleasant, had a hint of stubborn determination, a quality often mistaken for the strain thought to be natural in old maids. James had seen her before, in Clonakilty, the night he ran away; she made wonderful blackberry tart.

The noise rose again, shifted, was beaten down by the shushing of mothers and the glare of the odd father who had ventured out from the lounge. Colm, from his spot at the table closest to the meat, saluted Paddy with a wide ruddy grin and a wave of two fingers. Granny was still. James suddenly realized he'd seen this before. He also had stood there in the doorway with his mother, waiting. It seemed as if all of their lives had to pass through this kitchen to be approved. His granny swayed there, between shock and confusion. Her jaw hardened and the tendons of her neck stretched as she lifted one arm and pointed a crooked finger at her son.

"Ye do this..." she said, and all at once she noticed the woman was a guest, and there were ways guests had to be treated...and she hadn't been expecting company. Her hand fell to her dress – an old dress – and smoothed it. She felt her hair. What a way for a stranger to see her – she hadn't taken care of herself since the fight with Paddy.

Paddy and the woman were walking toward her: the future.

"Mrs. Cahalane!" the woman said, taking her hand. "I met ye first at Orla's wedding, and then when her Jenny was just born. But I've never been all the way out here! It's a beautiful place."

Granny stared at her, nodding, gathering her wits, glancing at her daughters, who were all stepping forward. She pulled her hand out of Eileen's. "If ye think –"

But her words were buried by a wave of greetings as her daughters crowded around. Susan barged in front of her mother-in-law.

"Lovely to meet ye, finally."

"A pleasure to see ye again, Eileen."

"Did ye see Orla before ye left? Did she say how her trip to Dublin went?" Susan said.

"Oh, she's still away. For sure she would have come, if she wasn't."

Granny pushed Susan away, fuming, but then Maureen threw her large body into the gulf.

"Thought we'd never get rid of Paddy," Maureen said to Eileen, grinning her sour jowly face into impossible girlishness.

"Whisht!" Paddy said.

"Do ye have a ring?" Rosie asked, pushing in between Granny and her mother, Annie, her tears forgotten.

"No, luv. We decided to use the money for something that does more than just hang on me finger."

"But ye *have* to have a ring!"

"Rosie!" Annie said, sputtering laughter behind a hand, catching the girl by the arm, steering her out of the way. Granny opened her mouth for another attack, but Bernadette came forward from the range, came out of her usual place of serving and hiding, to grab her mother's shoulder in a way which was far from the daughterly obedience she had sworn.

"You let him have a life, Mam, and be happy about it," she hissed into the old woman's ear. "You don't give your blessing, you'll have to answer to God for it, and he'll go anyway."

"Listen to her, Mam," Maureen said. "She's right."

Bernadette looked at the sister who hadn't spoken a kind word to her since she'd come home and turned away, took up her post at the teakettle again.

"Come, sit. Have a cup of tea," Susan said, ushering Eileen to the table. "I'm sure ye could use it. It's a perishing wind out there."

"Yes. Me hair has suffered. I should have taken Paddy up on his offer. He was going to axle grease me hair like he did his own!

Sure, but not one hair of his head has dared to move all morning."

The sisters laughed in delight at their new almost-sister, and laughed at Paddy as they had always done whenever they had seen him walking with a girl, whenever they had heard any gossip. His cheeks turned hot and pink.

"Lord, not – not even a *hurricane* could move Paddy's hair!" Annie said, her words garbled with hilarious tears and spasms, until finally, her laugh "went chicken" in a huge strangled intake of breath.

Paddy shook his head. "This is why I'm so late about this sort of business – because I could never take the embarrassment – Lord! Why was I *blessed* with so many...*lovely* sisters?"

"Paddy!" Eileen said, leaned over and kissed him on the cheek, which made his face roar red all over, and pushed the laughter in the room to an impossible volume.

Granny sat opposite them at the table, her body compressed as tight as her lips, elbows crushing her ribs, tea held with both her hands on the table, eyes drilling into her son. Dinner was served almost immediately. Bernadette carved slices of beef, Susan dropped potatoes on the plates with her hand wrapped in a tea towel, Maureen ladled cabbage and turnips, Annie poured gravy – "*Don't* put gravy on my cabbage!" James called – and Agnes word-whipped the children under control: "Shut your mouths and eat! Get over there, Dermot! Stop it, Liam. Take your hand out o'th' biscuit tin or I'll thrash you!" The teenage boys and girls ate propped against the wall while the children sat on the stairs or their mothers' laps. Bernadette didn't sit, but hovered, filling plates, taking an odd bit of dry beef rind and putting it in her mouth.

"That's a lovely dress, Eileen," Susan said. "Been a long time since I've been to Clon' to see all the nice things in the shops."

"I got it in Cork, with some other things," Eileen said, and glanced coyly at Paddy.

"What other things?" Paddy asked, touching her with his elbow.

"I'm not going to tell!" she exclaimed, covering her cheeks with her long hands, the gloves now laid in her lap. "You're the one that has to wait to find out!"

The women watched them, eyes sparkling, eagerly laughing at everything they said, as if Eileen had brought an entire theatrical group with her to put on a comedy, as if they hadn't had so much fun in years.

"You women..." Paddy filled his mouth with potatoes and gravy, then beef and gravy, then turnip and gravy, so he wouldn't have to talk, but then he noticed Bernie, a shadow in a corner of the kitchen, teatowel over her shoulder, bread knife in her hand. "Bernie," he said through a crammed-full mouth, "why don't ye sit down and eat? Ye never sit down. Sit down for once."

Bernadette smiled at him, turned away, sliced more soda bread.

James watched the woman who would become his new aunt. She was much older than his mother. She had a merry mouth and was self-conscious about her table manners, resting her knife across the rim of her plate, not leaning it against the plate like an oar. It was one of the things his English grandmother had insisted on back in Oxford. He decided he liked Eileen fiercely. Anger seethed up in him when he watched his granny chewing her meat on stumpy teeth, her eyes on her plate.

The meal went on with the sounds of silverware on cracked china, chewing, the squawk of small children, conversation which was less and less concerned with Eileen, more with the progress of the children at school, the sewing of clothes, the sick cattle, whether the amount of turf piled by the house would last through the winter and the new priest – like a vicious little weasel – down in Killaghmore. Maureen was unusually silent. She put her fork down.

"Ye can take the kerchief off, Bernie. We want to see ye."

The eating noises stopped.

"I been thinking. Here we are, about to welcome Eileen into the family, and we haven't even been welcoming with our own.

It's not like I agree now with what ye did, but we haven't been kind to ye, forgiving, haven't been Christian, and I've been the worst, and dragging the others with me. Maybe I shouldn't be saying this now, if you're embarrassed by all the people, but this is my shame, not yours. I've been treating ye badly, and really, what do I know of what ye've – what do I know? I'm telling ye, I – I want it over with. I want ye to belong here again. I want to *see* ye. I missed ye. Maybe if we stop being ashamed of ye, ye can stop being so ashamed of yourself. Ye don't have to wear the kerchief, not with me. If ye can forgive me."

He watched his mother put the tureen of cabbage on the counter. She always wore her kerchief when there were people other than her mother, her brother, and her son to see her. Her thin fingers circled the hard blue knot beneath her chin, her nails picking at it, pulling it open. She waited before sliding off the concealing tunnel of cloth.

There she was, a silhouette like before the accident, but her shoulders bent forward, bony, her wild hair bound tight. She was wearing one of her favourite dresses from England, the one she used to say matched her eyes exactly, the one she used to wear when she most felt like showing off. Her glass eye stared from its nest of scars, a different colour of blue.

Granny got up, grasped her hand. "Bernadette!" she insisted, called, as if trying to resurrect the old wayward girl who was buried somewhere inside. Bernadette stood taller, pressed her shoulders open, raised her chin, rested her eye on Maureen.

"Both of us born stubborn, but you were always the one to give in first – thanks be to God."

Maureen embraced her.

James's eyes stung: his mother standing straight, his mother, beautiful even with her damaged splash of skin, sharpened somehow, harder, prouder, pale as plaster with her suffering, her loss of weight, loss of flesh – she looked as if God Himself had purified her, turned her into one of her icons, the Queen of Heaven. He wanted to throw himself into her arms and bite a freckle from the tip of her nose. It would be salty, taste browny green, maybe, like his granny's seaweed. Maybe things would be better for her now.

❖ ❖ ❖

The men and boys left after tea and tea brack, the thick, moist, raisin-filled cake that Agnes had brought. The girls cleaned up the dishes and went off in groups of sisters and cousins, and the women took their youngest children home.

"Mam," Paddy said, taking Eileen's hand. "We're going for a walk. We'll go up to Colm's old place and have a look around."

Granny got up from her chair by the window and followed them into the porch.

"Well, does she have a proper kerchief, at least? No!" Granny exclaimed, looking at the thin city dress-up coat and little pillbox hat in a fury of repentant hospitality. "That thing'll never cover her ears."

"Mam, the wind's died."

"I'll be fine, Mrs. Cahalane."

"Nonsense! Here!" Granny yanked her big grey worsted cloak off its peg. "This has some warmth to it. Go on!"

Eileen's mouth dropped open. "I haven't seen one of these in years! Was it your –"

"My mother's, the mother I never met, given by her mother before her."

"I –"

"Wear it," Granny ordered, with angry generosity, part of her not at all repentant, wanting to make herself so. "Wear it!"

Eileen smiled. "I couldn't."

"Well," Granny said, ruffled, tossing her head, "ye've no proper shoes."

"I have them in me bag."

"Oh. Well. That's good then." Granny stood with Paddy, watching Eileen go to the car. "Jesus, Mary and Joseph. I don't know what to *say* to her. What did I say to Susan when she first came with Colm? Why is it so hard to give up the boys? The first boy?"

Paddy shifted his feet, kicked a clump of dirt off his Wellington boot, his hands slouching in his pockets.

"I was wrong. Always wrong," Granny said.

Paddy nodded.

"Ye can live here if ye want. Lord knows there's enough room and work, and we've got the electricity."

"Eileen wants a place of her own."

"Sure. Sure. Of course she does."

"Start off in Colm's old place. In a year or two, maybe, we can get the electricity. She's used to it, living in the town. They got a heater for hot water, even."

Eileen came back inside, carrying a brown paper package, already wearing a sturdy pair of shoes, her coat buttoned to the top. She gave the package to her future mother-in-law.

"Come on then," Paddy said. "We'd better walk if we're going to see everything before it gets dark."

Granny went back into the kitchen and pounced on the carving knife still sticking out of the lump of leftover roast. She slit the string, staining the paper with roast dripping, and went back to her chair to rip the paper off with her fingernails.

It was a pair of new field glasses, a miniature and expensive variety that was powerful but could be easily hidden. The tag was labelled "Rooney's Hardware, Clonakilty," Eileen's father's shop.

James heard Granny gasp, and was soon beside her, leaning on her shoulder to gaze at them.

"They're a little smaller than the last," she told him, her eyes skirting up past his face, "so we're going to have to take turns. Here."

She gave him the glasses and ushered him in front of her to look out the window. His mother, bare-headed, came up behind them as he took the first look through the new lenses.

"Well? Well?" Granny asked, poking him in the back with a scrawny finger.

"They're smaller, but they're stronger. I can see even the people on the strand! And there's a ship – way, way out!"

Granny seized the glasses, shooed him out of the way, held them to her eyes. They watched Paddy and Eileen walking down the road, arm in arm beneath one umbrella, as another blue storm began to fall through the sky. James lifted his hand to rest lightly on his grandmother's shoulder.

Paddy and Eileen were married a week before Christmas in the hill church of Clonakilty that looked out over the sea. During the homily, a silver pigeon, trapped in the church since morning Mass, flew down from the gallery, swooped through the nave, and out the blown-open doors.

In January and February the wind threw the blackened sea up the cliffs and the sky cracked open in perpetual waterfall. James soaked himself nearly every day going to school and then up to Colm's old place, now Paddy's place, for tea. It was a two-room stone house of unknown age with only a dirt floor, the thatched roof beginning to sprout weeds. It had taken a week to clean the place up and heat the damp out of it. When James arrived, often Paddy would be just taking off his coat, his wedding-barbered hair still making him look dapper, though it had grown an inch over his ears. Eileen, now obviously pregnant, stoked the open turf fire to keep out the chills. She took Grania's wedding present curtains off the windows – there was no one ever around to look in – and filled one of the kitchen cupboards with books: James Joyce, Evelyn Waugh, Thomas Hardy, and assorted newsprint romances. She got some worksheets from her old school so James could begin teaching his granny to read. She served tea in china she'd inherited from her grandmother: translucent and oyster-white, with tiny pink roses and gold rims. Once, she gave James store-bought Jaffa cakes she'd brought from Clonakilty, chocolate-topped and filled with orange jelly, forcing him to remember his long-lost British grandmother and father and friends, forcing him to run home early in rain that ran saltier down his face.

Sometimes, Paddy would dance Eileen around the kitchen or pull her into his lap, wrap his arms around her growing belly, and bury his stubbly face in her neck. James liked this, though it disturbed him like those sounds he used to hear coming from his parents' bedroom; he liked it when she scolded Paddy for scratching her neck, warned him about doing "things" in front of the boy, and for being such an animal. These were glimpses into the places beyond doors, the insides of houses he couldn't spy into with his granny's glasses. Paddy was changing. He talked more, and could stare his sisters in the face when they tried to make him blush. He let his big frame take up as much space as it liked, stretching his legs out under the table as if he was finally comfortable in his body, was no longer awkward in his manhood. There was a glint of mischief and carnality in his eye where before there had been sadness.

Sometimes, he took James to the pub on a Saturday afternoon. James liked it when they met Colm and John there. The boys made up blarney stories about the other farmers and fishermen in the pub, mimicking Colm's style of outlandish lying; how the fat man over there, Mick Brady, ate a whole goose for dinner, feathers and all, and how old Willie-Joe in the corner had to sharpen his few remaining teeth with sandpaper, because, really, he was a cannibal, and as strong as ten men, never mind the cane and his shuffle of a walk. Colm was always whispering questions about newly married life to Paddy and Paddy was sometimes embarrassed, fun to laugh at, would only say, "So good, it can't be legal."

James wanted to be like Paddy, peaceful of mind, strong of body. When Paddy was still with the cows at tea time, James ran looking for him. He would be milking with Bernadette in Granny's barn or further up in the hills when the calving began.

One rain-darkened day, James couldn't find Paddy. Dermot leaped at James from behind a sycamore, pushed him down into the wet grass and began punching his face, determined to cave it in.

"Ye fucking liar," he yelped, face dripping with rain and spittle as he brought his fist down. James curled into a ball, arms over his head, so Dermot began kicking with his steel-toed boots. James was nearly unconscious when he felt Dermot suddenly levitate. He saw Paddy above him, and a flail of arms and legs.

"What are ye doing?" Paddy yelled, jamming Dermot against the trunk of the tree. "Are ye crazy?"

"He's a liar! A tale-teller! I'm going to –"

Paddy tightened his grip and glanced at James lying in the road, the rain washing blood from his shocked numb face.

"James? James! Can ye *talk*, boy?"

James closed his eyes, head throbbing within the worst of his nightmares come true.

"Ye fucking bastard! I'll make it so ye can't see, ye can't talk ever –"

Paddy looked into Dermot's round vicious eyes.

"You're not afraid of me at all, are ye? Gentle old uncle."

Dermot looked at Paddy, puzzled.

"How old are ye, Dermot?"

"Seventeen."

"Well, you're a man then, aren't ye?"

For a moment, James thought Paddy would hit Dermot, his voice had become so cold.

"Then you'll be able to take the truth. Susan and Colm, they never loved you; they don't love you now. They pity you, and it's made you a useless, poisonous man. You hate this boy because you want to be the only near-fatherless martyr that I'm taking care of. But that's hate in the wrong direction, and if you're going to hate, let me show you the right direction. You hate your *father*, boy, because he hated your mother most of all. You go and talk to Colm about that. Let him tell ye the truth. Sure, the lies are pleasant enough for the rest of us but they haven't done you any good."

Dermot listened with his lips open, flabby, quivering.

"If there isn't room for both of you, then I'm going to choose. I'm finished with you, Dermot. You're on your own. And it's what ye deserve."

A low whimper came out of Dermot's rain-wet lips. It grew louder and louder, madder and madder, between his sloppy breaths.

"From now on, this boy tells me even one word, I don't give a damn, and I'll be coming for you. You touch him again, and *I'll* disfigure *you*."

Paddy half threw Dermot from him, and Dermot ran, stumbling, down the hill toward his parents' house. Paddy knelt by James.

"Can ye get up?"

Paddy helped him rise, then picked him up and started carrying him down the road.

"Jesus, what have I started? I shouldn't have said those things."

James swung his painful head from Paddy's shoulder, eyes squinting from the rain and blood and swelling, seeing trees, fields, houses, all slanted, jogging up and down in the wrong order. He thought of the swan that had been hit by a car on the edge of town, that Paddy had tried to bring home wrapped in a sack, that had died in his uncle's arms.

"This isn't the way home," he mumbled.

"We're not going home. We're going to the doctor."

<hr />

Everywhere, there were bruises. His nose was broken. His skin was torn above one eye and his lips were cut by his teeth — damn lucky he didn't lose those teeth, too. The doctor bandaged the eye to prevent infection, taped his nose, said there was no evidence of concussion. There was a fuss, of course, when he got home, his mother stricken, horrified, his granny enraged, angry at him for not being able to protect himself, angry at Dermot: "Ye should ha' kicked him in the nuts! Ungrateful little sod. I'll *murder* him." He'd remember the things she said for the rest of his life, because she told him what he was, that he was not a fighter, that he was like his uncle Paddy, a criticism that sounded like praise in his ears. Colm stormed into the house after midnight, screaming "What the fuck did you tell him? Why the fuck – now he's God knows where doing God knows what! Ye should ha' been there! All the lies I had to tell him! The bad seed. And that I hate *him*, not his mother! Jesus fucking Christ! What am I supposed to do to protect her? When half the men in this town think a woman never gets what she doesn't ask for!"

The day after, James was fascinated with himself in the mirror, the few black-knotted stitches protruding from the red wounds of his lips, the purple, blue and green bruise where there wasn't white bandage – worse, almost, than his mother had looked. He refused to go to school for the next week, and no one opposed him. He spent much of the days gazing through the rain with the field glasses, giving reports to Granny as she plucked and gutted an old hen or baked bread, watching his mother come and go in her new freedom, visiting her sisters, helping Maureen put up new shelves in her kitchen because Michael was too drunk to do it, giving Susan a break from the children, riding Paddy's mare down to the strand.

The real her, the before-the-accident-her, had not come back when she unveiled herself, but something was changing. There were still invisible plaster casts on her limbs, heavy with religion, whenever dancing was spoken of. Whenever she walked him down to Mass, arm on his shoulder, he could feel the weight of repentance, but proud repentance, as if she, too, embodied in her scars and glass eye, was wearing a crown of thorns that Jesus had transformed – twigs to gold.

"You're a better person than Dermot is," his mother told him on the first day he sat, injured, at the window.

"You fooled me for a while with your backtalk," Granny

grumbled, "your red hair. It's a bleeding good thing there are a few of us in the family that can protect ye."

"If you're going to be a priest," his mother went on, glaring at Granny, "ye must learn to forgive. It's what Jesus would do. Priests must try to do what Jesus did. Dermot knew not what he did. Say that when you pray."

To his nightly prayer of escape, now less ardent than before, James added a prayer that Dermot would die.

Horribly.

That he would feel his eyes rot to purple putrescent jelly, feel his flesh being gnawed from his bones, feel the worms and maggots munching on his balls and prick.

No one had seen Dermot since that night. James tried to talk to Paddy about what Colm had said, but Paddy just shook his head and told him not to ask. Once, when his mother wasn't around, Paddy said, "I should have just punched the tar out of him. It would have done less damage."

On the last day of his self-imposed quarantine, James spied his mother on the road, a letter clutched in her hand.

She was running.

He hadn't seen her run for a year.

The hole in his heart filled with fire.

His father was coming.

He raced out to meet her.

"From –"

"From St. Paul's School for Boys. In Cork City."

The heat burned out, dried his mouth. His eyes stung as if bathed in smoke. He was abandoned all over again: his father had thrown him into the winter sea.

He followed his mother, pulled along by her strange attitude of triumph.

"Get back into the porch! Ye'll wash me floor again!" Granny wiped her lips with a floury hand as Bernadette and James stood with muddy shoes in the kitchen, the envelope between them.

"Read it, James," his mother told him, her coat heaving with her breaths.

He read.

"I'm to go away to school?"

Granny dropped her wooden spoon, turned.

"I'm to go away?"

"It's such a good school, James, almost like England. Ye'll need letters from the bishop, ye see, to get into the seminary – and the best classes, things ye can't get here."

The best this, the best that. His English grandmother's words coming out of his mother's mouth. The cleanest floor. The shiniest silver.

"Ye'll not send him away?" Granny said, waving her hand *no*. "He's but a pup. He needs his mam, his family! And who's going to pay for it, I'd like to know! Where are ye going to get the *brass*? Ye can't –"

She stopped as if something, a piece of seaweed maybe, had blocked her throat. James saw his mother's eye glittering – disrespectful – felt the surge of new power in his mother's voice, the power that had been growing since Eileen's first visit.

"There they'll make sure he has a proper bedtime. And he won't be going drinking at the pub when he's too young for it, and no one will be scoffing at what the priest says, filling his head with – with stories." Bernadette pushed her wet fingers through her son's hair, grasped it, wanted him to go where he would be safe, safely God's...safely hers. "Do ye want to go?"

He looked into the wet halo of her plastic rain kerchief, her face eager. In a year, almost, he'd gotten used to the scars, but not the invisible damage, the holy well, the tangled ropes of rosary beads in her hands. Sometimes he would forget and race to her, bury his head in her lap, needing her smell, her touch, but getting a sermon instead. And it was worse when she lay in her bed, when it was his job to get her up, get her smiling, and he never knew when it was going to work, and it never worked for the first few days, and the same thing never worked twice – sometimes she would get up after he brought her tea, or maybe it would be reading his homework to her or reciting the lesson he had to memorize for Sunday school or telling her the town

gossip. Even saying he was going to be a priest, which was supposed to make her happy, didn't always make her happy. Even
his being good, acting good, didn't make her happy for good.
His lungs filled and emptied, filled and emptied and he didn't
know why he felt so suddenly, desperately tired.

He squeezed his eyes shut too hard, felt the orange pain of
the swirls and checkerboards he could see forming and dis-
solving on the insides of his eyes.

And Dermot could always come back.

"I'll go," he said.

He looked around his granny's familiar kitchen, the
moments of the past year becoming strangers to him. He had
never wanted to be here, had ached to run away, prayed to be
gone, so what else could this letter be but a kind of answer?
God's answer to his prayer. Could anyone say "No, sorry, God,
I've changed my mind?" The longing of his empty belly was
being met with only a few scraps – like the stories his granny
told of the starving taking what little they could get, eating
grass. This was his famine meal. And he would gnash it down.

All the muscles in his body tightened. His hands clenched
into fists.

"I'll go," he said.

The words cut him away.

The problems of the farm and Killaghmore didn't belong to
him any more. Here he was, almost twelve years old, standing in
his granny's kitchen: the sound of her beating the dough on the
counter, the whistle of the kettle, St. Patrick's claws on the slate
floor. He suddenly knew how much he had come to love it,
never wanted any of it to change, and he was about to change it.

"I'll write them this minute." His mother dropped her wet
coat on a chair, and hesitated – her son going away, away already –
then ran up the stairs.

She *ran*; it amazed him again.

He stood at the window with the field glasses. The world was
green. It was blurring, was wet, water filling his eyes, the rain
coming down.

Grania worked at the dough, puffing fogs of silent flour over the counter.

"It's not settled, boy, so don't go thinking it is," she spat, forcing her voice but sounding subdued, defeated.

It *had* been settled. He had settled it.

He went to watch her mound the bread onto the pan. She rested her thin shoulder against his. He was getting taller.

From then on, it was the spin of time. Spring took him to the grey slate cliffs where the dregs of the Atlantic winter crashed and foamed. The waves threw themselves at the flat rock face and fell back into the next row of waves, leaping twice as high with white tusks of spray. In the tiny hidden bays, sometimes swallowed by tide and wave, he picked baskets of carrageen moss for his granny to dry and chew like toffee in the evenings, giving her breath its familiar fishy reek. He turned twelve on the only full day of sun in March, a perfect Saturday they all spent cutting seed potatoes, *skiollauns* – a single eye per piece – and planting them in rows plowed up by Lizzy. Paddy finally released his crow, which he hadn't had the heart to do during the winter, lest another storm come to blow it away. Though it never talked, it still hung around the yard, strutting close to anyone who was working outside, cocking its sleek black head, waiting for scraps of raw meat or picking at the bugs that the chickens stirred up. Paddy and Colm slowly became friends again and the visits to the pub resumed.

"We're going fishing with Colm. His boat is ready," Paddy said, sticking his head into the kitchen at breakfast time. It was the first glorious day of May, a Saturday.

"His *boat*?"

"Sure, but it was a big secret – hidden in that shed of his. And ye never suspected with all that looking through the glasses? Colm has a lot of fishermen friends, and they've helped him

build a nice little curragh. We're going to float her out today, see
if she's worthy. Ye *canna* miss this, James."

The boreen was already a tunnel of blossoms with blue sky
above. They found Colm in the barn with John, admiring the
curragh, a boat of wooden lath frame with canvas stretched over,
a boat without keel or rudder, steered and powered by oars
alone. It lay upside down on two sawhorses where it had been
painted with hot tar. James remembered seeing it as a skeleton.

"Ah, Colm. I didn't think ye had the hands or the brain for
it. She's beautiful. Smooth and pretty as the top of your head."

"Get out, Paddy," Colm said, smiling at the compliment to
his new toy. He stood tall, proud, his big belly lapping over his
belt, hammocking in the billow of his tucked-in work shirt,
narrow eyes unused to words of praise, but flashing at the insults.

Paddy ran his hand over the black skin of the boat. James had
never seen anything as sleek.

"The faeries came and built her at night. Took them no more
than a fortnight!" Colm jabbed his burly elbow into James's ribs
and nodded vigorously.

"Sure they did," James said. "And they painted it with my pants."

They loaded the curragh onto the donkey cart and lashed it
with old ropes, then walked the donkey down the hills and
through the town to the bay. At high tide, the mud flats were
covered by relatively gentle water. The fierce shore-break was
broken by the sand dunes curling halfway between the cliffs at
the mouth of the bay. In the cleft of hills, near where the river
Tare spread itself into the sheltered sea, they walked past three
multicoloured tinker caravans, lines of flapping laundry running
between the nearby trees, a few horses and donkeys grazing
nearby. A smooth-haired dog with a belly of joggling teats stumbled up and rearranged herself in her grassy hiding place under
one caravan. They heard the milk-squeal of puppies.

"Ha!" Colm exhaled. "'Tis a soft day."

And it was, with clear sky, sun sparkling on the deep blue
water, swans with black beaks floating where the river met the
sea, the silt from the fresh water swirling brown, the surface

curdling like oil. The wind was picking up off the sea, hunching over the dunes, and blowing a skim of sand around their ankles, among the coarse blades of marram grass.

They left the donkey to graze on the dunes and launched the curragh into the estuary, gulls and gannets, curlews and oyster-catchers, crying above them.

Colm stepped barefoot into the curragh out of knee-deep water, sat and rocked it while Paddy held the rope that was tied to the prow. Even with Colm's fat body heaving about, the little boat was bobbing unconcerned, gleeful.

"No leaks, boys! We're away! I fancy mackerel, fried up with some spuds!"

"Ye better learn how to row the thing first, Colm," Paddy said, lifting the oars out of the cart. "Get in, boys and we'll row across to the other shore."

"Don't forget the jigs!" Colm ordered.

They rowed with the three sets of narrow oars, Colm at the back, Paddy in the middle, and James and John taking turns on the third seat near the front. They rowed in circles, in zags and spins, Colm uncertain at first how to stroke his oars to veer this way and that, the light, keelless curragh too responsive.

"That's what happens when ye get a farmer to row a boat." Paddy tossed the words at the back of Colm's head.

"Whisht!"

"Whisht!" James sputtered. "Whishshshsht." Like the wind.

Eventually, they were skimming through the choppy water, oars dipping and rising up out of the green.

"Kittiwake!" John exclaimed, pointing at a swooping bird overhead, showing off for James. "And that's a chough! He's a shorebird. Razorbill! Gannet! Ye know them by the way they shine like silver. Ye ought to see them swallow a fish!"

"Jellyfish!" James shouted, tugging John's sleeve. The transparent fringed bubbles – eyeballs – floated beneath the surface and slid away as they rowed.

It didn't take them long to come close to the opposite shore of the bay, its narrow pebbled shore shadowed with overhanging slate.

Weakened swells rolled past the dunes from the open sea, rushed at the land, clattering the pebbles, splashing against the curragh.

"You know the tides today?" Paddy asked, but Colm was already rowing again.

"We'll try just offshore, out in the open. See how she stands a bit of rough sea."

"No. Think better of it." Paddy took his oars and countered every stroke of Colm's so the curragh made no headway. "Cast your line here where it's calmer. Fish more likely to be here."

"It's not the fish. It's the waves. I want to see how she handles."

"Later, then. With one of them round lifesaver things. Without the boys. Without me. I'll stand on shore to fish your body out."

"No faith! Ye landlubber, Paddy. You're such a bleeding older brother."

"Here." Paddy handed out the fishing jigs, shaking them a little to disentangle the hooks.

"Watch, now and ye'll see a mermaid, boys!" Colm flashed his eyes over the water. "She'll sing so sweetly, and make ye leap into the water, and that's the last we'll ever see of James and Johnny. What! Paddy! Look who we've got in the boat! It's the Fishers of Men! The brothers James and John! The Holy Apostles!" Colm laughed himself red in the face and splashed a handful of water at his son and nephew. John rolled his eyes and looked at James. In wordless synchronicity, they splashed him back.

"Where's the anchor?" Paddy said.

"Anchor?"

"*Jasus.* Your little faery friends didn't give ye an anchor?"

"They've not finished yet."

"And ye got us all here in an unfinished boat?"

"She's *fine.* She *works.* She doesn't have maybe all the bells and whistles yet, but they're coming."

Paddy sighed and dropped his line, its bottom weight and tiers of feathered hooks vanishing straight down into the water.

"Better than fishing off the shore, no mistake!" Colm said in his own defense, but got no answer.

It was when Colm caught a small mackerel that Paddy noticed the boat had drifted. They were nearing the mouth of the bay and could see the waves crashing on the rocks at the base of the cliff and curling over onto the strand at the seaward edge of the dunes. The curragh met waves higher and higher with greater spans between them until it was rising and falling, rising and falling in a manner which didn't seem dangerous in the least, waves that would soon move them to the east, along the cliff and toward the dangerous swells crashing against the wet black rocks.

"The tide's dragging us out! Forget the fish!" Paddy yelled. Colm wound up his handline, then took the oars. "Pull, boys, pull!"

James and John sat side by side and strained at their oars, looking at each other now and then, fearing and desiring to be pirates, to be lost at sea, to be shipwrecked.

They fought the tide as it sucked the water from the bay, pulling the oars against a force that seemed to be getting stronger until they felt the curragh scrape bottom.

"Colm, get over to the side. Remember where the river flows when the tide is out? If we ground her, we'll be wallowing." James could see the mud flats through the shallow water, the soft hairy grass in places, the wormholes in impossibly soft mud. He'd tried walking on it once, just on the edge, and his feet were caught in its suck. When he was in muck halfway to his knees, he had visions of being anchored, of standing there stupidly until the tide came in, the cold water creeping up his body until it covered his head. He had to crawl out on his hands and knees.

They found the deeper muddy water of the river and rowed until they came aground in sand, far from where they first launched the boat. Paddy and Colm lifted the boat and carried it upside down on their shoulders, James and John running ahead through the shallows, carrying the jigs at arm's length, hooks swinging. Paddy and Colm deposited the boat on the sand, then Colm stumbled a few steps and rolled his body onto the grass.

"I won't be able to move tomorrow," he said, rubbing his shoulder. "No wonder them fishermen have such mighty arms! And a mighty thirst, I bet! The Guinness is calling to me. We'll just stop and wet the day before tea."

"Mighty arms," John said, bending his frail limbs into a muscleman pose.

"Mighty thirst," James said, guzzled back an imaginary Guinness and puked up imaginary vomit.

John threw sand at him.

They filed into McGovern's at four in the afternoon, donkey and cart tied in the square.

"Susan," Colm said. "That's what I'm naming her. Go out with a can of paint on Monday when I get me an anchor."

"Get the faeries to do it," James told him.

They spent the next two hours talking and laughing, telling stories, their skin rubbed and glowing with sunburn.

In their own homes that night, Paddy and James told of almost getting washed out to sea, John recited lists of the birds he had seen, and Colm kissed Susan, who was pregnant again. He made her sit and got the tea himself, sliced the bread, spread the jam for the little ones, and washed the dishes.

For James, it was an unprecedented day, a climax. For hours he had forgotten...forgotten the things he didn't want to remember: that there was a home, a country, a family, other than this one. Even lying in bed that night, face still raw with sun, he was his granny's own grandson, as Irish as they come.

❦ ❦ ❦

Eileen and Paddy's daughter, Lila, was born in June, in Clonakilty hospital – a bit early, his sisters whispered, for a December wedding. Eileen looked tired and overweight in a crocheted bed jacket. Paddy grinned madly, placed what looked like a small roll of laundry in James's arms. The bundle was warm, a bit damp, heavier than he had expected, heavier than he remembered. He held her a long time, silently remembering that other baby he used to hold. She was sleeping, her eyes in soft mollusk folds.

Paddy missed the wild bonfire night of Midsummer's Eve: fires and music and dancing all over the hills. Though she had avoided the revels last year, Bernadette came out to the fire, an arm linked through James's, her legs twitching, remembering what they knew, what her new piety no longer approved of. He watched one of her feet begin to tap. She didn't let go of him all night, and he memorized her blushing firelit flesh, the pink half moons beneath her fingernails.

Early July was all gardening and milking and whitewashing the house and barns, and fishing trips with Colm and John in the curragh.

"What if Paddy and Eileen and the baby don't come back before I go away to school?"

Granny was rubbing the cramps out of James's hands with a mixture of crushed rosemary and sheep's grease, her flabby-skinned thumbs sliding hard in his palms. He had taken over Paddy's share of the milking when Paddy took Eileen to the hospital.

"Don't be an eejit! He's got to be back for the haymaking, doesn't he? Can't blame his wife for wanting her mam at a time like this, for wanting the electricity – that electric clothes mangle. Hot water. All them nappies."

That evening, James spied Paddy coming up the hill from town, carrying a cardboard box. He ran down to meet him, tumbling over his feet in the cool fragrant dusk, gulping air like happiness. He leaped at Paddy, laughing, tried to knock the box out of his hands.

"Where's Eileen?" James was breathless. "Does Lila have hair yet? Or does she still look like Uncle Colm?"

"Stayed in Clon', James, the both of them. She's fine with her mother fussing over her for a few days."

They walked up to the farm, James kicking through drifts of fallen fuchsia by the overgrown boreen walls.

"Damned wet. It's a late haymaking this year."

"Oh, but it's been fine for days now! Paddy, look!"

James held out his hands, and Paddy peered at them.

"So what am I supposed to see?"

"My hands, Paddy! Look at the muscles! Uncle Colm says I've got milker's muscles! I thumb-wrestled John, and I won!"

"Oh, yes, sure enough," Paddy said, caught James by the shirt to stop his jumping, then examined his hands, pinched the base of the thumb, then shook him by the wrists, making his hands flop. "Look. See? Ye've got the wrists of a champion milker."

"Are we going to the pub tonight?" James knew haymaking season might be too busy for Saturday afternoons at the pub, but he desperately wanted to go.

"Nah! Don't ye think your mam and granny would like to see me for once? I stopped at the pub for a bit on the way from the bus, but maybe we'll try ye on Saturday once it gets too dark to work."

"Paddy's home!" James yelled to the house, then ran and opened the hall door. "Paddy's home!"

"We hear ye all right!" Granny screeched. "Ye don't have to split our ears!"

They sat around the kitchen table that night with cups of tea and the little vial of *poitín* that Granny kept in her bottom drawer for special occasions. Fueled, rather than damped, by Bernadette's strident protests, Granny let James have a few drops of it in a spoon, like medicine, and after it flamed down his throat he thought how possible it would be to go immediately to sleep.

They ate slices of gingerbread drowned in cream, and apples that Paddy had brought from Clonakilty. In the cardboard box were two dresses and some second-hand women's magazines Eileen had sent for Bernadette and Grania, a box of Jaffa cakes for James, and also an American book, *Huckleberry Finn*. In the bottom were a few of Paddy's clothes, and his razor. He shaved every day now, even the places under his eyes where the tufts of whiskers had been. Bernadette held her new dress up against her, looking down at the flowered print as if it couldn't possibly belong to her – maybe shouldn't belong to her.

They got up early to get the hay in, a job for every available hand. Even in his anger and depression of his first Irish summer, James had ridden the wagon, worked a pitchfork.

"You're sure you're not too tired for the pub?" Paddy said on Saturday night.

"We haven't gone in ages! Did you tell Uncle Colm? Are he and John meeting us there, or should we knock on their door?"

Paddy laughed. "I think they've gone on without us. Sure, but you're a happy pup. What's been wagging your tail?"

"Nothing," James said, excited about his first nighttime visit to the pub, even though his mother threw a stabbing look at him, then at Paddy. Would there be drunks and fights? Would the Guards come and throw them out? They walked down the hill to Killaghmore, the moon shining off the still sea in the sweet sliced green smell of an entire valley of hay.

"Pad-Pad-Paddy!" Colm called, waving his arm, his broad belly covered with red plaid. He and John were sitting at a tiny wobbly pub table that they'd pulled outside; the pub was too crowded and hot with thirsty farmers finished haymaking, and with the warmth of the day. Men spilled with the golden electric light into the market square, leaned against the front of the pub, glasses in hand.

John punched James in the arm as he sat down. "Guess who's joined the Volunteers," he said, with a little gust of breath that was filled with both pride and relief.

James stared at him.

"Mam got a letter yesterday from Derry – s'kind of in code, but *Jasus*, she's mad."

"Dermot?" James sat back against the rough stucco wall.

He had been trying to pray more in the past few weeks – real prayer that was not about Dermot's decomposition; he had been called, hadn't he? He wanted to know what that meant. Once, he sat in the church in Killaghmore and watched the long black-bird beings who were God's servants. He remained after Mass in the cold stone quiet, watching an altar boy gather the silver and linen – his own job every Sunday morning – and pace out of view. The priest turned God to bread, or was that bread to God? Christ had risen. Risen like his mother's bread in the oven, crisp, burnt sometimes. Were the holy wafers the bread of life everyone was going on about? Who made them? Angels with aprons baking them in front of the sun? Clouds could be puffs of flour. Mysteries were things he could never know, and he hated that, hated the confusion he felt.

God had taken Dermot away, answered another of James's prayers in a strange and disturbing manner. There had been little IRA activity since James had come to Ireland, so it seemed a historic and nearly defunct sort of organization to him, but he had been listening, absorbing a few details of supposedly secret family events: someone's dog that had been abducted and murdered so many years ago, the grand-uncle rotting in prison, the police raid of an arms stash on a farm between here and Bandon. He knew about the guns and bombs, and with Dermot joined up now, their presence became real, threatening.

Paddy fought his way into the pub and came out with two dripping glasses of dark stout. He began talking to a whiskery man, nodding his head now and then with a kind of energy that seemed alien to him. He put the beer on a table and wrote something on the corner of the man's newspaper. James watched, impatient for the drink and Paddy's wise, subtle company. The man went inside the pub, but then Paddy, like a sheepdog, cut another man out of the crowd and started talking again.

"Ah, he's different, eh?" Colm said. "Different already."

James, Colm, and John's conversation waned as they watched Paddy. There were rumours that his wife was turning snobbish – when was she finally bringing the baby home?

"I don't think this one'll show up at Finn's shop, but he might be interested in some of the big equipment." Paddy sat down finally, distributed the glasses. "Great thing to have a phone right in the house, Colm. Ye know, all them people in England, they have phones of their own. Ye should think about that."

"What – don't I think about things? It's me who buys the newspapers and *you* who does the borrowing!"

"I mean besides the politics. Things are starting to change in Ireland, like I never thought. James, wouldn't ye like a phone in the kitchen? It'd be good for Granny and your mam, especially now that you're going away, and there'll not be a man in the house. What if something were to happen?"

"Something's always happening," Colm said. "And I'm just down the road. So what do they need a phone for, for Christ's sake? *Jasus*, you're hopping on the newfangled things. Mam's got the bray of an ass. She can be heard as far as town."

"Boys!" called Michael, Maureen's husband, trying to jam his way out of the pub door. "I seen ye inside, Paddy! Is there truth in what I hear?"

"Now, ye haven't been listening to gossip, have ye?" Paddy didn't look at Michael. "I expected better from an *upstanding* man –"

"Falling-over man," James whispered to John.

"When a relation of mine can't –"

At that moment, an arm came out of the crowd of men around the door, and pulled Michael away. He was drunk, easily distracted, and in a moment, was laughing, slapping the man on the back.

"Ye'll always come back for the haymaking won't ye?" Colm said. "We're going to miss these little evenings, too, Paddy. I mean afternoons. Jesus. I can't understand how ye can leave the life."

"Whisht, Colm."

"I can't see ye boxed into a big town, in a shop all day, a house without fields, no chickens in the yard."

"Whisht," Paddy insisted, his head hanging lower at the mention of fields. "I hadn't told them up at the house yet. I was going to tonight. Never thought it was going to be the talk of the town."

James listened with an open mouth.

"You're staying in Clon'?"

"Looks that way."

"For how long?"

Paddy swallowed. "I'll be home here and there when I can. At haymaking for sure. But ye see, there's enough hands now. John's growing up, and Liam, and Agnes's girls, and there'll be less work once Colm gets his tractor."

"Hey, well, we'll see. They got milking machines too, and I like the sound of that," Colm said, gulping from his glass, rubbing a hand over his shiny head.

"And ye'll be needing the tools to fix them things when they break down, too. Don't forget what store ye'll be buying them at."

"No, not me."

"You're staying away for good?" James's voice rose higher and higher in disbelief.

"James, it's like this. I've been thinking about a lot of things. Lila especially. What's a girl going to do up in the hills but get married, and if she can't do that, can't find a decent man, well... Things are changing. Colm's going to buy a tractor to do more farming than the both of us. Everything's going automated with the money coming in from the Common Market. Soon, it'll be like England. Eileen wants Lila to have a better life, maybe go to university. We can make more money if Eileen goes back to teaching, and I work with her father at the shop, take it over. Finn isn't so young any more. He's been teaching me the books, says with a little more math in me brain, I'd make a mighty shopkeeper. He says I'll be good at it, knowing a farm like I do, knowing spades and pitchforks."

James fastened his eyes on one of Paddy's cheekbones, the place where a little tuft of whiskers had been. He began to swallow, couldn't stop swallowing though there was nothing but saliva in his mouth.

Paddy, leaving him, changing this place just as he'd come to love it, to call it home.

"Now, don't look at me as if I'm disappearing off the face of the earth. Who's moving to Cork City to go to a fancy boarding school? Eh? I'll be up here every month or two – staying in the house, in me old room – to make sure everything is fixed up and running."

"You'll never be home the same time as me."

"But we can plan it so we will. And ye'll come to visit us in Clon'."

"No I *won't*."

A spurt of laughter came from the crowd by the door. Michael tumbled out from between two men and caught himself before he fell. His eyes found Paddy.

"Things never change, do they?" Michael said.

Paddy ignored him.

"Ye heard what I said!"

"But I don't get your meaning, Michael."

"Well, let me explain. All of us – we think you're pathetic. Let your wife tell ye where to live, what kind of work ye do. Ye'll be the slave of her family! Taking orders! Living in her house! She thinks she's too good for us, being from the big town, and now ye think you're too good for us as well."

"I don't recall discussing the reasons *I'm* moving my family to Clon'. What difference can it make to you?"

"Your Eileen won't live in Colm's old house, not if she has to heat her own water, not if all she's got for company is farm wives."

"There's no electricity. I thought we could – but it's too far off the main line. It would cost – and a new roof? All we'd be working for, for the next twenty years –"

"Your own mother bore ye in a house with no electric light!"

"Don't we all want something better? Or maybe not. Ye promised Maureen the electricity years back. Ye promised her a cement floor and isn't she still walking in the mud in her own kitchen?"

Michael shook his head. "This has nothing to do with – Eileen, she wasn't ashamed of your lack of brass when she married ye! Was she thinking about all the land maybe? Selling it off? She knew what she was getting herself into! Ye let the women lord over ye! Ye always have. First your mother, then... So she doesn't have the hot water coming like magic out of a pipe! She married ye! She'll have to live where *you* decide, castle or ditch!"

"A ditch like ye keep Maureen in, then? That ditch ye call a house!" Colm exploded, his face bloating with years of anger. "Ditch, never mind. The only places now with dirt floors, they're barns ain't they? Sties. Keeping my sister no better than you keep your cows. That'll be the day she lets ye near the bed again – have another sickly brat of –"

Michael lunged at Colm, but the table was in the way, and two of his young drinking friends grabbed his arms. Paddy shook his head, played his fingers on the rim of the glass.

"...one to talk!" Colm shouted. "She don't like ye drinking your face off. Ye do it anyway and tell yourself it means you're the boss and she's not bossing ye. You're here at the pub all day every day because you're afraid to go home, and it's your own fault for being a jackass, not her fault for knowing it!"

Michael broke free and yanked the table up, throwing beer and glasses into their faces, knocking James to the ground. Colm got up and hit Michael in the jaw with all the ham-heavy weight of his body. Michael's neck snapped back as he fell, droplets of saliva spraying out in the bar's incandescent light.

"That was for *you*, m'dear Paddy," Colm said, massaging his knuckles.

"Come on, Colm. That's enough," Paddy said, getting up. "James? Ye all right?" Paddy put out a hand to help him up, but James refused it.

The four walked in silence. James could see Colm's fat, satisfied grin even by the light of the moon, but that soon faded. The silence became heavier with hidden words, other men's opinions hanging in the air. Colm and John left them to go home. James walked a little behind Paddy.

"Some men don't understand about marriage – there's no bossing people, women, around. Shouldn't be. He was only throwing words at me. Words don't hurt."

That's wrong, James thought. *You're* wrong. He wanted Paddy to have hit Michael, to have proven himself stronger, proven himself right. Let the women lord over you. Did everyone else love Paddy too much to tell him what seemed to be the truth?

James could feel his mother's hands on his back, steering him up to bed and through the rosary. They were clammy, hot. Were Eileen's the same way? Lila's? Grabbing, clinging, making Paddy leave him, changing the whole idea of his granny's house and the farm? James thought of himself alone in the house with the two mothers fighting over him. He would never be like Paddy. He swore it.

"Found a ride to Clon' so I can get there in time to go to Mass with Eileen. Granny's making breakfast early so we can all have a goodbye."

James smelled bacon in the morning, heard voices, didn't go down to breakfast even when his mother called him, even when Paddy rapped on the door.

He didn't see Paddy again before he left for St. Paul's School in Cork, cursed the window-glint of Paddy's adopted house as the bus drove through Clonakilty.

"In THE FIRST PARADISE
THAT LIES BEHIND THE MEMORY OF THE WORLD
THERE WAS NO CRUELTY..."

– H. W.

ST. PAUL'S School was a square of grey stone and blood brick walls, gravel courtyards and a thick-grassed playing field. The east side edged on a street of middle-class townhouses and a corner grocer's, a street that led down to the centre of Cork City. The north edge of the school grounds ran along College Road near University College and the west edge jutted into an area of mansions. St. Mary's, the girls' convent school, was further south, up the hill. Each school was rich enough to have its own large chapel, each sex entirely cloistered, ignorant, supposedly safe.

St. Paul's was devoted to tradition, the walls serving to keep boys in but also to keep foreign ideas out, even when these new and dangerous ideas came from the Pope himself. The trend to move chapel sanctuaries to central positions of the church so the priest could face, and better include, the congregation, was ignored; the sanctuary stayed firmly at the far eastern end of the cruciform chapel. The boys' showers remained without hot water. On Fridays, fish was served with potatoes and cabbage, not potatoes and carrots, not potatoes and peas.

A private "public" school, it was built after the turn of the twentieth century by the country's few wealthy Catholic families, donations from America, and church money. There was room for seventy boarders, one hundred odd day boys, and five year-round orphan boys, these charity positions ensured with specific instructions that accompanied an anonymous endowment. The school couldn't claim historic venerability, so the first Jesuit headmaster, Father Townley, saw to a great planting of ivy, Chinese wisteria, roses and Virginia creeper around every public facing wall and building, twentieth century brick gradually growing woolly with the green-bearded foliage of respectability.

In the nineteen twenties, having discovered a passion for fruit and for bending the limbs of trees (as well as boys) to his will, Father Townley brought a small pear cutting from his long-dead parents' home in Cornwall, and planted it beside the still-barren inner wall of the courtyard, training the growing branches along the brick with wire. It thrived for the next two years, partly because of his promise of a fate worse than death for any boy who so much as spat near it. Every year thereafter, Father Townley bought more and more saplings: fig, peach, nectarine, quince, Hedelfingen cherry, European and Manchurian apricot, Golden Russet apple, Japanese, European and Fellenberg plum – and pears. He fell in love with pears, their lush, shapely blonde fruit. "My Ladies," he called them, the fruit of medieval lasciviousness, the fruit believed to mimic the shape of the female body: Bosc, Beurre d'Anjou, Williams' Bon Chretien, Flemish Beauty. He studied the art of espalier, slanting his pears and quinces up the walls in straight cordons, bending his apples, plums, cherries, apricots, nectarines and peaches into wondrous fans and lattices against the brick, letting his fig trees grow wild in the corners, and still running the school with an impeccable authority twisted now and then with bright twigs of humour.

Picked by the masters and the orphan boys, Townley's amply rewarded "Fruit Slaves," the Townley fruit graced the tables of the masters every summer, was baked into pies, preserved in Kilner jars, and a special basket was always carried by Father

Townley himself, in a tiny battered Austin, to the Archbishop of Armagh every August on St. Oswald's day. It was this unceasing devotion with fruit that made one archbishop (no one can remember which) grant Father Townley his only wish: that he should be allowed, upon retirement, to remain at the school to tend his trees. The year Father Townley turned seventy-five, he moved his living quarters from the headmaster's suite to a tiny room overlooking the courtyard. He took a short vacation to England, returned, and waited for a shipment of thirty-five peach, apple and of course, pear trees, his first love, to arrive by ship at Cobh. He planted them all in one day before lying down to rest for two, the first of the young masters coming out to help him at nine in the morning, the second at eleven, and by one in the afternoon, all classes were dismissed, and the masters were along the wall with shovels and chicken wire and dirty hands as the boys played a huge ruleless game of rugby in the field, with ten balls and almost two hundred players.

Father Townley settled into his life of tending trees, concentrating as he never could before on fighting the brute-named fruit diseases which had plagued him for years – hard wicked names of brown rot, leaf curl, black knot, fire blight, crown rot – cutting out diseased wood, then fertilizing the roots with rotted dung from an old wooden wheelbarrow some boys had never seen him without. Remarkably, all but two of the saplings survived and Townley trained them in candelabra shapes, free-form flames, a white and pink heat of blossoms against the red brick. They began bearing bushels of fruit within a few years, more than the masters, the orphan boys, and the Archbishop of Armagh could pick and eat and preserve at the height of the season. After harvesting as much as they could, the masters opened the doors of the school to the poor, who carried away the apples and pears in potato sacks, in their pockets, in their hands. And still, there was more. Father Townley – already eighty-two, wizened to the size of a twelve-year-old boy, which made his nose and ears appear gargantuan – Father Townley, became a fruit vendor. He hired a donkey cart and a man to take himself, boxes of his fruit, and two or three overworked orphan Fruit Slaves, to the Saturday market. From nine in the morning to five in the afternoon, Townley sat beneath an umbrella in his soiled, leaf-smudged, black cassock, watching his boys put pears in the baskets of housewives, squinting and grinning with a mouth containing only one tooth.

He got more and more decrepit as years went by, as boys came and left and the youngest masters aged. Eventually, there was no one at the school who could remember what he had looked like as a man of forty, and his care of the trees began to suffer. He could no longer reach the top branches to prune their wild summer growth. He could no longer distinguish dead and rotting branches from healthy ones. He prowled the grounds of the school with his pruning shears and wheelbarrow, flakes of skin falling from his almost hairless brown-spotted scalp, decaying visibly, moment by moment, an object of terror to the youngest boys.

It was Father Townley who James first met as he entered the gates of the courtyard after walking the three blocks from the bus stop on the main road into Cork City. The old Jesuit had seen him through the wrought iron and waited in ambush for this new one who didn't yet know the rules. He stepped out from behind the wall and seized James by the lapels.

"A fate worse than death," he hissed into James's face, along with the smell of age and the sweet breath of pear juice. These words were thought to be the only ones the old man could remember from the English language.

James screamed, leaped out of the man's feeble grasp, and looked for a way of escape, the gate having swung shut behind him. He saw a tall priest standing at the top of a stairway, a Father Foley from Sligo, at thirty-three, the youngest Jesuit on staff.

"Is that James Young? *Young* James Young who was supposed to arrive on the half-one from Skibbereen? Welcome. And I see ye've already introduced yourself to the most respected resident of the school."

The next afternoon, hidden on the top of the maintenance shed roof, James and his roommates watched as old Father Townley began attacking a Virginia creeper with sailors' curses and a kitchen knife because it was creeping too close to one of his Flemish Beauties. Two of the masters talked the knife out of his hand and gently led him away to the hospital. He died that night, from a brain hemorrhage, three days before his ninety-seventh birthday. There were many people, particularly among his market friends, who believed he died of distress at being separated from his trees. Some said he was older than ninety-seven – a hundred-and-three, and some said he was a saint, that his body wouldn't decay, that within the gleaming mahogany of the coffin wasn't the shrivelling worm of death, but a body growing more beautiful, smelling of apples.

The school would never recover from its first headmaster, neither his life nor his death, and this was made manifest in the homage paid to his trees. Over the previous fifty years, every master starting at St. Paul's had been taught the rule of the trees. No one was allowed to touch them. No one was allowed to let a hurling ball knock against them or tamper with the wire that trained them against the walls. The masters all came to think of the trees as their ladies, the lost and precious things which represented everything they had renounced upon taking vows of chastity, on separating themselves from worldly feminine beauty. As they heard Townley himself threaten boys, so they also threatened them with the fate worse than death, a punishment no one had yet given or explained, a punishment forever lost in Townley's mind.

On the afternoon of the funeral, meant for mourning, James climbed the ladder of Townley's first pear tree, the almost sacred Flemish Beauty, the first lady, grown thick and doddering on the wall opposite the main gate. The masters were in their common room, a dark box of wood and shelves and books and the heavy knocking of an old wall clock. They were observing solemn silence together. Father Foley, always the restless one, looked out the window and screamed. It was a Celtic war cry he'd acquired genetically through long lines of pure Hibernian blood. Its shattering power nearly caused several more fatalities, shocking the hearts of the older Jesuits who were so startled out of solemn silence, they screamed, too. The masters charged into the courtyard, throwing outraged fists at James, who lost his balance and fell, grappling for handholds, bringing one core-rotten branch to the ground with him.

James lay at the bottom of a black well of cassocks, silenced by shock and the pain of a broken arm. The masters were at a loss. This was a new boy who obviously hadn't been taught the rules, not with everyone preoccupied with the death and the funeral. There had been minor incidents before, with broken branches, but no one had ever been caught, and no one had dared touch the first lady. Certainly, no one had ever encountered the Fate Worse Than Death. If James wasn't made an example of, given something far worse than an ordinary beating, the threat would be seen as hollow, and boys would climb the trees constantly, destroying them. And if the masters did happen to think up a fate worse than death, how could they explain it to the parents? Meting out a fate worse than death was politically impossible. And how could they strap a boy who was already badly injured? Those ignorant of God's Law are without guilt. Hadn't he already given himself punishment enough?

The older ones walked away to counsel together, clicking their tongues, aghast, musing on how fortunate it was that Townley himself hadn't lived to see this day. Father Foley took James to the hospital in the headmaster's Austin, observing the boy with quiet pity, wondering about his fate. The boys who had seen his fall wondered too, and word of his daring escapade spread through their ranks until even the oldest knew his name, whispered about him with gasps and shaking heads. James, like many condemned criminals, rose to the stature of a folk hero, and he did it *in absentia,* in less than an hour.

After the plaster had set, Father Foley brought James directly to the dark cherrywood common room. The masters had made a decision. The more reasonable brothers had prevailed over the more traditional, who favoured sound beatings for every infraction and demanded James receive double strokes. Headmaster Father Dunnigan put a cold hand on his shoulder.

"I don't think...you realize...what you have done," he said, halting his hollow tomb of a voice after every phrase. "So I shall tell you."

For the next ten minutes, he expounded upon James's hideous crime, and upon the mystery of the punishment no one had ever been evil enough to deserve – until now. Dunnigan stopped once he thought the desired level of terror had been attained by his small subject. James had turned white, making his freckles stand out like fallen autumn leaves on fine white sand.

"But this...the day the honourable Father Townley was laid to rest...happens to be the only day upon which infractions are required to be forgiven... It is what he wanted," Dunnigan said, clenching his hands behind him – almost crossing his fingers – during this one little lie. "If you want forgiveness...you may have it... Do you?"

James nodded: a kind of quiver.

They released him into the hallway and he made his way back to his room, painkillers still fuzzing his brain, silent to the stares of the other boys. He lay on his bed, face to the wall, cradling his plaster cast with his good arm while his roommates stood in an awed little coven outside the door.

"They broke his arm. *Jasus*. He broke a branch so they broke his arm."

The horrified whisper rumoured its way around the whole school, then around Cork City itself, producing a rash of obedience in the boys, and a rash of phone calls from the parents.

An eye for an eye, a tooth for a tooth, and a limb for a limb.

James began life at St. Paul's a hero, and his arm, a martyr. He couldn't resist embellishing, telling stories of a tiny room beneath the masters' wing, a candlelit sub-basement under the cold fruit storeroom. All he claimed to remember before he passed out was the sight of an anvil and Headmaster Father Dunnigan with a black hood and a huge iron hammer.

After prayers and a fifteen-minute breakfast, the boys attended classes from eight until three, when the town boys left for home. Dinner for the boarders was served at half-five (always with bottled fruit for dessert), and study was from half-seven to nine, when the lights went out. James sometimes traded fruitcake for an hour of listening to his wealthier roommate's radio: Radio Luxembourg in the night under the covers, a thin wire running to his ear, his head bobbing to the Beatles. There was a vigorous black market in sweets and cigarettes during the week because boarders were not allowed to leave the school grounds except on Saturday afternoons, and the town boys were glad to give service for a price. The school work was more difficult than it had been in the country, and he was glad of it, glad of the big library that permitted only thin stabs of loneliness if he paused too long between the lines of the books. The boarders spent the time between classes and dinner in the playing field, on games of hurling and rugby, or on getting into trouble climbing through the ivy to perch on top of the walls and watch the rest of the world go by.

"What the hell is that noise?" was the statement he'd woken to on the first night he was sleeping well, the little room still dark, his roommates still semi-alien beings.

"It's Young. He snores, sometimes, like a fucking demon."

The light flashed on, and he saw his three roommates, one standing in pale blue pajamas with his hand on the light switch, the others sitting up in bed.

"Snarls and roars and gurgles and never the same thing twice.

How'd ye get a nose like that anyway? More commando raids on the trees?"

James grinned. His face had healed from Dermot's beating, but he was left with the crooked nose of a fighting boy, its bridge flattened, the whole of it bent slightly to one side.

"Hurling," he said – or rather, *hurlin'*, in his best County-Cork accent, still feeling surrounded, alien, expecting the boys to be like boys in Killaghmore, expecting to be treated like the bastard of a fallen woman.

"Ah, hurling!"

"I got some scars meself."

"Think fast!" said the boy in the opposite bunk before hitting him with a pillow. "Ye think ye can shut it down for a bit?"

"Who can fucking sleep anyway? Ye heard the one about the two nuns and the priest?"

"Ye got that one from me, Douglas! That's me brother's joke, ye thief."

James watched their tired, homesick faces split into hilarity, faces that asked him to laugh, too.

"Your brother's got enough jokes to go around. Pretty boy here – his brother's to be a doc – those girlie pictures he gets from medical school in London – fuck."

"Better'n you, eh?"

"*My* da's a fuckin' General!"

"Fuckin' Second Lieutenant!"

"Shit, Mick here won't even tell us which jail his da' –"

"Hey, Young, what's your da'?"

James had been about to let his Cork County accent slip, the boys' eyes so open and sleepy, looking more like five-year-olds in their pajamas than rough gawky creatures about to crash into puberty.

"He's got land, near Clon'. Protestant landlord run off after the revolution. Me granda' bought it for a song."

He closed his eyes, crushed his father down, down, past his rib cage – the piece of his heart that had been torn out and couldn't be sewn back. He opened his eyes, filled them with what was here, what was now: three other smiling boys just as alone and homesick as he was, put his hand over his heart under the blankets.

For a year it was like this – school and more school, brown paper packages of Granny's tea brack coming in the mail, and shared out along with the cakes and biscuits the other boys got, a couple of weekends at Paddy and Eileen's house in Clonakilty, (James had forgiven him), Christmas and Easter at home, Granny and his mother fighting over him, the house oppressive with the uneasy partnership of the two women bored and irritated by each other, one washing while the other dried, one pulling James up to Mass, the other tugging him down to the beach or up into the hills, both sure he was getting too thin and overfeeding him, skimming the last swirls of cream off the milk to pour over his apple tart, vying with each other making the thickest custards, the richest Christmas cakes. His mother got her hair cut in town, shoulder-length and somehow curvy around her face, a swag of it falling sultrily over her glass eye, a style he saw on the back of one of Eileen's women's magazines: a woman with an impossibly tiny waist and wide skirt, hoovering an oriental carpet in high heels. "She's still a young woman," Paddy said, a warning tone in his voice, but refusing to elaborate. "Sure, don't listen to me. I might not know what I'm talking about." The first time she walked up the hill after her haircut, the crow had apparently flown down to meet her, then wheeled up into the air, cawing and screaming, not recognizing her at all. Bernadette still had her times of silence, times of shutting herself away in her room, making Granny almost crazy with the silence, making her exclaim, "Jesus, Mary and Joseph. I can't stand it. Do ye want to walk, boy?"

An intelligent, gentle, bookish boy, James was never bullied at school, mostly because of his heroic status in breaking his arm spectacularly, partly because his roommate Douglas was the main bully of his year, and partly because he was the fastest sprinter on the playing field. The older boys grinned and winked at him, called him Lady-Killer, told him which brothers to avoid like the devil himself. James was friends first with Aidan, who showed him the best moves on the hurling field, then with Douglas, when Mick went through a moody period after Christmas, and then it seemed they were all best friends with each other.

Just as James had gotten used to seeing less of Paddy, he began to see more of him. By spring, Lila, now past the new-born's greedy obsession with mother's milk, could toddle along holding one of James's fingers, could play a little on her own. Now and then, when the bus from Cork City stopped at Clonakilty, Paddy got on and sat beside James, saying, "Let's go home," and he would be sleeping in his old room as usual, bickering at the table with his mother, a newspaper and the remains of a greasy fry on a plate beside him. That summer, the first of identical summers for years to come, Paddy hired a boy from the agricultural college to help Finn out at the store and he and Eileen and Lila camped for all of July and August in Colm's old house, Eileen draping wet laundry over the prickly hedges, Lila stumbling after butterflies in the meadow, wearing a little bonnet because she was still even balder than Colm, had only a little peach fuzz to keep her warm.

James adored her, found a multitude of excuses to leave whatever job he was supposed to be doing – mucking out, whitewashing – to walk up the hill and lift her onto his shoulders and walk off again, Eileen rushing out of the house to hurl an extra nappy over his arm. The two of them would go off for miles looking for birds and nests, lambs and calves and kittens, going down to the sea to collect pebbles and throw sand, or off to the houses and barns to find her adored daddy, to let Susan or his mother feed her up on creamy milk, toast and marmalade and ginger biscuits. Sharing her with the others, Susan's and Agnes's daughters, too, was part of the pleasure: seeing her loved as she deserved, being the most darling baby in the hills. The only thing he wouldn't allow was Poor Snipey, Colm's favourite game to play with his own children. "Poor snipey, poor snipey," Colm would croon as he smoothed the hands of his little Brenda that were held together in prayer, pointing outward. "Poor snipey, poor snipey," then "Cock your tail up there snipey!" and Colm would slap her hands quickly if she hadn't jerked them away in time. James absolutely forbade this game with Lila, as it was inconceivable to him that she, that her fat little hands, should be hurt even in fun, inconceivable that anyone could ever want to hurt her.

The next year, that year of turning fourteen, the empty cavities of the school breathed with the uncertainty of disinfectant, waxed wood, and new, spilling hormones. On the surface were cold showers, uniforms, games of hurling and soccer, respectful greeting of the Jesuit masters, studies in the day and evening, prayers before breakfast and dinner and tea, and model altar boys fasting before Mass. Letters came from home. Boys recited paragraphs of Latin, Gaelic, Shakespeare, copied geometry assignments, stayed up whispering too late in the dark dormitories, smoked illegal cigarettes, shared little bottles of whiskey and *poitín* stolen from home, suffered the horror of wet dreams between foreign, monkish sheets, tried to wipe up the slimy wet with white handkerchiefs, endured their crusty pajama crotches until the weekly wash. It was all as it should have been, except for the advance of their illicit sexuality. The prudishness of their masters and parents forced shame and embarrassment on them, the sniggering evil of the female body, the irresistibility of breaking the rules.

James was surprised when he found himself wishing for the presence of girls, focusing on those body parts that lay teasingly, dangerously, under their clothes. How dangerous it was could only be imagined because even *talking* to a girl was a sin, and if the masters caught a boy, he might be expelled.

What must happen when one was *alone* with a girl?

Everything.

He knew what had to happen by the uncontrollable rearing of his ginger-nested adolescent penis – the horrific disappearance of mind and reason and clothing, the blackest sin of fornication expected and inevitable and impossible to stop.

The masters obsessed about hell and damnation, and "hygienic" practices. Once, during a class, Headmaster Father Dunnigan fixed each boy with a sepulchral eye and said in his subterranean voice, "If thy hand offend thee...cut it off." At the sound of the giggles the boys were unable to suppress, Dunnigan became flustered and batted through the pages of his Bible. "Saint Mark, chapter 9, verse 43. 'If thy hand offend thee, cut it off! It is better for thee to enter into life *maimed*...'" he shouted, his deep voice rising, frenzied, "'than having two hands to go into hell...into the fire that shall never be quenched: where the worm dieth not, and the fire *is not quenched*.'"

All mirth was extinguished. The boys were left crisp, brittle, their faces burning.

On the first warm day of spring, he and his friends climbed onto the high outer wall of the schoolyard and inched their buttocks along to a very particular location, a space a little bigger than the back of a plough horse, where they would be shielded from priestly eyes by the roof of the maintenance shed. They kicked their heels against the wall and the dead ivy that still clung there like dry shattered bits of centipede, and watched the day students from the girls' school pass. They sat there whenever there was time, whenever they could be sure of not getting caught, all in a row like birds on a branch, magpies cackling, competing with each other for the smoothest part of the perch, the first place in the pecking order, the first sights and rewards, baby birds, not quite malevolent enough for anything more than petty beastliness and harassment, not even worth a bullet.

James had begun their mischief the year before with the seagull cry none of the other boys could imitate, bird calls the only truly loud noises they could produce that would go unnoticed by the masters. Unless the girl they intended to tease was immediately beneath them, she might not even look up because the gull or the crow or the magpie sound was so familiar. Once, they caught sight of old half-blind Father O'Loan coming back from a doctor's appointment and they all scrambled to kick their legs back over onto their own side of the wall, then hung there on the edge, on their bellies and elbows, waiting, half hiding, strangling, as usual, on their giggles. Without thinking, James burst out with an angry *MoooOOah*, like one of Paddy's usually complacent cows outraged by the touch of icy hands on her teats. Father O'Loan stopped, looked behind him, looked up and down the wealthy residential street, baffled by the apparent presence of a Holstein.

A group of three girls turned the corner and began to walk down the other side of the street. Two were still twelve-year-old stick figures, but one was not.

"There. That one. Like to see her in her nip," Aidan said.

"Oh, yeah." Mick was clutching the wall edge with broken fingernails, his voice cracking with repressed lust. A fifteen-year-old among a group of boys about to turn fourteen, he was the one who drew soldiers with their legs blown off, battle scenes, bombings and decapitations. His eyes were dark-rimmed and he regularly shaved his few black whiskers, the sparse stubble looking like a crop of blackheads. There was a red lump on his prickly scalp where he'd popped a gloriously explosive and satisfying pustule.

"Ah, but look at her," Douglas said, knowing it all, the ringleader of the clan, a huge boy for his age with a little paunchy roll of fat bulging above his belt. He was the class clown, who'd been through more boarding schools than he could correctly remember because of an army father, a rich mother, an insatiable desire to step over boundaries, and what could only be described as cheerful, deliberate stupidity when it came to thinking about what might be for his own good. He was for immediate gratification. It was he who told the most filthy jokes, who got more than his fair share of detentions, and more than his share of Granny's tea brack. He had a habit of keeping one hand in his pocket, cradling the hairy bread-doughiness of his scrotum during morning Mass, Latin, Mathematics, and Composition. "She's not the kind, the way she walks all tight with her books squashing her titties. Ye know bollix about how to tell the hot ones."

"Fuck off," Mick said. "I know as much as *you* do, ye wanker."

"Go get her then." Douglas grabbed Mick's arm, jerked it toward the street, a fall of more than two meters, and Mick clawed back at him.

"Easy, boy! Hey!" Douglas shouted. "If ye make me fall off, ye'll have to pay for me breaking the pavement."

"You're a fat enough bastard, ye –"

"Fat?" Douglas exclaimed. "Them's muscles see –"

"If she's not the kind, she'll become the kind when I'm finished with 'er. They're all sluts," Aidan asserted, in his detached, medical manner. He was the rich boy, the blessed one, blond, childish and angelic-looking, cynical and racist. His father had taught him a passion for sports, horses, and women. His older brother, in medical school, sent him a regular supply of magazines that contained drawings of the female anatomy, the most important swatches blacked out by rectangles, pictures that frustrated as much as they tantalized. Once, half of a battered copy of a *Health and Efficiency* magazine arrived, which perplexed them all even more, containing pictures of women doing archery, playing tennis, and grocery shopping in the nude, and Swedish blondes who wore socks and plimsole shoes as they built a snowman. There were naked men, fat women, middle-aged women, women of varying beauty with varying breast sizes, but the problem was, all of them had their private parts neatly airbrushed away, giving them a plastic, doll-like quality. Aidan supplemented his already sizable allowance by charging fifty pence a glance, a price that remained firm even with his best friends. "Sluts. They want it worse than we do."

James grinned and jabbed Douglas with his elbow to make sure they knew he was with them all the way: in reality, he was completely confused. Listening to his friends, he felt as if he had never had any idea what women were really like, and yet impacted in his back teeth were still a few lumps of Granny's ginger biscuits – sweet discs of chewy, tangy love – and he was now in the embrace of a wool sweater that his English grandmother knitted him for Christmas two years ago, and that he had finally grown big enough to wear. Old women weren't the same as girls, this was true, but he had never stopped cradling his sister in his mind. Sometimes a woman walked past with a young child in a pram, and he watched them, secretly, almost as much as he watched the girls.

And then of course, there was his mother. He felt so sorry for her the first time he had left her for school. Every time he left her again after a visit he felt guilty because she cried. The worst thing was what he was learning at St. Paul's that wasn't being taught in the classroom. The girls who let a boy have his way were sluts. The girls who had a child without being married were ruined. Once, he'd ventured to ask her why she and his father didn't get married later, after he was born, and his mother told him that by that time they hadn't wanted to marry each other any more. Was that what it was to be a slut? What his mother, and of course his father, had done, had made him a bastard, but his conception had ruined his mother. And he couldn't deny that she was ruined. His mother the spirited, cursing, dancing, whirlwind was no more. How could he manage to snigger with the right amount of glee at the way a girl's breasts moved when his mother, by his friends' standards, was the worst slut there could be? But she *wasn't*. She was so religious now, was so... How could he not feel guilty when his very existence had ruined his mother's life? He couldn't turn time back, couldn't undo what his parents had done any more than he could change his own actions once he'd made them, once they were shuffled back into the realm of reality that was memory, the past that didn't exist except in his own mind. How could he possibly atone? It seemed that he had been the only thing that came out of her ruin, the only survivor of a terrible train crash. Surviving made him feel as if he had stolen something that shouldn't have belonged to him, and stolen it from his own mother. He had come out of the crash, and she was looking to him to make some good out of it all. He had a responsibility to her, but he didn't want it, shoved the burden of it away whenever he could. He was too young, too submersed in a Catholic childhood in a Catholic country, to be capable of blaming the church for making up the rules that condemned his mother to ruin and himself to bastardy. There were simply no other rules to go by. They seemed not the arbitrary rulings of a system, but immutable laws of nature and human nature, as fundamental as a pencil dropping from his desk to the floor.

The girl they were watching was pretty, curvy. He couldn't help but feel the tugs of his nerve endings, and unconsciously put his hand in his pocket, only to find a crumpled letter from his mother between his hand and his genitals. He was beginning to hate her letters, so full of Biblical quotations and hints at how lonely she was without him, as if his going away was some sort of deliberate act on his part. "Dear James, Dearest James, Darling James...forgot my cod-liver oil and dreamed of whales, if you can believe it...praying the novena to Our Lady of Lourdes...praying for your vocation...and how are your bowels?...been to the holy well twice this week...if you hadn't been so busy with Granny the last time...you go away, and know so much, and get so smart, and then you'll think I'm stupid...you must set the example for the other boys, James, lead them to God." He read his mother's letters and desperately left them places he hoped he'd lose them, stuffed them in his drawers, in his pockets where they disintegrated in the laundry, but could never deliberately throw them away. Sometimes pressed leaves or late-flowering roses fell out of the envelopes, tokens that embarrassed him. And what of his supposed vocation?

His mind was sometimes just a turmoil of fears and confusion. He was slowly learning about the alien world, the alien species he had been born into. How could Hitler have extinguished the lives of so many people, if he was really a man with a heart, with a soul? And then there was the Bomb. He couldn't get over the Bomb, remembered the horror he had felt when he first heard his father say that humanity could blow up the entire world, his first childish image of it staying with him even after he had learned the specifics of fission and fusion: the globe cracking open suddenly and bursting itself to smithereens, the fireball hanging in outer space. The reality was far more terrible: multiple mushroom clouds, melted oriental faces, atomized, vanished, men and women, cancer bubbling up for decades afterward. He could not fathom the travesties committed by adults in the same world they brought their children into – and this after the Irish Famine, history teaching no one any lessons. His mind rejected it. He tried to read book after book, but he couldn't seem to assimilate the information, wanted to reject the human race altogether because Father Foley said that those who commit all these crimes are completely human, no matter how much we would like to think of them as animals, monsters; "What animal murders his fellows at the rate we do? Where does such evil come from? I could say the human heart. I could say the devil and be right both times, if perhaps a little simplistic. I could say desire, lust, hatred, pride, list all the seven deadlies. I think of Hitler and that's how I know that all of us are born into sin and need Christ's redemption." James couldn't voice the fear that this produced in him, that every human being was another Hitler waiting to happen. That he, himself was. He clung to his confessions, clung to the idea of the Redeemer.

For the last few months terrible thoughts had been coming into his mind, coming between him and God; what if everything was a figment of his imagination, that there was no ocean, no land, no stars, no other people, but that everything was an invention of his own head, his life something that he watched as if it was on a television screen? He searched out Father Foley in this time of crisis, and the good father tried not to smile as he mused that James was a little young to be a full-fledged solipsist, but that he would search out a few good books for him; it had become apparent to the priests, if not the other boys, that James liked his books.

The girl with the books walked around the corner as the other boys jeered, asked her what colour her knickers were, shouting only possible because of the loud game of hurling going on in the playing field nearby.

"Shut up, ye eejits!" James hit Mick in the arm, nervous, having to make some contribution, his Cork-County accent now automatic. A few more girls came into view. "Her. Look it. The one in the middle."

"Oh, tits," Douglas breathed, scowling, and put his right hand back in his pants pocket.

Aidan superimposed what he remembered from his brother's medical magazines over the girl's clothes. "Oh for x-ray superman eyes," he said. He wanted to be a doctor, too.

Breasts were their main area of interest because the sexual organs were still too mysterious to become the chief spur of imagination. When they saw a girl, the first thing they looked at was the form of jumpers and jackets, trying to determine size, enjoying the bounce, imagining a feel. Only after this did they notice bottoms, legs, hips, hair, faces.

The girl James had pointed out was an excellent example of what they liked. Mick let his mouth open slowly. She was sixteen or seventeen, and abundantly curved. Though her school jumper must have fit her at one time, it was tight on her now, especially with her way of pulling her shoulders back. She stopped to look through her satchel, the other girls in uniform walking past. She checked to make sure the street was empty before hitching up her skirt to expose her thighs, unbuttoning her shirt as far as her jumper would allow, and tying her blue striped tie around her head. She was just as they imagined the Beatlemania girls might be, girls supposedly tearing at their clothes, girls screaming to have John or Paul's babies. The size of breasts, they believed, was directly related to sexual availability and enthusiasm; the bigger the tit, the better the ride.

"Now *there*, Mick," Douglas breathed, "is a hot one, I'm telling ye. Come one, come all. Ye go down there, ye'd get your hole, or a feel, at least. Go on."

Mick put his palms on the wall. "And get sent down." He wasn't going anywhere. He was afraid of his father, even though his father was in jail.

"Go on," Aidan said. "Steal a feel."

"You don't care about getting sent down," James said. "All yer talk o' quittin' and doing some real work for the country? Join the Volunteers?"

"Go on. She's wetting herself for ye. Go on," Douglas said, and laughed so loudly, the girl scowled at them and turned her back.

There was a thump. The boys looked down and saw James, far below, squatting behind the large, stepped buttress which jutted halfway into the sidewalk and prevented the hillside of earth and the stone wall that held it from crashing down into the street. The girl was intent on watching the cars that came up the street, and James darted up, snatched the tie from around her head, and was flying up the first step of the buttress before she began to give chase. Douglas reached down to jerk him up the final leap to the top of the wall. James twisted himself, sat, and put the tie around his neck; if he couldn't figure out what to say, he could at least do something.

"Give it back, ye little bastard," the girl demanded, hands on hips, directly beneath them. They stared down her open neckline into the dark place where her breasts met, creamy skin rubbing against skin. They hardly heard her screaming.

"I'll go to the priests! I'll go to your masters!"

"I didn't do anything wrong, did I?" James asked his friends. "I didn't say a single word to her."

They laughed and watched her furious flesh until a car stopped on the opposite side of the street and a thick-armed young man got out.

"What the hell –" he started to say, but the boys were already leaping to the ground, safe on their side of the wall.

"That's Donal Kelly, Frank's brother," Mick said, breathless as they ran into the boarder's wing, and into James's room. They slammed the door after them, then collapsed in helpless laughter. James held up the tie, victorious.

"The *winnah* of the blue and gold striped pennant," he cried, in what he called his Fucking Queen of England accent. "The Right Honourable Seamus Wilberforce Young."

The boys cheered; James did the silly voices, the impressions of the masters, whispered the funniest backtalk in the classroom, the masters whirling only to find the laughter swiftly doused, innocent faces everywhere. He was good at the deadpan, saying exactly the opposite of what he meant without a hint of sarcasm in his voice. He was the one with the mania for climbing the walls, for spying, who always had his eyes open, who could ferret out the most titillating bits of gossip – or tell the most interesting lies. He was red-haired, freckled, broken-nosed, skinny with long, speedy limbs, a conceited know-it-all with British pretensions, the one who had defiled the first lady, the one most generous with his tins of cake.

"Frank has been going on about that one, that girl," James said. "She's doing her leaving cert. She's eighteen. He told me. She's not allowed to go running around with anybody, but Donal, well...he's got her running anyway."

"The little whore!" Aidan said, delighted.

"Frank's been practicing kissing her on his arm," James said, as if releasing information he'd been saving. "Pushing his tongue into his fist. He was looking into the mirror in the jacks. Didn't know I was there."

"He was –" Douglas laughed, overcome. "Good on ye, Young. I'll mention it to him tonight, an' we'll see what he has to say for himself."

"Your middle name *can't* be Wilberforce," Aidan sneered.

The next morning, James was wearing a slightly narrower tie to class, a tie of the same colours but smaller stripes. The masters didn't notice, but it caused a sensation among the boys, a prickling of whispers and envy. James could only have excited more admiration if he had hung a brassiere from his belt. Soon, there were a few more boys with narrower ties, regarded as marks of manhood – the symbol of taking something else from a girl. The masters began to hear reports of missing articles of clothing from St. Mary's School for Girls.

James marked the passing of time by the change he could see in Granny. Except for weekends here and there, he would be gone, in school, for October and November, back for the Christmas holiday, gone again until Easter, then gone until summer, which he spent milking, haying, and fishing with Paddy, and going to the pub now and then. As he got taller, she got smaller. Her hair was becoming as thin as thistledown, her pink, spotted scalp looking cold and stony beneath. Her back was bending more and more, curling her head further down toward her breastbone, the pain of it destroying any inclination she might have had to good will. She was going deaf. She screamed her orders. Everything, including the radio, the presence of others, and the omnipresent rain, irritated her into tirades of swearing. What got to her the most was Bernadette feeding the birds, tossing Indian corn on the front step. Bernadette had taken over Paddy's role of caring for injured wild things, and James had hammered the bottom out of an old crate and stretched some wire mesh over the top and bottom for her to house her unlucky swallows. There seemed to be a constant supply of them, foundlings sitting unhappily behind the wire among her bedroom icons, shitting on Paddy's old newspapers, looking out the window; Granny complained that if she hadn't been attracting them to the house with the corn, they never would have flown into the windows in the first place. "Ach! She's going to feed the rats again!" Granny would shout whenever Bernadette carried a can of corn from the barn. When she couldn't bear being cooped up in the house any more, she'd disappear for hours, and when she came back, dip into her little bottle of *poitín* and stare out the window, field glasses in her lap.

The year James turned sixteen, his birthday fell on Good Friday, the day after he arrived home for Easter. On

Saturday, Murphy, the farmer down the hill, pounded on the door.

Bernadette was on her knees, washing the slate flagstones of the kitchen floor in the only long-sleeved dress she brought from England, once sky blue, now faded to powder blue, its cuffs worn through and fraying where they folded back. She stood up, her face glowing bright, ashamed, as the widower-man opened the door; he had been up to the house a few times since his wife died, to take tea and look at Bernadette. He was almost fifteen years older than she was, barely taller, and always wore a handkerchief with knots tied in all four corners over his scalp. She only ever stood with her arms folded in his presence, the small of her back against the kitchen counter, as Granny grimly encouraged him to eat more and more fruitcake while refusing to help him converse stumblingly about the weather.

"Best keep your eye on the old woman. She's out in Castle Field, waving a gun around. Better go get her before the Guards beat ye to it."

James ran to get Colm. They walked down past the church and saw her on the cliff, a silhouette against the sea, heard the crack of a pistol. As they came closer, they saw that she was shooting into the waves with an old sidearm. At the sound of every shot, St. Patrick hunched his shoulders and cowered nearer to the ground at the feet of his mistress.

"That was where we used to get the boxes in, Paddy," she said to Colm. "Right there on the rocks, and brought them up by pulleys. See? There's the iron still in the stone!"

There was indeed a system of old pulleys, orange with rust, jammed into a crevice on the edge of the cliff.

"Boxes of what?" James said.

"Guns! What do ye think? Grenades! Me father was the only man who knew this coast, knew the secret of the little harbour down there. Most people think that once you're in it, there's no place to go but back out to sea. T'was the old Protestant landlord used to haul up things he shouldn't. A smuggler, he was. This was the only place the Black and Tans never knew about for miles!"

"A nice little pistol, ye got, Mam," Colm said. "Let me have a look."

Granny passed him the rusty gun and the three walked back from the cliff, Granny pointing out the virtues of the particular kind of pistol it was, jabbing her withered finger at every part. Colm walked them home, but stopped at the door.

"You're not coming in for a cup of tea?" Granny said, offended.

"This is Dad's old gun, isn't it?"

"Of course!"

"I'm taking it home with me, for safekeeping."

"Sure, but it's safe enough in me own hands, Paddy! He wants me to practice. What's your dad going to think when he finds out? And him promising it to Owen, not *you*!"

But Colm was already walking, scattering chickens, shaking his head, knowing there was no point in telling her the men she spoke of had been dead for years; she would forget the novel information a minute later.

"I know what you're up to! But it won't work!" Granny screamed after him, the cords of her neck stretched tight. "There's more where that came from!"

Colm turned. He smiled. "Is that a fact?"

Granny laughed, ducked into the house, slammed the door, and watched her son through the window, wringing her hands. "He'll hurt himself with that bleeding thing. Never was a fighter, my Paddy. Like his granda'. T'was the rest of us – up to the rest of us to protect the peaceful ones."

"Granny?" James put his hand beneath her arm to lead her away from the window, from her agitation. He was a full head-and-a-half taller than she was now, and for every one of her age-spots, he bore fifteen freckles on his face, darkened and multiplied by a sunny spring in the playing field, and a few Saturdays pruning fruit trees. "Look at what I borrowed for you from the library in Cork City." He helped Granny sit in front of the big hardcover book on the table. "Can your read the title?"

She stared uncomprehendingly at the book. For the first couple of years he tried to teach her, she seemed to make progress. James would turn the pages, point to a sentence that he knew she could read, and wait for the meaning to burst out of her; "simple-minded!" she used to say, "I'm not a bleeding child!" Her favourite part of it all seemed to be yelling about the words that frustrated her the most: "Ye can't go having letters that change the way they sound for just no reason a'tall! *Jesus, Mary and Joseph.* How do they expect a person to learn it if they keep changing the rules? What about this putting a 'g' with an 'h' and making it say nothing or making it sound like 'f' or something else altogether?" The lessons had also become their excuse for spending time together, for keeping Bernadette from dragging him off to the holy well or to Mass: "He can't go, Bernadette. Here he gives me all this work – it confuses the b'Jesus out of me. How am I supposed to do it if he's not here?"

Now, she twisted impatiently in the chair, put her palms on the table, and looked up to see the plate of scraps for the dog still sitting on the counter.

"Lord, nobody's fed the dog. Why the hell didn't ye feed the dog, Bernadette?"

Bernadette pressed her mouth shut because her mother always fed the dog.

Granny got up and crashed open the porch door. "St. Patrick! St. Paaatrick!" she screamed, and St. Patrick skittered up – nearly a doggy heart attack – from his refuge beneath Grania's chair by the window.

"He's here, Granny."

"Eh? Lord save us. Put his food on the floor, then, will ye."

He put the dish on the floor and Patrick gulped it down.

"Come on, then, Granny. This is just your sort of book. Folk medicine. Here. This chapter's about baldness – you think you can cure Uncle Colm? Here, it says boiled mice and rotten worms."

"Agh. Go on, then." She sat beside him.

"You're reading. I'm helping."

"It's too bleeding hard for me. You read it out loud. Me eyes, don't ye know. Bad for me eyes."

"Bad fer me eyes," he repeated, but she had no humour any more. He read to her, but she seemed to have little energy. Every now and then she would exclaim, "Jesus, Mary and Joseph! It's a poultice of boiled onions that's for piles! Not that bleeding mess! Onions and oil and vinegar! Ye'd have them making a bleeding salad up your –"

"Mam!" Bernadette warned.

After she became tired of James's reading, she sat in the chair by the window. James watched her, knowing her hearing was going, her eyes were going, and that her mind was going too.

Bernadette put a hand on his shoulder, and he wondered what she would demand of him: More prayers? The holy well? A walk with her arm ivy-twined around his? An extra trip to Mass? He stood, watching his Granny, willing her to turn around and save him again, get up and bluster toward them, set them to work in opposite ends of the house, take him up Kilmoney Hill so he wouldn't have to trudge after his mother and her holiness.

"Well, what are ye looking at?" Grania said, catching James in the corner of her eye. "Am I a cat or a queen, however the hell it goes? Whoever the hell are ye?"

He stared at her, his eyes slowly blurring. She often got mixed up with the names of her children, but she had never not known him; he had always been too different, too new, too troublesome. He watched her age-spotted hands shake as they held the field glasses.

His mother's hand slid around his shoulder, squeezed.

"I think your hopes are a little high, James," she whispered into his hair. "Old people can't learn as fast. Sometimes they can't at all. You and me – we might have to be helping her a lot more."

He pulled away from her, went out to the barn, and sat on Paddy's milking stool, head in his hands. St. Patrick found him; Bernadette must have let him out. The dog tasted the salt freckles on James's face, then found the one tear that he had allowed to escape: a pink silk lick into the corner of his eye.

Midsummer's Eve was a red snapping heat against James's face, shadows moving cooler across his eyes, fiddle music in his ears like a kind of sharper fire. The darkness was warm as an animal's breath. St. Patrick barked to the other dogs across hills furred black with night.

Murphy sawed away on fiddle, his son on squeezebox, and Sally, one of Agnes's girls, twittered on tin whistle. The music was loud, but got lost in distance – nothing but air between earth and the endless outer space above them – and beneath them, too – ultramarine pricked with stars. Beneath the world under his feet, James felt an eternity of distance.

He had helped pile the trash for the bonfire, the broken crates, oily rags, the cleared brambles and brush. He and John had gone to the pub by themselves for a pint before dark, waiting for the party to get started.

It was the teenage girls with their little sisters and cousins who were first step-dancing, or simply hopping around in the grass, then their mothers danced with each other – even Bernadette in a dress Paddy's Eileen had given her – spinning two and two with Susan or Annie or Agnes, feet moving faster and faster until the stumbling and laughter; Bernadette was full of joy; her own little...grown-up boy was home again, finally, for the summer, and she felt so young, a girl again. The old men and boys ventured to show off later, after a few swigs of *poitín*, kicking their feet high into the thick sparking air. James could see five more fires in the hills, glints in the eye of midnight, flickering with shadows, bodies passing in front of the flames.

Granny was sitting on a kitchen chair, clapping her hands, singing. Granda' Murphy had his teeth out, his nose folding down, almost hooking over his mouth like a beak. Susan's youngest – her eighth – watched all with his little open fish-mouth. All the girls' faces were big-eyed in the shadows, young deer shy among the leaves, the sycamores antlering up behind them among the stars.

Girls: his cousins and neighbours. All the girls in the world. He prowled among them, long-armed, long-legged, watching like an adolescent wolf, half hungry, half afraid. During the year in Cork City it was a sin even to talk to the likes of them, but now, what could he say? Nothing, nothing...but *oh*, the bareness of their insteps in the grass, smooth, salty, his tongue remembering the pearly insides of oyster shells – tender knees and thighs seen under the cotton flip of skirts, tender biceps and necks.

Another of Agnes's daughters was supposedly off visiting her aunt in Clonakilty, but was really at the Catholic maternity home in Cork. If there had been a salmon in her belly, it had changed to something else, something not seen as princely. How his friends at school had laughed when he told this overheard story – it wasn't the fish, but the girl who'd gotten caught. How hard *he* laughed, embarrassed, because wasn't it almost the same thing as what had happened to his mother? As what had happened to him? And where would this baby end up? Would it ever know the arms of the girl who bore it? Would the poor innocent ever know which family it had been cast out of?

He darted his eyes from ankle to ankle, slid them up legs, saw his mother dancing – the first time in so many years. She had grown her hair long again. It was molded to smooth curves by the coil it had been in, its frizz tamed, redder in the firelight, but with a strand or two of grey: smoke instead of fire. She held her arms tight to her sides, moved only her legs, but how she moved! Every kick, every back and forth sway of her ankles, met the clap of hands, her feet flashing out, never where he expected them, behind, to the side, and sometimes in a devouring reach up and out, beating the grass flat beneath her.

A mighty dancer. The boys were all after her when she was a young one.

Remembering this, bringing it alive in her mind, making it *now*, she was happy. She was desired by all, her scars and shame forgotten, dancing again, finally! It was flying, was racing, was her body laughing. And she was still a young woman, after all. That part, she didn't have to imagine.

She stood beside James when she was tired, accepted the glass of *poitín* and white lemonade from Grania, drank too much. She looked up at James's face; he was so much taller than her, now. Every time he came back from school, he was different, his face slightly metamorphosized – the distance changed from eye to mouth, from ear to chin – his voice cracking deeper, his clothes an awkward fit. He was still growing, still stretching those limbs that didn't seem right to be so long, those limbs that had grown inside her body. Once, his hand was so small it didn't even fill her palm, its fingers creeping up her fingers every time they measured, his skin so fine, so smooth, so spotty: her son, her little freckled beast.

She remembered nursing him, remembered how it was to have his small, perfect body all her own.

She rested her hand, measured the span between his neck and his shoulder, slid her palm slowly down his back. She had been his age, had been just so beautiful when she gave birth to him. He was only seven years younger than Victor had been when they'd... Was this how Victor would have looked at fifteen? When the war was on? Afraid of being called up if it lasted any longer?

"I'm twice your age," she said.

But really, she was fifteen again, and there was no harm in remembering.

Her hand moved down his back, so naturally there, so naturally possessing him. She sometimes touched him like this – it seemed she always had – and he would move away as quickly as he could, would avoid her when she smiled too gently at him, was in one of these sentimental moods. He shifted his feet, but her hand was an unblinking eye upon him, down the small of his back, his hip, his thigh.

He moved away, put out a hand to stop her hand.

"Don't...there, like *that*."

His hand had moved so quickly, had almost slapped hers, as if she had done something dreadful. What was this dreadful thing she had done? What? Nothing – nothing like *that*. No. It was unspeak – she was his mother. He was her little boy. She held her hand in the air, between them, the fire snapping, the fiddle screeching. Her face darkened from the shock, receded further and further into the cover of night, until all he could see was the dim whirlpool of her scar.

"How dare you. How – I'm your *mother*."

Hot fire-burned, cinder-smoked air clogged in his lungs. How dare he feel like *that* at her touch, his *mother's* touch. He wanted to pound his head on the earth, break his skull open on a stone.

She ran from the fire and he followed her.

"I'm sorry. I didn't – I – I'm sorry. Mother! Mam! *Mammy!*"

She stopped. He waited for her to forgive him, to turn to him, to touch him; he knew now that he wasn't to dislike it. He put his hand against the shuffle of slate wall beside her and she took it, twined her fingers into his and clenched their fists together.

Her little boy.

In his final year at St. Paul's, James was eighteen, a tobacco addict, an exemplary scholar, a striking young man in spite of his broken nose, and some would say also in spite of his cheeky red hair and freckles. It seemed to the masters that he had matured beyond the childish pranks of his youth. Father Foley in particular had watched James with interest, knowing he was to go into the priesthood. Surprised that James displayed little zeal for his calling, Father Foley decided against discussing his thoughts. James had a powerful mind and a strong will – both characteristics of the best priests, and going into the seminary wasn't a commitment in itself, but an exploration. If the priest's life wasn't for him, James would only find out by examining himself.

Saying goodbye at the end of the year wasn't as difficult as he'd thought. Many of his friends were already gone. Douglas had been sent down two years before after the last-straw offense of calling one of the masters a faggot. Mick vanished from school in January, the week after Bloody Sunday, in the roar of horror and anger that awakened so many Irish Catholics to the zeal of revolution. Aidan persistently failed his physics and chemistry exams, his cool exterior cracking open in panic at the prospect of never becoming a doctor. He was caught with a girl from St. Mary's when he should have been studying for his most terrifying chemistry final. The masters prevented him from taking the rest of his exams, and he stormed off to his mother's house in Dublin. In a one-time performance, James entertained his remaining friends with impressions of particular masters. Headmaster Father Dunnigan's tomb-voice was everyone's favourite – James saying *"Dona nobis pacem* (grant us peace) with onions and potatoes," the good father having gained a considerable amount of weight in the last few years. Inspired, James went through a whole mock Mass, adding more and more food to the simple meal of bread and wine for Dunnigan to devour – legs of lamb, bacon and cabbage, mutton stew, apple pie and cream – it was the last supper, wasn't it? Even Father Foley, the only master present, laughed himself hoarse. It was James's last stand as a schoolboy, and it was all the funnier because his intentions to become a priest had become well-known.

The graduation party degenerated into a drinking binge at the house of one of the day boys – a secret from the masters. James got himself completely drunk for the first time in his life.

He wandered the house trying to find the bathroom, opened the door to a little wood-panelled office instead; the honey-glow of the wood shot him back to his grandmother's house in Oxford.

There was a phone, sitting on top of a phone book.

He looked up the country codes, dialed.

He heard ringing, then some kind of noise.

"You arsehole. I'm grown up, now. I'm a man. No thanks to you."

After a moment the operator said the number was no longer in service. What had happened to his father? Where had he gone?

He was drunk. The next day, it was easy to convince himself that he had dreamed the whole thing.

That summer was glorious. The heat of the afternoon and the smell of warm grass was made more intense by the memory of every past summer, every past cutting of hay. The first week in August, he went with John to a dance at the MoonStar Dance Hall. A warm and windless evening, they walked on the road-sides, crushing through the drifts of fallen fuchsia, the blossoms still hanging above them, lifting their skirts to show purple petticoats, spreading their pistils and stamens like the tarts they must be to dress like that.

John had grown taller than his father and his asthma was less troublesome. The farm work was making his muscles taut, and with Dermot gone, there was no one to take away his confidence. He was the eldest son, now.

James's hair was a shaggy over-the-ears version of the Beatles cut and he had a freckled variety of his father's tall, aristocratic face. He stood impossibly straight, a habit jabbed into his subconscious by his English grandfather's walking stick. He opened the door for a girl as he entered the hall, polite, gentlemanly, exactly as his English grandmother taught him so long ago.

But listening to the whisper of fabric, of nylon stockings, leg against leg.

He stood near the row of refreshment tables, watching the daring girls in their cheap polyester minidresses from Clonakilty, the more conservative girls in their homemade out-of-date bell-skirted crinoline dresses, watching all the bare necks and collarbones, round smooth arms, strong peasant ankles. He recognized most of them from school, and he knew the boys, too, most looking uncomfortably pink and clean, but some smelling of muck. James was still a little afraid of them, so he took refuge in the kind of snobbishness he'd learned at his big city school. The laughter he heard breaking out within the little groups was silly, uneducated. They had never been away, lived in the city. They had been taught a second-rate nun's curriculum. They weren't scholars. They didn't know the sons of rich men. They stood near the walls looking just as lost as James felt, even in their own town.

The band on stage where James had once played bingo, was a collection of too many ragged-haired young men. There were two lead electric guitarists, one bass, one drummer, an accordionist, a saxophonist who kept wandering the stage without anything to do, and a boy bashing on a tiny electric organ with silvery fold-out legs. It was an amateur show band hired for the parish dance from Cork, but they were nothing compared to what he heard on Radio Luxembourg, nothing compared to the professional show band that James had heard here last summer. They played a mixture of stolen pop tunes and threw in slow dances and electrified Irish jigs in an attempt to make the older dancers happy. The best part about it was that their sound equipment kept blowing the breakers and clapping the hall into darkness, girls squealing, boys laughing. Once the band unplugged the required number of instruments, the evening became much less exciting. Matronly chaperones wove through the wallflowers selling raffle tickets for a large box of Rose's chocolates.

Liam shuffled up beside John. James took an automatic step back.

"How'ye," Liam mumbled, and gave James a curt nod, pretending he wasn't already drunk.

"Bit early to come for a dance," James said. Regular show band dances only got started around midnight after a night of ale and talk at the pub.

"The old biddies need their sleep," John said. Two girls came up to the table and bought orangeades, the boys' eyes following them.

"Hm?" Liam said. His eyes swayed over to John after an attempt to look down the bosom of the girl beside him. She left with her orangeade and his whole body lurched in her direction. He glanced, sly, back at James. "Ye hear Dermot was home for a day?"

James shrugged. He couldn't show himself afraid of ghosts.

"Says he's in Belfast now."

"Has he shot himself in the foot yet?" James wished he hadn't thought of that: Dermot with a gun.

There had been rumours. Years ago, Michael, Liam's father, had a dog, a stray, not even a cattle dog, a thing of no real value to anyone, a smart little creature that had one favourite trick. If Michael would cry out, "Do ye love me, Lucky?" the little dog would hurl himself up and off his knee and into his arms. It had gone missing one winter, had been found strangled, hanging by a rope from a tree down by the river. Over the years, there had been speculation, a couple of suspects identified. A few months ago, one of them, a twenty-five-year-old Protestant boy, had been found dead, run over by a car near the mass famine grave at Skibbereen. This was thought to be Dermot's, and perhaps even Liam's, work, not officially IRA, but symbolic of the same sentiments. The Volunteers came from somewhere, and this was where: wrongs and then greater wrongs, more and more wrongs, private, individual. Revenge can be as patient as you please.

Liam's eyes, puffed and blurred with whiskey and contempt, gleamed at him. He was a handsome, dangerous-looking young man, squat and brawler-shaped. Whenever he saw Liam, James could still hear the taunt of bastard, the insult to his mother.

"Bastard," James called him, his voice obscured in the band's new song, a grind of electric noise.

"What?"

"You bastards have the guts to ask for a dance?"

"You tell me, Mister Cork City. Come on. Let's see how ye do."

Except for shopgirls and cousins, James had still never really talked to a girl. They were all soft hair, deliberately enticing masks of lipstick and powder, the swell of breasts and hips, their clothes revealing more of the sensual differences than they obscured. Girls frightened him, the way they giggled to each other behind their hands, seemed to know something he didn't. Were they laughing *at* him? His hair and freckles? His ears? They seemed to be teasing him, keeping something from him, dangling their bodies in front of him.

He examined them, their dresses, their exposed ankles, arms and shoulders, then – *Jasus* – in the opposite corner of the room was Deirdre McAnenely. Dermot's old piece. Had they done it? If she was doing it six years ago, how much more was she doing it now? His heart beat against his ribs. Every nerve rose to the surface of his skin. His penis tightened like a muscle, and he shifted his legs to let it do what it had to do, hid its bulge with his jacket, an animal moving inside his clothes. He had always avoided McAnenely's spirit grocer's for fear she would be standing behind the counter. Sometimes he glimpsed her in the town, and a current of guilt and lust cycled through his body. It wasn't fair that girls like her should look like that, like movie stars, poster girls, angels. She was wearing her hair up and her dress was a froth of pale peach beneath a low-cut bodice, beneath the brimming roundness of her breasts, the plunge between. A hot one, by Douglas's standards; if they don't mind you looking, they don't mind you touching; they wouldn't show it to you if it wasn't for sale. Her ankles were narrow, as fleet as her smile – and the way she laughed, twirled in front of the other girls to show herself off. She had to be nineteen or twenty, almost two years older than he was. He looked around to see who else was staring at her. No one, really, or maybe he couldn't tell. Maybe these country boys didn't know where to get it.

Now or never. He walked up to her and she looked at him, then away, blinking, wearing enough makeup for two. This was her way; the strategy of women. She wasn't going to twist him around her little finger, make him follow her around like some puppy. He gazed into one thick stripe of rouge on her cheek-bone when he asked her to dance. She allowed him to lead her onto the floor where a few couples were stumbling, fixing their eyes on their partner's ears, hair, or on a bit of air or imagination. They shuffled through a slow dance.

Her warm flowery perfume touched him all over.

She knew what she was doing, oh, she did.

He led her outside when the chaperones looked too busy to notice. It was lovely, a perfect night, dark blue as a mussel shell. He told her there was a field where they could watch for the lights of ships, and then speech seemed impossible; he was terri-fied. Wasn't this supposed to be an act of silence? How did you get from walking this far apart to...to... Didn't Douglas say they wanted to be taken? That *no* meant *yes*? Or was it *yes* meant *no*?

"Did ye know I been goin' to your mother's class?"

"Class?" He looked at her, so real beside him, having thoughts he couldn't imagine.

"Sure. The dancin'. The real old stuff. It's supposed to be coming back, you know. With the patriotism, with the Gaelic. I guess it isn't really a class. We saw her, you know, Midsummer's Eve. Just some of us girls go up every now and then to bother her. I can't get the – whadya call it – ankle sway? Not for the life o' me."

She looked down, and in the light of the moon, he saw her narrow feet, tight together, high on their toes, her heels lifted right out of her high-heeled shoes. His mother had taught Dymphna a little, and he could remember her dancing along the sidewalk, kicking her little legs high in the air, full of joy, full of nothing but the desire to dance, full of nothing but her own desires. Dymphna hadn't really wanted to learn, was always trying to get away from any sort of lesson, was always off doing her own dance, a willful little thing even at the age of four. That was what girls were like: his sister, his mother, his grandmother, his darling little Lila, who was now almost inseparable from her skipping rope. An only child, wrathfully unable to share with her cousins until only recently, she was regarded as spoiled by her aunts who had too many children to really get to know any of them. She wasn't like most of her other cousins, puppies tumbling over each other in the dirt; she was dreamy and used to being alone, was never allowed to eat sweets between meals, stay up past bedtime, or neglect to brush her teeth. To her, the hill country above Killaghmore was a special, almost mythological, place. If there was anything he knew about Lila, it was that she was her own little self. In spite of James, she *would* play Poor Snipey, and she had a wicked slap when she played with Colm, getting him every time; put a rifle in her hand someday, and she'd make a mighty sniper.

Their own selves; that was what girls were like. He shook his head, clearing it as well as he could. What an idiot, after all, was his old friend Douglas.

"My mother, she's got rubber ankles, rubber legs. We had the television, back in England. I remember one show, some of these stretches. Yoga? She used to be able to tie herself in knots, one leg up behind her head –"

There was a scream, and then some shouting, coming from behind them, back down the road.

"Sounds like something's wrong – some girl –"

"*Jasus*. It's Father Coghlan. Run for it!" She darted ahead, but changed her mind, the sound of running feet coming closer, the light of an electric torch beaming around them. She managed to leap the ditch and get up over a gate in the stone wall, her dress and its crinoline glowing in the darkness. James followed, crouched with her behind the wall.

"What –"

"Shh." she put her forehead against his hair, her lips to his ear. "Father Coghlan. He's a lunatic. Goes sneaking around on the nights of the dances, trying to catch people getting up to things. Him and his chaperone ladies. He's awful. Should hear him in the pulpit. If there wasn't a devil he'd have nothing to talk about. Oh, God. Me other shoe. And me poor dress. Ye see this –"

"I know you're around here somewhere!" came a sharp voice from the road.

The torchlight grazed the edge of the rock wall and the gate they'd just climbed. Deirdre clapped her hand over her mouth. James could hardly keep from laughing; they were about to be caught – caught at doing nothing – and it felt as if he were twelve again, hiding, spying.

"Ha!"

The torch flashed on above them and Deirdre shrieked; the priest had scaled the wall and was almost on top of them. They ran, laughing, up over the gate again, then down the road, rushing back into the hall. Deirdre tugged his hand and he looked at her, one high-heeled shoe in her hand, the other gone, her stocking feet muddy, a shred of her crinoline hanging down behind her. The band was going at full volume, the dance floor full of people trying to dance to some American surfing song, twisting their hips, moving from one shy foot to another. James began to breath easier, put his cold hands against his hot cheeks. Deirdre pointed at the chairs on the side of the hall and James shouted that he'd meet her there with drinks; "Is it fizzy lemonade you like then?" He headed for the refreshment table, feeling in his pocket to make sure his money hadn't fallen out.

"Enough!"

There was a loud crash on stage and the music stretched and fried and was abruptly unplugged.

"Enough! Enough!"

The unamplified shouting was sour, puny after the sound of the band. The skinny young priest – the one described by his granny as a vicious little weasel – stepped through the black-wired chaos of the stage and hurled one of the electric guitars to the dance floor. There was a yell of pain from one of the band members as he leaped after it.

"Enough of occasions for sin! I have proof now! Proof! How hard need the devil work when there is *dancing*?"

The priest whirled and seized the saxophone, yanking its owner by the neck-cord to the front of the stage.

"I had nothing to do with it, Father – whatever it was," the saxophonist whimpered, awestruck. "I didn't even play me number yet."

The priest unhooked the saxophone and leaped to the dance floor, his long black robe flying. He stalked through the crowd, leaving a wake empty of cheap jackets and flowered fabric. James got outside just in time to see him lift the saxophone high over his head, like Moses would have lifted the tablets, and hurl it into the big silty puddle from last week's downpour, a brown lake in the gravel of the parking lot. The priest stood, breathing heavily, his hands curved and ready at his sides to capture more errant instruments and send them to their righteous deaths.

"Jesus said, 'Thou shalt not tempt the Lord your God,' so even your presence here is a sin! Even if ye didn't feel any...when ye, when ye...when ye dance," he faltered, the nature of the sin too filthy, too embarrassing. "Or ye've been causing others to sin! With your bare arms and legs. The shame of it! What are ye looking at? Get out! Go home!"

James made his way through the confused tides of people, but a wiry hand grabbed him by the collar. He twisted to see who it was, but couldn't because of the crowd and the strength of the hand. The hand propelled him past the open hall door, where the matrons were hurriedly drawing the lucky raffle number.

"You! I seen your red hair in the lane! Like the burning fires of hell! It's him, I swear it!"

James almost twisted free, but then a huge woman – a Mrs. MacManus – caught his arm between her own and her vast spongy ribs.

"What are you doing? Let me go!"

"Not until your parents know what you've been up to. Not until I've called the Guards!" she said, and the two self-proclaimed avenging angels propelled him up the hill, the priest with his wiry, spiritual strength, the woman with her suffocating bulk.

"I saw ye's, coming out o' the bushes after the screaming. That poor little one all a-crying, with her dress torn, and I smelled it on 'er, I tell ye, there's no mistaking that smell. What're ye shaking your head for?" James twisted again, saw the priest looking at him with bared teeth as if he might bite him.

James stopped struggling. "You've the wrong man."

The priest raised his hand like the paw of a large cat and his cassock flapped stiff and black, sending a breeze of old wool and sweat into James's face immediately before the blow that stung like a thousand grains of shattered glass. The priest threw him into his granny's house as if it were the pit of hell and he was about to be stoned, crying out that he had forced a girl, had been caught in the act, out-shouting James who proclaimed his innocence. His mother backed into a corner of the porch, her hands over her face, shaking her head in disbelief. Granny, in her flannel nightgown, went for the broom, struggled to untwist the wooden handle out of the bent-bristled head. She couldn't remember her grandson's name, but she knew enough to beat him. She cornered him on the other side of the porch and felt the weak clatter of the broom handle on his back, his head, the walls, before she abandoned it and substituted her hands, the flat impact and drag of them on the back of his head, on his heart. Even in his outraged innocence, he wouldn't grab her wrist to stop her, afraid he would break its brittle bird-bones. "Hell gapes for boys like you," she said.

Paddy, home for haymaking, came in after them and caught his mother around the middle, lifting her high, her arms still flailing.

"What in the name of –"

"They think I –"

"A girl attacked –"

"– not like a gentleman with –"

"It wasn't me. Just ask –"

"Cesspit of the MoonStar –"

"Sure, hang on – I'm just up from Agnes's. It was her Sharon was hurt. And she's named the man. From over to Glandor. One of them Costellos."

James let his shoulders drop and shut his eyes in relief. How could they think that possible of him? How could they have thought *he* – but Sharon. She was maybe five years older than him, and he didn't know her very well, but he knew she was good-hearted. During his first summer, she had always made silly faces across the room at him whenever he seemed to be lonely.

Granny curled her fists against her breastbone and Paddy set her down. Bernadette took her hands from her face and wept. "I knew it couldn't be true."

"Ah. Right, then," the little priest said, twitching his head once to the side as if adjusting a switch on his primitive brain. He shoved at his black sleeves, which were pushed up past his elbows to show his lean forearms, and, still scowling, left the house without apology.

Mrs. MacManus didn't know what to say. She looked around and stumbled into the kitchen, then came back with the dish-cloth to dab at James's split lip. He took the cloth from her and she bowed out of the house, saying, "Sorry, sorry, goodnight, then."

"Agnes's Sharon. Little Sharon. Ah, no," Granny whispered. "We got any gin? Sure but she'll need a few doses of juniper before – I've got to get –"

They all followed her into the kitchen, where Bernadette fussed around making James sit, making him a cup of tea, trying to get him to agree to a plate of eggs and bacon. Granny gathered what she thought she needed in a canvas bag and headed out the door in her plaid house slippers. Paddy and Bernadette looked at each other.

"You go with her," Paddy said, and Bernadette snatched up her cardigan and was gone. "And you," he said to James. "You need a whiskey, not a fry."

They sat with their tumblers across the table from each other. Summer's heat had stuffed the kitchen with smells, the milk souring too quickly in the pantry, sweat and turpentine hanging between the freshly painted walls, flies bouncing against the new robin's egg blue of the ceiling, moths fluttering around the bare light bulb.

"How's Sharon, then?"

"Beat up and bloody. Worse off than you. Too ashamed to call the guards, so it's lucky the others done that for her. Though that bleeding priest doesn't make much of a witness. Ha. It'll get talked of everywhere now, and go nowhere. But at least her parents won't be able to blame her...that much. What am I saying? They'll blame her anyway, for just being there, for showing her ankles to a man. Oh, God. History repeats itself."

"What do you mean?"

"Susan was forced when she was a young one – by McAnenely. You know. The spirit grocer. No one but me, Mam, and Colm, knows. And maybe that's wrong. Did ye ever wonder why ye never saw him drinking any place but his own shop? He's afraid. Colm almost killed him. And maybe things would be better if he had. Or at least – Colm's castrated plenty of cattle. Better that they don't get the chance to reproduce themselves. Rid the world of these fucking animals."

James remembered Deirdre's father handing out licorice from behind the counter, while the old grandfather – the first man he'd met in Killaghmore – filled his rotting mouth with Guinness. Deirdre's father seemed an ordinary enough man, a bit silent, nothing to hint at a molten core of evil.

"Susan was from a poor family. Dirt floor in the house. Poor as tinkers. Course, she was too frightened to tell them at first, and then they saw her belly growing. They didn't believe her. Threw her out of the house, into the winter. They didn't have the wit or compassion to send her away to have the baby, quiet, in one of them church homes, without all eyes upon her, to send it for adoption. Girls have died like that. She was Maureen's bosom friend. Colm loved her. Both too young to start a family, but married to save her. And then Dermot was born. Susan couldn't bear the sight of him, hated him, especially when he was inside of her, kicking. Saw her once behind a wall when she thought she was alone, crying, beating on her own stomach – that's nine months of raping she went through. What can be done with a child like that, eh? A baby was found washed up on the beach, years ago. It was said a man over to Bandon dug one out of the bog once, cutting turf – sure, such good Catholics we are. Colm tried to give him for adoption in Cork. They were going to tell your granddad the baby died, but it didn't work out. There's no getting away, when the whole town is watching ye, and the church, too, and your grandfather thought Dermot was his first grandson and doted on him – even though he had a face nobody could figure. Susan was sick with the nerves, heart-broke a long time, but she got out of it. It wasn't poor Dermot's fault – and what a smile he had when he was a little baby. She and Colm started to feel sorry for him, guilty, spoiled him by giving him his own way because they couldn't give him any love. And then John came along, their own, and then the others, and they wanted to forget he was even there. Toward the end, all Colm wanted him for was work. Ye heard him – 'He's my boy. He'll work in my fields.' My *boy*. Never my *son*. And all Dermot ended up doing was throwing the pain onto others, onto – well, that's what happens when ye force a woman."

When you take her.

"Why didn't you *say* anything?" James demanded, angry now, realizing no one had told him anything about this, save Douglas, Douglas and all the other ignorant boys picking up their information from ignorant men. Stealing ties, stealing kisses, stealing feels, taking. The whiskey burned his throat, burned the cut in his lip, the raw parts of his mouth that had gotten crushed against his teeth. He could taste the whiskey, but it didn't wash away the taste of his own blood. Could he have been guilty? Would he have done the same thing? All this time being taught by the Jesuits, had they all been learning how to behave like animals? A fly caught itself on the brown curl of fly-paper that hung down from the ceiling by the window. It buzzed in terror, finding itself among the dried up corpses of so many of its fellows, in its grave before it was dead yet.

"Irony is what it's called. Maybe God's justice. McAnenely married my poor Fiona, had one daughter, no son to take over the store. Doesn't know his own son who has the name of another man. Irony. Not justice. And so Biblical, too. The sins of the father visited upon the son. That poor boy. God knows where he is, now. Deirdre is Dermot's sister and they don't know it."

"Why didn't –"

"And Susan, still. How does a woman live within a mile of a man who did that to her? Have to go to church, put money in the plate when he's the one passing it around, giving her a saintly smile. Some of the women, they want it that way, too. It's not supposed to happen, so they pretend it doesn't. They blame the girl: *ye shouldn't have been dancing like that, looking like that, giving the men permission to take what they want.* It happens to their daughter, they'd rather throw her from the house, keep the reality of the thing a secret, so their husbands don't go off killing each other all the time, so their own devil-man is still around to earn their bread."

"You never said –"

"Poor Fiona. She didn't deserve to live with a man like that. A man –"

James couldn't get Paddy to look at him. Eileen had miscarried their second child a few weeks ago and the strain and suffering had made Paddy look like an old man, the power drained from his large frame, the lines in his face dragged with exhaustion. He was once again in his old choppy, lank haircut, his head now a nest of dandruff and worry.

"Why doesn't anybody talk about this? To boys. How –"

"Ye learn from the Bible, from the Church. People don't know *how* to talk about these things, and I'm no different."

"Where in the Bible?"

Paddy didn't answer, poured him another whiskey when he was finished with the first – or was it the second – knocking the lip of the bottle against the tumbler, overfilling the cup to drain the bottle. Beat-up and bloody. Things like that had never been talked of by his friends. The girl only pretended she didn't want to. But what if she really didn't want to?

"Is she ruined, then?"

"I don't know. I don't know. One of the ladies brought her home and no one was going into such specifics. Whether he got as far as that. If she thinks she's ruined. If others think she is."

James had only been fed the extremes at school. There was only the rule against fornication pitted against the delight of their spinning hormones. No meant yes: this idea made refusal impossible. The boys at his school were forbidden to talk to girls. No wonder it never occurred to them to listen.

He and Paddy finally went to bed. The shock of being thought guilty hadn't worn off. In a way, he was guilty. He lay in his bed with the light on, his eyes tracing the familiar cracks in the plaster of the ceiling. He had covered himself and his clothes with the blankets, but his hands were exposed, and he couldn't bear to look at them. What did the priests say? To look upon a woman with lust in your heart was the same thing as adultery. To want to take...was the same thing as taking. The intent was the same thing as the act in the eyes of God.

He didn't feel vindicated. He didn't feel good. He felt like filth. His body was a pile of shit that he was lying in.

James fled the house after several sleepless hours, long after Granny and Bernadette had come back from Agnes's. On his back, still tingling, were the places Granny had hit him with the broom. It was as if demons had possessed her to show him his possible fate if he continued on the path of sin, if he continued to ignore his vocation: furies beating him, hellfires burning him, his loved ones no longer recognizing him, but hating him, hurting him, cursing him. He wandered through the boreens toward town, touched his skull where the broom handle had bashed up a lump, sat on a wall here and there, watched the sun rise – terrible accusing innocent colours of pale pink and peach, the colours, almost, of Deirdre's dress. He watched people go into St. Mary's Church, Killaghmore, and finally went in as the others were coming out, knowing he was too evil to be with them, to take the wafer in his mouth. The priest had already tidied the altar and was gone.

For the last few years, he had been so proud, so sure of himself, so sure he was a good person, with all his good examination results, with all the praise of his mother and grandmother. What had really been happening to his soul? He'd hardly thought of it. The idea that he was God's, that he didn't belong to himself, was too much for him, and he had taken refuge in his friends, in running on the playing field, in the pictures of girls smuggled into the rooms. At first, becoming an adult was too far in the future for him to believe it would really happen. He had been a child all his life, after all. The God of his masters was the same God that he used to feel in the wind, when he was still a boy of twelve, when he walked up the hills with Granny, though he had never thought to divide them, never questioned the right of his grandmother to question the Church or the Bible or the priest. There was no other way to think than Catholic, one form or another of it, more or less devout.

But why couldn't he just be a farmer?

He thought of Sharon, of whatever brutality she suffered, with confusion, all the things his friends had joked about coming back to him; rape was impossible because a girl could run faster with her knickers off than a man could with his pants down around his ankles. Last night was his Pandora's box. Someone had taken the lid off, and all sorts of horrors flew about him into the world. He was seeing more things about the human race than he ever wanted to, things that disgusted him, that set something tumbling inside him that knocked other things over... Why did his Aunt Maureen sometimes have bruises on her face and arms? Why were girls not supposed to leave the house at night? Why were women afraid? He had known all these things before, of course, had listened to the news, to the bombs going off in the North; he knew about the mass graves of the Nazis, had heard of the woman killed by her husband in Cork City for some imagined adultery, the atomic bombs that could be released any moment with a flick of a resentful Russian or American finger. It had all been so distant before, the beating Dermot gave him having become little more than a bad dream, the fields of home so green, the cows grazing peacefully in the pastures and children going to school...and now his sweet Aunt Susan having the child of a rapist, the child a lost soul, an abandoned baby, a bastard, in a way, like him, but much worse off. How much didn't he know? He had never read the Bible from cover to cover. He didn't know the extent of the works of the devil, the extent of God's goodness. All at once, he *had* to know. All his love of books, of *knowing*, condensed into wanting to know himself, to know humanity and all the horrors and wonders it was capable of. Suddenly, he understood the desert fathers, the early hermit-monks of Egypt who had tried to get as far away from humanity as possible, whose main desire was to quit the whole human race and its ugliness; they felt contaminated by it. He thought of Deirdre with shame, remembering her hot sweet breath in his ear, his thoughts of doing something to her, taking something, even only one kiss.

He had gone inside with the vague idea of confessing to a priest, maybe even the vicious little vandal priest, and prayed for courage before going into the confessional, a ruddy upright coffin that smelled of mildew. *Bless me, Father, for I have sinned.* He stumbled through what he'd done, sins of intent, sins of the mind. Though he knew that all sins were committed against God, he felt as if he had committed them against his sister, the only girl he had ever completely known, and then forgotten in his adolescent passions. Was she watching him from heaven? Maybe she was really better off to be there already. Were all girls, then, his sisters, since he had lost her? He could hardly hear the priest in his wretchedness, made an effort to memorize the grocery list of a penance the priest gave him, wondered whether he had shocked the priest or bored him, and stepped out into the grey stone air of the church. He had expected his penance to be some nearly impossible task; he wanted to suffer, needed to suffer, but he had this list of prayers instead, as if he were a child caught lying. The priest *had* sounded bored, tired...hypocritical. The vandal priest was the only true kind of priest.

He paced back up the aisle, dropped into a bench, pulled down the kneeler, and knelt on it. If he had a list of prayers, he would say them, double them. He could find ways to suffer.

"Hail Mary, full of Grace..." he began, then got off the kneeler to feel the floor under his knees, bone on stone. He slid his fingers along the smooth wooden rosary that used to be his mother's, and chanted the prayer over and over. Once the pain started to ruin his concentration, he sat back on the bench.

He couldn't bear the idea of Sharon's life destroyed, couldn't bear the idea of wreckage. But if he was innocent, why did he feel such remorse? And why was he here, useless to her, and to everyone else who would suffer along with her, everyone who loved her now and would love her in the future, her unborn children, the child she might have now?

Imagine being the child of a rapist, conceived by murder, almost, your mother wanting to erase you, kill you, too. His feeling of revulsion for Dermot began to dissipate.

Was his sister better off out of it all, in a place she would never suffer? The loss of her, the one childhood companion he could have had in his own family, was as terrible to him now, as his first loss of her. She would be eleven now, the age he had been when he left England, the age he had been when she died. She would have been sharp as a little tack, her halo of strawberry blonde hair grown out into long braids, her knees just as skinned and bruised as they had always been. She would still be a child, and now, he was grown.

He had grown up without her, had left her behind. She wouldn't know him if she saw him.

The thought was senseless, was some other kind of punishment he was inflicting on himself, imagining her alive and four years old, fresh from that day of grubbing up worms to murder the baby robins. "Who's your best friend?" he used to ask her, and she would always say it was him, James, her big brother Jamie. And would she even know him now? He began to cry for the first time in years, telling himself not to be stupid because he hadn't had any sleep, and maybe he was hungover, or maybe he was still drunk on the half-bottle of whiskey he had finished off with Paddy. He was crying for the birds. Wasn't his sister safe home in heaven, flying on her angel wings like the little bird she was, where no hurt could ever touch her, far safer than him?

The door of the church banged closed and he heard footsteps, hard woman's heels on the tile: bang, bang, bang. The rhythm angered him. Why did women always have to go and remind men of their different bodies, different sounds, motions? Women should only ever wear soft-soled shoes.

Though the church was empty, the woman knelt directly behind him. His body tingled with the strangeness, felt her there, inches behind him in an acre of lonely space. She knelt and began the whisper of her prayers, one nostril plugged, her breath whistling: his mother.

He couldn't recognize a word she mumbled, his body instinctively recoiling, sickened by her proximity. Her prayers touched the back of his head, murmured their way around his neck. She was praying over him, and he was to know it, to submit to her will, to God's will. He watched the cold grey stone angels tethered to the walls. They were hard and painful to him, their slick weight weighing him, their perfection shaming him.

He was so very tired.

What he had once thought of as the sentence of the priesthood, a kind of curse for being more bookish than other people, a dead end to life, became his only possible life. The thought of knowing what he was to do, knowing where he had to be, suddenly became immensely comforting. He had been running away, like Jonah. Now, he would give himself up – give up his body – to be swallowed into the great-bellied whale of God.

"...HOW BEFITTING...
THAT THOSE WHO HAVE RENOUNCED
ALL FELLOWSHIP AND SERVICE OF MEN...
SHOULD THEMSELVES RECEIVE
THE GOOD OFFICES OF DUMB BEASTS
AND A KIND OF HUMAN MINISTERING."

– COLGAN, *VITAE SANCTORIUM...HIBERNIAE*, H.W.

İAMES received his small room on the second floor of Humanity House, St. Patrick's College, one of the grey stone Georgian wings surrounding St. Joseph's Square, a landscape of European conservatism: straight paths, clipped yew, and roses.

St. Patrick's College, Maynooth, County Kildare, was a Catholic seminary founded by the British colonial government during the early nineteenth century, shortly after it lifted its total ban on Catholic worship in Ireland – a quick about-face from shooting priests, to ordaining them. The British Protestants feared the loose political morals of the French, the way the rabble had taken over and severed the king's neck during the revolution. They feared the rabble far more than they hated the Pope, and the establishment of this first Irish seminary staunched the flow of Irish boys into France to take their vows of poverty, chastity, and obedience, and to perhaps absorb too much of the spirit of foreign *égalité*.

After the orientation, James fell into the routine with the other new boys, got used to the bells that measured the days, the early mornings with their sleepy-eyed prayer and meditation which could flow gently to dreams or daydreams, both unacceptable. Then came Mass, then breakfast, and then work, silence, exercise and rules. He had decided to take a degree in history in addition to the required philosophy. Real clerical training wouldn't begin until after he had his history degree, after three years. Then, there would be four more years of study leading to his final vows. The clerical students, the First, Second, Third and Fourth Divines, walked the halls in small peaceful flocks and seemed to know so much more than he or any of his peers. These boys were an odd collection from all over Ireland and a few from elsewhere: the tight-lipped virgin-faced boy from Louisiana, the dark, chubby, matronly boy from Brazil, and the handsome local boys, lovers of hurling and their mothers, a loss to the girls of Limerick, Meath and Armagh. Some of his classes included two elderly Sisters of Charity and a handful of lay students. Maynooth had recently opened its doors to ordinary students because of the drop in the number of boys who wanted to be priests and the resulting need for money. It was wonderful to study among those who wanted to study, and to learn from men who were impassioned for knowledge. It was wonderful to be respected, to be known as Mr. Young of Cork even though he made it clear he would sign up to go into the missions, an intent seen as admirable. He wanted to get as far from Cork as possible, throw himself back into the world his mother had taken him from. He fantasized of going to Africa, Australia, Canada, thought of wild places, kangaroos and grizzly bears, lions and wildebeest.

He learned for the joy of it, putting his head down and looking neither left nor right, the three girls his own age in the college not obtrusive or beautiful enough to present a distraction. He told himself he was through with sin, tried to believe he had been forgiven for all he confessed. But confession was no remedy for his poor sinful body. He thought of Deirdre McAnenely. He couldn't help it. He thought of the few moments they spent whispering and giggling in the field, thought of the tickle of her breath in his ear, on his hair, the feeling of her elegant hand within his own. When he pushed his hands beneath the blankets to touch himself at night, it was impossible for him to think of anyone but her, her smooth black hair and pale doll's face. If only he could find some way of making himself stop. Why did women have so much power? Was this the same power in his mother's hands, in Granny's fierce rule over Paddy? Was this erotic gravity what was buried in the darkness of every woman's body? He couldn't pick out the hook Deirdre McAnenely had embedded in his groin. It pulled him awake at night, and he would deal with himself, then wash his hands with the perpetually cold water from the taps. Constant study, sports, and cold showers weren't enough to keep him from waking. All the same, he thanked God for the mercy of the confessional, for without it, he would be heaping the sin of mental fornication on his young back, would bend like a sapling under a weight of snow.

The college almost immediately became home. He didn't realize he was being seduced by the physical world, by its beauty. His sense of belonging came from the atmosphere of learning but also from the facades of the buildings he inhabited. Each step he took was like turning a page in an old book, his eyes on rich stone and brick, oak floors in herringbone patterns, arched windows nestled in Virginia creeper turning ruddy in the autumn, spires, towers, things he dimly remembered from Oxford. Why did the buildings look like this? When were they built? He looked through books of old engravings, became familiar with the orders of Greek architecture, plain Doric, scrolled Ionic, and the foliage of Corinthian, observed them reappear throughout the historic structures of the west, filled his head with the forms of the wealthy building class. He wasn't allowed to go into town or off into the countryside. He never saw cows any more, or mucked-up boots, or worn dishrags, or decaying thatched farmhouses, or fields overtaken by ragweed. Instead, there were the playing fields, the gardens, and St. Joseph's square, with its geometric paths, yew trees clipped into the shape of cold green flames, roses with red blushing edges and hearts of golden cream. The cold damp air of autumn smelled of mud, and was filled with the black sweep of crows in their cassocks, mocking the priests from the crown of the chapel.

His thrill at the splendour of the chapel mingled with his love of God. The peeling paint in the cloister hadn't prepared him for what lay beyond the chapel doors. He walked inside, and his mouth opened, receptive as a lover's; even the sunlight spilling from the windows was sparkling holy wine, and around him were jewels. The altar was made of rose and white lace-carved marble like thin frozen milk. Saints floated above him in blue and red skies of stars as the oil-painted Lord progressed to his agony along the walls, the Stations of the Cross making death itself beautiful. His comrades pushed him into his place in the choir stalls, and he sat surrounded by polished wood carved with foxes, squirrels, stags, and other Irish animals, surrounded by black wool and tender enraptured faces. The ancient rituals were enacted. Seven priests baked and pressed God's body into bread and blood-wine, then swallowed them.

"'How much do you love me, Lord?'" the boy to his right whispered to him in a surge of devotion during Mass, in wonder at the profound height and depth and breadth of God's love. "'This much,' Jesus said, stretched out his arms as wide as they could measure, and died."

So many words, so many beautiful words: gorgeous, seductive lines of love that were miraculously true, that he was trying to think of as if he heard them for the first time, to propel himself to weeping gratitude; take up your cross and follow me, for my load is easy and my burden is light. Lose your life for my sake and find it again. Blessed are they which do hunger and thirst after righteousness: for they shall be filled. Greater love hath no man than this: that he should lay down his life for his friends. Be not afraid.

The nuns sat across from him. One held her hands to her chest, bending over them as if she held a bird in the wings of her fingers: the Holy Spirit. He felt the organ music like rain pounding through him.

He went to the chapel whenever he could. He memorized it with joy, as if he too was one of the angels arching out of the walls, immortal. He knew the sound of the caretakers cleaning the roof above the striped ribs of the barrel vault, the clatter of a fumbled broom handle striking the slates, the stiff feather sweep of straw and deep-voiced laughter, the thudding landings of pigeons and boots.

His favourite place was the Lady Chapel behind the altar, where the Blessed Virgin's initials, BVM, were written in the tiny stones of the floor. The walls, too, were mosaic. The images of the annunciation, the birth, the assumption, and the crowning of the Queen of Heaven were made of tiny knives of glass, even the Virgin's gentle face and peacefully ecstatic eyes. Most of the glass was blue and gold, detailed with turquoise, ultramarine, creamy bubbled white, red, brown, old pea green, and shards of black that divided diamond, flower, and fleur-de-lis from sky and robe and face. When the angel announced Mary's divine pregnancy, the Holy Ghost descended upon her in a unicorn beam. Her halo was gold-rayed and white, and there was an urn of glass lilies between her and the divine messenger. The cold alcove smelled of melted beeswax. Wet silver light came through the leaf-shaped windows, brighter on the side of the invisible sun.

When he had trouble concentrating, when he thought too much – which is not the same as meditating – when he got discouraged, when he desperately needed to know that God knew what was going on even when he didn't, when he was feeling lost, when the rosary didn't help, when he couldn't bear to repeat *The Lord is my Shepherd* or *I shall lift up mine eyes unto the hills* yet again, he read the first half of Psalm 139, read it so often he had it memorized in the first two months. It began, *O Lord, thou hast searched me and known me,* and his favourite part shook him with the power of God itself:

> *Whither shall I go from thy spirit? or whither shall I flee from thy presence?*

If I ascend up into heaven, thou art there: if I make my bed in hell, behold, thou art there.

If I take the wings of the morning, and dwell in the uttermost parts of the sea;

Even there shall thy hand lead me and thy right hand shall hold me.

If I say, Surely the darkness shall cover me; even the night shall be light about me.

Yea, the darkness hideth not from thee; but the night shineth as the day: the darkness and the light are both alike to thee.

For thou hast possessed my reins: thou hast covered me in my mother's womb.

I will praise thee; for I am fearfully and wonderfully made: marvelous are thy works; and that my soul knoweth right well.

He had to stop there because the psalmist then rattled on about God smiting his enemies, and James thought, as a priest, he should not have any enemies.

He learned so much in the first year, learned how to turn each of his thoughts into a stone skipping over the vastness of God. The blades of grass, the green of their photosynthesis, the filaments in the feathers of every wing of every sparrow, were miracles. He longed to walk in cities again, to marvel at God's children, every face created so different, every eye, mouth, hand and heart, millions upon millions of miracles in mankind alone. History and the beauty of mankind's works had also taken him and he absorbed them, astonished, without judgment. His survival depended on not judging. He couldn't think of the fact he wasn't always thinking of God, especially while meditating in the chapel. He couldn't think of the fact he wanted simply to learn, more than he wanted to take his vows. He couldn't question the existence of God, for the thought would have made priesthood, and schooling, impossible, pulled his life out from under him. He wouldn't know what he was going to do with the next day, the next week, the next year, wouldn't know where he was going to go. Back to Killaghmore? His sudden move to Ireland when he was eleven years old had made him deeply conservative, had made him fear change; change was loss, was chaos. Change was a drunk driver coming to kill you before you'd met the happiest day of your life. He asked his mother to keep praying for his vocation: she had added to her prayers the Novena to Our Lady of Knock, for Mary was the Great Believer.

Another year of study. Boethius, Erasmus, the history of the Church, the Renaissance, Michelangelo, the Enlightenment, Latin and more Latin, Greek, the French Revolution, Voltaire, Goethe, William Blake, Immanuel Kant, Cardinal Newman, World War One and Two, the Cold War, Vatican II. He snuck out to the pub sometimes with his classmates, though clerical students weren't allowed out of the grounds, and were even less allowed in the pubs of Maynooth, because they might get drunk and embarrass the college. He made friends with boys who were pious, who were uncertain, who were rebelling against the priestly urge they found so strong in themselves. He talked to the priests about the trouble he was having with meditation, trouble keeping his brain from galloping around, thinking about all the fascinating things there were to think about.

The IRA had exploded in the late sixties and early seventies, split apart, and one half, the Provisionals, were detonating bombs timed with Japanese alarm clocks, and chopping independent fiefdoms out of Northern Ireland. The Protestant paramilitary groups and the British forces had begun, or continued, or were adding to, the horror. Priests weren't supposed to take sides, which was a relief, because he didn't know who to blame and his heritage made him guilty on both sides.

The second summer, he got a job as a tour guide in Castletown House, the local tourist attraction in Celbridge, the next town on the way to Dublin. He loved touring the visitors through, loved telling them the history of the place, gossip that produced smiles and shocked faces. This had been the house of one of the Lord Mayors of Dublin. Here, the famed writer Jonathan Swift walked, and perhaps did other things as well; Swift's very *very* good friend Vanessa, the Lord Mayor's daughter, had planted the grounds just for him. James was fascinated with the architecture, the Greek columns and balustrades, the frescoes and paintings, the tapestries and furniture. He reminded the members of his tour groups not to touch anything, not to leave the oil of their skin on the precious objects that almost seemed to belong to him; he told them of the acid one little touch would leave behind, so much acid accumulating from the touches of thousands of others, decaying the objects, increasing the ravage of time. Most of all, he was happy to pretend to be an independent, employed man. On his lunch break he would ramble along the Primrose Walk, the Yew Walk, lie on the grass in Vanessa's Bower, and think of what it would be like to have a job, just any job, for the rest of his life, to earn his money, to do as he pleased. Allowed to board at the college over the summer, cycling to Celbridge every day, he wondered what it would be like to have his own flat, cook his own meals, maybe have a very, *very* good friend, but then he was back in school, and had no time to think, except about his granny.

When he went home at Christmas, she was looking more shrivelled, her back crumpling, bending her neck further and further forward so she had little choice but to stare at the ground when she walked. Every muscle and tendon stretched to their limits, bone grinding on bone, the discs in her backbone crushed and aching, she walked to escape the pain of sitting, of lying down. She was forever roaming the lands of distant memory. Castle Field, above the cliff where her father had hauled boxes of munitions up the rock, was her favourite place, though sometimes people saw her in Colm's fields or up the side of Kilmoney Hill, St. Patrick loping circles around her. She always came home for meals, never lost herself, knowing the hills better in her senility than anyone else. In every cup of tea, she poured a shot of whiskey or *poitín*.

The spring James completed his final exams in his history-philosophy degree, he came home for the month of June, intending to go back to Maynooth in July to work at Castletown House. He travelled on the bus wearing brown woolen pants, a navy tie and a white shirt that both darkened and intensified his weedy red hair, which now grew all the way around his face. The hippie movement had infected the clerical students, who were enthused with Vatican II, with freedom, with the heady expectation that priests would soon be able to marry. It was 1975. They wore peace pendants, grew their hair long, and spoke of civil rights, though they weren't allowed to march about them.

He entered the kitchen to find Granny hard at work making tea for two white-faced young men who sat rigid-backed on the settle. It was surreal: the modern beatnik world invading the turn-of-the-century kitchen. One had a tweed cap and a fuzzy little goatee. The other had curly shoulder-length hair and a single gold hoop earring. Their backpacks were propped by Granny's chair under the window, and their feet were bare on the cold slate floor. Granny turned. An old rusty pistol swung in her apron pocket and banged against her legs.

"Who the hell are you?" she demanded, the way she usually greeted James. The young men gasped.

"James, your grandson."

"Right. Righ-et," she said. "Sit yourself down and have a cup of tea, won't ye?"

"Who are they?" James asked, and the men stared back at him.

"From the Volunteers. Found them on the cliffs, on the run from the Black and Tans – soaked to the skin they were! So I made them to come home for a cup of tea."

Sure enough, two old waxed coats, obviously not very waterproof, were spread on chairs and drying in front of the range. Hanging over the oven handle were two pairs of grey wool socks, and beneath them were the hiking boots.

"Who are you?" he asked.

"I am Dieter," said the one with the goatee.

"Franz," said the other.

"From Heidelberg," said Dieter. He shrugged and looked at Granny as she buttered thick slices of soda bread, as the gun swayed inside the threadbare cloth. The German boys never took their eyes off her.

"Here," she said, and banged two plates in front of them, each filled with eggs, rashers of bacon, black pudding, and a pool of extra-special canned tomatoes in juice. She put the tray of tea, cups and saucers, buttered bread, jams in glass jars, and store-bought shortbread biscuits in front of them, then poured out their tea.

"Sugar?" she asked. They nodded apprehensively and fiddled with their forks.

Granny settled back to lean against the counter with her own cup of tea and lit a cigarette.

"Well, eat, why don't ye?" she shouted at them. "You're both thin enough to see through!"

The young men tensed and began stuffing egg into their mouths, eyes moving from the gun, to her face, to James.

"Is good!" Dieter said abruptly, eyes popping as if he had just remembered his manners, bits of eggs spraying out of his mouth.

"Good!" repeated Franz, bobbing his head.

"Here," Granny said, holding out another cup of tea for James. "There's enough hair on your face, isn't there? Ye look like a monkey."

"Where is everybody?" he asked carefully, the house silent except for eating, the kitchen cut off, isolated by the gun.

"They'll be back," Granny said, the thought just occurring to her, and she hurried toward her window, shoving over one of the dirty canvas backpacks. She dug her field glasses out of her knitting and peered down toward the town. "Nobody, nobody. The Tans have to come through the town – unless – Declan, go run, check the hills behind the house and come tell me. Thank God ye've come. We've got to warn me father!"

"I'm James."

"Yes, yes. Go quickly."

He left by the proper entrance door in the lounge. Granny sat in her chair, pistol in a ready grip in her lap. The German boys cleaned their plates, ate bread and jam, tea and biscuits, and then sat watching their grim gaoler finger her revolver. When she had captured them on the cliff she kept repeating that they shouldn't worry, that she was prepared to hide them as long as was necessary, that it was the least she and her father could do. While they were still trying to decipher her English, she whirled suddenly, shot at a phantom; the rusty old gun worked. They were unnerved by her abrupt explosive presence, had almost been at ease while she was cooking for them, brewing tea, as if they were visiting an eccentric aunt.

"Are ye finished?" she said.

Dieter nodded.

Franz, the pet of both his grandmothers, took a risk.

"Vas so good. Is more?"

For a moment, he thought he had made a mistake, and she would think he was imposing on her poor generosity, but then the most enormous pleased smile spread over her face, and unthinking, she deposited both the field glasses and the revolver in her knitting and made her way to the range.

"As much as ye can eat, boys! All me hens lay an egg a day! I've got enough bacon to see ye through the autumn and into the winter!"

Outside, Bernadette and Colm virtually leaped upon James.

"What's happening in there?" his mother said. "Your brilliant uncle lost his cool and threatened her with the Guards. She shot a hole in the wall of the lounge!"

Colm grimaced, put his thick fingers on his temples and squeezed his head. "My foolish brain."

"Your foolish mouth!" Bernadette snapped. "Where did she get that gun?"

"She's expecting me back inside," James said. "What do you want me to do?"

"Leave the doors open," Colm said. "When ye think ye can occupy her with her back to the lounge, go into a fit of coughing – pretend you're choking – and we'll come in."

"*Colm* –" Bernadette said.

"You think it's not dangerous *now*? If they talk too much, she'll not know their accents. God knows what'll – go, boy!"

James came back into the kitchen where Granny was frying twice as many eggs as the first helping, the pan crackling with bacon fat, the eggs getting brown and lacy, yolks lying open and vulnerable.

James was about to say, "no one around back," when he saw the gun handle sticking out of the nest of grey wool. He took a shortbread biscuit from the tray and, munching it, settled himself on the chair, the knitting, and the gun.

And only then did he imagine it might go off.

"Achhh," James began, putting his hands to his throat during a series of convincing choking noises and writhings. Even the German boys leaped up to give him rib-cracking thumps on the back, and Granny was panicking, rushing for water, yelling "Bend him over a chair! Hit him in the stomach!"

Suddenly Colm was in the kitchen, and had his mother wrapped in his meaty arms.

"The Tans! The Tans!" she screamed at the German boys. "Run for it!"

"I'm sitting on the gun."

Colm released his mother, crashed through the chairs and Germans, and had the gun in his hands before Bernadette rushed in.

"I can't believe this thing shot a bullet," Colm said, turning the old revolver in his hands.

"Where's Mam?" Bernadette said.

They saw her through the window, scuttling through the yard, scattering the chickens, sliding on the gravel. They ran, lost her behind the barn for a few moments, then saw her trying to clamber over a wall – a wall she'd scaled many times in her youth, one that was too much for her now. Her brain refused to make allowances for her aged body. She got halfway up, then fell back, releasing an outraged cry of pain and rage.

She screamed and cursed when they tried to lift her, so James raced down to Killaghmore for the doctor and a stretcher. Bernadette remembered there had been a pan on the range and went back to keep the house from burning down.

She found the German boys eating eggs, expertly turned, with more crooked slices of soda bread. The pan had been drained of its fat and was soaking in a sink of hot soapy water. The boys washed the dishes before they left.

Grania Pearce Cahalane, a woman of uncertain age, was registered in Saints Hospital in Clonakilty that evening. She had a broken hip and elbow, was nervous, exhausted, and couldn't remember how she got there. The blue and white habitted nursing nuns refused to get her the cigarettes or the whiskey she demanded, but pumped her as full of morphine as her stick body would allow. Drugged sleep was the only thing that could silence her cursing.

"She'll never walk again," the doctor told them, and after a week in the hospital, she caught pneumonia.

James and Bernadette took the bus often to see her. James held her hand with its thick, striated fingernails, and read to her from an old second-hand book called *Beasts and Saints* he'd bought in Dublin. "These are stories of the mutual charities between saints and beasts, from the end of the fourth to the end of the twelfth century..." Sometimes she was able to listen, but often, she fell asleep. James kept reading anyway, thinking the stories might enter her dreams. There were the desert fathers who kept lions as pets, after the ancient thorn removal from the paw trick, or saints that used crocodiles to raft from one side of the Nile to the other. There were fox-monks given to gnawing the slippers and holy books of their human brothers, a cow that had no food other than what she licked from a saint's cloak, a monk's cat that had grown so huge on the eating of fish that it became a sea-cat, a monster, and the monks had to pray to Jesus to send another sea monster to fight with it, that they might go unharmed. Saint Cainnic read from a book held safe in the antlers of a stag. The Blessed Ammon walked into the desert and led back two dragons to wait in attendance upon him at the monastery gate. St. Brendan's white spirit birds flew, their wings chiming like bells, their voices singing only hymns. St. Kevin raised his hands to heaven in prayer and when a blackbird alit there and laid an egg, the good man remained motionless until the whole brood had been raised safely. James's favourite was the ordinary housewifely saint, St. Werburga of Chester, who gathered up the bones from a man's goose dinner, told the flesh and skin to grow again, held the teeming resurrection of it as it fledged suddenly between her fingers and flew away.

He told Granny what he needed was St. Coleman's fly, who would sit on a line in an open book and keep his place if he was called away.

Her fingers were weak, unable to hold her glass of water, shaking more every time she took a handkerchief to wipe her sticky mouth. Her hair, its white unscarfed frizz, clouded her stony scalp. In her mind, between long stretches of medicated sleep she was a girl again, flicking the rumps of cows with a willow switch, driving them into the barn, forgetting all that had taken place since childhood. Only now and then did she have moments of lucidity, but these were mundane, disappointing.

"Watch! Ye'll upset that!" she said to the nurse who was putting a bedpan on the side table.

"Can't think where I left me handbag," she said, gesturing, twitching one hand in the blanket so Bernadette would go to look.

Once, she saw James's face above her. She frowned as if trying to find something behind her forehead. A sharp sweetness came into her eyes before she sighed to sleep, peaceful at last after an hour of horrible coughing; someone was holding her hand.

She died in her sleep four weeks after the accident, almost fifteen years after becoming a widow. It was agreed that she should be buried in her grey worsted cloak, but James didn't think this was good enough, so he wore the cloak one last time, making his way over walls and through hedges, deliberately swinging its hem into the puddles, the holy water on the highest hills, tearing bramble branches to snag into it, wafting it through beds of ragwort bursting with pollen, old St. Patrick confused, running around him, barking at ghosts. He watched his aunts wrap her in it, over her best Sunday dress, so she wouldn't be cold in the ground. He tucked a rag of carrageen moss into her hand so she wouldn't be hungry. The funeral was attended by half the town, more people than could be held in the small hillside church.

The sun was hot, striking everyone hard on the head. James helped carry the casket from the church to the open grave, then went to stand with his mother in the warm wind that was blowing straight up from the south. He squinted beyond her, to the edge of Castle Field where he could see crows soaring in the updraft coming off the flat cliff face. When had he last seen Paddy's crow? It had become Granny's crow, following, picking bugs as she hacked her way through the vegetable patch, because, as his uncle said, the two had so much in common. It had come around less and less, then finally not at all, perhaps because it died, but he preferred to think it had just forgotten about them, had gone off with its other companions, allowing him to imagine its immortality. Suddenly, one of the crows flipped on its back, its wings half furled, and dropped like a stone before it flipped over and shot up again. They were all doing it; joyriding. He had never seen them do that before.

"It's not –"

"It's not our place to discuss what's fair and what isn't," Bernadette said, looking at her son, lifting her hand to cover her glass eye, an instinctive act she wasn't aware of.

"Why can't we?" he demanded, even though he was about to enter his first year of clerical training, about to become a First Divine. Father O'Griofa went on about how his granny's name, Grania, meant "Grace," but what was that? It only showed that he had never known her. Ashes to ashes and dust to dust, and the ceremony was over. It was bad enough for her to die, but for her to die stupidly – from climbing a wall after that comedy in the kitchen, the outside foreign world crashing in suddenly to kill her – how *could* God? That death should come at all, but that it should come with such disrespect.

"Ye see off in the corner where the ground is uneven?" his mother whispered. "That's where they buried the babies, long ago. The two stones there, I don't think even Granny remembered which was which. One is supposed to be my brother Brendan, who should have been maybe two years older than me. The other is my sister Angela, who, they say, never took a breath."

He hadn't known. He shivered as he looked at the anonymous slabs of slate, the ground around them uneven, filled with children's small, unmarked graves.

He left his mother to find Paddy, moving through the crowd, watching Eileen put her arms around Lila, a tall girl of nine.

The night of the wake, she'd been put to bed in Paddy's old room, where she slept half the time in the summer. Five minutes later, she was at the top of the stairs and Eileen had to put her to bed again, and five minutes later, Paddy took his turn. This went on for half an hour, until Paddy said she was asking for her Jamie.

"Why did she have to go?" she asked him, the question his own mind had suppressed as being too childish to bother with.

He had no answer for her or himself, though he should have, if he was to become what he was to become – something about the sin in the garden, a snake, and the eating of an apple, but all these things seemed irrelevant. "Why *now*? Why does *anybody* have to go?"

She climbed into his lap, something she hadn't done for a year or more, and he examined her face, the sharp-boned beauty of the Cahalanes married to something softer, more generous, a family that no longer wore its history of starvation. The metamorphosis of her face was miraculous to him because he went for months, sometimes, without seeing her; her face was different every time.

"I don't know. I don't know..." he said, shaking his head. He was just as disturbed as she was, Granny's body lying on the kitchen table that had been draped in sheets and moved into the lounge, half the town there, coming and going, drinking and eating, spending time with the old woman before she left her home for the last time, left the house she was born in. Lila began to cry and he started talking about heaven, tried to quote a few lines from the Bible for her – about there being a time to be born as well as a time to die, about Christ dying for all so death would be no more, but nothing helped. He couldn't find any way to comfort her. All he could do was hold her until her tears had run dry.

He must have looked very sad to her; she put her spread-fingered hand to his cheek, then very gently, placed it on his hair, then his ear, then his neck, and back up to his hair again. "Baby octopus," she said, playing a little girl's game they used to play so long ago, he had almost forgotten it. He reached down and held one of her icy feet. With difficulty, he persuaded her back to bed, then went down to get a hot water bottle and smuggled up some cake for both of them. He searched for an extra blanket, hesitating outside Granny's empty room before going in to take possession of the rag quilt.

"You just need something more to weigh you down, or you'll be floating up out of bed again," he said.

"Don't go, Jamie. Stay with me 'til I go to sleep."

He sat beside her, nowhere in the world he would rather be, and told her the story of Saint Brigid, the little girl saint of Ireland, who amused herself by taming wolves. Finally, turned to the wall under the rag blanket, surrounded by a dark snow of cake crumbs, she fell asleep. James could hardly leave her even then, because there she was, her hair flung in all directions on the pillow, thick curly streams of it above Granny's blanket: his granny as a child; Lila had red hair. And a glory it was to her.

Now, across the graveyard, he watched Lila crying in her mother's arms. He felt his inability to have given her any words of comfort was the most dismal failure of his life – his personal failure – not the failure of religious philosophy. He couldn't think that, in the case of death, comfort was impossible.

He walked among the yews, seeing so many people he hardly ever saw any more. With a shock of fear up his backbone, he recognized Dermot, completely changed except for his cold, carnivorous eyes. Dermot had lost a lot of weight. It was strange to finally see the bones of his face clearly, like looking at a skinned animal that had worn fat instead of fur. He seemed distilled to his truest essence, was hard-muscled and lethal-looking. Dermot met his eyes and grinned viciously. James saw his teeth, rotting now, spread a little too far apart, one of the front ones cracked off at an angle like a misplaced canine, shorter but sharper. He was escorting two very ancient men that a few people recognized – men from the old IRA.

Paddy was standing next to Dermot, and James made himself walk up to them.

"Ye look good," Paddy was saying. Dermot nodded once to him, stood tall when he looked at the IRA men, old heroes, men whose acceptance of him was automatic because of his supposed relation to the dead woman, her dead husband, her dead father. James thought of the irony: Dermot mourning a woman he wasn't related to, carrying on the work of a family to which he didn't rightly belong.

"It was she who told me where to find them," Dermot told Paddy, proud and cold. "I am a Patriot because of her."

Paddy nodded, mute, as the old men turned to cross the graveyard and Dermot turned a moment after, as if by instinct, as if there was an invisible collar around his throat, and an invisible leash.

"Came out of violence, end in violence," he muttered to James, with a shudder. "If he doesn't kill others he'll be getting killed himself. Why do ye suppose she wrapped him up in *that* particular family tradition, eh? Was it out of the goodness of her heart? Give a lost child a place to go? Jesus. Aw, I abandoned him, too. I – but *she*..."

James had never seen Paddy like this, seething, more and more thoughts boiling up about what Granny had done to Dermot, the baby boy who hadn't wound up buried in the bog. His eyes found Dermot across the graves and he tried to imagine the fat swelling his cheeks – baby fat. Was there no way, then, to bring him back? To give him some other sort of life? James put his hand out, almost staggered with the swirling reversal of his emotions: fear and revulsion turning for the first time to compassion. Was this the moment he began to become a priest?

"She sent this boy who didn't belong to her, sent her *grandson* she didn't love, to his death. She sent him off to be killed. There he is, walking around, but she's murdered him. With malice and forethought, she has."

Paddy rammed the heel of his hand against a sun-baked, lichen-covered cross. He drilled James with his eyes, as if wanting to make sure his anger lived on beyond his own body, in the mind of another, wanting to make this betrayal of his mother a public thing. His brows hunched suddenly, as if he finally understood.

"And Dermot – he and the spirit grocer's girl. They never...did they? Way back. The first year ye came? That *was* a lie, wasn't it?"

James shook his head, and then the good holy boy in him suddenly panicked, because it was partly lie, but partly truth, and the lie part was told by someone he wasn't any more. Everyone was wandering away from the hole in the earth, back to the house: his mother and Susan, Maureen and Agnes, Eileen and Lila, Mr. Murphy and Mrs. McGinty, Colm and Orla, John, hand in hand with Deirdre; they were engaged.

James stayed. He turned to see Paddy striding away from them all, arms swinging as if he was marching, leaving James, leaving Grania before she left him, before the digger man could throw his first shovelful of earth.

That was the worst part, when she was put into the cold dark ground.

James's body cracked and caved in, and was still emptier, his arms around his stomach, a famine hollow: everything he wanted and needed and would never be allowed him. The whole of her absence now came to him, the slow vanishing of her mind when she didn't recognize him, when she no longer remembered to take him up Kilmoney Hill, the wild snapping spirit that had hung on to the end. His gift of reading, of another kind of sight, had come too late; Grania forgot the words almost as soon as she had learned them.

She was buried beside her husband, near her father and mother, close to the graves of her other children, the ones that hadn't lived, the ones that James only met here, now – small Brendan, and Angela who didn't live long enough to take a breath – the children she had buried in her mind and refused to talk of. It changed his whole idea of her, increased his love and his pain, almost burst him wide open. He imagined her in heaven, finally cradling her newborn daughter in firm, young arms.

❖ ❖ ❖

"She was a pagan," his mother had said, the night of the funeral, "as near as you can be to one in this day and age."

It was all he could think about for the rest of the summer,

living in his little cell-like room, cycling to Celbridge every morning, touring people through the great house, watching the clouds with their grudgingly released beams of sunlight. After weeks of denying it, he found he no longer could. She had not gone to confession or to Mass in years. Once, before her mind had gone completely, he'd heard her refer to the Bible as a load of codswallop. You couldn't get much more pagan than that. And then there was Paddy's accusation. James reasoned that Paddy couldn't be considered the best judge of his mother. After the way she'd run his life, prevented him from marrying his first love, he could be forgiven for harbouring resentment. Was sending a boy off to the IRA equal to killing him? She had said she'd murder Dermot; he could remember clearly that he wished she would, when he was bruised and his nose bandaged and he had nothing to do all day but think vengeful thoughts. He had never imagined she'd do it, yet never thought her incapable of it. If he sat back, removed himself as far as he could from his own interest in the matter, he could see that she was guilty on both counts, paganism and murder, at least murder in her heart. Not accessing the mercy of confession, like he did, these sins must have remained in her heart when she died.

And yet, he loved her. Harsh as she was, mean and cruel at times, illiterate and resentful, full of pride and sarcasm, he loved her, in spite of all these things, and because of all these things, and because she had loved him. She had seen him, too, for what he was, and had not been able to help loving him, somehow, though she tried, as he had tried not to love her. And what was he? Nothing much. So if *he* could love Granny, why couldn't Jesus Christ? Why?

He knew the answer, of course. Jesus offered her his love, and she refused it.

She would never rest among the saints. There was nowhere for her to go but hell, but into everlasting torment. He hadn't really thought how horrible this would be. He had never been in excruciating pain but for a few hours, when his nose was broken, when his arm was broken, but he knew that forever was too long to be in pain. And he knew that he could never be happy in heaven knowing this, never be happy in heaven without her.

※ ※ ※

August was a dish into which the clouds poured torrent after torrent of rain. At the age of twenty-one, James was about to become a First Divine. His mother came to visit, to pick him up on their way to do a pilgrimage to St. Patrick's Purgatory. She was to stay at a small guest house in Maynooth while he took her on a tour of the college, then Celbridge.

"Horrible day," she said to him, when he met her at the train station, peering out at the grey clouds, the streaming rain.

"Horrible day to you, too," he said, nodding in greeting.

It became the joke of the week. Whenever she reached for him, tried to hold his arm too tightly, he would say "Horrible day," and she would erupt in giggles and say "Good day, to ye! Horrible day to ye!" He couldn't stand it when she grabbed on to him as if she was an old lady needing support. The joke and her laughter allowed him to take that one step away, allowed him to find something on the opposite wall of the hallway to move toward – a graduation picture from 1912, perhaps, a grid of photographs of grey pasty faces and priestly collars.

"All them cobwebs in your room. Ye haven't been killing the spiders, have ye? It's bad luck."

"No, Mother."

"Your granny never killed a spider. Some of them women in England getting their girdles tied in a knot, screaming at them."

"Granny? I saw her take swipes at cobwebs with the broom! The –"

"I know she's in Hell," Bernadette said, quavering, whirling the old wedding rings around her fingers, repeating the panic in the letters she had sent to him over the summer. "Or she's almost there. In thousands of years of purgatory. With her profanities. And she was more faithful to bingo than to Mass. And the questioning of things and Beings which should not be questioned." She blew her nose and tucked the hanky back into her sleeve.

"Whisht, Mother," he said. They were in the library. "Solemn silence, remember?" James darted his eyes to the sides. The Fourth Divine at the table was undisturbed, still moving his lips over a book, chewing on one of God's softer truths.

"Better pray to Saint Jude, Mother. He's lost causes," James whispered, then, warned by the sarcasm he heard in his own voice, looked at his mother quickly. Had he upset her? "Look up," he said because he wanted to make sure she was happy, unable to see her mood because the lights were glaring off her transparent plastic rain hat as she looked down, fiddled with the hanky in the sleeve of her cardigan. "See the beams, Mother? The wooden tracery and carving? Isn't it beautiful?"

She lifted her eyes briefly, then turned to smile at him. Her face was pale, her skin smooth, with only the beginnings of wrinkles around her eyes and mouth. The scar around her false eye was not so noticeable any more, but she was almost forty. Her sharp, sword-like beauty was no longer softened by youth, and had become a collection of knives. Her jaw was two blades joined at the tip, her sharp cheekbones jutting and aggressive, making the softer flesh beneath look sunken, her shoulder blades jabbing out against her cardigan like the sliced-off stumps of wings. Even her nose seemed to have thinned and sharpened. The fire in her hair was beginning to fade to grey.

"I read some books on St. Patrick's Purgatory. Did you want to look at them yourself, or just for me to tell –"

"Ye don't believe in the indulgences, do you?" her voice breathless and quick and worried whenever she spoke of pious things; the holy wind that blew her soul was always full of fear, for the soul of her son, for the souls of those she loved. "All your fancy modern thinking. Well, ye might change when we're through with the pilgrimage. A lot of time to think and pray about it. Maybe that's another reason why God wants us to go. Where did ye say the Ladies' was?"

He offered his arm to her in penance for the thought that the pilgrimage was really just another excuse for her to hang on to him – thinking up a new holy well to march him around, a penance that took three whole days. He took her out of the library and through several hallways to the hastily built Ladies' next to the chapel – an afterthought, a room renovated after the nuns were already attending classes and going to the hotel off-campus to do their business. When she came out she asked to go back to the gardens.

"What are you going to do now, Mam, with no one to look after?"

She sighed as they walked back outside to the roses she had so admired.

"Have to be a farmer, I guess, a third part of that hill being mine – yours really, someday. Who'd have thought Mam so canny with that lawyer, years ago? You can be sure Orla wishes she'd paid Mam a few more visits. And me sister in America, too. Pity about Annie, though. And nothing to Maureen either, for, you give something to Maureen, and right away, it belongs to Michael anyway. There'll be hell to pay for that. And poor Agnes, always the good girl, the very picture of Mam, and she gets nothing to chop up among her girls. We figure that's what Mam didn't want – the hill chopped up and sold. Paddy thinks Mam loved the hill more than any of us – leaving us to *it* instead of the other way around. Me and Paddy and Colm, the farmers. Got me own wellies, already. Someone has to milk the cows. The young ones, they're going for jobs in town, now, getting cars. Agnes's Siobhán, she wants to go back to nursing after the baby's old enough, and I can help out, you know. There's always some-thing to do."

She brushed the back of her fingers over a full-blown double rose, peach at the edges of the petals, deep pink within. "Until, of course, you get your first parish. Cooking, keeping the manse tidy, that'll be a full-time job for sure."

The manse. Where they would live together, of course, when he became a priest. His eyes widened and he put both his hands to his face as his lungs filled with too much horrified air. She was still a young woman, could live for another fifty years, and she would live with him until the day she died.

"James."

It was a few seconds before he turned and realized she had stopped far behind him to breathe in the scent of yet more roses.

He watched her hurrying after him on the gravel path.

She would never let him leave her behind.

They arrived in Pettigoe, Donegal, then changed to the pilgrim bus that took them to the shore of Loch Derg.

The clouds were dank grey blue. They sped in from the northwest, released a sharp thin drizzle at times, then held back, reserving their cold wet misery. The low mountains were covered with bracken and bog and pines except for the dark grey brown granite rocks which bared themselves, sparkling with rain and mica. The lake was brown as milkless tea under the clouds, tainted with the reddish iron-tinge of its water. Tossing through the wind were the sounds of pilgrims' voices. Almost a hundred waited on the dock. Many were quiet, preparing for the ritual. The ferry, rowed by only two men, was bobbing toward the dock. The air smelled soaked and weedy. James tried to clear his mind of its tourist urges, but he was too curious, and had read too much, to become solemn just yet.

In the middle of the lake, was the island. St. Patrick's Purgatory was a name that had inspired terror and disbelief throughout medieval Europe. It was said to have sparked Dante's *Divine Comedy* – at least, James thought, its lower reaches. For perhaps a thousand years, there was known to be a cave on an island in Hibernia, at the very westernmost point of the earth, the place of the death of the sun, the place where one could visit purgatory, demons, and the dead. A pilgrimage to the Purgatory was reputed to be the worst and most terrifying penance, the last chance for the most desperate of sinners. It was once the entrance to Hell itself in Celtic mythology and a place of pilgrimage long before the takeover of Ireland by Christianity, the takeover of the lake by Christian monks, and the replacement of the Druid gods with God.

But now, in 1975, the island looked like a floating city. It was crammed with a basilica, hostels, docks, and concrete extensions over the water.

"It looks like it could sink," James said.

"Whisht."

James and his mother jammed into the boat with another eighty or so pilgrims – there would be over a thousand doing penance with them – and watched Station Island grow bigger as the boat moved over the water.

They were all prepared for the symbolic three day descent into hell, the most gruelling pilgrimage still performed in the Christian world. He and his mother hadn't had anything to eat since the night before, and the first crab-pincers of hunger were picking at his belly. It would be physical hardship, deprivation of food and sleep and warmth, only the chants of the rosary to sustain them, Mary always full of grace. There were some things James thought he would have difficulty with in being a priest, but rituals weren't among them. After three years of rising for Mass every day at seven in the morning, James had come to love the hypnotic prayers that warmed him when he was half-asleep in a cold morning chapel, the beauty of God's power and love finally coming through to him after he slogged through the boredom of yet another morning the same as so many mornings. After ten or twenty or thirty Hail Marys, she *was* the Queen of Heaven, blessed among virgins, as if the repetition of words had made her so, and everything intoned by the priests *was* sacred, and the bread *was* flesh, and the wine *was* blood.

James looked at the faces of the other pilgrims. He saw piety and gloom, simplicity and hope. There were a lot of old women in clear plastic rain hats. Some were all in black, and these widows were the most solemn, James imagining the white skeletons of their husbands still dancing in their hearts, working at fishing lines or ploughs. There were old men and middle-aged women dressed in fine wool, a few young men and women, and fewer teenagers accompanied by parents. A scrawny, red-haired child in a yellow raincoat drowsed against her mother. Sometimes a wave would slap the side of the boat and wake her with its fine spray, and he remembered his first fishing trip in the curragh, on that soft, warm day so long ago, Paddy presiding gently over all of them, he and John like the apostles, the fishers of men.

"It's bad luck for a red-haired woman to be in the same boat as a priest," his mother informed him, too loudly.

"She's hardly a woman, and I'm hardly a priest."

"I'm not talking about her. I'm talking about me – and the priest behind ye."

James turned to see an old man in a black cassock that was specked with tiny, even blacker, moth holes. His puffy red hands were resting in his lap as he watched his fellow penitents with equally puffy red eyes, nodding and giving encouraging smiles to all.

"He'll be one to lead a group in the all-night vigil," Bernadette said, sure of it, stabbing her index finger into her leg.

The priest put a hand to his mouth and made a strange hideously convulsive movement with his face, to spit his teeth into the palm of his hand. The priest put the set of false teeth, still stringy with saliva, in his pocket, where James thought of them clattering with cold. The priest relaxed, his smile now caved in, fleshy and elastic.

"Bad luck," his mother muttered.

"Why? Will you do the priest damage, or will it be the other way around?"

"Whisht, disrespectful," his mother accused, and he shut his mouth. "Used to be said, too, that if ye slept while at the Purgatory, ye'd go to hell for sure."

"Don't worry, Mother. *Please*. We're doing something that pleases the Lord, right? We're doing it for Granny, to lessen her sufferings. So He'll take care of us. Don't worry so much."

She nodded and James sighed, relieved because she was relieved.

They took off their shoes with all the others after stepping out on the pier and listened to a monk explain the rules of the tiny island: quiet: bare feet: no sleep except at designated times. James followed the crowd into the basilica to visit the Blessed Sacrament, the bread-body of Christ. Hundreds of people were already immersed in repetition ahead of him, dispersed around the island's many sites of devotion. Some recited in Latin, some in English, some Gaelic. He was surprised by the pain and the cold already arching up his bare feet. The rocks of the island were worn, but still uncomfortable, and he looked forward to numbness, for the time he would be too tired to be interested in the place itself so he could pray in earnest.

Aeneas and Orpheus had been here. Supposedly. James looked at the walls as if for their graffiti. The legendary knight Owen from King Arthur's Round Table had come here because he deserved the heaviest of penances. Not only was he a violator of churches, but he had killed the husband of the lady he loved, then deserted her. After Owen, not-so-legendary men from all over Europe braved distance and disease, hunger, thirst, thieves, murderers, the rumour that the cave, the island, the lake, didn't exist at all, that they might wander forever, looking. They walked the last miles barefoot or on their knees – Hungarian, French, Spanish: Guarino da Durazzo, Godalh, Sire De Beaujeu, Sir William de Lisle, Georgius Crissaphan. In order to enter the cave, they were required to obtain permission from the local bishop, who took their money, whose duty it was to dissuade them from their plans of descent, for it was said many had entered the cave and never emerged. The prior of the island's monastery also took their money, and implored them to give up their plans, but if they were still determined, and not completely reduced to poverty, they entered into the ritual.

There used to be fifteen days of fasting and prayer while the monks told terrifying stories of demons and torture, and of pilgrims who never emerged from the dark. Then, after Mass and a sprinkling of holy water, the penitent was led with litany to the mouth of the cave. He was given a last chance to reconsider, blessed by the holy men, then locked inside, all light shut out by a heavy wooden door. The next day the procession would return and the prior would unlock the door. If the penitent was waiting there, he was joyfully led back to the church for another fifteen days of vigil and prayer. If the penitent wasn't at the mouth of the cave, he was considered lost forever, and the door was locked again.

James felt safe because the cave had been filled in and he would only be here for three days... But the ancient penitents met those they knew among the dead. This worried him. He was afraid of his mother seeing ghosts.

After the visit to the Sacrament, he flowed in the river of penitents to pray at the vandalized cross of St. Patrick, a battered pillar of knot-carved stone, its arms and head now made of iron. Next were prayers at the cross of St. Brigid, after which he and his mother turned together to the lake and renounced the world, the flesh and the devil. After circling the basilica four times and the repetition of seven decades of the rosary, each decade including one Our Father, ten Hail Marys, one Glory Be to the Father, and one Creed, James was in what he considered to be the holy emptiness inside his soul, the place he went in meditation and the endless Masses of his life at Maynooth. It was now that he knew nothing, trusting in God to do all the knowing for him, like when he was a child lying on the strand, cloud shadows scudding over him. He never had to move or change: heaven on earth, a heaven in prayer.

He flowed among the other pilgrims around the penitential beds: six rings of stone, the ancient foundations of beehive monk's cells dedicated to saints Brigid, Dabheoc, Molaise, Columcille, Catherine, and Brendan. The ritual at each circle was the same. Three paced circuits with three Our Fathers, three Hail Marys and one Creed, then all repeated again while kneeling at the entrance, all repeated again in three circuits of the inside of the bed, and repeated again kneeling in front of the crucifix in the centre. Around and within the beds, the stones were sharp, and the ground steep. James started to get mixed up in his prayers. On his third bed, he couldn't remember whether he'd said two or three Our Fathers, and so forced himself to do another circuit to make sure. His knees were raw already from the rocks. The drizzle turned to downpour.

"Hail Mary full of grace. The Lord is with you. Blessed are you among women and blessed is the fruit of thy womb, Jesus... Hail Mary full of grace. The Lord is with you. Blessed are you... Hail Mary full of grace. The Lord is with you. Blessed are you among women and..."

He could hear the splash of countless bare feet in the rain, pacing around and around in circles, and was no longer sure he would survive the day, let alone three.

And the penitents met those they knew among the dead.

William of Stanton met his sister and her lover who scolded him for not allowing them to marry. Archbishop Fitzralph was collectively bidden by the dead to remove one of his most objectionable interdicts, though no one knows exactly what the dead were objecting to. Georgius Crissaphan brought secret messages from the dead for King Edward of England, Pope Innocent the Sixth, and the Sultan of Babylon.

"Our Lord was in Hell for three days. And we are here for three days," his mother whispered behind his ear, making his flesh shiver. "And this is nothing. Nothing to what *she* is suffering now."

His granny, who would like to be laughing at them both from the thick blue clouds. What would her idea of heaven be? The clouds rolling into green hills, a house with a big turf fire and a huge cup of spiked tea, and stories, and spying down on all of them. And maybe even a few reading lessons, just so she would have something frustrating to yell about.

His mother placed her hand on his arm, and his body and thoughts stilled, waited for her to remove her touch. Her fingernails were beginning to show faint ridges, an almost imperceptible sign of aging: delicate girl nails becoming an old woman's claws over sixty or seventy years.

He repeated the Creed, then knelt on spines of shining grey stone in a puddle of water and started the same prayers all over again.

There would be only two meals of dry toast and black tea to look forward to in these three days. There would be no sleep that night nor the whole of the next day when he would be praying, walking, kneeling in the rain. He thought of the stories he had read: how knees became bloody, how people fainted, got infections in their feet, in their lungs. All had to make nine complete circuits of the island, nine "stations," which meant a total of 360 rounds of the individual prayer sites, kneeling fifteen times each round, reciting 2000 prayers, 63 decades of the rosary. Penitents had to attend two church services each evening, and that night, almost all night, they were to recite four complete Stations of the Cross in the basilica.

He finished his rounds of the penitential beds, then went with his mother to the water's edge where they said five Our Fathers, five Hail Marys, and one Creed, before kneeling and saying them again. They went back to St. Patrick's cross for more prayers, then back to the basilica to pray for the Pope's Intention. The first of his stations was over. He would have to do eight more. He and his mother separated to follow pilgrims of their own sex to the segregated hostels for a piece of dry bread and a cup of black tea, the only food they would get until the next bread and tea, twenty-four hours away. He threw spoonfuls of sugar into his tea, the only extravagance permitted.

Then back to the basilica to start his second station, his mother already far ahead.

He was wet and shivering, got tongue-tied sometimes, and had to be silent a minute to collect his thoughts. He heard lapping water, wind, torn throats, and the voices of people no longer aware of themselves. He was losing his determination and sense of purpose. Why did God want the same words after the same words after the same words? Why did He want suffering from those He loved? The rain pelted down, splatting cold on his scalp – sent directly from heaven. He should have been afraid to come to Loch Derg. It was a test of his spiritual fitness, a test of soul rather than a test of knowledge. Had his soul been tested before? Only in life. How good had he been at life before he entered the enforced cloister of the college? Not very good at all.

Louis de Sur saw demonically beautiful women singing and dancing, carrying crowns, and playing chess in the nude. Others saw souls gnawed by serpents, straddled by toads, hung in fiery chains, hooked through their "sinning members," boiled, spitted, impaled, lead-dunked, and thrown by storms into lakes of ice. Was this what God, the good Lord Jesus Christ, was doing to his grandmother? Forever?

Was this what she deserved?

He buried his mind in the rosary, concentrated on picking his way around the most painful stones.

He counted his beads.

Grey air, grey water, all around him.

Why should pain help him?

If he was going to be a priest, he should know this.

He should know everything.

He couldn't get back into the meditative state and he mouthed his prayers, watched the people around him who seemed so sure of themselves.

The old priest with his removable teeth was pacing, circling. His face was intense, brown-spotted, eyes watching the air strangely, his nostrils hairy and arched like the eyebrows of a sur-prised man. He walked into the water up to his knees and rubbed his soft swollen hands in the cold wind, sometimes bending painfully, dipping them in the lake and holding them out in the air to freeze. Did this willingness to suffer show the priest's goodness? Had the priest done something terrible and did he need forgiveness? The Maynooth priests frowned upon superstitious pilgrimages that reeked of past pagan tradition – holy wells, even St. Patrick's Purgatory itself.

His mother was following the priest. She also put her hands in the water and held them out to the rain. He turned away.

There was a pregnant woman on her knees in front of St. Patrick's mutilated cross, swaying and entranced. Why did she want God's favour? To get a better job for her husband? To have a healthy child – the child she was starving now? The teenagers were all probably praying for good marks on their exams. God knew what. What was the point of wandering in the rain?

He attended the six o'clock church service. After his third arduous journey around the stations of the island, he stood to watch the sun set behind Croagh Breac in a clearing of sky between rain and mountains, the air red and wet, the lake calming.

His mother found him among the hundreds at the nine o'clock service, and they knelt together under the massive stone vaults of the basilica, lit now with a few dim bulbs and clutches of candles. He was praying, his elbows on the ledge of the pew ahead of him. She touched his back, let her hand rest on the tweed between his shoulder blades.

He couldn't pray with her hand there, couldn't think. He was so hungry and tired and her hand was pure, painful gravity upon him – *take it away, take it away* – a stone pressing through to his heart. And then her hand began to move. Where would it go? When would it stop? He must not, should not, could not move. He cried as her hand caressed him from his shoulders to the small of his back.

As if his tears had begun first, and she had reached out to comfort him.

When it was time to begin the night vigil of the Stations of the Cross, she steered him toward the group surrounding the old priest, pushed through the crowd of forty-odd people so they could be near him.

"My son, James – Seamus, is at Maynooth," she whispered to the priest. "Can he be of service to ye, Father?"

James began to shake his head, but the old priest held up a hand and gazed at James with his red eyes, examining his soaked-to-the-knee trousers.

"He can follow me. Stay beside me, young man, and learn," the old priest said, in a clear gentle baritone. He smiled then, broad and innocent, the teeth once again inside his mouth.

They began.

James followed the priest and listened to him dutifully, though he had the Stations memorized since he was a boy, though hunger was squealing in his stomach, deafening him. First Christ's condemnation, then the whole sequence of carrying the cross, being relieved by Simon of Cyrene, washed by Veronica, falling, falling, and finally being hung on the cross, dying, descending, and descending into the earth, all strange things to make so beautiful in coloured glass – bruises and blood and death – stained light falling on their shoulders, at their feet. James watched the floor sometimes, moving his bare toes through blots of bloody red and pools of blue, the glass lit from the outside by incandescent bulbs.

After the first round, the pilgrims were allowed a fifteen-minute rest. James went outside. Many pilgrims were leaning against the walls of the basilica, flapping their arms to shake out numbness, hoping the cold wind would keep them awake, glad the rain had stopped. It wasn't yet two in the morning. A bearded man offered him a cigarette, which he took, grateful. He watched the smoke – dragon's breath – leave his mouth.

"They're bad for you," his mother told him, though she still smoked the odd cigarette herself. She was beside him, having forced her way through the pilgrims around the door.

He held out the cigarette and she took a long breath through it. After the second Stations of the Cross, he went outside and smoked again, and after the third, he smoked again, begging his tobacco, taking advantage of the pilgrims' generosity; they were all suffering, all thinking about the suffering of Christ, all willing to offer what little comfort they could. It was almost five in the morning, and the nicotine dulled his nagging desire for food and sleep, made it possible for him to drag his exhausted mind open and pay attention the next time around.

The penitents recited, swift and mumbling and without enthusiasm, as they repeated for each station:

"We adore Thee, O Christ, and we praise Thee;
Because by Thy Holy Cross, Thou hast redeemed the world."

The red-pawed priest intoned the rite of the first station in his devoted baritone: the Condemnation by Pilate.

"Pontius Pilate dares to condemn the all-holy Saviour to death. No, not Pilate; but *my sins* have condemned Jesus to be crucified. O Jesus have mercy on me and remember thou didst choose to die that I may have eternal life. Let me so live that when I come to die I may find thee a most merciful Judge, an all-loving Redeemer."

James watched his mother with furtive eyes. Her hair was still long and thick, perpetually tied in braids and knots all her waking hours. Her old coat, the threadbare clothes that she brought from England, had become her pride – she had conquered her vanity. She was clasping her blue hands to her breast, a look of contorted guilt, shame and sorrow on her face, as if she had pounded the nails into Christ's hands and feet herself. He saw others looking at her, noticing the scar, wincing, pitying, counting their blessings, loving her for loving a God who could do this to her. That's what omnipotent meant, didn't it? All-powerful. All things were done by God's hand.

God's fist.

God's claw.

Where was the cave of this Holy Island? He could crawl into it now, and hide forever, and any of the caves would do – pits the monks had dug to replace earlier pits that had been filled in by shovels and surges of anti-pilgrimage fervor in the church. He would even hide in the one that Oliver Cromwell's soldiers were said to have shat into, for which the Catholic God smote them in their hinder parts with dysentery and the foulest flux – hide from his mother, from God, from his hunger, hide and sleep, and sleep forever.

The penitents repeated one Our Father, one Hail Mary, and one Glory Be. "Have mercy on us, O Lord; Have mercy on us."

"Isn't that His job?" the old priest whispered to James, startling him out of his dreaming. "Isn't it a rum thing to be reminding Him of His bleeding *job*?"

The priest walked to the next station and the penitents shuffled after him. He led the rite again, his baritone shrunken into crackles and rasps. As they walked to the third station, the priest took James by the wrist, addressed him as if he were God.

"Why is it, Lord, your priests can't be human? Have human passions and comforts...family? Why is it?"

A snaking shiver up James's back. Awake as he never had been before.

"We adore Thee, O Christ..." the penitents intoned. The priest spoke the third station, pulled James by the wrist and walked on.

"Why, Lord, do you have us suffering through these nonsensical chants?" the priest hissed into his ear. "Does tedium please you? Will it do us any good?"

James sucked in his breath; to think he'd thought the same thing only hours ago! He tried to pull his wrist away, but the priest's hand was thick and raw and clammy, closed around his wrist like clay. They stood at the fourth station, Christ meeting his mother:

"Jesus, the Man of Sorrows, meets Mary, the Queen of Martyrs...*Oceans* of grief *deluge* their hearts as they face each other. They suffer thus for my sins. O Jesus, O Mary, bathe my sinful soul in a *sea* of true sorrow for my past offenses. In all temptation I will say: 'Jesus, Mary, *help* me!'"

The priest gave the words too much life and feeling, a mockery when juxtaposed with his doubts: soap operatic, melodramatic, embarrassing.

"Why, Lord, do you have us suffer at all?" The priest asked James, blaming him gently, squeezing his arm, as if out for a stroll with the Lord himself. "You created us knowing we would sin as free creatures. So you created us to sin and you *torture* us for it?"

James's eyes went black; all these things he had been trying to shut his mind to. What could he do if he doubted? If he couldn't be a priest? How could he return to the farm? Would his life dissolve into day by day by day with the cows, shunned by humanity, watching John and Deirdre have baby after baby after baby? Tramping around the holy well with his mother? Watching her across the dinner table and wondering if every shadow that crossed her face was his fault? Wondering how he could possibly make her smile, or even comfortable enough to leave her bed, her room, the house?

And where was his father now? Dead? Drunk to death?

Pilgrims met those they knew among the dead.

All the faces around him were pale and haggard, starved ghosts. James couldn't hear the words properly. The rite of the Stations of the Cross swarmed and mingled with the priest's doubting questions, with James's own doubts, turning him whiter, weaker.

"...die a thousand times rather than have the misfortune to fall again into mortal sin!"

If sin is misfortune, you have no control of it; fortune, a pagan idea, like chance, God punishing for no reason.

O Lord, there are those who are born into hopelessness, who live in hopelessness, who sin without your forgiveness, and they go to hell therefore, because of the fact they were born. What kind of God *are* you?

...inflamed with love...I may shed tears of blood...tears of blood...tears of blood.

What is the point of torturing us poor buggers in hell forever, for sin accumulated in a life of a few years? Surely we cannot be so bad or important. Seventy years of sin, and therefore an eternity of torture?

Isn't that, *O Lord*, overdoing it? Just a little?

...true Christian mortification that I may love only Thee...

Thee Thee Thee, the divine pronoun. For Thee I live. Jesus, for Thee I die!

Are we really creatures of free will if we have no choice as to whether we are born? Born to enter into God's circle of pain and sin and righteous retribution? What is the good?

Like Jesus, I too must lie in the grave. But Jesus rises in triumph on the third day. My buried Jesus, grant eternal rest to all who sleep in death. Have mercy on me and grant me the grace to rise to a new spiritual life, that dying to myself now, I may rise gloriously with thee on the last day.

The penitents buried Christ at the fourteenth station in a tomb of brown shards of glass and James ran out of the basilica, through the walking sleepers, to the men's toilet. His bowels exploded out of him until he was empty, utterly, though he was still sick, still felt like vomiting, still felt he needed to strain, to squeeze out the entire contents of his body cavity: bowels, liver, lungs, and heart. He sat on the toilet, and it was a long time before he was composed enough to leave, to go to the eating room and drink cup after cup of rusty lake water, "Loch Derg wine."

It was seven in the morning.

He couldn't stop thinking.

Sleep would not be allowed for another fourteen hours.

A disappointed Dutch monk from Eymstadt complained to Pope Alexander the Sixth that he hadn't seen one vision the night he sat huddled in the small cold dirty hole the monks passed off as a cave.

Visions. If only James would be so lucky – so unlucky. Visions to tell him what was true, what to believe.

He had to pray his stations, pace from one penitential bed to another, recite more endless Paters, Aves, practicing his Latin, his Gaelic. What kind of God?

You *knew* Adam and Eve would eat the apple.

What was eating an apple anyway?

Disobedience.

They were *disrespectful.*

Do what you're told. Don't do what you're not told.

Follow the rules and you won't go to the Hell of God's creating, a pit of snakes and burning ladders grinned over by a supernatural bully with a snotty nose, the bully who hits you without explaining the rules of his game, the rules which all players are too stupid to understand because they only make sense to He who made them: Divine Mysteries. James erased the image of Dermot from his mind.

"Our Father who art in heaven," he prayed too loud, to drown his mind. "Hallowed be thy name. Thy kingdom come. Thy will be done on earth as it is in heaven..."

He prayed and prayed, but there was no way to know what to ask of God.

Not a God who behaved like this.

His mother thought Granny was in Hell. But Bernadette thought Heaven was waiting for Bernadette. How could she be happy there, knowing others – her own mother among them – were getting their fingernails torn out? Getting white-hot iron rods shoved up their anuses, their eyes raked out? How could anyone be happy in Heaven knowing this?

"Holy Mary, Mother of God, pray..."

There was something *evil* about the way God was running things.

"Our Father who art in heaven, hallowed be thy name. Thy kingdom come. Thy will be done on earth as it is in heaven. Give us this day...give us this day our...and forgive us, forgive us."

He wanted to go on strike, a spiritual hunger strike, would refuse to strive for heaven until God got rid of the trap door, the dungeon, and His dragons waiting beneath.

James finally walked to the basilica to find a spot of wall to sit against.

Multitudes were walking, dazed, trying to be active, afraid to stop moving, afraid of sleep. James thought about sleep. How had he taken this blessing so for granted? If he could sleep, he could wake and maybe all this desperation would seem the product of a tired, suffering mind. One was supposed to suffer at Loch Derg, and suffer in any way one was disposed to; would he, too, be straddled by a toad? Naked women playing chess – where were they when he needed them? Would he receive God's orders directly from the decaying maws of the dead? There were yet two more required stations of crosses and beds. Beds. He imagined St. Brigid asleep on her penitential bed, green as grass growing in the clefts of the rocks, Brigid shrunken to a tiny baby, rocking in the arms of another baby, a twin who was grown older, who was his dead sister, who looked like his mother with an eye dangling, and a scream – another scream and his mother was throwing the baby at him, a four-year-old flying though the air, his sister splattering bloody over the rocks of the island, then coalescing, rising into the sky to become an oyster-catcher, black with a red stick beak sailing up, then diving, diving open-beaked at his throat –

"Wake up!"

The thud of a bare wet heel against his leg, and James popped his eyes open. The old priest was standing beside him.

"Be awake and watch therefore," the priest told him, voice cracked and somber, destroyed by the night of prayer, "for the day of the Lord is at hand."

He couldn't believe the priest had kicked him. He stood and watched the priest wander away to stand ankle deep in the still lake. The rest of the day he spent wandering stupidly over the rocks, wading in the water, watching the gulls, listening to the low talk of the penitents, to the muttering prayers of his mother who was never far away. He closed his eyes whenever she was forced to wipe her nose with the back of her hand. Hardship, to her, also meant no handkerchief.

More kneeling and praying. Endless. There was toast and tea again, a church service at six and another at nine, and after, he fell into the abyss of his bed – a real bed with springs and blankets, not with rocks, grass, rain, and a cross.

He woke to a bell the next morning and was surprised to find himself in such a strange place. He drank reddish water (the blood of the saints?) and stood a long time in the lavatory as urine poured out of him. Two more rounds of the stations, his stomach cramping; he followed the stream of penitents into the basilica, then to St. Patrick's cross, then St. Brigid's, then to the beds. On the first round, a hole finally wore through the corduroy on his right knee. He concentrated, counting beads, aware of how bad he smelled every time he moved his arms. One round, and a rest, another round, always waiting in line to begin each bed's prayers, the stations crowded by people trying to do their penance in time to catch the train from Pettigoe.

After he said his final prayer, he couldn't help but sit, astonished by his accomplishment, feeling he'd earned something – maybe not indulgences, but something – victory? Relief came to him, and happiness, almost. He had slept, felt rested, if weak, his head throbbing, his stomach empty and howling. His memories of his doubts were fuzzy, and in the front of his mind was a meal, the future plate of food that he imagined was waiting for him in a tourist restaurant in Pettigoe. Bacon and cabbage and floury white potatoes and chips and green beans all smothered in a rich brown gravy – he never used to like gravy – and maybe apple tart and cream, and tea, and beer, maybe... He swallowed saliva. He saw the old priest, red-eyed, nodding benignly to people, then stooping to scoop a handful of gravel into his pocket.

"He's crazy," James whispered, amazed, relieved. "Barking mad." He almost laughed.

The boat was coming, heavy oars splashing, to ferry them out of purgatory, back to life.

His mother stood beside him, both pairs of their shoes in her hands, her kerchief flat and dank, her seeing eye in a dark sack of hunger. She was staring at him, adoring him, biting her smiling lips: her son, her life.

His unclean mouth tasted like sour milk. Another four years of study, and then she would come to live with him wherever he went, wherever the church sent him. She would be the only woman in his life until he died. He shut his eyes, leaned against a wall, let the hard cold stone press into his back, chilling him further. He prayed for God to bless and keep him, to be merciful to his poor grandmother. Who was he to think his prayers weren't working?

Bernadette pulled him to the dock, elbowed her way through the crowd so they could be among the eighty to leave on the first boat. He thought only of his meal, seated himself behind his mother on the narrowest seat at the back of the boat. The old priest jammed in immediately beside him, nonchalant, one eyebrow raised.

The devil could also appear as an angel of light.

"Ye'll have to get out and wait for the next one, miss. Sorry," said the hard-mouthed, tweed-capped man standing at the oar nearest the dock. He held the young pregnant woman by the hand and helped her out of the boat to stand again with the pilgrims on the dock. "There you go, Father," he said. "Can't have an expecting woman on the boat with ye."

"I never heard that one," Bernadette muttered.

"Sure, man, that's no matter! Pagan stuff and nonsense!" the old priest called, outraged. "Get back in the boat, miss! The state of your – it's me who should be getting off."

The tweed man shrugged and helped her back in, then pushed the boat away from the dock. The oars began lifting and splashing. The priest stank of unwashed age and damp wool, and James turned away to face the fitful water and the dull steel rain that pattered on the waves. His mother hunched forward on the seat ahead of him, sleep taking her. A few people began to sing with shivering lips:

> Oh! fare thee well, Loch Derg,
> Shall I ever see you more?
> My heart is filled with sorrow
> To leave thy sainted shore...

The priest stood and looked at his watch, the wet black sail of his cassock flapping against James's face. He stepped on, then over the edge of the boat, disappearing through the balloons of dark cloth that jerked away immediately after him, a faithless Simon Peter unable to walk on water. The large boat hardly wobbled. The splash disappeared into the splashes of the oars.

"He's gone! He went over!" James shouted, and the rest of the pilgrims turned their dull, deprived faces toward him.

"Who, dear?" his mother asked, awakening.

The oarsmen, the only other people who had seen it happen, turned the boat around. They drifted, listened...the wind slapping in their clothes, the silent beginning to pray.

The students said the after breakfast prayer, and solemn silence, a blanket laid over them since the night before, was thrown off. The day of voices dawned slowly. Chairs vibrated on the oak floor of the dining hall, and greetings and laughter were subdued, though some of the students hadn't seen each other since spring. The deans frowned upon unchecked boisterousness. It wasn't respectful or priestly. It wasn't conscious of the seriousness of life or the suffering of the world. A young cleric had to cure himself of noise before he would be able to contemplate, to meditate, to assume his future office. Even though the priests weren't always listening, the students were aware there was Someone who was. It was this Someone that the students were supposed to be most concerned about; however, the Good Lord wasn't the one handing out caveats – "cats" they were called. Three cats and a student would be thrown out of the seminary.

Accumulating enough cats would take too long, James thought, as he watched his friends, watched himself. The skin of his hands, between the freckles, was the colour of bone, as if the demons of purgatory had stripped his flesh away, and he was all bare ivory and nerves. He had hardly slept for a week.

Francis Crowley, the top Fourth Divine, was speaking about the deaconate retreat he'd been on in Culdaff. He was blond, pale and cerebral, his eyebrows raised permanently in concern. He brushed toast crumbs from his lips.

"I had heard it was possible to dwell completely in prayer, but it had never been allowed me before. It was a breakthrough – a gift. Every act, every step, every breath of the day, was part of the hymn."

Francis stumbled over his words, unable to convey what he had felt while walking one day when the wind blew up a storm and the waves were the power of God crashing against his soul.

Francis spoke as a man in love.

If James became a priest, his mother would be the only woman in his life, ever.

He couldn't stop swallowing, though his cup of tea had long been empty.

James could see various shades of understanding on the faces of the other students from Cork – the older ones nodding in appreciation, the younger ones amazed: an entire day in meditation? Impossible. Most of them could barely manage a half-hour before daydreams began to plague them.

Would it change Francis to know that priests could slip as easily into the cold deeps of Hell as anyone else? Would it change Francis to know someone he loved was embarking upon eternity in Hell? How dare God make things so simple for Francis?

It was his anger at God's cruelty that turned to disbelief. James believed in goodness, in rightness. An eternity of suffering for a few miserable years of disobedience? Perhaps eternity was also too long for anyone to be happy. He would give up his place in Heaven, annihilate Heaven itself in order to annihilate Hell, Heaven's shadow. He would give up his place in Heaven to save his granny from Hell, would sacrifice his own need to hope for eternal, blissful life, as if he could obliterate both by stopping believing in them. Heaven and Hell was a system that couldn't be true because it wasn't good, wasn't *right*. Even his disbelief was confused, had elements of his old faith. At first, it was a kind of spiritual hunger strike; he was punishing God by rejecting him, by withdrawing his faith and love because of God's corrupt rules and regulations. He could either believe in God or in goodness, so he made his choice.

So, no Heaven and Hell. Why were they invented in the first place? Because people couldn't conceive of their own end, couldn't bear the idea of *not being*?

There was the worst part of it all. Where was his sister, then? The terrible thing was, that to annihilate Hell was to annihilate Heaven, and therefore not only his own eternity, but also his sister's. To save Granny, he had to give up his sister's afterlife, her compensation for only living to the age of four. Now, she was really gone, not waiting somewhere for her mother and father and brother, not singing with the angels, but nowhere. He gave up his hope for a deity that could transcend time and decay, had to finally allow the drunk driver to snatch his baby sister into oblivion. Death was the end, equally for everyone, and in that way, was fair in a way that life wasn't. It was terrible to finally have to say goodbye to Dymphna. He had no choice but to join himself with the modern, secular view of the cosmos so despised by his teachers, the view that has no place for Heaven or Hell or immortality, has nowhere to put the dead except history.

No God, no Jesus. No one was up in the sky to save him, to keep him from being a beast instead of a saint, to keep him from the evil that was in his own heart and in the heart of every human being. Exhausted and confused as he was, he would have to save himself.

He prayed to the God he no longer believed in, to the God he was certain didn't exist, to give God one last chance, asked God to answer his questions, allow him to hold to his faith, asked God to vindicate Himself, prove that His was the good way. He prayed because wasn't Mr. Young of Cork, a First Divine, too deep into it for the loss of his faith? And what about his mother?

He prayed, but Jesus didn't appear to him. Jesus didn't show him the spear-wound in His side, so James could not put his hand within it.

How strangely easy it was to leave Ireland after all: start walking, buy a ticket with the money he'd made from his job at Celbridge. He watched his hands move, watched his feet walk, watched the waves rise and fall and fall away as the ferry took him from Dublin back to England, as he made the passage that he'd so longed to make as a child, as he came back to what he thought of as the modern world. He bought sausage rolls and meat pies and chocolate bars and cups of tea from the cafeteria on board. He watched all the people, the little girls with their white socks and black shoes, the little boys carrying toy trucks, the mothers with their big purses filled with store-bought biscuits and sweets in twists of colored paper, the fathers with their newspapers and cigarettes, the few young men from America and Germany, with their dirty canvas backpacks, their hiking boots, their plimsole sneakers and umbrellas tied somehow to the mounds of what they lugged around and deposited in the aisles. He felt strange beside them, so properly dressed in corduroy pants and white shirt and tweed jacket, envied them their shoulder straps because his battered suitcase was hard to carry. He met a fellow from New Zealand, on his way around the world, seeing the sights, paying his way by shearing sheep. He could hardly conceive of it because he did not feel free, did not think of himself as free. Untethered, maybe, falling, maybe. What an adventure his first ferry trip to Ireland had seemed at first, with his mother, and the cloth bag of food, going off to someplace he had never been before. Once, he examined the British passport his mother had worked so hard to get him so he could go on the clerical students' trip to Rome in November; it seemed hardly necessary now, him a British citizen going back to Britain.

Where else could he fall to, after all? He had to see if his father had really drunk himself to death, or find out what had become of him if he was still alive. If he was still alive, would his father speak to him, own him, be happy to meet him again? His mother had thrown him up into the air over ten years ago, and he was simply falling back down to earth, falling to the only place he could fall to, England, his old home.

It gave him comfort to touch his chest lightly where his hand would naturally fall while crossing himself. He caught himself saying a prayer now and then, and stopped, shut his mind down as quickly as he could. When he thought about it, what a relief it was to let his mind go, after all, to allow himself to think whatever he wanted to think, without having to jerk his own reins, jerk himself back to God, back to proper kinds of thought. He averted his eyes from young women, then reminded himself this was no longer required, but could not help feeling he was doing something dangerously wrong when letting his eyes rest in their soft hair, on their lips, their delicate fingers and ankles, on the way the faces of the watches they wore slipped around their narrow wrists, always attempting to look shyly at the floor. Was there really nothing wrong with this? He could hardly believe it.

Now and then, the ferry would crest a slightly bigger wave and a burst of spray would explode up, past his window, sparkling like rain when the sun dips under a storm cloud in the evening. He was so thankful for the water's beauty, but had no one to thank, and the emotion swirled within him without an outlet.

It was then that he thought that Jesus Christ, or at least, the idea of Him, could be the greatest loss of his life, greater than the loss of father or homelands or grandparents. He had lost his faith that there was a divinely inspired plan for his life, lost the particular sense of safety this had given him. He had lost the idea that he was a good person, a good person because he prayed, went to confession, followed divinely inspired rules, and fit the template of Catholicism over his soul and pressed himself, hard, into it. He had no idea what he might do: after all, hadn't he just overthrown the Ten Commandments? The greatest sin of all was supposed to be disbelief, because it allowed in all the other sins. He had no idea what was a good thing to do or a bad thing to do, or whether he was on his way to becoming another Hitler. He was travelling with a stranger, himself, and he was frightened.

Once back in England, on another bus, he was excited by the numbers of cars, such modern cars, more even than in Dublin, and other kinds of mysterious machines everywhere, on the wharves, the building sites, on the lorries. The bus station in Oxford looked familiar enough. He wandered around on his first day, trying to orient himself, trying to see all the smaller things he remembered, the less dangerous things: St. Aloisius Primary, the churches, the colleges, the playing fields, the punts, the river. He circled. He would start slowly. The old phone number was not in service, so his father was probably not in the little semi-detached house any more, the house he and Dymphna had grown up in. It had been to the east of Carfax, was down a long road lined by old Victorian brick houses with little carriage courts in front of them behind low walls. The ivy was thick here and there, the gravel weedier than he remembered; things had gone downhill in the last ten years. He kept walking, too terrified to find his father just yet, but wanting to find the house, to look at it, maybe wait around to see what stranger went into it. He couldn't find it at all. What he found was a new roundabout and a building site with a placard announcing the Sainsbury's that was to be built. He had avoided going to his grandfather's house, afraid of the wreckage of time, afraid of finding them dead and gone, or his grandfather's hacking cough, his grandmother's shaking hands, blooming horribly into whatever disease would take them. Now that he had seen what had become of his house, there was nothing else left for him to do but seek out his grand-parents, no way of avoiding a confrontation with what he had missed, with how this world had gone on without him. He went back to the youth hostel to think.

The hostel had a large kitchen with hot plates and pots for cooking, a common room, and cavernous stairwells that had once allowed fine ladies to make dramatic descents when the house had been a stately home and not flooded with cheap green carpet. Its rooms now contained clusters of bunks and shabby young men and women in their late teens and early twenties trying to find themselves, most of them unable to find their stash of clean underpants.

He sat in the kitchen, the greasy, vinegar-stained newspaper from his fish and chips crumpled on the table beside him where his elbows rested, his hands holding his head up. There was a man – a boy – from Spain giving a monologue to anyone who would listen as he tried to feed his stiff strands of spaghetti into a pot of boiling water much too small to hold them. He laughed, a staccato *ha-ha-ha-ha* as he talked about the strange British and their tea: "PG Tips! PG Tips! *Ha-ha-ha-ha!*" A little group of Americans had gathered around him, listening and laughing as they ate their late-night snacks; it was almost eleven, and most of them had cooked their dinners long ago. The trash bin was overflowing with cans from sardines and baked beans in tomato sauce, the remains of sausages, eggs and bacon, carrots and cucumbers, apples and pears.

He shifted over a little when a girl set a small paper sack on the table beside him. She sat down and arranged her purse and newspaper in front of her with a sigh of contentment, as if she was finally, *finally*, where she was meant to be.

"So, what planet are you from?" she said, opening the bag and taking out a white floury scone dotted with raisins.

"Pardon?"

"I mean country. It's just that you look more like an English schoolboy than a backpacker."

"Ireland."

"Well, that explains it. Amazing that you people dress like that and still go on killing each other."

"Like wh – well, you know, it's not all of us," he said, blushing because she was a pretty, liberated American girl, with the gleaming white teeth so unusual in Ireland, and because of Granny, and Colm, and Dermot, and because he was close enough to see the six – seven – freckles on the tip of her nose.

He put his arm with its rolled-up sleeve beside hers on the table. "Quick. Freckle contest – I win!"

She laughed and wrinkled her nose. "You looked so *sad*," she said, as if people were almost never sad, as if it was a state of mind prevented by the North American weather.

He couldn't answer, couldn't speak. Sadness. Was that all this was? What about lostness, abandoned dreams, bereavement, broken faith? He didn't suppose those things were allowed in her country either. Even though they spoke the same language, he doubted she would be able to understand a thing he said.

The lights flicked off, then on, and everything abruptly changed; girls leaped up, gathering their belongings, and boys wolfed the last of their food. The lights would be turned off in the whole building in five minutes, and if people couldn't get into their beds by that time, they would have to stumble in the dark.

"Shit. It's eleven." The girl got up, folding her newspaper. "You know, I came in late, the latest, in fact. They had to open up a whole new room for me. I'm in it all alone."

"Well. That's good," he said, thinking of the snoring din of his own room, following her out of the kitchen, through the other milling backpackers, all trying to get to the toilets and back to their own beds. "Then you can...sing."

"It's funny you should say that."

She took his hand and led him out of the crowd, all the way up the ornate set of stairs, and through a door. It was another big room with battered plaster walls and pale green wainscoting and six sets of metal bunks. The roof was white, angling down around them, pierced with dormer windows. To his surprise, she did begin to sing, a pure boyish soprano, clear and lovely and bright as a cloudless sky, but with the heat of the sun as well. His sudden burst of joy shattered when she hit one particular note, the same note he recalled from his favorite version of the *Donna Nobis Pacem*. Her singing could then do nothing but remind him of sacred music, remind him of his friends – choirboys and clerics – remind him of the faith he had left. She had such a lovely voice, a happy voice, though it made his face contort with pain, broke his heart, made him wish he were deaf. He could not put his hands over his ears, he could not ask her to stop, and she flew up into a celestial wind of trills and arpeggios, and then her own soaring cadenza, leaping octaves, mingling all the desire and suffering expressible in three, four, maybe more languages – so dazzling he thought that this was all he could ever want to hear into eternity, and all he could ever want to see: a graceful young woman, her mouth open to heaven, spilling a heaven that did not exist – unless within her own soul – in the pale shadows of the curving roof, the deepening night of the window, the trees, and the stars. The lights went out, and still she sang, her voice softening, softening, until he startled at the silence that came at the same time as her touch.

He woke beside her at dawn, the dim sunlight slowly coming in through the east dormer, throwing patterns of shivering oak leaves on the walls. He moved closer to her, though they were already touching, unable to get enough of touch itself, soft skin, soft flesh, soft hair, another life against his own life. He had almost nothing to compare it to, only the remembrances of early childhood in his father's arms, mother's arms, the odd careful embrace measured out thereafter. Whose arms did he dream of resting in when he was a child, when he was crying, his heart torn? Didn't the Jews dream of the arms of Abraham, an embrace that surpassed that of the grave, an embrace that recalled the arms of the all-loving parent, an embrace that, to them was the very sum of paradise? And now that he was a grown man, the passion that came with embracing, holding and being held, his mind stuttering, stumbling, his heart shaking. He could hardly breathe with all the microscopic stars swirling in his limbs, whirling in the back of his head and down his spine. He held his hand over her cheek, not close enough to touch, only to feel the warmth, only to marvel at the girl who had let him touch her life, her being.

His eyes traced the details of her face, the freckles on the backs of her hands, her limbs all still safely enclosed; he hadn't allowed her to remove any clothing, had kept his tightly buttoned around him, had curbed his instincts to merely worrying at the edges, tugging at her collar to touch the skin that lay further along toward her shoulder, pulling at her shirt until he could smooth his hands up her bare back. But then, there was always the thought of what he could do next, and then after that, the fabulous terror of not knowing what she would allow him and what he would allow himself, her shirt untucked and his hands already beneath it, her breasts against him and so why not against his hands, his face, why not? He could hardly get enough. She took him to one of the beds and he lay down with her, smoothed his hands over her thighs, becoming stunned by the curve of her haunch. He froze. He could go no further.

He was still paralyzed by the overwhelming shame of his own body, of her body, of what bodies did, of the danger of bodies, of the way they made other bodies, the bodies of babies. It had taken him ages to fall asleep; he hadn't slept in the same bed with anyone since he was a child afraid of nightmares in the warm tunnel of blanket between his mother's and father's bodies. He had been too excited to sleep, had been in too much pain. Gingerly, so as not to wake her, he had tried to relieve his suffering, his lust, but had been unable. What if she woke and saw him? This wasn't something he had ever done in the presence of another, and he felt so ignorant, so inexperienced, so contaminated and confused by everything he had ever heard, everything that had ever been implied. He didn't know what was true any more. Was she one of these modern girls so infected by the secular world that sex was no more than a handshake? Or were these stories merely the rumours spread by hopeful, leering, young men? And what of other forbidden things like, like...he hardly knew the right word for them – rubbers? How could he even talk about that to a girl? Sin piled on sin, and he still had sin in the back of his head all the time.

And then, he didn't know what he was doing. It was the man, somehow, who was supposed to do everything, wasn't it? But if the man barely knew what to do? Would she laugh? She had laughed the night before, called him old-fashioned in a fond sort of way, told him he was sweet. He could bear that, but...what now? What would she expect or not expect? What was he supposed to do now? If she woke, would she hang onto him, claim him like his mother claimed him? If only. The thought filled him with such hope, such dread, that he had to dispel it. Why would she want him? What good was he, failed cleric, unemployed nobody from the poorest country in Europe?

And where was his father?

And if he went to his grandparents' house would he find they were all dead?

It took him many minutes to convince his legs to move. Only the strongest potion of confusion, terror and shame could have made him leave her, the touch of her.

And he left.

The door of his grandparents' house opened briefly, and there was his father – alive – in pajamas, bending down to pick up the newspaper that had fallen out of the mail slot, then standing for a moment, seemingly to assess the weather as he pushed the drooping hair back from his forehead, to breathe deeply before going back in. It *was* his father, but in an insane sort of way, his father in theatrical makeup that aged him, his father with grey spun throughout his hair. James could hardly take it in. A cold wind blew through him, blew away all the desire and confusion of the night before, left him with only the chill of the unrequited love of his childhood mingled with rage.

How ardently had he longed to be just *here*, to come home? How ardently had he longed to know that his father was longing for him, too?

But what if he wasn't? Of course, he wasn't. Why would a grown man chase after a useless boy, after all? His father was a grown man, had the freedom of grown men, could have come out for a visit any time he wanted. James breathed hard. He would knock on the door, and then he would never have to again, would never have to torture himself thinking of it again, could leave it all behind.

He knocked.

What if his father didn't recognize him, didn't believe him when he said his name? Would James shake him, hit him, batter him full of the pain he'd almost forgotten about from so long ago? James didn't know what was inside himself, what would burst out. Was he only coming to scream the screams he had written into his childhood letters, the letters his father had ignored?

The door opened, and there was his father again – shorter than James was – his father reaching for the door frame to steady himself. How strange to look down on him, how strange, how false, the wrinkles around his eyes, the mole on his nose, how –

"She said you left the... She said you might come."

They didn't touch.

There were a few moments when too many things were happening at the same time as they stared at each other, his father retreating, almost falling, back into the house, gesturing with his hands for James to come in, looking as dumbfounded and terrified as an actor who has forgotten his lines, James tearing his eyes from his father's hair, the familiar hank of it that had lapsed over one eye again, looking down at the mat, wiping his feet because he didn't dare just walk in, not into his grandfather's house.

James found himself unable to speak, sitting in the lounge that was still the same, the memory of his grandmother's elegant operatic laughter around him like a sudden delicate tornado, her voice educated, accented, ignorant of planting potatoes, making hay, measured by the odd thump of his grandfather's cane, his grandfather, so tall above him, the light of the crystal chandelier shining off his white hair – there, the same chandelier, the same light – the same India carpet under his feet, the mirror above the fireplace, the painting by the follower of Constable, the oil-painted clouds blurred with one hundred years of coal smoke, the books on the table – had to be his father's – eighteenth-century prints, art nouveau stained glass, reproductions of ancient dead-reckoning maps. There by the fire irons, he'd played with his cars, and there, in the brocade chair by the window, he'd read his books when the adult talk became too boring, and there the wall Dymphna had drawn upon with her Christmas box of real artist's pastels, his grandfather having no gruffness or cane-thumping for her. Here everything finally was, his old life, his other life, the world he had left, the cars, so many cars, driving past to London on Headington Road.

"So...hm. What are your plans, then?"

He looked incredulously at his father. Was that all he had to say?

Victor was sitting too still, too straight, in the big protective armchair: stiff upper lip. His eyes darted around the room with the perplexed look he always had when someone called his attention out of a book, the sagging wool jumper not quite hiding the extra weight around his middle. He shifted, fumbled in his pockets and tried to light a cigarette, the flint in the lighter sparking again and again without flame. James's grandfather had never been able to light a pipe with the first match, either.

There was the seducer of his mother, James thought, the man who had left him to the mercy of Ireland.

"Hm. At any rate, you decided the church was not for you, hm?"

James nodded, didn't dare say anything until he could be sure rage wouldn't blast from his mouth. Why was his father asking such mundane questions? Didn't *what happened* matter to him? What happened to them being father and son?

"It was alright, then, over there? Were you happy?"

"Yes," he managed to say, because it was true, before his entrails rose up into his throat, because it was a lie, too, because he didn't trust himself or his father, didn't trust his own eyes or ears, could hardly believe in this room, its old tea parties and crackling fire and Christmas carols and dancing and the cigar and brandy smell of his grandfather, that was almost, almost there, the way they used to stop speaking when the housekeeper came in to set a fresh pot of tea in front of them, the French doors into the dining room, the hardwood and carpet instead of dirt and slate, morning sun shining down in a shower of prismatic hail from the chandelier, hanging heavy and dangerous above them...as if he'd succeeded in crawling back into a wondrous dream, and it was beginning to turn surreal, nightmarish. There, still propped in a corner of the room, was the cane that had thumped the rhythm to all those records, had made the needle jump and scratch. All over, everywhere, were his father's books, boxes of them, stacks of them, in the corners, on tables and chairs, filling up even some of the windowsills. Through the doorway he could see the little oval telephone table, much smaller than he remembered, its curved carved bars near the floor connecting its delicate legs, the little table that he loved to hide under because it was really more like a shelter made of branches. How very small he must have been to be able to fit in there.

"Where are they?"

"Ah," his father said, and cleared his throat, the sound of it so lost and familiar to James that he had to ask his father to repeat the words that came after. "Father died three years ago. Mother's senile. In the home. Doesn't know me any more."

Even though he was prepared to hear something like this, he had to shut his eyes. After this, nothing his father could say to him could be more terrible. The house he'd grown up in had been demolished, and his grandfather was dead and his grandmother was as good as. This was not home. There was no such thing.

"She didn't tell you?"

James shook his head. *She.* "She wrote to you, then?"

His father nodded. "To mother, more, especially when I was...unwell. A telegram this time. When someone at the semi-nary –"

"She's written to you all along?" James's voice was high, incredulous. He'd assumed that had stopped long ago. The sound of a siren came through the windows, closer, a city sound he wasn't used to, wailing in his ears.

"I sent you letters, too," his father said. "I mean, after I was...well. Didn't you get any of them? Didn't she –"

"No," James whispered, his throat hollow.

"I suppose I knew all along you hadn't. You never – I wish – it makes me hate her. I don't want –" Victor's lips spread back over his lower teeth and he began to shake. A tear rolled down into his mouth. "I sent you something for Christmas. Every year. Good clothes, not like – she did let me write. She wouldn't let me come. I don't know whether I *could* have..."

"You wrote. You paid for my...those clothes she said were from catalogues...I thought the diocese...she said she'd sold Grandma's silver, jewelry that you'd – and I wrote to you. *I wrote to you.* The first year. Until after you didn't come. Until I'd lost hope –"

"She just...left." Victor looked out the window, then at the floor, could see only a wild strong-armed girl with hair brighter than blood. "I kept going over it, every day. I did everything she wanted. You and...raised Catholic. I thought I did everything. What didn't I do? Did she tell you? She never told me. And I asked her in every letter, for the love of God! She kept saying she needed time, for me to stay away, just another year maybe. Then another year, then another and another. And I...drinking myself into oblivion. How much worse could I have made it all if I had hunted her down?" His father's eyes asked him as if he knew, as if he was the only other one in the world who could possibly know. "And then, years after, I was too ashamed to... Do you hate me?"

He didn't know any more. He didn't know at all. He hated his mother. It was his mother who had done this to him, to them. His father would have come, but for his mother and her fanatical religion – but no. No. He couldn't think that way, let his hate swing back on just her, for who had been the drunkard? How could she have gone back to him, to *that*?

A movement caught his eye and he turned his head to see a middle-aged woman in a dowdy dress coming in from the hall with a purse and a paper bag of shopping. His father stood and James followed his example.

"James, this is Edna."

A look of wonder came over her face and she hesitated, looking for a place to put down her things before taking both of his hands in her own.

"It's you, then, is it?"

He nodded, uncomprehending. There had always been housekeepers in his grandfather's house.

"You must be so tired. Are you hungry?" she said. "Would – tea, at least? I can make you some eggs. We've got some ham in the –"

"I could use a whiskey," he said, only half joking, then took a quick breath; he hadn't meant to test his father like that, but the words were out and he didn't want to take them back, and now, yes, he did want to test his father, resentment finally seeping to his surface, into his words, so he could hear it, feel it, cherish the ugliness of it.

"Sorry," his father said. "I don't keep it in the house any more."

"So, then you *didn't* drink yourself to death."

"Please don't upset him," the strange woman, this stranger-woman demanded, as if it was her business. "She must have told you about the hospital. How he didn't speak after...after your sister...after you and your mother... Did she turn you against him?"

"Edna –"

"I'm sorry, Victor. But I dare say she has. You *never* should have... You were an invalid for a long –"

James watched his father push his dull blond hair from his forehead, all his childhood fantasies fulfilled: his father loving him after all, but prevented from coming to him, carried off by the demons of drink. At least, that was the excuse his father was using. It didn't make him happy. It made him despise his father for being a weakling.

"Your health, Victor. You must calm yourself." Victor darted a helpless rebellious look at the woman who was hovering, protective, repositioning his collar, then pushing on his chest to make him sit again. "Oh, she would have been back all right! If you hadn't kept sending her that money. Mark my word, it was the money she wanted, Victor. She would have been back. For a time. And then what would have become of you?"

James stared at the woman, finally understanding, looking at the ring on his father's hand, the ring on hers.

"Edna thought I should stop writing altogether. Hm," his father said, making that familiar noise, now exhausted and despairing, that James remembered from his childhood. "Edna thought I was going to have another breakdown. But I didn't, did I?"

As he watched his father, listened to all the words, the tones of voice, James's life tumbled over and over.

Victor wasn't the seducer. He was the seduced, had always been seduced, would still be waiting for that terrible sword-faced girl to come back, to slash him open again, if it wasn't for this woman, who was, of course, his wife, his real legal wife, his recently wedded wife. It didn't seem possible that he still had hope that his mother and father would get back together, hope that everything would be fixed, mended. But there was his father's wife.

"I was stolen," he said to them, to himself. "*But you let her.*"

James's lungs began to heave with dry hot anger, every breath a rasp in his throat. He was getting too much oxygen, was hyperventilating, was looking at his father, the lounge, was seeing none of it. He promised himself that neither his mother nor father would see him again, hear his voice, have news of him, know where on earth he was. And neither would her country, the family he should never have belonged to, and that religion. That time when he tried to run away – why hadn't he kept on going? Stolen money? Gone to a police station and lied, or told the truth?

The woman was watching them both with that iron will he had come to expect in older women where their men were concerned. James thought she must be one of those brusque women who fed on the uncertainty of a man, who had come to his father because she needed to marry and *he'd* do, once she'd done the work of convincing him.

James turned his head toward the door. "Maybe you should just forget I ever came," he said, the words tasting like blood in his mouth.

Victor cleared his throat, wiped his face with a handkerchief, pulled himself together.

"I know your birthday, know the day..." he made himself say his daughter's name, "poor Dymphna was born. I know exactly how old you are. You are twenty-one years, seven months, and...and thirteen – fourteen days."

James walked from the room, walked from the house. All his anger of the last ten years had found its righteous object, found its voice, which was silence. He rejected his father as he was first rejected by him, some primitive subconscious circle he had to complete. His first feeling was triumph, knowing he was striking a final blow. As he had rejected God, so he punished his father by withdrawing his love.

"...WHiLE JEROME DiES...
THE LiON RENDS HEAVEN
WiTH HiS BOOTLESS CRiES."

– H.W.

H E walked out and somewhere behind him he heard his father call his name for the first time in ten years, and then he ran, jagged, jerking down every corner he could find, faster and faster, his suitcase dragging on his arm, hitting his leg.

"Bastard, bastard, bastard," he said, bruising his father, bruising himself with the word, knives in his breathless lungs, his eyes blurry, running into more and more rage because only now, only now, after more than ten years did it occur to his father to come after him. And it wasn't only his father, but his mother, too, connected by letters and wireless all those years, keeping it from him, using it to chase him down now: she said you might come, *she*. He slowed finally, walked under rain and flapping leaves.

Those leaves; the horse chestnuts of his childhood compounded the pain blossoming in his chest. They gusted and teetered above him, moving, moving, almost making the horizon move with them – but where was the horizon? The road cut a slice down through the park, and all around him were thick stone walls, the buildings of the college city stacking up into view. He swayed with them, nudged one of the walls with his shoulder, off balance, then kicked at the fallen, driven-over horse chestnuts, the reddish brown crush of them that looked like so much dog shit. Where was he going? Back to the hostel? He'd packed everything. Everything he had was hanging from the end of his arm beside his sodden shoes and pant legs. Buses and cars steamed past him. The street hissed at him under the dull pewter sky. He'd never been able to imagine further than this, further than seeing his father.

Where would he go now?

Back meant Ireland, home now meant Ireland, but the thought was thunder and lighting, a burst of terror down his backbone.

When he got to Haymarket Street, near the bus station, he finally felt as if what he was doing, what he had done, was run away. He had no idea where he was going, or what he was going to do. He had no plans, no ambitions, not for the immediate or the distant future. The future was as blank as the area of his mind that had once held his faith in God. The rest of the day, even the next hour, was a blank, a desperate hole in his head, as if a gunshot had blasted an opening in the screen of his vision whatever direction he turned.

"Holy M – oh, no."

He shook his head to fling out years of habits and walked faster. There was no one to pray to. He couldn't even rely on himself; without the rules of Christianity, how did he even know he was a good person, a capable person, a worthy person? His goal of finally reaching his father had masked the lack of anything else, any other resource he had. And his mother was pursuing him over the wires, and there were wires everywhere. He looked up and there they were, over his head hung with sparrows, in the walls of all the houses, in the red phone boxes. He felt his mother's hand around his wrist, and he ran again, as if he were about to miss his bus, ran through the station, looking for something, some sign that would tell him where to go, and then he saw her, the girl, his girl from the night before.

She was sitting on the cement, looking out at the buses in their bays, her back against a brick wall. She took a drink from a small carton of milk, waxed paper and the remains of a pastry on her rucksack beside her. She wore a little skullcap of multi-colored knotted string, but this morning her sheet of red-brown-blonde hair was tied in a low ponytail and pulled forward over her shoulder to disappear down the neck of her loose cotton shirt. She saw him and glared, her eyes condemning, her brows lowering, and he remembered how he'd snuck away, left her in the early morning dark.

He was walking straight toward her. He could not turn. For a second, he thought the only thing he could reasonably do was hurry on by – an unfortunate accidental meeting after a more fortunate accidental meeting, but he couldn't tear his eyes away from the eyes that sent him to Hell, was perversely attracted. He couldn't escape her outrage, his guilt, didn't know where to run, hadn't anywhere else to go. He continued walking and knelt in front of her.

"I'm sorry. I'm sorry for – I had to see my father..."

It all came out of him in a few minutes, his whole story, the burden he didn't have the strength to carry. He laid everything in front of her, all of himself – the stolen child, the lost boy, the almost priest. He knelt and if he hadn't allowed his story to fall at her feet like some sort of penitential offering, he would have collapsed. She interrupted him gently, with her hand creeping into his wet hair, a corner of her mouth turning up.

"Nah...thought you'd *scarper*, did you? Love that word. Heard some guy use it in Edinburgh last week. *Scarper*. Grab the money and run. You British. Well I suppose you did invent the frickin' language."

"It wasn't like that. I'm...a bit confused, I –"

"Yeah – no. I'm just teasing. I remember you, lost schoolboy. Cut you some slack. My parents are divorced, too. Going back to London?"

He swallowed, may have given a ghost of a nod.

She tilted her head to the side and looked up at him with her big, clear, grey eyes, slid her hand from his head and put it between her neck and her long smooth hair. His mouth had only just been there.

There was a tingle down his spine, a fainting kind of fog in his head. All he wanted was her, every part of her body that he had touched or overlooked. He didn't know a thing other than this, but it was all right. He sat beside her and shivered as his arm slid against hers.

✤ ✤ ✤

It rained so hard, it was barely daylight, was a beautiful wet darkness, black and silver like hard-rubbed pencil. There was so much rain, every car shone its headlights dazzling into his eyes. The long bus whirled at every corner, stone buildings spinning behind sheeting rivers of rain down the glass. He had never felt joy in rain like this. There had never been rain like this, steam clouding the windows. They raced in their own cloud, were blown by their own wind to another kind of heaven.

She let him put his arm around her, and in that double seat, they shared each other's shoulders and arms and legs and hands and mouths. He put her pack on his lap against the raining wet window and she lay against it, the small of her back pressing his thigh, his arm around her waist, his lips in her hair, and the rain beat down and ran away, shimmering. A swirl of her light hair stuck to the damp window. He had never had hair like this in his hands. He wound twists of it and let them go, combed his fingers up along her skin, lifted her hair into the imagined wind.

His heart raced and ran, and ran away. What could compare with this, with this girl, this girl? This girl in the rain.

Yvonne. Not American, as he'd guessed the night before, but Canadian. Half-French Yvonne. Yvonne of the pale eyes, like a bright overcast sky inside: her unknown inside. Yvonne of the seven-no-eight! freckles arching her sharp nose, and the hair that could not make up its mind, blonde or brown or red. Yvonne of the white teeth, the North American smile, the small hands with the long fingers, the tiny feet in her battered, ridiculously sturdy sandals, the tan corduroys covering her legs, fraying where they had dragged in the dirt at the heels, wrinkling wherever she decided to bend. Oh, how cold and trembling her arms were, and she dragged a denim jacket from her pack, disrupted everything, just to fit herself into it. She looked at him for a moment, then sat back, rested in his arms, asked that he scratch her back just beneath one shoulder blade. He could feel it move like a shark beneath the water of her skin, and he remembered the night before, her bones moving against him.

That night centuries ago.

Yvonne of the canvas purse with all the pockets she rummaged through. Yvonne of the Swiss Army knife and the battered journal with the thin blue lines on each page and the mystery novel and stale newspaper, and lip gloss and sunglasses and packet of sunflower seeds, and cake of blue eyeshadow, and *Europe On $5 A Day* book, and collapsible umbrella, and loose change. Yvonne of the extra orange she peeled for him with strong stained fingernails, sour with rind. He wanted to eat her.

Yvonne, the mistress of the world. The world was her oyster and she could eat a thousand of them, a thousand of this, a thousand of that, wanted to fly over Greenland again and again, had to visit Paris just once before she died, and Rome and Athens, and, well, everywhere. She had just missed seeing Bob Dylan at the Isle of Wight concert, and she was so disappointed she really was going to *die*, and if her mother thought she was going back to get serious about opera, she must be out of her mind. There were people starving in the world. There were people fighting for their freedom, and he should know, being from Ireland. There were people fighting to *stop* fighting. People fighting for peace. She was one of these, she thought. Even her father said she was a political animal, like him, not a musical one, like her mother. She thought she was finding herself. And she had found him, too. Maybe you had to do nothing for a while before you were able to discover what it was, exactly, that you wanted to do. Get away from all the voices telling you what you should do, and listen for your own voice.

In a way, his happiness was impure, was almost a fury; he hated his mother for pushing him to give this happiness away, give desire away before he even knew what it was, hated her for the seminary, for the idea of this girl's beautiful body being sinful.

There were braided yarn bracelets around her wrists, in colors mismatching her hat, and a black leather string around her white throat holding a long vein of polished turquoise. She tied her hair back, but as she swerved her head, as she laughed and gesticulated, her smooth hair began releasing itself from the elastic, slowly fraying, draping around her small face in an illusion of modesty. He thanked and thanked and thanked the raining sky for her, for finding her again, the only terror in his heart the idea that it might never have happened if he had looked away at the wrong moment, if he had entered the bus station from a different direction.

He had hardly slept all night, and no matter how much the movement of the bus lulled him, he did not sleep, though she did, shut her eyes and lay her head against his neck. He held her, kept her from slipping to the floor when the bus stopped at traffic lights, when they swung through the dim city of London and stopped at the station.

He was so happy, he didn't care if he ever slept again.

And he hardly slept at all for the next week of nights, exhausted as he was with joy and frustration – staying in the Earl's Court Hostel in one of the men's dormitories while she was miles away in the women's, trying to snatch kisses and touches wherever they were: Madam Tussaud's, the Tower of London, the British Museum, being awake and mad for her half the night while other men snored and muttered in their sleep. Instead of sleep, his waking hours took on the hazy, melting quality of dreams, dreams of ecstasy, dreams he could dream forever.

Four years of contact with earnest young men thinking of death and salvation and troublesome Catholic doctrines had not prepared him to come back to the modern world. He followed her everywhere – to the newsagent's, where she bought a paper, some gum, and a bottle of fizzy orangeade, to the grocer's where she bought apples and carrots, milk and buns, to the little park where she lay on her stomach to read about protests in Northern Ireland, about justice and freedom. He read over her shoulder that The Who was playing somewhere, and Led Zeppelin. Something was going on in Downing Street and in the Cold War, more boat people were leaving Vietnam and Prince Charles was seen with yet another girl. They went all over London and it seemed he could never remember exactly how, had lost his sense of direction because they kept surfacing from the underground like burrowing animals, the patches of city he saw unconnected to each other. She led him through the streets and subways, because he could not navigate, could hardly jump on the subterranean trains fast enough before they were moving again, taking them away. The modern world had gone on without him, it seemed, and with every step he became more dependent on her, bound heart and soul to her.

He thought they were the same – practically the same – human being walking side by side in two bodies. She would swing his arm and he would nudge her shoulder. She would undo the top button of his shirt and on a windy bridge he would twist her long hair into a rope and feed it down the back of her collar so it wouldn't whip her in the face. Between Big Ben and the Parliament buildings she taught him to do the Groucho Marx walk using a sausage roll as a cigar. Along Portobello Road she made him buy a Bob Marley T-shirt and some second-hand jeans and he bought an antique tortoiseshell comb for her hair, which would not stay in, but slipped through the smooth strands like fingers through water.

He talked, and it was effortless, not like he had ever talked to any other girl. He talked the way he talked when he was a child, his mind so full of the new things he was seeing, joining the things he had been learning from books, that he could hardly talk fast enough to get the ideas into words. Everything he said seemed to fascinate her, even when they were just walking, looking from building to building, at the walls rising up around them, walls with passageways, traffic lights, cars, buses, subways and trains speeding around them, underneath them, layers of passageways and lives and trajectories, everyone going in their own different direction.

"Those columns. You see them on the face of that building? Doric: the oldest of the Greco-Roman orders of design, stone versions of the original ways of building with log posts. And those with the curls at the top, Ionic, the ridges carved down them supposed to be a fancy version of the lines left by tools on the trees after stripping the bark off. The Romans, they used to sacrifice chickens and predict the future by looking at their guts."

"Don't be disgusting."

"It's true."

"God."

"And whenever someone would take the name of the Lord in vain they would tie her to the back of a pig and run it through the streets of Rome until she cried out, "Stop, stop! May the pigs eat my –"

"What?"

"Just joking you."

"You're such a turkey."

She would push him because he was terrible, terrible, telling her things, some of them boldfaced lies with the straightest face she had ever seen – that Irish blarney she had heard about – and he would push back and they would wrestle on the grass of some park like puppies under the miraculously risen sun, wrestle as he had with his baby sister. He told her about Dymphna, was about to think of her small grave back in the city they had left, but opened his eyes on his girl instead, and let himself be dazzled. Around the pupil of each of her eyes, sparkling in the grey were little flecks of yellow visible only in sunshine.

"Say that again," she would say.

"What?"

"In your accent. Irish-English, whatever it is. *Just joking you.*"

She said the way he talked tickled the inside of her head, and she would pretend to swoon, go limp in his arms. This inspired him to give her everything, his Queen of England accent, his impression of Father Dunnigan stumbling over the sin of self-abuse, but his best impressions were of his granny and his uncle Paddy, Granny shrieking and shrieking over a muddy footprint in her kitchen, but his uncle's calm sleepy voice describing a house as it burned down around him: "Sure...but I think the roof's about to cave in, now. There it comes, righ-et, just as I thought. You see, then, how the beam is strikin' me head, and me hair is catchin' on fire... And sure, isn't it a good thing the rain has been uncommonly wet for the past few days?"

The night before they were to leave for the ferry, she went to see a West End show, *Guys and Dolls.* Her ticket had been reserved before she came to England, but the show was sold out. He walked her there, then, waiting for her, he wandered the theatre district as it got later and later; for sure, now, they wouldn't get back to the hostel before lockout, would have to stay up all night or sleep in the park.

Or sleep together at last in one of the little hotels near the theatres.

He first looked everywhere for a late-night drugstore, then for the little rubber sheath that was still illegal in Ireland, finally having to ask the clerk, who reached under the counter and put the packet of Durex in a little bag. James was unable to look him in the eye as he put his money on the counter.

Yvonne was surprised when he led her into their room, all white coverlet and eyelet lace, and they were both nervous, as if it was their honeymoon.

"Have you...have *you*?" he said, "because I haven't...you know coming from –"

He showed her his purchase.

"Oh. I'm on the pill."

"The pill? Oh. Good...good."

That sort of thing was still hush-hush where he'd come from – back in time – and was the devil's work, but out in the modern world, talking about it was like talking about lunch or cold medicine.

"You're a bit freaked out, aren't you?"

He exhaled.

"Well, I've got a surprise for you, too."

She produced from her canvas bag what he thought was a tiny wrinkled cigarette. It wasn't tobacco. It was even better. They undressed each other in a cloud of smoke.

❖ ❖ ❖

They didn't sleep at all that night, but the next night, on the overnight ferry from Dover to Calais, he slept. He slept with his hand over his grateful heart and the passport in his shirt pocket. He slept in spite of the fact that he slept on the floor, flattened maroon carpet marked with black areas of impacted chewing gum, cigarette burns and faded flowers. He slept in spite of the constant flow of passengers past him into the small casino, the smell of sweating hippies, the talk and laughter of the people sitting around him. He could sleep through just about anything, now, though not for long.

❖ ❖ ❖

"Wake up."

"Mmm?"

"Wake up."

He opened his eyes, but it wasn't Yvonne shaking his shoulder. It was Marilyn.

Yvonne had told him about her on the bus. *Mmmarilyn.* Whenever Yvonne said her cousin's name she rolled her eyes, raised her eyebrows and sighed as if she was talking about Marilyn Monroe, or about someone who was the complete opposite of Marilyn Monroe. *Mmmarilyn* from *Mmmanitoba*, a place she described as pre-civilized, a place in which the nineteen-sixties hadn't yet arrived.

"Wake up, the ferry's going to dock soon," Marilyn said, in her solemn, even voice, assuming, like her, he would want to be awake and ready to watch the exciting event unfold, to tick it off on his traveller's to-do list, to be first in line to disembark. Her round face was cut in half by her equally round wire-rimmed glasses, framed by two thick black braids that covered her ears. Rising late from their luxurious expensive West End bed, he and Yvonne had rushed back to get their things from their hostel locker, almost too late to meet her cousin there so they could catch the Dover train together. Yvonne had introduced him as her lover: "Marilyn thinks I'm *scandalous*," she said, and Marilyn had merely stared at him quietly, furiously, sitting on the steps of the hostel as she ate warm fish and chips from its newspaper. She seemed so strikingly ordinary, next to Yvonne, that he couldn't help staring at her trying to gauge her qualities. Was she short, tall, fine-boned, wide-hipped? He could interpret little beyond her camouflage of baggy pants and untucked man's shirt. Yvonne quickly whispered, "She's only nineteen. She's terrified of travelling alone."

"Any later, and I would have had to go *by myself*. Any later, and you would have spoiled *everything*," she finally said, once they were in their black taxi with her naively big new backpack like a fourth person sitting beside them.

"Come, on, *wake up!*" she said.

He sat up.

"Where's Yvonne?"

Marilyn glanced to the right, and he saw her, standing almost in the middle of a double doorway, talking to someone. A man. Another man.

He was beside her in a moment. The man was speaking in a thick French accent, saying, "He can't sing, Dylan. He may be some kind of poet, but he can't *sing*."

"Guess what?" Yvonne said, grabbing James's arm. "We can stay at his place if we buy the food and do the cooking! His name is Yves – that's who I'd be if I was a man! He has a flat in Paris, can you believe it?"

Yves was leaning against the door frame with only his shoulder blades, sheltering a black guitar case at his heels. His shoes were new and expensive-looking black leather, though his jeans were faded and his jacket old-fashioned wool. He was tall and thin, and his head was a little too large, and held a fabulous collection of longish black curls that organized themselves miraculously, softly, carelessly. James disliked him immediately.

All the way on the train from Calais to Paris Yves was half-turned in the seat in front of them talking to Yvonne in French (she could speak French!) while James looked from him to the back of Marilyn's head, the white chalk-line parting of her hair straight down the middle, two braids dividing her head in half. The autumn fields near Calais were dead and brown and endless, without hedge or wall or habitation, sometimes, like a house without walls, without ceiling, blasted away by what? The wars? The modern era and its giant machines and gasoline? The trip gave him a feeling of endless acceleration, the dull roaring sound of going over the rails, the rare buildings and trees close to the track faking punches at him as they hurtled past. Every ditch, every guttered rail-end of town they passed, even the weeds and litter comforted him: places that would have sheltered foxes and rats.

Yves laughed at something Yvonne said and he looked at James.

"She keeps saying, 'oo, la-la,' and 'mon Dieu!' because she thinks that's what they say in France, and they do, a little. She is – what – a Quebecois taking the piss out of us, eh?"

James did his best impression of Marilyn, staring at him evenly, solidly, mutely.

"You don't understand her," Yves went on. "How you let her walk around in those shoes, eh?"

Yvonne had brought only one pair of shoes, thick-soled boys' leather sandals that mocked the delicacy of her feet, her small bones. Her feet were getting thorny and callused, weather-beaten, had a few cracks of dirt that couldn't be washed out. She had packed no socks.

"It's almost October," James said, "but she doesn't care if she catches her death."

He put his arm around her because she shivered sometimes, and the fields were drenched here, too, and he loved her and people like Yves had to understand that.

"You think *this* is cold?" Yvonne's face was flushed, excited. "Sorry. It's the uniquely Canadian snobbery, the only one we've got. I once went to visit Marilyn in Manitoba. It got down to minus thirty-five. Her dad used to walk from the house to the barn – through the snow – in his sock feet."

"No," Yves said. "I mean your shoes are *ugly*."

Yvonne's mouth dropped open and she slapped the arm Yves had lain across the back of his seat, slapped it again as he raised it to defend himself.

"Good shoes!" he shouted. "We are getting you shoes in Paris. Beautiful, *feminine* shoes. And then you will be perfect. *Oo, la-la! Mon Dieu!*" He kissed the tips of his fingers extravagantly.

She literally squirmed. James had his arm around her, and he felt it, felt it happen in every part of her body at once, saw her nose wrinkle, her eyes smile, her mouth quiver. She turned to James. "He's seen Dylan. And Cream. And zz Top. *And* the Beatles just before they broke up."

Yves snapped his fingers and pointed at her. "My friend Phillipe, he just come back from the 'States. Saw Alice Cooper: *Welcome To My Nightmare*."

The train dropped them off on the outskirts of Paris at five-thirty in the morning. The Metro station wasn't open yet, but it was raining, so the entire train population had to huddle together at the bottom of the dirty cement stairwell against a folding metal fence like animals who have not had enough sleep, enough food, enough fresh air, lost animals trying to get back into their cage. James smoked his fourth-last cigarette; he was running low on money because of that hotel room. Marilyn dutifully recorded events in her travel journal, the book on her pressed-together knees, sitting on her pack on the steps. Yvonne talked to the other backpackers in the crowd as if they weren't complete strangers, in a voice that James thought sounded stupid: Yvonne the songbird chirping away. He could do an impression of her. Were all North Americans like this? Marilyn didn't seem to be.

Where are you from, and where are you going, and where did you get those cool sunglasses, and I lost my pair off the Tower Bridge and do you think I should have gotten a Eurail pass and what does it say in your book about sleeping on the beach at Nice?

The Americans and the Australians and the Germans answered her, elaborated on travels of their own. The air was full of the distant rushing sound of the waking city in the rain, and with the details of other people's lives, people they would never see again.

Yves watched her, guarded his guitar case, smoked like James. Yvonne focused on each person as they spoke, nodding, smiling, her face, even the way she breathed, displaying her attention, her empathy, in just the way he remembered the night they met. But then, she was looking only at him. Now, a little gust of wonder escaped her lips when one man told her about his narrow escape from a small avalanche in northern Italy. She bit her lip when a woman described being swarmed by beggar children in Marseille. She laughed when a boy told about maneuvering his sister's stuffed bear into a photo he'd taken of the Pope.

It was all so wrong, such a chaos of irrelevance. His own life was just another story getting lost among all these other stories, all these details filling up Yvonne's head, pushing him out. She was too open. She was dangerously open to everyone and anyone.

No one could be more lost than this, James thought. The grey raining dawn brought a man up from the dark Metropolitan tunnel to unlock the fence, crush the folding metal diamonds of air to the side, and turn away from them without a word as they began to descend with their weights of luggage, not knowing where they were going. The girl he loved, whom he had known for a week, laughed as he walked faster and faster, and he passed billboards full of giant lips and eyes and bare limbs and pots of cosmetics and spectacles and hard varnished fingernails. They paid for tickets and followed Yves, the man they had only just met, onto a train, and they tunnelled faster and faster into the earth and Marilyn wrote it all down even though nothing happened, nothing until another bright train full of people passed them, flashed bright faces, and then was gone, as fast as an electric light snapped off.

What would it have been like if he'd had more than half an hour of sleep? If Yves had stopped talking? If Yvonne had stopped hanging on his every word?

What would it have been like if God was still in Heaven? If there still was a Heaven?

They surfaced onto the Left Bank and Yves led them to a counter where they stood and drank coffee and ate swirls of pastry dusted with sugar and looked out the open door, where each black car hushed past them through running, falling water. People passed speaking the language Yves and Yvonne were speaking, the French he could not understand. He went down a narrow stairway to the toilet, and found the door was coin-operated, so he had to go back and ask Yves for money, and then there was no toilet seat, only hard porcelain with bolt holes, and nameless damp on the floor. He sat and leaned his head on his hands and then suddenly heard knocking and Marilyn's heavy voice.

"Are you okay in there?"

He jerked his head up. "Yeah, fine. Be out in a minute." He must have fallen asleep.

"The guy up there. He's waving his arms at me like I have to get out now that I'm finished eating."

"Yeah, yeah, I'm done. I'm done."

Upstairs, she gestured at the three backpacks and his suitcase.

"Let's go into the entrance of that church across the street."

He looked around.

"Where's Yvonne? Yves?"

"You were taking such a long time, they went off to look at something. Something about maggots. Said they wouldn't be long."

"Maggots?"

"Allez, allez," said the man behind the counter, sweeping them out with his hand, a corner of his mouth turned up, but his eyes hostile, glancing at the mound of damp luggage.

They dodged the cars to cross the street, the cold rain slapping their scalps through their hair, each with one pack on their back, another piece of luggage jouncing in their arms. They dumped their loads in the corner of the small vestibule, a shallow cave they sheltered in like primitive men still too simian to build anything themselves. James gave the knobless door a little push: locked. Marilyn, self-contained, arranged herself on her big pack and took out her journal. For some reason this got to him, made him stand flat-footed in front of her, sighing, shoulders sagging.

She hasn't seen anything yet. What could she possibly have to write down?

"Which direction did they go?"

She looked up at him, her eyes huge behind the round lenses and her brows pinched together a little. She hadn't noticed. Whatever she had going on in her head was far more interesting.

"What if we never see them again?" Marilyn whispered, her shoulders hunching all the way up to her ears, her fingers white at the tips, scrunched around her pen. "What if they don't find us at the café and then leave, and we don't know where he lives?"

James leaned out of the archway, groaning in exasperation, examining the street for any sign of them, any sign at all. Wasn't there some nineteenth-century bar called Two Maggots that all the famous painters had gone to? If it was on this street, it didn't have a neon sign that would cut through the downpour. The only people on the street now were running with their umbrellas.

He was almost hit by one. No sooner had the old woman rushed into the vestibule and shaken and shut her umbrella, than there was another, and another. The locked door was pulled open from inside and they entered: morning Mass.

Mass. His mother obsessed with it, his granny avoiding it, so much a part of his childhood, of his education, he could almost taste the wine and wafer. The sadness was so strong, so physical, was a hard hand crushing his throat. He used to know where love and safety came from, and even if that was a lie, the illusion of knowing had been precious.

He sat beside Marilyn as if she were just another part of the wall – actually, she was a closed door, a locked room he wasn't in the least curious about – and he couldn't believe it when the pipe organ started up. Of course it would, why wouldn't it? But why couldn't he be left alone? Why couldn't he run away from it, stop thinking about it? Why did his old life have to follow him everywhere?

Then he saw that Marilyn wasn't writing. She was drawing. She glanced upward now and then and James raised his eyes to the center of the little groin vault and saw the medallion, some animal-demon's head carved in the center.

Monster.

What was that? The game he and his mother used to play when there was nothing to do, when they had nothing but a pencil and a piece of paper: You draw the eyes, I'll draw the nose.

Monster.

There was another little demon in the far corner, a demon at each corner of the pitted stone ribs, and in the arch above the door were more demons in relief, demons on one side of the God of Judgment eating each others' flesh, tearing each others eyes out, clawing upward to grasp the feet of sinners and drag them down to Hell. But on the other side the saints and saved simpered, gave little smiles of triumph, didn't care at all that others were going down to everlasting torture.

He got up, stillness unable to contain his anger, and stalked into the church. The bent heads of the old women seemed to be saying, "Don't hurt me, don't hurt me," and he marched down the side aisle feeling like an invader, an apostate who had not genuflected, no matter how much his knees instinctively wanted to bend, his eyes darting here and there seeing familiar things that were all changed in meaning now. All of history was changed. A little side chapel held a glass case with a reliquary in it, silver-gilt, with a rock-crystal window. Inside it, he could see a bone. Shin bone of Mary Magdalene, or Saint Christopher, or whoever. Come worship it. Come give us money.

He had never felt such rage; his mother and father were only pawns, herded sheep, innocent lambs, compared to this system of centuries of greed and lies, this system that had contributed to splitting them apart, twisting them into the forms they now took, and twisting him and his life as well. His head was on fire with it. If he'd had a sword, he would have wielded it like a crazed man, whirling and hacking in all directions, not caring who or what he destroyed.

Some Englishness, some childhood instinct, was the only thing that kept him from at least yelling obscenities at God's henchman, the dog-collared *francais*-droning priest, before he paced back into the vestibule and found Marilyn still alone, the rain still falling. Anger seizing up his mind, his bones, until he didn't think he could move; he might have been just such a priest, wearing just such a collar. He stared at the water rushing over the street, the rain like the precipitant of a dark poisonous mist, the city metallic grey, taxis rushing, and then the pious procession of women coming back through the vestibule, bowing to unfurl their umbrellas one after another in genuflection to the rain god, their line dance almost comic as they retreated to wherever they had come from, wearing grooves in the street, Mass every morning for years, for centuries, and who knew what variety of madness it served to cover up? Wasn't his entry into the priesthood an extension of his mother's guilt or pain or whatever at her marriage or nonmarriage? He'd been walking the path she'd laid down for him and he'd never thought up any direction for himself. The church taught there was only one path, and to stray from it was the easy road to damnation. But here was Paris. He'd never imagined Paris before. Had he turned right or left off the path? It didn't matter. There seemed to be thousands of intricate directions now. Beside the café across the street was a book shop – every book a direction – and beside that was a greengrocer, half the fruits from other countries, other directions and philosophies and religions.

Where was Yvonne? Was she going to come back, or was he stranded here with Marilyn, no French money and nowhere to go?

He looked out the archway, a thin spray from the drops that struck the upper sill cooling his face. Down the street were restaurants with shuttered windows, clothing shops, men shoving away the steel screens to open for business, a tobacconist, a newsstand, a bakery, all other directions. He had never been able to think of himself becoming a baker, a person who sold newspapers, a man who worked in a factory making clothes, a taxicab driver. His mother and the church had blotted out everything but themselves, had held him so tight, he could not look to either side.

He peered through the rain, up past the slate roofs and saw yet another steeple.

It made his pain and rage almost unbearable because it was beautiful, so beautiful the way stone seemed to float up into the sky like that and remain motionless for centuries. He wanted to see, *had* to see, the rest of its carved harmony, but he knew it would break his heart because there would be more fanatical women worshipping in it, terrified of everlasting torture, more parts of dead bodies inside it, mingled with gold and rubies and alabaster, soaring vaults, rose windows, paved mazes, candelabra drenched with molten wax, carved wood and melded bronze and all manner of physical tribute, all the glories of the works of man aimed toward heaven, all the booty of the ravening ecclesiastical system, and how could he hate it all and love it all at the same time, and where was the dividing line between the beauty and the lies?

He stood in the middle of the room. Marilyn finished her drawings, shut her book, got up and stretched, easing the cramps out of every part of her body. She began circling the edge of the vestibule, circling him, dragging first just her middle finger, then her ring finger, over the carved stone, her eyes not lost in thought, but alert to all thoughts. It irritated him to no end: didn't she know she was playing a part in the destruction of the very thing she was admiring? The stone walls were blackened with the acidic oil from so many other fingers, the pillars of the door frames carved into smooth twisted ropes, their capitals carved intricately to represent – he hadn't seen it before – twisting lions, open-mouthed and crying and digging; they were St. Jerome's lions who had dug a desert grave for Paul the Hermit. Marilyn walked past him and curled back down on her pack to slouch against the wall. She put her hands in her lap and began to pick at a hangnail, then raised it to her teeth.

"I wouldn't worry too much," she said. "They probably haven't gone to get a room. Yet."

He took a shocked breath; this was a thought that he, the good little seminary student, had been incapable of coming to on his own. He'd thought Marilyn was some sort of uptight religious conservative. She looked back at him with her usual deadpan, but with an expression of deep and languid mischief beneath.

"You're terrible," he whispered, as the last vestige of his British grandmother's sense of decorum rattled with jealousy and terror, and some small, unspeakable thrill tingling the back of his head.

It would be an hour yet before they came back, Yvonne drenched in an ecstasy of Parisian streets, of rain that she said was "wild," Yvonne full of éclairs, glutted with unconscious passion, her smile gentle with the sheen of being admired; Yves barely took his eyes off her, glancing up to hers whenever she spoke or laughed, but his gaze always travelling down to take in the raptures of her form, the ghostly slip of her arm beneath the drenched white shirt, the way her worn corduroys caught and hugged her hips, the fold of her leg, when for some reason, she found it necessary to grasp her ankle and bend it up to the back of her thigh. She actually twisted her hair in her hands and wrung rain from it, spattering the floor in front of them.

"Oh, don't you just want to be here forever?" she said, as she threw her arms around James, not noticing his rigid, pale face. He held her too tightly, crushing his outrage into her – how could she be so happy, how *dare* she be so happy after leaving him alone for so many hours? She gasped and pushed away, laughing.

"This is crazy. Us with all our stuff. Yves says he'll get us a cab."

He took his anger out on the girls. During the next week he led them through the Louvre, past ancient icons, a Duccio altarpiece from northern Italy, a Raphael Madonna, played the venomous tour guide, even though he knew he was being ridiculous. So many paintings of annunciations: "Look out Mary, God is coming, and you won't believe it, but..." Battered wooden altarpieces, Christ dying here, dying there, eating for the last time, praying for the last time, raising the dead, serving fishes, drinking wine, riding a donkey, getting baptized, lying dead in his mother's arms. James looked and looked, his eyes gulping rich sculptures after paintings after jewels, eating and overeating with his eyes as if looking for a death by gluttony, but the food only made him hungrier, could not stop the burning inside him. And these were just the physical objects. He hardly dared think about all the words of the Bible, begin counting the crimes of the mind.

Honour your father and mother. But nothing about parents honouring their children, only an exhortation not to spare the rod, or you'd spoil the child.

Honour your father and mother. That meant don't disobey, didn't it? It always had in his mind. Honour them even though they may be madmen, murderers, pirates and thieves, kidnappers, nose-pickers, closet-drinkers, finger-twiddlers, time-wasters, or child-haters.

How could he fight it except by battering himself bloody against it, this religion that had been around for almost two thousand years before he was born, this religion that had taken his mother away from him, his father away from him, his whole life away from him, this religion that slandered his body and the bodies of women, god-created bodies but twisted sinful all the same, that said nothing of slavery, of owning the body and mind of another human being? And yet, how could he, one lonely Irish boy, deny the ages – what was supposed to be the wisdom of ages? How could he resist the goggle-eyed Christs from the seventh century, the cracked wooden Christs, the ivory Christs, the Christs encrusted with gems and pools of colored glass, the Christs surrounded by chunks of lapis lazuli and pearls cast from the repentant necks of medieval matrons, some jewels with holes to indicate their vain former lives as bracelets and necklaces? For an ecstatic, dazzling, five minutes, he believed again, between one Madonna and Child enthroned in beaten gold – five hundred years older than he was – and another, a Raphael Madonna with two plump babies playing at her feet, the Christ Child and John the Baptist. But then he saw Saint Sebastian, poor Saint Sebastian, stuck full of arrows, and he remembered the female saint he'd seen in a book once, holding her severed breasts on a plate in front of her like a Sunday morning fry-up, bacon excluded.

He couldn't escape from Christianity, so he flung himself against it, anywhere, everywhere, in the rich ornament of the royal chapel of the French kings, St. Chapelle, with its gem-studded walls and sheets of floor-to-ceiling leaded glass, or the crypts, filled with bits of bone and chips of true crosses. He hunted down the sins of the church so he could stare at them, remember them, never be fooled again by them, cry them out in the street to heal the world of them, take the power of them out of people's hearts. How could people just *sleep*, unconsciously anticipating their breakfasts when beneath every rock in every museum, every church crypt, was a small vial of Mary's mother-milk, or a shrivelled bit of Christ's foreskin, religious charlatanism dabbed with rubies and etched with gold? Perhaps God saw the little sparrow fall, but now James waited for the car that would drive over it, and the crows swooping down for the roadkill.

The place that amazed him the most was Notre Dame. High up on the towers, the strange animal gargoyle-devils, larger than any man, loitered as if they were bad boys waiting to make trouble, cast out of God's house, flung out of heaven. One was a winged chimpanzee leaning on the balustrade with his chin in his hands, bored by all the goodness inside. Another was some sort of man-wolf-dragon that clutched a smaller demon in his claws as he devoured it without even the mercy of killing it first. James felt a strange affinity to them, imagined how they had watched the city for almost a thousand years, witnessed history being made, seen every building built, silently listened to the pigeons and crows and sparrows, unable to die, unable to believe, unable to enter heaven again.

In a way the girls were the jury and he was presenting the evidence. They were the impartial ones, and if he could show them everything, *everything*, they could make the final, impartial pronouncement and then he could hate all of it, give it all up, even the praise of God in the works of man, burn down the soaring chapels and throw the ancient paintings on the pyre, torch his past and get on with the rest of it, what he couldn't imagine, the rest of his life.

He would point out something to the girls – a scrap of cloth or bit of bone behind a rock-crystal window – and say, "People used to actually believe in this, would bring offerings and pray in front of this little bit of trash. Why? How could they believe this?" and say it as if all these people lived hundreds of years ago, say it as if he had never been one of them, though it had only been a little more than a month. "You think people *decide* what to believe?" Marilyn asked him once, a clue that the girls were beginning to get fed up with this sort of talk. He kept an eye on Marilyn now, knowing that behind her glasses, behind the usually shut doors of her expression, there was far more going on than he could imagine; he caught it now and then, a darting of her eyes, a half-wry smile, and wondered if she was laughing at him. Once, he saw her looking at him out of the corner of her eye and she didn't look away, let her eyes rest in his too long, as if she didn't care if he caught her looking because she'd just as soon set a match to him.

After the first day, he no longer minded Marilyn's presence; she didn't talk much, and what she did say was curt, intelligent, sometimes very funny in its dumb-striking forthrightness. Marilyn became his accomplice in his obsession, dragging her finger down a page in her guidebook, telling him where the next crypt was, the next museum or ancient building. At first Yvonne exclaimed over his knowledge, his gossipy information on Cardinal Richelieu, St. Louis, and medieval thought, but she was becoming more and more silent, dragging her feet, talking about what a shame it was that Yves had to work all the time. Marilyn prodded her with a cousin's familiarity, saying, "Get your behind in gear, flower-girl," which Yvonne always found infuriating: "The expression is flower *child*." It was Yvonne, though, who kept them going, playing mother at lunchtime, saying, "Let's find someplace to sit. Let's find a bistro that has steak and *frites*. I've always wanted *real* frites – or a nice baguette, some brie, wine and fruit. Have a picnic." Under her care, they didn't exhaust themselves. Every afternoon, about four, she said, "Let's go have a little monk," because James had told her that cappuccino was named after the dark brown and white habits the Cappuccin friars wore. Weary, he was able to sit down at some café she found, and Marilyn was able to take the big black camera from around her neck and put it on a red-checkered tablecloth, lick the milk foam off her spoon, and eat *pain au chocolat*, or a little ramekin of *créme brulée*. Every time James worried about his dwindling supply of money, Yvonne reassured him: no rent at Yves' place, and besides, all three of them would be off soon to pick grapes in the countryside in the little town her mother and stepfather had honeymooned in three years ago. That had been the plan, part of the reason for meeting up with Marilyn, since London. Only a few more days and it would be time for the vintage. When James was down to his last few francs, she led them off their planned route for a couple of hours, scouting out streets with rich-looking offices and cafés, threw her hat to the sidewalk, and began to sing.

James hardly knew how to stand, where to put his hands, so dumbfounded was he at her North-American fearlessness, and then at the beauty of her voice, so clear, so arching and flexible, the way her lips moved around the words...just the way she sang for him that first night. Her voice seemed so much lower than he remembered, and then it climbed higher, in ecstasy, not so high as to amaze them, to leave them behind, but to lift their spirits with hers. He could almost see the bird of her voice when she made it flutter, and he knew it was going to fall, and he couldn't bear waiting for it.

"She's a contralto," Marilyn said, too loud, into his ear. "Those are nineteenth-century French love songs. She did them for her fourth-year performance."

He shook a little, to get Marilyn's lips away from his ear, and then he saw the businessmen, the office workers, coming out of the big glass doors as if looking for something, their seeking faces finding the face that belonged to the voice.

"Lunch hour," Marilyn said. "Boy, she knows how to do it."

James watched the men, and a few women, too, pause as they walked past. The men seemed to be there almost as much to gaze at her face as to listen to her voice. A few chose to sit in the more expensive outside tables of a nearby bistro to listen while they ate. These were the ones who threw the most money into her hat. Out from underneath his admiration for her courage and her talent, crept something else: embarrassment. This was so public. Wasn't this practically like begging? All his unconscious British snobbishness and class-consciousness, his inheritance from his father's side, seeped around him, clenched his ribs. After an excruciating hour, Yvonne came to him, smiling, with her hat full of money, telling him to hold out his hands, but he held them up instead. No, no, he couldn't take money from her, from a woman, not money she earned that way.

The next day, the plan was to go back to the Louvre; they had not seen Michelangelo's dying slaves, and Marilyn *had* to draw them. He and Yvonne were going to leave Marilyn with the slaves and then go to find all the galleries they hadn't seen. The day had started slow. The night before, Yves had taken them out to a discotheque, Yvonne had drunk too much wine, and she had a headache. She led them off to find proper lattés and croissants first, and they sat in the little café waiting for her Aspirin to take effect. Finally, they were walking along the Seine, nearing the Louvre; James was dreading the moment he knew was coming: Yvonne paying his admission. If they could get that part over with quickly, he imagined he could forget it quickly. But Yvonne remembered she had forgotten to buy her morning newspaper. They turned down a side street, and she heard music, blues saxophone. She changed direction, and the search for a newspaper became the search for the saxophonist, who, conveniently, was playing just across the street from a newsagent. Yvonne circled the musician, bought her paper, went back to buy some gum, crossed the street, and tossed a few francs into the man's saxophone case.

The music stopped abruptly when he said something to her. Marilyn and James waited for Yvonne to come back across the street, and after a minute, when she didn't, they crossed to collect her. James caught his breath, then blew it out with force when he heard what the two were talking about: bands. The Stones, Pink Floyd, Genesis, blah, blah, blah, with the fervour of fanatics. That was practically all she and Yves and Phillipe from downstairs talked about, only about French and European groups, too. The saxophonist was American and this seemed to give Yvonne the chance to really get going. Dylan, Dylan, she loved Dylan and the whole folk thing. Paul Simon, Joan Baez, Joni Mitchell – she was a Canadian! And what did he think of Elton John? Marilyn seemed ready to burst. She looked at James and took a deep breath and he could see the devilry rise up in her.

"Come on!" she shouted. "Let's get *on* with it, you shameless hussy! Are you going to flirt with every musician in the city?"

Yvonne's mouth fell open and the sound that came out of it was an involuntary gasp of outrage. She grabbed Marilyn's arm and marched her across the street, James close behind. "How *could* you?" she said in a dagger-like whisper. "You are so embarrassing – this is – this is *Paris*, for God's sake. You'd think you'd have some idea of the proper, the civilized, way to behave, of –"

"Oh, come on. It's not like you're ever going to see him again."

"That's not the point! How – he and I – if you're not going to go back and apologize, then I'll – and maybe, maybe, we can just finish our conversation, if you don't mind, if you don't have to go somewhere important to save the world or –"

"Oh, whatever. See you at the Louvre, then, and if not, back at the flat."

And Marilyn, who had been too frightened to travel by herself, left.

Of course, James could not leave. He had no money. And he was worried about Yvonne, the way she seemed to have nothing in her head but bands, like some sort of religion, the way she was ready to take up with anybody who spoke the same fanatical language. He stood and looked around; one building featured stone lions snarling at him, and another, half-naked voluptuous women. Everywhere, there were discarded yellow Metro tickets, cigarette butts, and so much dog shit on the sidewalk. Outside of the museums, he didn't really like Paris. The air hurt his eyes. It was grey and wet and its rain tasted of cars and trains and carbon monoxide; its wind was too steady, too far inland, didn't breathe with the ocean and its waves, didn't have the gusts that made it alive, awake.

Yvonne eventually finished talking to the saxophonist. Her mood had improved and she almost skipped up beside him to kiss him on the cheek.

"Hasn't this just been the best morning after all?" she said, "Getting rid of *Mmmarilyn*, just drifting, seeing the *real* Paris, the real –"

"Yes, yes, I know. The *real* Paris. It feels even more like a cliché now that I'm here. Everybody talks about it: the city! the women! the art! The Seine! The intel*lec*tuals! The immorality!" James realized people talked about it as if it were a delicious hell on earth just as ballads sang of Ireland as earth's lusher, greener, heaven. "Come on, Yvonne. We don't have time to talk to every stranger on the planet."

Her mouth dropped open again, but no sound came out if it this time. He pulled her by the hand and met Marilyn in the Louvre lineup. Yvonne paid his admission, slapping the money hard on the counter.

"You know," she whispered, "I used to think it was artistic to be depressed, to be one of those angry young men. Now I think it's a pain."

❖ ❖ ❖

On what James assumed would be their last day in Paris, he woke early, at five in the morning, and could not get back to sleep. He had saved one of the best things for last, La Musée du Cluny, the old Archbishop of Cluny's residence and the Roman ruin beside it. It was supposed to contain a lot of medieval church art as well as the recently found heads of kings that had been lopped off the facade of Notre Dame during the French Revolution; even stone monarchs could not escape the guillotine. He could hardly wait.

Yvonne slept beside him on the floor under a heap of blankets. Bedding down in Yves' living room, they hadn't made love since that first time in their West End hotel room, over a week ago. Even as his mind tortured him over religion, his body went on yearning with its own animal mind, taking its turn tormenting him with its wordless memory of everything they had done. He knew he would be addicted forever to what the priests had been so afraid of, helplessly ensnared by his corporeal self and the entrance into the hot velvet darkness of another human being, her skin turning inward where sight had to be abandoned to touch alone. If this were really the cliff of perdition, he would leap off it a thousand times. There she was, only inches away, and he could do little for fear of being caught. Every day, he managed to catch a few moments with her, kissing and touching, never in a place or at a time that would allow his skin against hers. Last night, Yves had been out, and Marilyn had gone off for a shower just as they had gone to bed, but Yvonne had simply turned away from him. "I've got my period," she'd said.

Marilyn snored softly on her back on the small sofa beside them, her glasses still on her face, her feet sticking up above the arm rest, her big backpack propped in the corner like a small mummy, clothes and other bandages fraying out of the top. She always seemed to go to sleep with her glasses on, though they were usually folded on top of her journal by morning and her body turned toward the wall, her hip like an ocean swell under the old, pink, boiled-wool blanket that had faded to the color of skin.

Overwhelmed by his own furies, Yvonne filling what was left of his attention, he still absorbed the details of Marilyn's presence because he couldn't help it, because they were living in the same rooms, the same streets. Every morning he saw her sit on the edge of the sofa and stretch with the blanket wrapped around her, dragging her bare toes over the dusty wood. She wore that blanket as a mink wears its pelt, claiming the flat was too cold, missing the big fireplace of her childhood home. It was a family legend that, as a baby, she had escaped her crib one night and her mother found her the next morning sleeping on the hearth in a big pile of dogs and cats. Sometimes, Yvonne and

Marilyn would sit on the couch together and talk about the summer that Yvonne's parents got separated and she came to stay on the farm. Yvonne would wrap her arms around her and Marilyn would grin tolerantly and rub her hair against Yvonne's: "Just like sisters," Yvonne said. And just like sisters they fought a little, Yvonne calling her a goody two-shoes and a smarty-pants, claiming the teachers made her skip a grade because she frightened the other seven-year-olds. Marilyn bared her teeth and knocked their naked knees together and told her she only said those things because she was a birdbrain herself. "Oh, *meow*," Yvonne replied.

Marilyn went about in her deliberate ways, twisting the ropes of her hair in her fists, turning them into braids, padding around the apartment, dragging her fingers over the velvet wallpaper as if she tasted everything with touch while Yvonne chattered on, flitted here and there, picked up this and that, a shirt, a shoe, an apple, and tried to decide what she should wear and what she should eat, involving James in every decision, asking his opinion of whether it was likely to rain, whether he thought there was any truth to astrology, and what he thought he might have been in a past life. Sleeping in the same room with two women was the sort of thing, that, to a seminary student, would seem beyond exciting, beyond sinful, but he hardly knew what to think of it. It wasn't sordid, wasn't anything, really, but haphazard, as if he and the rest of the people in the world were being shuffled like cards.

He got up quietly in his undershirt and pajama bottoms, and walked from window to window. It was a big attic apartment in a narrow building at the top of endless stairs. All around were similar buildings of similar height and age, a couple of cracks in the plaster above, the ceiling sloping down around the windows seemingly with the sole purpose of bashing his head now and then, whenever he stopped paying attention. There was an edge of dust on the old wood floor around the rim of the room and a couple of crisp dead plants in tin cans on one sill. As the overcast sky brightened, the napping pigeons on the roofs flew away,

and there were people to watch in the street, more and more
people; later there would be a foaming sea of people, draining
down the holes of the Metro station, as if the city were flushing
like a giant toilet. He quietly slid the window open in the cold
shadow of the building, listening to the sound of traffic, the
depth of sound beyond the immediate rushing cars, the deep
sighing of it for miles and miles, the city's blood and breathing
and life force. There was the taste of car exhaust in the air, croissants and coffee, and the hard-crusted bread that hurt his gums
and made his jaw ache from so much chewing. It had stopped
raining after the first day, but the weather had stayed overcast
and dull. Some sort of front, some high-pressure system, was
keeping the pollution from blowing away, and their hikes from
sight to sight filled their lungs with toxic fumes that gave them
all headaches, coal smuts alighting on their foreheads after spinning in the air since the turn of the century.

He walked to the window on the other side of the room,
where a cat appeared every day at dusk, silhouetted against the
twilight, looking for pigeon dinner. On this side of the apart-
ment, under the cramped fire escapes and three stories of
washing lines, deep down in the building's secret grassy garden,
were huge horror-story insects and welded iron electric guitars
made by the landlord's son, Phillipe, who lived in the basement
with his arc welder. He came up every night with wine and stories and Yves would grin and shake his head and Yvonne would
scream with laughter as James and Marilyn looked blankly at
each other. Yvonne had to translate constantly, so it seemed half
the thoughts in her head were no longer her own, but Yves or
Phillipe's. Often she would put a hand on her cheek sympathet-
ically and tell them that some things could not be translated.

The first night, they had all sat around on the floor with a
couple of bottles of wine and the bag of pot Phillipe had
brought up. Desperate, furious, jealous, he had swallowed his
wine in gulps, taken deep breaths of the smoke, done anything
and everything to try not to see Yvonne and Yves' intense conversation, to try not to think. He thought "I'm having *poitín*:

a little pot," as the room whirled around him, Phillipe constantly moving closer to Marilyn, pestering her to drink more
wine, Marilyn getting up to find another place to sit, to pace, to
go off to the toilet. Phillipe began to make a big deal of the fact
Marilyn shared only Yvonne's English ancestry, and, knowing
little English himself, was trying to teach her French words as he
attempted to place his hand on her leg, her back, her cheek:
jambe, dos, joue. Befuddled, James lost track of who was going
where, who was talking to whom, until, at one point, he
thought he saw Marilyn climb out the window and he found
himself on the edge of the sill, stumbling onto the fire escape,
asking the first in a series of stupid questions.

"What in God's name are you doing?"

"Don't these people ever sleep? I was climbing the walls in
there."

There was a dim light in the bottom of the courtyard, and
she was streaming down the stairs beneath him, the blanket
flowing out behind her, translucent, the sculptures gleaming
here and there with wet, casting shadows, becoming wholly alien
in the night.

"What are you going to do down there?"

"Look at the sculptures."

"Why didn't you just ask Phillipe? There's stairs inside where –"

"Because then I would have to look at Phillipe, too."

He watched as she climbed over the railing at the bottom,
lowered herself nimbly, then dropped to the grass, almost to all
fours, her legs buckling, sprung, to catch her. The beam of a
hand torch flashed on behind him, casting his shadow huge over
the courtyard and the opposite walls, and someone was yelling
in French, maybe thinking he was a cat burglar.

"How are you going to get back up? You're not even
wearing –"

She stood and turned her face up to him, her eyes reflective.

"Go away," she said, and vanished into the dark.

He went back to the window on the public side of the house,
sat on the sill, and watched the cars that were somehow more

elegant that the ones he'd seen in London. He'd never thought how much they looked like skulls before. Every man and woman who passed beneath the window wore hard-soled shoes that hammered into his head. An hour passed.

Yves opened his door wearing only pajama bottoms, as usual, nodded to James and went into the little corner kitchen to boil water for coffee. Yvonne stirred and woke as if she smelled his presence, smelled the absence of his shirt, woke for the sole reason of looking at his bare pectoral muscles with the dark hair to match the curls on his head.

Her fascination with Yves made James clench his teeth, made him grip whatever piece of furniture was nearby. Yvonne talked on and on about how Yves was just like she knew a real Parisian would be, even though he was born in Caen. He, she said, was *quintessential* in the way he valued culture, and even style. When they were lost that first day, he commented on the appearance of women in the street, making his comments to the women them-selves, because, as he said, beauty is every man's business. She was never more fascinated than when he practiced his guitar, a necessary two or three hours every day. Often, first thing in the morning, he would come out of his bedroom, dangling his guitar in his fist like a spear, his shoulders hunched, ready for something, then sit on the floor with his back against Marilyn's couch and begin to play – songs composed by himself, of course. Yvonne would wake and lie, luxuriating in the blankets, while she watched his strong arms and large, delicate hands as he prac-ticed placing his fingers decisively for various bar chords and hammer-ons, his music modern, yet exotic, with reflections of flamenco. Now and then he rested for a moment, shook his fin-gers, then raked them through his black curls discontentedly. She touched his left hand once, as it depressed the strings for a particularly difficult B-flat, pressed the soft veins and taut, rayed tendons.

The morning began as usual, all of them taking turns going down the hallway to the shower Yves' flat shared with the apart-ment across the hall, someone making a trip to the *boulangerie*

up the street for baguette, Yves leaving to teach his guitar classes
before Marilyn had packed everything she needed into her day-
pack, checked her film supply, filled her bottle of water.

"Can't we just stay *in* one morning?" Yvonne said quietly, as
if knowing how outrageous this would sound to her companions. James looked at her, puzzled, because he couldn't understand the little whine in her voice. Soon they were all out on the
street, Marilyn matching his hard, obsessive stride – wanting to
see *everything* – while Yvonne lagged behind in a kind of dreamy
melancholia.

She paid for him to enter La Musée du Cluny, and all the way
through the archbishop's apartments he could not forget the
shame he felt. Once they were in the proper museum, with its
glassed-in display cases, he was fine, had found his voice, was
commenting on the collection; everything was *cloisonné* or
champlevé enamel, or gilded copper, even the intricately carved
covers of books. He explained to Yvonne how the men in the
workshop at Limoges would carve away the metal, make shallow
empty pools for each separate color, each separate fold of cloth,
or fleur-de-lis, or peacock feather, then fill the depressions with
coloured glass beads, then heat it all in a kiln to melt the glass
that would freeze into place forever, becoming little pools of
man-made precious stone.

Then he saw the book; it was a medieval bestiary. He was
stunned. It was the first-ever attempt at an encyclopedia of animals, was open to the page where a sciapod hopped on his single
giant human foot through the desert, a twin image on the next
page showing how the creature would lie in the scorching sun to
rest, using his foot as a parasol. A museum attendant appeared
too close beside him, excused himself, and, with a key, opened
the display case and turned the page gently with white-gloved
hands. When James saw him about to lock the case again, he
made page-turning gestures, got tongue-tied as he tried to get
Yvonne to tell the man, ask him, implore him, to turn a few
more pages. The man shrugged as if he couldn't care less, but
closed the book, and started from the very beginning, rattling

on in high-speed French that Yvonne attempted to translate. Half of the paintings were of animals the artist had probably never seen, not all of them purely mythical. James was amazed to see the elephant with a snake for a trunk and huge leaves for ears, a sharp-snouted whale with jagged little teeth, a curling mermaid with a pug-dog face, and a camel with a man drinking from its hump. There was the unicorn of course, but also the basilisk, a black and yellow reptile with fatally bad breath, hatched by a serpent from a rooster's egg.

"I knew a guy who could kill with his breath, too," Yvonne said, and laughed, but James hardly heard her, he was so enthralled. It was like that first time, that first book, the *Book of Kells,* when he knew what he wanted, and what he wanted was to *know,* to know everything, at least everything he *could* know; he had prayed a fervent child's prayer: this was what he wanted for his life. Here was something old, and it wasn't something purely Catholic either. This was secular, or as secular as anything could get in an age in which the only science was religion. This was mankind trying to know everything, doing the best it could with the information it had.

And maybe that was all Christianity was, too.

The book was like the churches they had just seen, made in the supposedly dark ages, using half-forgotten, half-bastardized Roman and Greek ideas, and ideas grown individually, anonymously. Medieval people had wanted to know everything, everything, just like him, and he wanted to know everything about them, too, from the only things they had left to the world: their work, their buildings, their pictures, their stories. One of the few books he carried in his suitcase was the book he had read to Granny as she lay dying, filled with stories and woodcut pictures of saints and their animals. In the *Book of Kells,* there had been strange animals, too, intertwined with the letters. Had anyone ever gathered a book of these together? Had anyone ever studied the way the legends of an even more ancient Ireland had crept into Christianity? What had been so holy about the holy wells before the first mention of Christ on the island? Had anyone ever thought about the deer-god Tuan? It was the sort of thing he could do. Now that he had thought of it, how could he keep from doing it? What would it mean? More school. Graduate work. The thought made his heart rev with ambition.

The man turned through all the pages, then found the sciapod before closing the case. James told Yvonne to tell him that it was the next page that he wanted, but Yvonne yawned.

"Oh, can we really just go to the Eiffel Tower this afternoon? My eyes are buggy from looking at all this little stuff. I think I have museum overload. I'm going bananas."

They made their way into the bigger rooms of the museum, the ones with the tapestries and sculptures. Yvonne stayed in the middle of the room, looking around, up at the ceiling, giving a little twirl now and then with outstretched arms before she found a padded bench to lie on, one arm draping down to rest on the floor, one foot twitching. James and Marilyn went from object to object until they found themselves in the Roman part of the museum, a ruin glassed-in and roofed-over, with a few objects here and there, the biggest of which was an enormous carved bathtub or sarcophagus – not even the experts knew which – curved and polished smooth inside and outside, a tub that could hold a few senators at a time.

Yvonne came up behind them.

"You know, Yves has a few days off next week. With all the cloudy weather we've been having, I don't think it's even time for vintage yet, and besides, we've hardly really seen anything but the insides of museums. I want to stay another five days – a week."

James looked up. "I've got no money. How can I possibly let you –"

"Don't be silly. When I can just go off and sing? Don't you want to take advantage of a real Parisian tour guide?"

"Yvonne wants to take advantage of him."

James turned abruptly at the words he'd barely heard. Marilyn. Her eyes met his for the briefest of instants, and he caught the knowing little upturn of one corner of her mouth just before it vanished. The jealousy he'd been trying to suppress rose up and panic poured into him: his girl, his lovely girl, the only one in the world. He turned back to her, but she was gone. He stopped breathing. She had been standing right there – *there*!

"Yvonne? Yvonne!" He shouted, his voice echoing back to him in the huge stone and glass chamber. "Yvonne!"

Reality seemed to have abruptly shifted, making her vanish. Maybe he had imagined her all along in his fever of losing his life, his religion, his family. He had gone mad and missed out a couple of weeks of his life to find himself – where was he? Was this really the place he thought it was? Had the devil been using the image of a beautiful woman to tempt him further away from God?

He heard laughter, not the evil laughter you might expect in a horror story, but light, delicious, and childish. He took a step and looked into the tub. There she was, lying with her hands folded over her breasts, laughing and laughing. "Boo!" she said.

"Get out! This is a museum, not a playground." He reached in and grabbed one of her arms and pulled as hard as he could, jerking her torso up from the stone bottom. Didn't she know the tub was a hundred times older than she was? How could she just climb in?

"Let go! Let go of me!" She pulled back, grabbed the arm he held with her other hand. He was stronger, and he dragged her, swivelled her, pulled her backward out of the tub.

"You don't do that!" he shouted. "What's wrong with you? Part of your, whatever it is, American cheek? This is a museum, for God's sake! You don't just go and do things like that, just go up and talk to anybody, go and live in some stranger's house!"

"You hate me because I'm happy and you're not!"

"You're going to get hurt. Someone is going to hurt you. Some people in the world –"

"*You* hurt me. *People* in the world. Like you! You're the one that hurt me!"

He let go of her, horrified, red marks around her wrist where his hand had been. *He* had hurt her.

She rubbed her arm, held it up to him, her eyes savage.

"*This*. Look at this. This is mine. *Mine*. See it? See all the other parts of me? All of it is *mine*. You have no right to it, to grab it, to put it anywhere that *you* would rather have it. It is *mine*. It's me."

She ran out of the room, the stone and glass cavern, her footsteps small but echoing, and James followed her, but only in his head. He couldn't move.

He'd hurt her.

He finally started after her, but it was too late. She was running. She had run out of the museum, and she was gone. The street was empty of her.

Marilyn came up behind him, panting a little. He started to walk, looking up and down every street they crossed – so many streets all around them. It was no use.

"I'm so sorry," he mumbled to himself.

"You're going have to watch that, that redhead temper," Marilyn said, matter-of-factly, invulnerable, calm as a nun.

The rain he hadn't noticed before began to rush over him, pound his head.

"There's that church near here. The one we wanted to see. It's over this way. I think we better run."

❖ ❖ ❖

Inside the church, Marilyn dug into her pack and handed him a book – his own book, the one of saints and beasts; he'd forgotten he'd put it in her pack the night before because of this very church and what her guidebook said about it.

He let his arm hang with the weight of the book: how could she think he could go back to being a tourist after what he'd just done? "I hurt her," he said softly, with shock, with shame, and he thought of his uncle Paddy, the gentlest person he knew. Without religion, what was he turning into?

"You'll see her tonight."

He watched Marilyn walk ahead of him down the church's left aisle, another of God's long dark caverns, stalactites and stalagmites so huge they joined midway to form columns and piers. Why did they make these places to seem so much underground, or inside of a body: tunnel vaults, groin vaults, stone ribs? It was a series of tubes for a monstrous burrowing worm, sightless and venomous, a parasite so much bigger than the puny minds it really inhabited. The worn stones down the middle of the aisle showed its trail, where it had dragged itself through its lair, day in, day out, for almost two thousand years. And here, all around him, the work the worm-god, dragon-god, demanded in tribute from its legions of terrified worshippers; the smooth pilasters on the wall were capped with ornately carved capitals of acanthus leaves and the triangular spaces above them, the spandrels, had little scenes on them. He saw one of the desert fathers holding out his hand, feeding a lion a bunch of dates. The next spandrel held the story of the hermit who fed loaves of bread to a wolf every day and had his hands washed after his meal by the wolf's soft, paper-thin tongue. Marilyn was looking at the same image, had climbed up onto the base of the pilaster, and was attempting to reach the wolf's paws with her hand.

"Will you stop touching everything? You're driving me mad. You keep touching the stone like that, the acid from your skin oil will make it decay faster."

She hopped backward to the floor.

"I don't know what you see in her, anyway. She's my cousin; I love her, but she's fluffy. Like her pastries. She's light as a feather."

His eyes stung with rage. Nobody could insult her like that, could say anything against his beautiful lady, his songbird; nobody could hurt her. But he had been the one who had hurt her the most.

"She didn't even write some of her essays that got her through university. Her boyfriends wrote them, or bought them for her. Not that she asked them outright or anything, no. But she charms them, like that lady you told me about in the unicorn tapestry. They lay their heads down in her lap, just like the unicorn. They just fall into her lap and she tames them. Sure, she's fun, she's pretty, she's – well, maybe I *do* see what you see in her."

She said it with a deadly implication, a salacious snarl on her lips, said that what he saw in Yvonne was what all men saw in her – her body, sex. How *dare* she, when all week he'd been sleeping not three feet from her, from both of them, and had behaved like a choirboy? How dare she bring that up now, and make lust itself surge inside him, a wave lapping over his anger and washing toward her: the wrong girl. Sure, he stayed under his blanket the longest, waiting for the girls to get up and step over him with their long bare legs, his head spinning, directionless, unable to prevent every cell in his body from enjoying their beauty. Sure, he was mad to get at Yvonne, but he was in love, and to imply that men were only this madness, to imply that this was all *he* was, how dare she? He looked at her; he had always had the urge to smooth his thumbs over the lips of any girl he found attractive, as if wiping away whatever was there to keep those lips from meeting his own. Her lips were beautiful, full without suggesting a pout, and for a moment he forgot everything else in imagining how the lower one would feel between his tongue and his teeth as if it were a lobe of blood orange. He looked away quickly, what he had done when he was a seminary student training himself to renounce desire itself. How dare she call that up, call his body to her, when it was so wrong, when he worshipped her cousin?

"Just *shut up*. Shut up. You have no right to say anything to me about her. She's –"

"Fine. I'll shut up. It's your life, anyway. Who gives a shit?"

Marilyn left the aisle and stalked off across the apse, shoving and crashing her way between two of the neat rows of chairs. James walked deliberately to the next spandrel toward the brighter eastern end of the church, the choir empty of singers. Carved above him was a man, a saint with a disc-like halo and there was some strange animal with another animal in its mouth. He practically broke open his book, paged through it quickly and found a nearly identical woodcut: Saint Macarius and the Hyena. The weeping Hyena mother was holding her blind baby in her mouth, imploring the saint to heal it, which of course, he did. Thereafter, the hyena would not kill any more, would eat nothing but carrion. James read: "And the old man perceived in his heart that it was the purpose of God who gives understanding to beasts for a reproach unto ourselves."

His heart could have stopped.

He thought of all the things Granny had shouted at him in her first fury after he'd been beaten almost senseless by Dermot so long ago, almost half his lifetime ago. "Ye should ha'! Ye should ha..." Granny shouted at him while she stood, shaking, looking at the bandages, the crusted blood. "Ye should ha'. You're like my father," she said disparagingly. "Like your uncle Paddy."

"What're they like?"

She grunted: he should know by now what his uncle Paddy was like. But he wanted her to say it, whatever she was thinking: that they were all cowards? Or weaklings?

"*What is he like?*" What am *I* like?

"Not a fighter." She threw the words at him, soft words as if to soften a blow, but a negative all the same. He was lacking. She shuffled toward the door, frowning, her mouth twitching, her eyes looking around for something, someone who no longer existed. "No. Gentle," she finally said, her voice slow, almost suffering. "A gentle soul, he were."

And that was always how he had seen himself, always been proud to be. He couldn't lose that. He wouldn't. Not after losing everything else.

Why had he grabbed her? He had never hurt anyone before in his life, at least not like that, never thrown the first punch, never wanted to. Why had he become so angry? Why had he reacted as if she had desecrated something holy? It was a stone sarcophagus that had been out in the rain for almost two thousand years. What could a light girl like Yvonne possibly do to harm it? Even though he was no longer a believer, what was still holy to him was the past.

That was it.

That was *him*, that part of him that he could still recognize from his childhood. He had lost everything but that, the one thing that was still him, that would always be him, the one thing that he loved the most – history, the only place left where the dead could live on. Maybe he did worship it in his way. He had history and he swore he would have his gentleness back, would hold on to these things until the day he died.

"Oh my God," he said, as his head sagged, and he put up his hands to cover his face. He couldn't believe his feeling of relief. He could let himself love the form of a cathedral, a book, a Raphael painting of the Madonna and Child. This was no longer forbidden him as an apostate. All of these things, though they might be religious objects, were still the work of men and women who had lived and were loved. All these things were evidence of them, were part of the journey of past generations.

❖ ❖ ❖

He found Marilyn in one of the little grotto-chapels beyond the sanctuary, leaning her shoulder against a relief carving of a female saint who held a box in her hands.

"I'm sorry, Marilyn. I...haven't been myself for a while."

"She's your first, right? First girlfriend?"

Embarrassed, his breath rushed through his nostrils. "She tells everybody?"

"I'm sorry, too. I should have been...nicer to you. I mean, my first time, it was hard, too."

"You fought?"

"No. He – I liked him for so long, before, I could hardly speak to him, and then after, you know, we'd been together – sort of – a month, he just...went."

"Didn't tell you why?"

Marilyn lifted her hands as if she wanted to put her arms around the saint. Even in the grey light, he could see her cheeks were burning. She put one against the saint's cold stone hip.

"This wasn't very long ago, then?" he asked.

She sighed and looked away and her chin twisted, dimpled, as she pressed her lips together.

"He just said, 'So long. Been nice *playing* with you.'"

"Och, Marilyn." For a few moments, there was only the hollow cavern sound of the church. "That any man would have the temerity to toy with *your* wrath –"

"As if I was a *thing*, as if all he –"

"Marilyn, ye *must* know that he was an arsehole as well as an idiot. Everyone must tell you that."

"Well –" the word cracked in half in her throat. "I never told anyone else." She grinned, teeth clenched, and moved away abruptly, grabbed the saint's robe with the claw of her hand and swung herself in an arc. "You see, it isn't just the flower children who have *experiences*."

"Marilyn. Ye *must* know it. Come to believe it in your soul. Say it once. Let me hear you say it."

She took a deep breath. "Arsehole!!" she roared, and it echoed far into the church and came back at them until they were both laughing because it was just the right thing to do. "I don't even know what that means. Is it the same thing as asshole?"

He could barely answer, he was laughing so hard; she had shouted a curse in a church, and it was almost as if he had been able to do it himself.

*   *   *

They didn't see Yvonne, not at five when they came back to the flat, not at six-thirty when he and Marilyn started banging around in the kitchen trying to make supper, not when the sun set just before seven. James was terrified. Yvonne hated him. She would never forgive him. She had gone out, and in her mad fury, had stepped in front of a bus or fallen in the river.

Without Yvonne, he and Marilyn were pathetic cooks, especially pathetic French cooks. When Yves came home, he took one look and immediately rushed into the kitchen and wrenched an egg – as gently as he could – from Marilyn's fingers as she held it high and was about to smash it against the edge of the little counter.

"Merde, non! Ici. Not like that!"

Swearing in French under his breath, he pushed a few of the bowls aside, then looked at them, and sighed.

"Never mind. Out."

James and Marilyn went to the far side of the room, where Yves directed them, left the little corner kitchen to him. James sat on the windowsill and looked out. No Yvonne.

"Marilyn," Yves called, and piled cutlery on the table. "La," he kept saying, as he told her where to put everything.

By the time they sat down to cheese omelets and the salad Marilyn had hacked up and thrown together earlier, it was dark, and James was so upset he felt like he might vomit. He took a bite of the eggs.

"So, what made you want to become a music teacher?" Marilyn asked.

"I am a *composer.* I teach so I can eat. We all have to teach," he sighed morosely, forbidding further discussion.

They ate quietly for a little while, except for James, who could barely swallow. Yves cleared his throat, let his head fall to the side, and looked at them with a little smile. He was going to test them again with his own special kind of rhetorical question.

"I was on the Champs-Elysées. Fucking tourists. All the garbage in the street. And around here. Algerians are moving in everywhere. You can hardly see the whores on St. Denis for the fucking Algerians. What do you think? Is it worth it for Paris to be so brilliant, to be the center of the world, so that so much trash has to drift in?"

Yves finished off his slice of omelet quickly with his elegant hands, hardly seeming to rush. He pushed his plate away a little, sat back. James braced himself. At least, in the midst of Yvonne's incessant translations, he didn't actually have to talk to Yves.

Yves took a sip of wine, looked from Marilyn to James with the air of a bored boy about to prod two small animals with a stick.

"And you," he said to Marilyn. "In Canada you..."

"I go to art school. I'm going to be famous."

James watched Yves try not to smile patronizingly.

"You Canadian girls. A little bit lumberjack, eh? You should go shopping. Like I tell Yvonne. You wear man's clothes, men can't tell there are wonderful things beneath. *Vive la différence.*"

Marilyn stared at him in disbelief, picked up one of her dark braids and held it like a paintbrush.

"I have hair."

"You go. Where I tell Yvonne. *Leetle* black dress. Nice shoes. High heels. Even *you.*"

"You can't tell I'm a *girl?*"

He tapped two cigarettes out of his pack and held one out to her. "Come on. It don't bite."

Marilyn considered it.

"My father calls those things baby soothers."

Yves pulled his arm back, nonplussed. He forced a laugh through his teeth, trying to appear to find Marilyn amusing. "You think too much," he told her, dismissive, a snarl on his lips. His eyes darted to James.

"So, what make *you* want to wear a dress, eh?" He flicked a black curl off his temple with his middle finger. "You give up a girl like that to wear a dress?"

"What?" James said.

"*Sacre*...your *ho*liness. A priest...he fall. He is defrocked. And a frock is a dress, no?"

"That was before... It was a long time ago."

"*Pardon.* Yvonne, she say like, she *corrupt* you, she rob you from the church's cradle. How many French women want to have a priest? Millions. You should take advantage, eh? Throw them a little Latin, a little...forbidden fruit? Tortured guilt? *Agony*. Women love it."

Marilyn rolled her eyes and got up from the table with a groan just as the door opened. A foot appeared, or rather, a boot, tall, caramel-coloured suede with a squared-off toe and small platform heel. The rest of the leg appeared, tan corduroy pants rolled up to the knee.

Yvonne's head appeared around the edge of the door frame. "Whad'ya think?"

James was out of his chair and beside her immediately.

"I'm sorry," he pleaded, in a whisper.

"I'm not talking to you," she hissed back, before striding past him into the room. She wore the boots, a wrapped cardigan with matching suede panels and belt, and her long hair was mounded up under the big pouf of a brown corduroy hat, the brim pulled low over her eyes.

"Bravo!" Yves cried.

"I went to that shop, you know, the one we saw that first day trying to find Deux Maggots..."

"The boots – *magnifique*. Look at the leg. *Mais non!* You buy the sweater too large..."

They lapsed into French as Yves criticized her, pinching the excess knit around her waist, taking her hand, holding it high, and moving her around with it, then pushing her toward the big oval mirror on the bedroom door so he could stand close behind her and reposition her hat with his palms.

"Oh, my god! I almost forgot!" Yvonne bumped past him and ran back to the door. "Come on in. Don't be shy!"

A young man, nodding and smiling, came forward from the dark hallway drawing a young woman by the hand.

"They're from Montreal! They live, literally, around the corner from me. I saw them at the Eiffel Tower, and kept thinking, hey, I've seen them before! Isn't it wild? Thomas, Helén, this is Yves. He's got a *band*."

They introduced themselves in French, and immediately Yves was all over them, bringing wine, talking rapidly in French.

Phillipe came in and everyone ended up sitting on the floor on the blankets where he and Yvonne slept. There was more and more wine, then, and more pot. He didn't partake of any of it this time, and noticed Marilyn didn't either. He couldn't recall her ever taking a toke. He watched Yvonne, talking, laughing, enjoying herself as if he wasn't there, as if nothing was wrong. Did she think that this was it, then? Is that how people got dumped? Just a bit of yelling and he was supposed to go away? Marilyn got up and grabbed something out of her pack and left for the toilet. Yves got up, took her journal, and sat back down. She came back, dressed in the shorts and baggy T-shirt that she slept in, and when she began to sit, her legs folding beneath her, she saw Yves paging through her drawings. In a fluid, feline, half crawl, half stretch, she pounced, was across the floor and back again, the journal snatched up in her hand.

Yves gasped, recovered himself. "What, you afraid I find out all your secrets?"

"No. I'm afraid you'll read all the nasty things I've written about you."

She smiled at him and he smiled back uncertainly, all bared teeth, two cats, hackles raised.

James moved off the blankets amid the commotion, crawled behind Yvonne and carefully fit his face into the angle between her head and shoulder.

"I'm sorry. It's all the, you know, things going on in my head, the –"

"Yeah, I know. You have a lot of problems, don't you?"

The hardness of her whisper silenced him.

"Take it easy," she said. "You need money. We'll go to the vineyard tomorrow."

❊ ❊ ❊

The next day, on the train, Yvonne still wouldn't speak to him. He sat beside her, and she stood, stepped over him with her long boots, and sat in another seat. She slouched down, with her knees propped on the back of the seat in front of her, and read a French newspaper she'd picked up off the floor.

Marilyn looked at him, rolled her eyes.

"Move over."

James slid over to the window and Marilyn sat beside him and put her journal in his lap.

"You can look if you want."

He paged through, glancing out frequently as the train rattled slowly out of the city under a dull sky. She was good. She had drawn the *Mona Lisa,* a few studies of the *Dying Slaves,* bits of sculpture from the fronts of buildings and churches, snuck portraits of strangers in cafés, several of Yvonne, one of Yves, and even one of him, all of them asleep; so that's why she left her glasses on when she went to bed; that's what she did, prowling around at night. He hardly knew what to think about this, never having felt vulnerable and a little spooked at the same time: that she had stared so long and hard at him while he had been oblivious, that she should know his face so well. He looked at her and she smiled, half mischievous, half guilty. At the front of the book were art-school studies, a few nudes, which shocked him a little, and drawings of horses.

"That's Snickers. She's mine. That's Bounty. He's a Shetland. Oh Henry died last year. He was almost eighteen. I shouldn't look at these. It's making me homesick."

She shut the book as she pulled it away. James leaned his head against the cold glass. Everything was going by so slowly, all the empty fields, the little towns with their sooty, ornate houses, lead roofs, peeling shutters. He had been speeding, running away, but since his fight with Yvonne, time had stretched into endlessness. Every moment she wasn't speaking to him was eternal; he could feel her silent, angry presence across the aisle, and he longed for her smile the way he might have longed for a glimpse of the sun during a rainy Irish winter. The train stopped at every little town, every small station with dead weeds shivering in the gravel at the side of the tracks, broken bottles near the edge of the platforms.

"I used to be really religious, too. But first-year anthropology took care of that."

He nodded. It was impossible to talk about it. He looked at his hands on his knees, then at Marilyn's. He'd never noticed how dark she was.

"Sure, but how did you get such skin, Marilyn? You're brown as –"

"It's the mixed blood: Turkish, Afghan, maybe even Mongolian. I figure every Ukrainian's got some, the way the place used to get invaded. I'm probably a descendant of Genghis Kahn."

He examined her: the black hair, the round face, the inward-looking, stone-steady eyes with their slight but unusual slant, their brown shadowed irises with yellow flecks around the dark matrix, the fierce outspokenness that could demolish anyone in her path; no one messes with the Mongolian hordes. But now, he also saw compassion in her eyes, a place for him to shelter during this one particular storm.

"I am a Parisian compo*zaire* and you *air not.*"

He laughed – it was remarkable – because she *had* Yves exactly, had him between her teeth and was giving him a good shake. He smiled at her for trying to cheer him up, but there was nothing she could do. This all reminded him too much of the way he felt when his mother stopped speaking to him, to every-body, and stayed in her room for days, and he blamed himself, tried to find a way to bring her back, bring her close, make her happy, make everything alright again.

The seats emptied as they got further from Paris. After a long time, he saw the land change. There were hills, then patches of sun. The towns began to seem brighter, many of the houses built out of pale limestone. The train began following a river, and the river brought them upstream into a valley, and there, on the slopes, were the vineyards, rows of trussed vines running up the hills. James glanced at Yvonne, who was looking away, out of her own window. They must be getting close. It was a relief. Maybe she just needed time. After a few days of working together in the sun, being away from all the distractions of Paris and people obsessed with bands, they would be all right again.

"St. Jean Sur Yon," she said to Marilyn, deliberately not looking at James. They waited for the train to slow as it pulled up alongside the town, then dragged packs and suitcase from the overhead rack. It was midafternoon and they were starving. Yvonne led the way through the narrow streets. They came to a little square with two trees in the middle and a fountain between them.

"That's the house we stayed in," she said, pointing to one of the little two-storey stone houses, the only one whose shutters were freshly painted white.

"You and your mother and stepfather," James said, trying to get her to acknowledge his presence.

Yvonne rewarded him with a glance and a curt nod. He began to breathe easier.

"Strange to go on their honeymoon, eh?" he said, echoing what she had told him before, trying to get her to aim her animosity elsewhere.

"Oh, I wanted to come to France. They got all their stuff over with in the first couple of weeks, I think. I only came after that."

"She came by herself," Marilyn said, awed. "When she was seventeen!"

"There's the *patisserie!* They had the best croissants."

It was as if they were back in Paris again, and it was lunchtime. Yvonne spoke to the storekeepers, and they loaded up a paper bag with croissants, cheese, a thin gnarled sausage, three carrots, three apples and, of course, éclairs. James carried the bottle of water in one hand and the bottle of wine in the other. They ate while sitting in the shade on the edge of the fountain.

"It was July when we were here. Of course Burt had to go to every other blinking nowhere town in the area, go to the markets, do all the things the locals did. Can you believe he actually made me go to a donkey race? Some town over in the next valley. Now, is that nothing to do, or what?"

James laughed. It was just the way she used to talk on their first bus trip together.

"He did teach me how to make an omelet, though. Oh these are just so good. I could eat a thousand of these," she said, taking the first bite from her éclair, then chewing, rubbing the cream from her lips with the heel of her hand. "Why is it some people think that whatever happens in small towns is *unspoiled*? What does that mean, anyway? That they've been doing it so long, not even they know why, so it becomes somehow religious?"

Yvonne was really talking to herself, or talking merely to make noise, to make less room for anyone else to say anything.

"So everyone stuck here is somehow better than anybody who left for the city. So this is some kind of heaven, right? And, say, the thought of the Rolling Stones or Andy Warhol spoils all that? It was like he wanted to turn a whole town of people into his pets or something. Put them into a vacuum chamber and pickle them so they couldn't ever change. Take them home for his friends to sample at his authentic wine tastings. Here – have a bite of Jaques the blacksmith, Jules the baker. He still wants – Burt wants – to give up the office. Been looking for just the right land ever since. Goes on and on about limestone soil and getting the right grapes. Blah, blah. He met Armand at the winery and he couldn't stop talking, like someone had given him speed or something, like he'd just met a long lost brother. He and Mum went there every day after that, tasting, learning how to prune, hiking up and down the hills with Solange. God. I'm not sure why I even came back. The money. Right. At least it was only a week before we went down to Nice. The beach was amazing. Mum thought she saw Faye Dunaway at a big hotel downtown. Isn't it stupid? When I came in on the plane, they just picked me up in the rental car, and I didn't even care about seeing Paris. It didn't make a difference to them either. Come on. The vineyard is a couple miles down the valley."

She took a last swig from the bottle of red, hoisted her pack, and walked off, leaving Marilyn to clean up the papers and apple cores, James to carry the water and the remains of the wine to balance his suitcase.

Cobbles and the odd bit of crumbling asphalt gave way to whitish, jagged gravel and damp-darkened clay potholes after they left town. There were no clouds. The atmosphere had the bright clearness of the edge between summer and autumn, dry roadside grasses and leaves beginning to yellow, the contrasting colour pouring more blue into the sky. The road ran beside the river. A few cars passed them, honking through their clouds of pale dust. Now and then they walked by a lane with trees on either side, tall, thin, Lombardy poplars, pines, or an unfamiliar kind of pollarded tree with thick limbs knuckled at the ends where thin sapling branches sprayed out bouquets of leaves. The sun felt hotter than James had ever known, even though it was already four in the afternoon; there was no water in the air to block the radiation. James put his hand on his neck above his collar, could almost feel his freckles seething, growing. There was only the sound of their feet on the coarse gravel and the odd caw of a crow and the distant sound of a car somewhere up the hill beside them. Yvonne picked up the odd stone and threw it into the river, sometimes ran on ahead a little if she glanced back and he and Marilyn seemed to be catching up to her. Finally, she stopped and waited for them beside a lane where there was a crude hand-painted sign in French, with a sloppily painted bunch of purple grapes.

"I think this is it. Mum wrote I was coming."

They walked up the lane, Yvonne frowning a little as if she might be mistaken; it had been a few years, after all. They went up, the road becoming steeper until finally it curved around to follow the contour of the hill. The river was far away, now, and they were surrounded on all sides by little fields of vines, fields full of almost-Irish hedgerows but with posts at regular intervals in the middle of each hedge, and the earth between hardly earth at all, but composed almost entirely of stones, thick, flat, like broken, prehistoric eggshells. And under the leaves, not hidden at all, were the grapes they would pick, small, blackish, and dusty. They each spontaneously stopped to pick, to taste one: seedy, too intense to be sweet. Yvonne smiled at him then; they all smiled for some reason. This was the next adventure: vintage. This was the work they would be doing, and the sun they would be doing it beneath, and the view across the valley was so beautiful. They were the happy peasants in a French impressionist painting. Soon, they would see the grand chateau.

But it wasn't a chateau. It was only the village co-op. The building was a big shed made of stone, with a corrugated metal roof. It was set back a little from the side of the road behind a small, gravelly courtyard with weeds growing along the wall. To one side was a pile of rusting machinery and barrel hoops, and a stack of grey, decaying hay bales. A small tractor and trailer was on the other side. The door opened and a woman carrying a stack of three plastic boxes struggled out. She put them against the wall, then straightened, frowning, a hand on her lower back. She was in her late twenties, with dark hair and skin, dressed as a farm wife in tall rubber boots and a baggy flowered dress with a man's denim shirt over it.

"Solange!"

The woman turned, looked at them, and smiled.

"Ah!" she exclaimed, opening her arms, talking rapidly in French. She embraced Yvonne, kissed both of her cheeks, pushed her arm's-length to look at her, exclaiming all the while. Even though James couldn't understand a word, he could tell what she was saying just by her gestures: How you have grown up! Your hair is longer! You are taller!

Yvonne introduced them, and he and Marilyn each got their kisses, then exchanged glances: the French and their kissing. There was a torrent of conversation which he had no hope of understanding, and the woman led them all behind the building and up a short driveway to a farmhouse half covered in scaffolding. The only things in the yard were a pile of sand and a small crusty cement mixer.

"Vintage isn't going to be for at least another three days," Yvonne said, turning to James and smiling, raising an I-told-you-so eyebrow. "But we can stay in the bunkhouses and help out with the cooking. She says there's other stuff to do, too."

Inside, the house showed its true age. The limestone step between the low-ceilinged entry hall and the kitchen was worn into a curve by hundreds of years of boots, and the big fireplace was dark with soot and bits of ironwork: hooks and spits and pokers. There was a rough line between old plaster and new plaster through the middle of the room, and the outside wall was a bank of windows above a big wooden table. There was even a window in the ceiling. They dropped their packs in a corner and sat, with glasses of wine and apples and cheese, as Yvonne and Solange talked. They heard the door open and a man, balding, of about thirty-five, walked in carrying a large cardboard box of groceries.

"Oh, Armand! *Voici!*" Solange said, and the man looked them over, his mouth opening in wonder when he recognized Yvonne.

He put the box down, and bent to kiss her gravely.

In the confusion that followed, Yvonne had their French hosts practice saying "farm boy," and James came to understand that he was to get the rest of the food out of the truck. There was a lot: eggplants and red peppers – things he had never seen before – tomatoes, celery, carrots, onions and potatoes, a crate each of apples, pears and peaches, big sacks of flour and sugar, a few wheels of cheese, brown paper bags filled with bread, spices, baking powder, chocolate, glass bottles of milk and cream, sacks of beans and lentils, loops of sausage, and slabs of meat in brown paper, tied with string.

Whenever he entered the kitchen with another box, the contents of the last had already been stowed away. Yvonne was chopping something at the counter, and Marilyn was kneeling beside an open trap door where Solange appeared with two plucked ducks in her arms, their heads still on and covered in green iridescent feathers.

"I can do it if you want," he heard Marilyn say, before he went back for another load. Each time he went back into the kitchen, its configuration of people had changed. He didn't see Marilyn again until she was standing in the yard, in his way, with a big ceramic bowl of reeking offal in her bloody hands. Her shoulders were bare and a large bib-apron was tied tightly around her; her body was as elegant as Yvonne's, but stronger-looking, more wiry. How had he never noticed before? Then he remembered the night they had gone to the disco, Yvonne all show, jumping and flinging her hair, but Marilyn so subtle, it had taken him until the end of the night to notice how she moved, her whole body rippling like waves on water.

"Can you go in and find out if they want me to save the liver or anything else? I got blood on my shoes."

James laughed in admiration; he couldn't imagine Yvonne eviscerating a duck. Soon, in the kitchen, Solange was hacking the ducks apart with a big knife and Yvonne was watching, her upper lip curled. He could have kissed it.

"Farm boy," Armand said, after James dropped the last of the boxes on the table, and James followed him outside again, and down to the big shed. He helped Armand take the rest of the plastic boxes outside and spray them clean of spiderwebs and dust, taking turns with a garden hose blocked with a thumb, then stacked them on the back of the truck and in the trailer. They went around to the other side of the building where there was another yard and an open garage door. Inside, there were big steel drums, and a machine he could only imagine to be a modern winepress.

"Armand!"

A man in a dirty boiler suit came out from behind the machine, gesturing angrily at it, talking with such emphasis that he had to be swearing. The machine was shiny enough to be new, but that didn't mean it worked.

"Ahh..." Armand said, and grinning at James, he made gestures as if to pull out his hair, then took him by the shoulder to steer him back outside. They climbed into the truck, and were soon bouncing down the hill, hitting every rut and pothole, the plastic boxes rattling behind. In town, Armand stopped suddenly and got out, waving his hand for James to stay. He knocked at a door, then knocked louder, then gave the door a little kick, and then came back into the truck. They were off again, through the town and over the tracks, over a small bridge and up the other side of the valley. Suddenly Armand slammed on the brakes and the truck slid in the gravel, twisting a little sideways before it stopped. Armand leaped out and shouted to an old man walking among the vines. The man broke into an awkward run: he wasn't as old as he looked. Armand leaped back into the truck and stepped on the gas just as the man jumped in among the boxes. Armand drove, biting the side of his thumb, muttering what must have been more evil French words. He glanced at James, smiled solemnly, and lifted one hand off the steering wheel, palm upturned, to heaven. His face became philosophical, though his driving remained frantic. They drove back, stopping behind the co-op at the garage door. The old man in back got out, and the man inside met him beside Armand's open truck window, a relieved look on his face. They talked heatedly for a minute, the truck still running, then Armand drove away again with James. They stopped halfway up the hill and unloaded some of the boxes, stacking them upside down in the grass. They drove again, and unloaded again, did the same thing again and again until the truck and trailer were empty and the sun was already down. James was exhausted, but filled with the look of the gentle valley, its strips of vine hedges and pale stony soil, filled with open sky and fresh air, his muscles filled with tension and release from good work.

The kitchen was warm, brimming with thick meaty smells, candles reflecting off the big dark windows. Yvonne was cutting bread, Marilyn leaped up from the table to dish out the contents of a casserole, and Solange opened her arms to her husband, who embraced her, putting a hand on her stomach. James narrowed his eyes. He had not seen it before because of her loose man's work-shirt; Solange was going to have a baby, not soon, but sometime in the next year.

"Ah! You!" he said, opening his hands toward her middle, his inability to communicate in French making him almost tongue-tied in English.

"*Oui, oui,*" she said, and Armand grinned and muttered something which made her slap his arm with the back of her hand.

Yvonne translated: "He said, 'we're hoping for triplets.'"

A baby. This was, somehow, the completion of everything. It made him suddenly happy. Without thinking, he said, "Would ye look at that!" to Yvonne, and she smiled back as if they had never fought. They all sat, and he ate, and was warm, was dazzled by the candles, the voices, the good wine. It was very good, the wine. Everything was good. Yvonne was even sitting beside him, and he held her hand, pressed his nose through her long, every-coloured hair to find her ear, whispered to her how he had been trying for so long to apologize to her. She barely let him talk, told him it was okay, okay, to never mind, kissed his cheek. He was eating something he'd never eaten before, beans and sausage, and what must have been the duck in some rich sweet sauce. And there was a bitter, leafy salad, and crusty bread, and after, an apple tart – the apple slices laid in a kind of pinwheel spiral, like spinning sunrays – apple tart with cream, and then more and more wine, more cheese, oil-sweating cheeses on a wooden platter with strange knives. Armand and Solange and Yvonne laughed and he and Marilyn rolled their eyes at each other, and it felt like a small happy family, like the time he remembered from before Ireland, before everything – maybe like the family he and Yvonne might have someday.

A family. Children. *Him?* This had always been barred to him, as his mother's son, as a priest. He had never been able to imagine it before. He couldn't take his eyes off Solange, how she laughed and ate and got up to get a cloth to wipe up a spill of wine, all while unconsciously creating new life within her. He wanted to throw himself to the floor and weep with gratitude to the cosmos, so drunk he was. He was just a man, but he could help, would go off hunting for Yvonne and lay at her feet whatever she desired, hare or salmon, haunch of venison or plate of pastry. Even if he had lost everyone he loved, with a woman he could make a new family, children that he would love even more. He would carry them in his arms forever if they cried and his arms would never get tired. A girl he thought of first – for what good are boys, really? And he would raise her fierce, so that no bad thing would ever happen to her, make sure she learned karate and to fire a pistol, and show her what gentle men were like so she could find one of her own someday. He could almost see her through the window in the wind-washed night, staring down defiantly from the trees she climbed like obsessions, chasing birds, collecting leaves and old nests, spying out over all the lesser mortals. Such a being she would be – to him, at least, her father – such a heavenly being that she seemed as if she might take flight through the deep rippling night, dark as the future; in the glass there was a reflection of himself.

Of course she would hate him someday, for a while, when a teenager. All children did. But she would forgive him eventually, wouldn't she? Why? Why would she?

Because he wouldn't abandon her, ever.

But he would let *her* go.

He looked at Yvonne, the mother of his imaginary children. Maybe there would be time for them to take walks up these hills, maybe to another little town he'd caught sight of down the valley. They would explore all the ancient little streets, taste the bread, maybe go fishing in the river. He was exhausted. He could hardly believe they had been in Paris that morning. After the meal, they picked up their things and Armand led them, his arms filled with blankets, down a short path to two small bunkhouses.

"Ah, *non, non!*" he said, laughing wickedly when James tried to follow the girls into the first one.

"*Les filles, ici, mais les hommes, avec moi.*"

James managed to grab Yvonne and kiss her cheek, her lips, and her forehead, before Armand took his arm and steered him into the next little house. Armand turned on the single bare bulb. The little room was built of unpainted concrete blocks and held six bunks. It was a little cool, but James was so tired, that when he woke the next morning, he didn't even remember making his bed or getting out of his clothes. Sunlight slanted in through one of the dusty windows and James lay still for a few minutes, his happiness unchanged by the passing of night, though, yes, the headache was there, and he would suffer for all that wine. He walked outside, taking a look around before going behind the bunkhouse to relieve himself in the tall grass. He went back inside and stepped on a piece of paper. He must have stepped over it without seeing it on his way out. It was the drawing Marilyn had made of him, torn carefully from her journal. That was nice of her. It was a good drawing, too. He hadn't realized how much he'd gotten to like her, to respect her active mind that only revealed itself here and there between her long silences. He still felt that he hardly knew her at all, that there was so much still hiding behind the darkness of her eyes. He smiled to himself. For the first time he thought of the possibility of Marilyn. But he loved Yvonne, and now that she was out of Paris away from all the musicians – but he'd better get dressed. He looked at his watch: half-nine! And he'd gotten the impression there was a lot of work to do.

He dressed, walked to the house, and poked his head into the kitchen, but there was no one there, just a place for him at the table, a baguette, a pot of jam, and a coffee cup with a saucer placed on top of it. He went down to the winery, but there was no one there either. He thought he saw Armand's truck and its dust-cloud going into town. He went back to the house, sat and began his breakfast.

Solange came in with a basket full of herbs: rosemary, thyme, parsley, and a smaller one of tomatoes.

"Ah!" she said, and took his cup, poured the milk from it into a saucepan, and began to reheat it. She felt the side of the coffee pot with her palm and nodded once to herself.

"Solange," James said.

"Mmm?" She didn't look at him, but was placing her eyes and her hands here and there on the counter, as if she had lost something that should have been in plain view.

"Where are the girls?"

"Ah!" Solange seized a little jar from the top of the stove, opened it, and grated some nutmeg into his cup.

She must not understand him.

"Uh, Yvonne, Marilyn?" he said, trying to accent the names, say them the way she had said them.

Solange came toward him with his cup now filled with steaming milk and coffee and a floating dust of nutmeg.

"I – sorry," she said, struggling in English, then looking at him for the first time, frowning, sorrowful. "She say...tell you s...*scarpered*?"

He was running down the gravel road, its steepness lengthening his stride, making each footfall more jarring. They must be in the town, if not already on the train, on their way back to Paris, back to Yves. She was just a girl, after all, her head filled with music, maybe chasing fantasies of being in Yves' band, opera turned pop. She was just a girl, so how could he make her understand that those things were all naive, all dreaming, that he was the one who could make her happy? Maybe she had talked Armand into driving them down, maybe he had only missed them by the time it took for the truck to go down the hill, maybe he had been watching them run away, and not known it. It was the pain of this thought that made him suffer, even more than the pain in his lungs, as he ran, almost all the way, gasping, into the little train station. There was no one there, not even in the ticket booth. There wasn't even a schedule, not even a piece of paper tacked to the wall to tell travellers when trains arrived and when they left. But why would there be? It was probably common knowledge. A train out in the morning, and in at night. Only one destination. What travellers would come here? He walked out onto the platform and looked down the tracks toward Paris: gravel and dark oil stains and broken glass. He had the urge to just start walking, but all his things were up at the bunkhouse.

And he had no money. And there wasn't a soul around who would lend it to him. What would they say up at the co-op if he asked? *We should pay you to go away? Just give you enough money to escape from the work we need you to do?* That was what they would say, if he could even make himself understood.

The way back was so much longer than he remembered, he was afraid he had passed the lane, was walking off to who knows where. His mind frantically ticked away, planning, plotting. He would have to work for awhile. How long? A week, maybe. Get enough money just to get away and find her. What other choice did he have? None. None. His thoughts whirled and then stopped, because they could find no other place to go. He knew what he had to do, and then he thought of nothing; his mind was numb as he watched the river, the vine rows, the lanes he passed until he finally found the right one. With a crazy last hope, he went into the girls' bunkhouse: no rucksacks, no blankets. He walked slowly back to his own little house and saw the drawing, the portrait of himself asleep, unaware, innocent, looking very young. Suddenly he turned the drawing over. There were only a few words, hastily scrawled:

Sorry. She made me. M.

He caught a cold, barely slept that night because of the coughing. The next day a couple of French boys and a black Algerian man arrived and invaded his bunkhouse, and their snores and his coughs let him sleep even less; he had never seen a black man up close before. The day after, more French boys arrived, and a whole family of Moroccans, father, mother, and two teenage sons. And still, the grapes were not quite right. They saw pickers across the valley on the west-facing slope, but the timing had to be perfect, and the weather was good.

When vintage finally came, when Armand came in from the vineyards after tasting the right amount of ripeness, vintage was all there was: work and food and wine and the suffering of his muscles. Up before dawn, they were in the vineyards picking before the late sunlight finally found the bottom of the valley, he and the French students and black Algerians and Moroccans who filled the bunkhouses, the old women and men and wives and husbands and teenagers and local odd jobbers who talked almost constantly as they worked, who treated it as some kind of party. They began at the bottom of the rows, one picker on each side, sometimes having to clip away excess leaves to get at the heavy bunches of little grapes, almost black under their dust, filling the plastic baskets slung from their shoulders and shuffling through the weeds over the pale stony earth, steeper and steeper as they went up the hill. James's only shoes, his black seminary oxfords, had stood up well to the travelling, but now, covered in dust and the juice from fallen grapes, they looked as if he'd found them in a back alley. Jean, a big local boy, walked up and down the rows with a huge plastic container on his back, taking the picked grapes down to the waiting trailer to dump them, with a twist of his shoulders, into the boxes. After a couple of hours, when Armand came up in the truck for another load of grapes, he brought breakfast and they all sat by the roadside, silently gorging themselves on the ham and egg pie and milky coffee poured from a big stainless steel urn into melamine cups. The glass jugs of water and cheap acidic wine were always there, left along the side of the road, and as they sweated, as the sun got higher, they drank more and more. The first morning was a blur, his senses overloaded with the smells of wine and hot grape juice in the sun, his wasp-stung, sugar-coated fingers sticking together with the mixture of juice, dust, and grime, sneezing now and then from the mould spores that puffed up from the bunches he was picking, the background hum of the foreign language mingled with the barking of dogs, the buzz of cicadas, the cry of magpies, the sound of tractors and trucks. By lunchtime, when they all sat beside the road with long crusty sandwiches filled with sausage and some kind of chutney, his grey shirt was covered in purple stains and his back ached horribly. Only then did he notice what the rest were wearing – old clothes he had already assumed, but they were all old *blue* clothes. By the time the sun had begun to descend, his face and hands were burnt red, which so shocked one of his Moroccan roommates, that he immediately took off his big straw hat and flicked it across the vines to James, too late.

They all returned sitting in the trailer behind the truck, bouncing over the potholes, drinking freely from the jugs of wine, to the waiting feast set upon big pieces of plywood and sawhorses in the winery yard. There were steaks blackened by fire, sliced potatoes disintegrating into some kind of cream sauce, green beans with butter and crushed almonds, apple tarts and fresh rosy peaches, melting cheeses and nuts and more and more wine until the locals went home and the rest fell, exhausted, into their bunks. James could not sleep even though his coughing had abated and he was almost used to the noise of the night, several different nationalities of snoring. Pain scorched over the backs of his hands and neck, and he shoved his pillow off the bed and let his palms rest on the surface of the blankets. He had not slept properly for days – for weeks, really – was losing faith in his ability to sleep. It was this that kept him awake the most: the terror of not being able to sleep.

The next morning, mist filled the valley, and for the first hour, they moved through it, surfaced slowly from it as they shuffled up the rows, until the sun burnt it away. James worked, the pruning shears reminding him at every snip of his work with Father Townley's pear trees so many ages ago in Cork City. His movements were already automatic as he built another layer of purple stain on his fingers, the rest of his skin still torture-red, not yet beginning to peel. He looked up now and then, sometimes down to the football field in the little town where boys spilled out to play when the distant bell rang, sometimes to wherever the next game of grape pelting or spitting had begun two rows over, always near a particular girl with eyes both bright and smoky, her hair knotted into a sensuous curling tail that rippled down past the small of her back. This made him think of Yvonne and her probable flight to Yves, made him suffer far more than his skin or his muscles or his back. He would go back to his work, lifting leaves, clipping bunches, taking care not to nick the big woody trunk of the vine or clip his fingers; someone made this mistake every day and had to go back down the hill to the house to get the wound seen to by Solange or one of the other women helping her in the kitchen. Half an hour later they would be back, the cut-off finger of a rubber glove around their wound and its bandage, carrying a basket of something – apples or pastry – for them all. He was grateful for the work, not because of the money, but because the few days before it began had been unbearable, filled with thoughts and fears and jealous rages; all he had been able to do was walk higher and higher up this hill and that, as if he thought he could escape *up* if he couldn't buy a ticket *out*, hoping some power or demon or wind might mercifully pluck him off the top of the highest rock and take him entirely out of the world.

What would Father Townley have thought of him now? That old Druid-Catholic he had barely known but for rumour, that gentle reactionary, the man who had directed his footsteps by arranging buildings and pathways and trees, who had built walls to keep out any kind of change, who had never threatened the wild things with a fate worse than death. James heard that before Townley had gone senile, he wouldn't even kill the worms that ate the leaves of his pears, would pick them into a bucket and give them to the fellow who did maintenance, not knowing, or not willing to know, what was done to them. *Let not thy right hand know what thy left hand is doing*, and the maintenance man was his left hand, crushing the worms under his boot. This quote was about the unselfish giving of alms, but it worked as well if you didn't want to know about killing, didn't it?

What would Father Foley have thought of him now that he was so fallen from the heaven the church envisioned for him? Father Foley was such an intelligent, compassionate man.

Would he be capable of reclaiming James's tormented soul? Or would James redeem Foley from a life led in an intricate network of blindness and rationalization? Could James convince him to think past the dangerous questions of suffering and Hell and the sins of the church, the ones theologians merely gave up to be the mysteries of a God whose goodness was inconceivable to puny mortals?

The third night was tense, the stars now clouded over, now visible, lightning sighted once beyond the west hill. Morning was no better, the remains of thundershowers hovering, threatening to build up again in the heat of the day; they almost ran to get their baskets. James could feel the fear in the air; wet was no good, one of the students who could speak a little English, told him. Wet made the grapes rot. They would pick in the rain if they had to, pick in downpours and risk the lightning. But the clouds blew away. They picked as usual, ate their meat pies with pickles, drank their wine and water, ate pastries filled with custard and cream and let the crumbs and powdered sugar snow down their filthy stained clothes.

He noticed it on the fourth day; his heart beat strangely. His night-fear of not being able to sleep was infecting the daylight hours. Behind everything he thought or felt was a buzz, a vibration, of nervousness. He was so tired, and now, what was it? He felt frightened all the time. But of what? Of not being able to sleep? The thought of sleep obsessed him. Why couldn't he? Was he going mad? How could he make himself sleep? That night, he had just gotten to sleep, and the thought "I'm sleeping!" woke him. He went behind the bunkhouse to urinate, went back in, was buzzing, buzzing, thinking "I'm not sleeping, not sleeping. I'm too afraid of not sleeping to sleep." Lying awake, he got up again and again to make more trips behind the bunkhouse. Why did he have to piss all the time? Oh, God, and what should he do, repeat a prayer to the empty universe?

On the fifth day, he was clipping off a large bunch of grapes that he had almost missed beneath the leaves, when the suddenness of the pain and his uncontrollable cry made him leap back, made the other pickers look up. What animal hadn't they told him about that would hide among the grapes and bite like that? His rage at the inscrutable French and their language only abated when he looked through the blood at the base of his index finger to see the clean cut, saw matching blood on his shears. Jean was behind him suddenly, clucking his tongue.

"Tante Anne," he said, and gave him a little push down the hill. James carried his basket to the bottom of the row and left it there, then began to walk back to the winery.

This is it. No more, he thought. Five days of work, almost twelve hours a day, would surely give him enough money for a train ticket back to Paris. Then he could persuade Yvonne out of her almost religious music fanaticism, bring her back to sanity and himself, and...what might happen after that was hazy. Anything that might happen after they were together again would be fine with him, as long as she was with him, laughing again, letting him gather her hair in his hands. Maybe they would come back here to work the rest of the vintage, to get the money to travel further south. Hadn't she said something about Rome? Rome where his old Pope lived? Anger and confusion rose in him again, and he tried to shake it off, think about seeing it all, the ruins of the ancients, Saint Peter's itself. Whatever, whatever. He was done with grapes and the sun and peeling skin for now, the road he walked littered with sweet crushed purple, buzzing with flies. He walked up to the house, finding Tante Anne sitting on the step by the kitchen door shelling peas. She was Solange's great-aunt, could speak the most English of any of them, had married a Scottish soldier during the First World War and returned to the village from Glasgow after he died. He held out his bleeding hand to her and she made a face and grunted, tossing her head in the direction of the door.

She washed the wound and the rest of his hand in soap and hot running water and he waved it in the air to help it dry. He yelped as she painted on the iodine, then she bound it in cotton bandages. The wound was too close to his hand to benefit from the remains of the rubber glove, so she wrapped it in some kind of rubbery plumber's tape.

"I'm going to go now, back to Paris. How do I get paid? Do I just talk to Solange? or Armand?"

"You go *after* vintage."

"But I have to go *now*."

She grunted and laughed and shook her head, which made the big grey bun of hair at the base of her skull sway. Solange came into the kitchen carrying a box of baguettes.

"Tell her. Tell her I have to go and need to get paid. Tell her."

Tante Anne said something in French that made Solange look suddenly at James, an expression of perplexed outrage on her face. She began talking fast, waving her hands. Armand came in and soon began to talk angrily, aiming his words at James, coming so close to him, James backed up, was almost afraid.

"What are they saying?"

Solange and Armand managed to stop shouting, motioning Anne to talk for them, Solange folding her arms tight across her chest and leaning back, Armand gripping the edge of the table with his big purple hand.

"You come early and eat their food – this is trouble for them. You want to leave early. Nobody leaves early. Vintage is not done. A big crop. You come to work vintage, you work vintage. You work all of it. You get paid at the end. You work Armand's vines, but he manages some fields for others, and you work them too, and not all money comes from him, you know. It's a co-op."

"That's it?" James could hardly comprehend what he was hearing.

Armand threw his hands in the air and walked out of the kitchen. Solange shook her head and began attacking a baguette with a big serrated knife.

"But how long is that? How long will it take?"

"Two more weeks," said Ann. "A little more."

"But I have to go *now*. My girl, she's all I've got. I've lost everything else. I mean, everything. You don't understand..."

Two weeks. Would that be too late? How could he endure another two weeks, knowing Yvonne and Yves were together, that Yvonne was sinking further and further into his world of bands and dreams of sudden rock and roll fame? He was trapped.

He paced back to the vineyard and picked up his basket again, numb, staring. Hedges and more hedges, walls he couldn't leap over. The green striped hills reminded him of Ireland, the winding roads, the stone-built villages. He could hardly work, his hand painful, too bound up, and Jean sent him back to the house to help in the kitchen. He sliced zucchini, then tomatoes, then eggplant, using his left hand more as a weight put on the vegetable than as a hand able to grasp it. Solange set him to work cutting an enormous amount of raw beef into cubes and passing it through a meat grinder while she chopped onions and herbs and worked on pastry, laying out ten pie tins on the table. She bustled about, usually turned her back to him, handed him new things to chop, her lips tight. When he was done, Solange said something to Anne, who grabbed James by the wrist and took him down to the winery yard to the long metal barrel cut in half and filled with ash, burnt black on the inside. He was to clean it out, and build another fire. Anne told him how to do it to make the deepest charcoal. He worked and glanced up at her now and then as she set the long table, crunching over the gravel in her old lace-up leather shoes, swollen ankles spilling out over their tops, apron and loose flowered skirt blowing in the wind. A brown and white spotted dog James had seen here and there every day followed her around, back and forth to the house, then ducked under the table now and then to pick up morsels of food from the night before. Dogs loved where the food was, so women became their mistresses. Tante Anne was swollen and sagging, wasn't at all like his old granny, but now he could see they were exactly alike. The wind blew heavily in the chestnut tree above him and he looked past it to the hedges, the vine fields and the hills.

She began to talk to him, about the ball of lighting she'd seen fall to earth and roll down the hill between the vines when she was a little girl, about the lousy communists that were infesting the town, about the ditches filled with mutilated soldiers fifty years ago, about the fields that grew thicker, greener, fertilized with the blood and bone of thousands of men even younger than himself, about her brother Alzare who died, and her brother Gaspar who died, and her cousin Theo. The only people not watching their loved ones die were the ones who had died first.

"And you. Ireland. In the next war – neutral. How you stand back when there are people murdered?"

He shook his head at her accusation; it was before his time.

She came up to him and took his wrist again. "Everyone loses everything."

He jerked away, the constant buzz of fear inside him turning suddenly to terror. He was trapped. He could go nowhere. He couldn't even sleep. He was back in Ireland again, Ireland with the water turned off and the heat turned up, Ireland without clouds, with only the contrails of distant airplanes to block the sun, Ireland located a little closer to hell.

For the next two weeks, he would be their boy.

The ninth day.

Jean walked across to him and bent a little. They were picking on a steeper hill today, the vine rows across the incline in small terraces. James emptied his picking basket into Jean's larger basket and Jean straightened and walked on. "Tankyou," he said in English with a big grin. He made a point of learning to say thank you in the language of every foreign picker, but made a little face when he turned away because James looked awful.

First there had been the streaming cold, then the blazing red sunburn and peeling skin, and now, the dark circled eyes, staring, then flitting around, like birds frightened by a gunshot. He used to look like a lost schoolboy, but now he looked like someone not completely right in the head. It was impossible not to notice. No one had talked about it yet, but the looks had started, the meeting of eyes, then the quick glance at James and the meeting again. Maybe one of the girls would roll her eyes or frown a little in concern, one of the Moroccans shrug his shoulders. Sometimes James would stay in the field when the rest had piled onto the back of the truck with the jugs of wine, looking forward to dinner. He would show up later, when everyone was full, take a plate of cold food back to the bunkhouse and eat only half of it – all he wanted was to be alone – while the others moved closer to the dying cook-fire to drink more wine. They noticed he was strange, but they didn't necessarily notice he hadn't always been so.

Some made more of an effort, put an arm around his shoulder when they could, joggled him a little as if shaking some sense into him. Even the girl with the smoky eyes took aim once, hit him in the back of the neck with a slightly mouldy grape, left a mark.

He could hardly bear it.

He wished someone would ask him what was wrong with him, because he asked himself a thousand times a day, and would have replied, "I don't know. What do you think?" If only he knew, then maybe he could find the cure.

He didn't feel safe inside his body any more. He vibrated with a terror he couldn't stop like one could stop the ringing of a bell by taking it in one's hands and hanging on, being still. He couldn't find the source of this fear by searching his mind. It was as if he had lost his skin and the fear entered him from outside because there was no proper boundary to keep it out. His nerves shook and rang and shivered. Sometimes he moved slowly, trying to slow them down, sometimes quickly, trying to drown them out. He no longer bothered agonizing about Yvonne, about what he could have done differently, how he could have avoided their fight in the first place. The invasion of his psyche, his body, completely eclipsed any other concern, even his terror of not sleeping, though he couldn't sleep with all this going on, the silent clanging that began in his head and filled his body with panic. Run, run, he sometimes thought it was saying: Alarm! Danger! But from what, coming from where? And where could he run? He would work, clip and pick and dump his grapes, and his head would hurt more and more, his jaw clenched, even the roof of his mouth seeming to have muscles perpetually tightening. Sometimes he couldn't stop swallowing or was aware of every time he blinked his eyes, or could not get his shoes to fit properly: always his socks bunched where his little toe met the leather or there was a stone he had kicked up inside one, or the laces were too tight and bit into the top of his foot.

What was he afraid of? Was he afraid of people? Of himself? Of being grabbed by Tante Anne's swollen fingers? Even when he was asleep he was not alone, seven other pickers snoring in the beds around him, above him, André and Guillaum and Henri and Robert, and the Africans with names not even the French could pronounce. He could barely sleep with all of them around him, got out of his bed only when the last of them had shut the door so he would not be jostled getting his toothbrush, so he wouldn't have to come so close to touching them. Why was he like this, he who had lived with roommates since he was twelve, at school, and then the seminary?

What was even more terrifying than this terror itself, was that he couldn't control it. It had taken over his life as he could only imagine permanent madness would seize its victim, shake him and tear him, and chase him until he ran into the river, never having learned to swim. He was helpless, his brain, his emotions, rearing up against him and running away, and would he always be like this, his heart pounding whenever someone walked past, spoke to him, even just sat on the road where he could see them? He was going mad, and he could tell no one, had no one to tell, no one to help him, and just the thought of *people* frightened him even more, bent his head further down as he worked. As if he had gained an extra sense overnight, he was aware of the person harvesting in the row behind him, and the one in front, could feel their proximity, heard every snip and rustle of leaves, shivered when they drew nearer, worked faster. He dreaded the time when the slow-walking Jean would come up beside him for him to dump his grapes into the basket.

Almost nowhere could he be alone, and alone was the only place he could get a little relief from the torrents of fear. He almost felt safe when he locked himself in the lavatory on the edge of the house nearest the bunkhouses, almost felt safe when he escaped from the jovial table after dark and ran down the lane to the river, sat in the ditch in the middle of the tall grass where surely no one could find him. This would relieve him a little, skim the foam off the top of his great depth of fear, but did not cure it.

Something thwacked him in the side of the head and he glanced up to see the girl with the smoky eyes retreating around the end of his row. Her name was Bernadette, the same as his mother's, something that he had remarked on the first day, and viewed with horror ever since he had noticed the similarity between this place and Ireland. Of course there were Bernadettes in France. Saint Bernadette was from France, and it was a Catholic country. Nothing unusual about that.

He put his head down and worked.

Sometimes he tried to distance himself, to figure it out coldly; so: he had run away from Ireland, and he was back, now, trapped in Ireland. How could he stay here, trapped, without going crazy?

He worked – that was his penance – but as soon as he was able to concentrate on picking, drown out the vibration, he would be even further back in Ireland, would look up and see hedgerows and stone walls instead of vine rows, would know his mother was watching him. What did that mean? Had she died, and was a ghost, and could ghosts find anybody, especially the ones who had wronged them? Had she died then, when he had vanished? Had the blow been too much, had they been so entirely conjoined? He would put his head down and work, and look up expecting Dermot to be standing there grinning, or

Paddy looking at him with sorrowful eyes: he had failed them. He would work, and as soon as he would forget, he was back home, and Granny was still alive and his bedroom floor was cold on the bottom of his bare feet and he was hurrying to put on his clothes because he could smell the bacon frying. This was what terrified him the most, when the fear had gone so far inside him, it became one with him, it became almost possible to forget it was there, to forget he had to find out what it was, forget there was a dragon inside him waiting to come at him at night, a dragon he had to kill.

The twelfth morning, he was up and dressed and down the hill by dawn because he could not bear to be awake in his bed any longer. He heard the tolling of the church bell and walked into the town, following the sound, until he could see the steeple rising up above the houses. He almost turned around then, but could not help himself. He went up to the facade of the little church to see what he knew he would find: carvings over the lintel, devils and angels, saints and God. He moved back when it seemed the early Mass was over, watched old Tante Anne walk into the square and sit on the edge of the fountain. Another woman, one of the ones who sometimes helped cook, joined her. Something made him walk up to them: perhaps envy.

"Why do you go?" he asked, gently, as if she would understand all the complexity behind his eyes, all the other questions that hid beneath this simple one.

There was a perplexed look in her eyes. "Everyone goes," she said, then considered. "It's peaceful. I had five children."

He nodded. It was getting late. He had to get back to start work with the others, or Armand would think he'd run off. Just then, the truck came into the square, Armand picking up the ladies so they could get up the hill to begin cooking breakfast. James thought to hide, but it was too late. Armand waved him over.

He looked exuberant. The tension between them since James asked to leave had dissipated.

Armand was talking to Anne, and she turned to him.

"He say, enough workers now. Most of the fields done and the weather good. He talk to the others at the co-op, and will pay you tonight after another day's work. You can go!" She raised her hands, and clapped them together, looking from James to Armand as if to say, "What a generous man! You see how everything turns out well!"

And before he knew it, he was in the back of the truck and they were going up the hill. Had he thanked Armand? He couldn't remember, could hardly think because, instead of being relieved, his panic had increased. Leave and go where? To find Yvonne who didn't want him anyway, where she might not be anyway? Go out alone into the world like this?

He worked. They all worked their way up the steepest slope yet: his last day, his last time. He didn't feel any safer, though the cage door was open now. He would carry his panic with him, he thought, forever, until he threw himself into a river – the river down there like the estuary back in Ireland – or threw himself under the wheels of a car because he was alone in the world and alone in his terror, at its mercy.

Word got around that he was leaving early, and after supper, they wouldn't let him retreat into the bunkhouse, but raked the coals together on one side of the barrel and threw more logs on. Vintage would be over in a few more days, and no one objected to a warm-up party. Armand brought out his little accordion and one of the men from the winery tuned his fiddle, bow pointing at the stars, plucking the strings over and over. James sat on a bench watching the fire leap, lighting up the big chestnut, watching the few couples that came forward to dance: arms around each other and spinning, or gravel-shuffling, shy.

Bonfire night.

He watched the girl with the smoky eyes dance with Jean. One of her friends came up to him, then another, and each took one arm to pull him up, make him dance.

"No, sorry. I don't feel like it," he said, but of course, they didn't understand, pulled harder. He twisted his arms, wrenched free. "Mine," he said, holding his arms up, away from them, and walked out of the firelight. *Mine*, the word Yvonne had given him.

Mine, he said, as he opened the door of the bunkhouse. Mine. He turned on the bare bulb and sat on his bunk. Mine. All his body was his. All his mind was his. All his life was his. And his soul. Deep down, he had always thought he was his mother's. Did all children think this or was it only him? Was it because she'd stolen him once from everything he'd loved? Was it because of the way she held on to him, touched him, demanded he allow whatever caress she gave, wouldn't allow him his own body? Was it something deliberate on her part – or demented – or did it just *happen*? Mothers, deranged or not: men fled to a male god just to try to escape the power of them.

Mine. Every time he whispered the word, it cut his fear down. He said the word, believed in it over and over, and he could feel his fear slowly shrinking away.

Mine, he could say, if he ever saw his mother again, his priestly teachers, and his little Irish town. He didn't have to protect himself by being alone. He didn't have to run away from people, from anybody. He could just say this one word and say it again and again, and turn his back if it wasn't heeded.

Mine.

He fell asleep without taking his clothes off, or even his shoes, woke the next morning not remembering hearing the others come in during the night, woke knowing exactly what time the train left for the city.

He had to find her.

Of course, they really had nothing in common. He could see that, now. She had a right to be obsessed with bands, if she wanted. It was her life.

But he had to find her, to tell her that she'd saved him. With just one word.

She saved him, she saved him, and then what? He belonged to her, now?

He retraced his steps: the train, the hills, the vineyards, the fields, the towns, the city of Paris, the Metro coming up from under the earth. He had money for cigarettes, now, and he leaned against the wall of their local boulangerie where he could see the building. It was the afternoon. He stayed for half an hour, smoking, and saw no one.

He walked down the street to a bar, drank a warm glass of weak beer, and ate three of the hard-boiled eggs from the dish beside the cash machine. He went back out, bought a bag of every kind of pastry she liked and sat on a windowsill to have another cigarette. He saw Phillipe across the street and turned slightly, hid until he went inside. He stayed there until one, then two, then five in the morning – she had to be just about to return from whatever night escapade they had gone on – the disco, a party with a local band, a show or a movie. The longer they had been in Paris, the later Yvonne wanted to stay out. He knew his luck. If he left, she would return a minute later. One by one, he ate all the pastries. He left only once the city began to wake and he was almost dying of thirst. He walked until he found a small hotel, fell into his bed, and slept into the afternoon.

He saw Yves return about six from teaching. He saw no one else. He went to bed at midnight, was up at six, watching. Yves again, Phillipe. No one else, all day. He couldn't ask them. It was the last thing he wanted to do, something he might have to do. The silence of her absence descended upon him. It was the quietist thing in the world, Yvonne just not being there.

He spent the next several days like this, up in the morning to see who left Yves' building, back in the evening to see who returned, wandering Paris in the afternoons when the sky was a flat, slightly smoky blue, or overcast, or frankly raining, the leaves on the trees crumpled to brown, falling around him. Now and then he spent the money to go up the towers of Notre Dame and rest with his elbows on the balustrade, watching the small cars and smaller people, their noises getting lost in the dull roar of the city, then erased by the big bells behind him that rang the hour, the half-hour, and the quarter-hour, vibrating his insides, almost deafening him. So many people: that one down there – the tourist sitting for the caricature artist – could die tonight, and it wouldn't affect him. He would never hear about it. How many people would care? Ten? Twenty? Fifty? It hardly mattered what happened to him, did it? He said this once, out loud, to one of the demon-gargoyles, one of the other fallen angels, just to see if anyone would notice. Now and then, a tour group, sometimes elderly men and women, sometimes school-children, would come up in identical hats, the guide imparting the standard hunchback/ bell-ringer/ architectural gossip. There weren't many tourists left in the city in the fall, but those that came had to come here, would flood around him and then drain away, leaving him alone or almost alone for half an hour or more. It wouldn't occur to any of them that he had been there for half a day. It wouldn't occur to them that *he* was the hunch-back, crippled in mind if not in body.

One day he decided to stay up there as long as he could, to risk permanent hearing loss, to see the way the city changed, trace the shadows. After looking out for half an hour, he walked around, took his bottle of water out of his pack and drank, ate some bread and cheese. As he looked down the face of the church, all the foreshortened edges and bumps merged together into a kind of vertical landscape, a scorched desert of soot-blackened stone, with flat plains and bumpy mountainous rhythms, a strange design or logic that couldn't be interpreted. He had never looked straight down the building before, and his head whirled and tickled with the vertigo: the human mind was not made to look at the world this way; it seemed to short-circuit, flip back on itself, substitute the feeling of falling for the actual event.

He realized suddenly that there was nothing in his head. He had lost everything, now even his thoughts. It didn't terrify him the way it had at first, in Oxford, when he had run from his father, from the misunderstanding that his life had been all along. His rage at his father was dissipating; he wouldn't want to be married to his mother either.

Looking down, suspended in his own personal vacuum, there was nothing but him and space.

He could jump, of course.

Maybe that's what the ticket-takers would begin to think, if he came up every day and stayed too long, if they even noticed people any more. But why would they?

He could jump, like the old priest at Loch Derg, end the nothing with nothing. That would be the only thing he ever had to do again, and everything had become such an effort.

He shut his eyes. What a relief. He opened them again, walked up beside his favorite gargoyle, the one eating another gargoyle, leaned on the balustrade, and shut his eyes. He put his chin on the rough, decaying stone, and peered over the edge at the vertical desert. He shut his eyes.

But hadn't his mother tried to kill herself? After his sister died, before they ran away to Ireland. The broken mirror. All that blood. It seemed to him he had never thought of this before, refused to remember.

He stepped back from the edge, made his way down the winding stairs.

Two days later, it was miraculous. It was Marilyn, though he didn't recognize her at first because she was so far away, striding down the stairs into the Metro station. She must have left the building a minute or two before he had arrived at his post.

By the time he'd gotten down into the tunnels, she was gone, trains leaving in both directions, sucking subterranean winds after them. He ran back, up the street, up the four flights of stairs and pounded on Yves' door. Yves opened it a few moments later, a scowl on his face.

"Oh. It's *you*."

"Marilyn's back. I saw her. Where's she going?"

"She say *Place de la Concorde*. She say people-watching." He drew on his hand with a finger.

"Thanks, thanks," James said, breathless, then, with an afterthought, "and Yvonne?"

"Pfft," Yves said, spitting air through his teeth, throwing an angry hand into the air. "Who knows? She come back. She fly away."

James ran, caught the Metro, watched his sunburned, shell-shocked face in the windows that the cave-darkness turned to mirrors: filthy clothes stained with blue-purple blood, an expression beyond terror, more like wide-eyed numbness. He put a hand – the one that was still bandaged – to his eye, and when he took it away he almost expected to see it transformed, turned to an orb of glass in a sunburst of scars; shouldn't he bear a mark where lighting had struck him, too? It had struck his father when Dymphna died, widened the hole that he'd been pouring his drink into. It had struck their mother, and the electricity had splintered down, shattered her to her soul, where the wound had festered and rotted. How was it that he was only marked on the inside? How long would it take him to heal? To go on with his life, with his schooling? How could he do it all alone? Was it even possible? How long would it take him to fit himself back into the lives of the people he loved – Paddy, Lila – and the people he hated but loved anyway, because he couldn't help it?

He came up to the surface and somehow made his way, darting and hesitating, across the eight lanes of traffic to the acres of desolate concrete oval, its obelisk and fountains. Cars and water rushed around him, the battering sound of a hundred torrential rains in the late October sun. She wasn't there, not at the foot of Cleopatra's needle, not at the edge of either fountain, where naked bronze madwomen crushed writhing fish to their bellies. Where? Where was she? He ran through the traffic again, onto the Champs-Elysées, under the grey haze of thousands of bare autumn twigs and branches, a giant horse rearing on a plinth, one futile man trying to restrain it. There was no one around, no one for her to draw; he would never find her here, tourist season over, lunch hour not yet arrived. She had washed her hands in one of these fountains and he had seen her slap them on her blue denim thighs, handprints, paw-prints, invisible for a second, then darkening. They had been here before, after their first trip to the Louvre, and had gone to the right – or was it left – to find lunch. On the right he could see a bridge over the river, so he went to the left, unable to run any more, hunching over, his side aching, his heart aching, not knowing why he was so desperate to see her, to see her *now*, even though he could have waited as he had for over a week, waited for her to go back to Yves'.

He didn't know why until he saw her and his heart leaped like a child. She was sitting at a streetside café table, leaning over her journal. He walked slowly until he was able to see her face, her hair loose, a dark hood that framed the eyes he hadn't noticed until their last day on the train, complicated eyes of microscopic stained glass in sunlit ambers and browns. She held her pen in purple, wasp-bitten fingers and chewed the end of it now and then, between bouts of drawing, the Rue Royale receding on her page. On the white tablecloth was a cup of cappuccino, its saucer holding a pool of milky coffee. She set the cup on a napkin, tucked her hair behind her ears, and lifted the saucer to her lips to lap up the excess, but her elbow grazed the table and the coffee spilled into her lap. The sound she made was half moan, half growl – it mustn't have been hot enough to hurt – and then she threw her head back and laughed. He laughed then, too, silently, all the breath he'd been holding shaking out of him at last.

The building just beyond was ornate, baroque, with a heavy staircase and lions perched on sand-coloured cliffs. The city was quiet here, seemed to contain mostly space; the area of tables was deserted but for her. The lions waited at a respectful distance, waited for the crumbs that would fall from her table.

ACKNOWLEDGEMENTS

Biblical quotes are from the King James Version. Some are deliberately inaccurate, such as when they are in the thoughts of a character, who would remember a quote imperfectly, like a real human being.

I owe much to Helen Waddell and the circumstances that allowed *Beasts and Saints,* her wonderful book of translations, to fall into my hands. These stories are the spine of this book. I am indebted to Constable and Company who allowed me to quote from the work.

Many thanks to the Saskatchewan Arts Board, for the partial C grant, back when I was young and foolish. Thank you to the staff of the Banff Centre Writing Studio, who helped me turn this book in the great swerving directions in which a first novel must often travel; the first-time novelist ventures into a vast country without map or compass. I am grateful to the Saskatchewan Writers Guild, the Saskatchewan Artists/Writers Colonies, and the good people of St. Peter's Abbey, Muenster, for giving space and time and community. Thanks especially to my wonderful editor and writing teacher Edna Alford, who a long time ago, told me that everyone loses everything.

I owe the completion of this novel, and the chance to complete my life to the beneficence of all Canadian taxpayers and the system of Medicare, the doctors and nurses and staff of the Royal University Hospital, Saskatoon, its emergency and surgical departments and the Saskatoon Cancer Center, my oncologists, Dr. Hasagawa and Dr. Fibich, my nurse, Tamara Weigel, and my surgeon, Dr. Andrew McFadden. I owe a huge debt of gratitude to my Cancer Center volunteer driver, beautiful soul, Denise Martin, and all the other people who looked after me and my family without hope of reward during those eleven months when every day was an emergency and I could not look after my children: Patrice, Honor Kever, Judith Wright, J. Jill Robinson, Sue and Curt and Caty and Megan Williams, Amy-Jo Ehman, Liz Martens, Marc Menzer, Barb and Fred Phillips, Kim Rothery and Paul Christensen, Trudy Einarsson and David (Stormy) Williams, Heidi Arntzen Sheehan, Tom Bowman, Pat Bowman, Donna Bowman, Yvonne Marien, and the others that I remain unaware of because I was in the hospital, or simply too ill. I will never forget. If you're still missing any of your Pyrex dishes, do come around; I am keeping them safe for you.

In regard to the writing of the book, I wish to thank May, Liam, and Helen Burns, Stephen and Fidelma Foley, Aidan and Annie Foley, Angela and Bernadette, little Susan who danced with me at the wedding, Father Michael McManus, Father Kellegher, Sister Dolores of the Ursulines, Agnes McNulty, Bridget Boyd, Danny and Eileen Cahalane, Bob Kelly, Patricia O'Driscoll and the tinkers who camped on Warren Strand Road, the nuns of Mercy Convent, Rosscarbery, Willie-Joe and Agnes Hayes, the Decoursey family, David Hynds and his dog Lucky, and his other dogs who weren't so lucky, Dominic McNamara, Peter McAnenely, and the priests and students of St. Patrick's College, Maynooth. Thank you to Kathleen O'Mahony who plucked me off the side of the hill of Glandore in my distress, took me home and fed me, and played her fiddle. Thank you to all the other people of Rosscarbery and Downeen, Kinlough and Cliffoney, Maynooth and Dublin, who harboured me and my questions and allowed me to listen to their voices. Thank you to my husband, Colin, who helped me steer clear of Irish cultural potholes. Thank you to the generous heart of my son, Alex, for granting permission to reveal our secret game, Baby Octopus. Thank you to Doreen Bangerter, and her dear departed Ernst who taught me to ring the cathedral bells of Ross, the most joyful noise I have ever made.

My eternal gratitude and devotion to Yvonne and Donna, to my father Jim, to Colin and Alex and Jo; your love truly keeps me alive.

And love, always, to McGinty, who lives in Ontario now, going to medical school.

The Father Townley section in Chapter v was previously broadcast on the CBC Radio arts program *Gallery* in 2000. It was also published under the title "The Irish Book of Beasts" in *The New Quarterly*, Vol. xx, No. 4, 2002, and later reprinted in *Best Canadian Stories 2002*, Ottawa: Oberon Press, 2002. It was read by Mary Eileen McClear in the *Hermione Presents* series, Stratford, Ontario, 2006.

Beasts and Saints translations by Helen Waddell, Constable and Company, London 1934, reprinted 1960.

ABOUT THE AUTHOR

Bernice Friesen is a writer and visual artist whose poetry and fiction have been published in numerous periodicals, such as *Grain, CV2, Prairie Fire* and the *Capilano Review.* Coteau Books published her poetry collection *Sex, Death and Naked Men* in 1998. The title story of her book *The Seasons are Horses,* won the Vicky Metcalf Award for Best Young Adult Short Story in Canada.

Bernice Friesen was born in Rosthern, Saskatchewan and now divides her time between Saskatoon and Hornby Island in British Columbia.